THE TALES OF DRACO
The Six Pieces

ALSO BY JORDAN B. JOLLEY:

The Tales Of Draco: Rise Of The Dragon

Fairy Tales, Fables & Other Short Stories
(Collection 1)

THE TALES OF
DRACO

— ∾ —

THE SIX PIECES

JORDAN B. JOLLEY

LUMINARE PRESS
WWW.LUMINAREPRESS.COM

The Tales of Draco: The Six Pieces
©2020 Jordan B. Jolley

Printed in the United States of America

Cover Art:
Cover Design: Melissa K. Thomas

Luminare Press
442 Charnelton St.
Eugene, OR 97401
www.luminarepress.com

ISBN: 978-1-64388-581-0
LCCN: 2020906492

To Amanda Hansen and John Abbott

TABLE OF CONTENTS

PART 1

THE CABIN ON THE LONELY BEACH

Prologue 3

The Final Day 13

The Wizard's Truth 28

The Pacific Shore 40

Lost in a New Land 50

The Strange Visitor 56

Loose Ends Meet 69

Plans Unfold 79

The Face of the Enemy 88

David & Goliath 99

Written on a Cloth 110

The Viewing Ring 115

Larson's Attack 134

The Spying Dragon 144

Discovery in the Junction 153

'To Shiloh's Pass, We Bid Thee Farewell' 167

Chase of the Darkscales 186

PART 2
The Search for the Six Pieces

Help on the Way 209

Sorrow 225

The Tree & the Abyss 231

The Commencing Fight 239

Bridging the Gap 243

Elemek's Visit 255

The Blue Blade & the Lightscale 261

Pierre 271

Ice Caverns 276

Friends Come Together 289

Razden Awakens 294

Trahern's Charge 300

Under the Mound 307

Rendevious Atop the Cliffs 313

Battle Atop the Cliffs 323

No Easy Journey 334

Escape from Kimberly 350

Battle of Manti-La Sal 357

On to Mt. Ellen 373

Tensions Rise 378

The Militia & the Grun-Haere 386

Coming of the King 399

Closer to Pearl Forest 410

Epilogue 415

The Tales of Draco Glossary 417

PART 1

THE CABIN ON THE LONELY BEACH

PROLOGUE

The sun sank below the horizon of Elsov, painting the sky with glorious hues of lavender and purple. The planet of the blue ring, Alsov, smiled down on the enchanted forest. The ground in that forest was soft and cool in the late summer evening. Songs of mysterious creatures rang throughout the expanse of the woods while fireflies danced about with their yellow orbs of light. Along a well-kept road on the outskirts of Pearl Forest sat a small eating establishment. There, a young dwarf dismounted his white mare. The dwarf, scratching his trimmed beard of red, took a breath of the fresh, clean air. The wind blew cooler as each day passed, telling him that the summer season was due to close. After another long breath, the dwarf tied his horse and entered the restaurant, where he found many others like himself. Families were dining at the tables and booths while other groups were playing card games or dancing to the musicians' upbeat music. The dwarf silently made his way to a vacant table and sat down.

"Good fortunes to you, stranger," said the waiter, approaching him. "And what brings you here this fine evening?"

The dwarf rubbed his eyes. "A long day's what brings me here. I've decided to take my supper at your establishment."

The waiter chuckled. "Very well then. What can I interest you in for your supper? If I may make a recommendation, I'm holding a special this week: past dusk, it's twice the food, half the price. There's a fine selection of vegetables along with any sort of meat. Now what will you like? Take what your belly can hold."

The dwarf thought for a moment.

"Hmmm… the berries of any bush are fine by me. Put that in a salad. And meat? I must say any hunted beast'll make me happy.

Surprise me with that one, too."

"The berry ain't a vegetable, but I can provide that," said the waiter. "And meat, I'll surprise you for sure. And what about a drink?"

"My thirst has been quenched. I'll skip that, thank you."

The waiter said no more and left. The dwarf sat by himself, watching others in the restaurant dance and sing. Flutes, accordions, and banjos provided the lively music. The dwarf was humming to the tunes when the waiter set before him a bowl of blueberry salad, topped with a sweet yellow dressing; and a plate of juicy roasted grouse drenched in brown gravy. The dwarf thanked the waiter then took a bite into a leg of the grouse. The salted gravy and chewy texture gave the dwarf a strong appetite to clean out the salad and finish the plate. He ended his meal with a polite belch, patting his chest.

"Ahh! Pardon me. The food was delicious!"

The waiter chuckled again when he returned.

"I work hard to prepare it," he said. "With the special and quantity of food, that'll be five pennies. I also need your name."

The dwarf reached into his satchel and pulled out six small coins. He dropped all six, the extra one he paid as a tip.

"So, it would've been ten pennies for only the grouse. A good value if you ask me. And my name is Fenson Katque."

The waiter picked up the six coins. "Enjoy the rest of your night, Mr. Katque."

Fenson stood from the table. Thanking the owner one more time, he left the restaurant to its merry atmosphere. As he untied his horse, he could still hear the music from inside.

"A lovely evening this is," he said to himself.

Fenson slid his foot into the stirrup. When he was secure on the horse's back, he continued down the path until the restaurant was long out of sight. Alone again, Fenson felt content. One might mistake the dwarf for a Nibelung, but nothing could be further from the truth. When Fenson was young, he vowed that he would only do what he believed was right and stay away from evil desires. To that day, he had lived up to his vow the best he could.

His horse moved quietly past bright, glittering trees. Some of the speckles of light drifted from the trunk and floated past Fenson's head. He felt the magic all around him. Despite the evening hour, there was enough light to guide his way. The horse's slow stroll soon evolved into a brisk trot. Down the path Fenson went with his teeth exposed by his smile. He laughed as his mount leapt over a small stream and landed in a patch of thick, soft grass. Farther and farther he traveled through the forest. As he ventured onward, the colorful sky melted into darkness. He knew that in the distance, hidden by the night, were rolling hills. Fenson slowed down, his happy mood faded. Something was out of the ordinary. It was quiet. Too quiet.

There was no question about it; danger was near.

Fenson slowed his breath then climbed off his horse to let her graze. Making no noise, he searched for anything threatening. After a minute or so, he found an old house sitting atop one of the hills. The clapboards were rotted and there was a large hole in the roof. It looked as if the house should have been abandoned years ago, but a dim light flickered through the window.

Someone was inside.

"The luck of myself," Fenson mumbled. "Who would be in such a sorry-looking house?"

He tip-toed up to the open window. He hesitated to look in, not wishing to be seen by whomever or whatever was in there. Instead, he pressed his ear against the wall. He cringed at the sound of dark laughing and disgusting snarls.

"Hahahahahaha! It really took you that long to slay the rat?" a deep voice cackled from inside the house.

"Rat yourself!" said another voice harshly. "I've killed more'n you. 'specially the young 'uns."

"Yes, but the young 'uns don't count."

"'course they do! They're the ones who think they're so brave an' strong. Ha! They're the expected heroes who pretend to lead the battle. I pick 'em off one by one; quite amusing."

"Oh, shut your mouths!" a third voice growled. "We've also lost some o' our own comrades! I'm still quite annoyed. The grøls in Pearl Forest are still roaming free. That dwelling is a long three day's journey from here, and it's been a challenge to recapture the snots. It's all because of that numbskull of a dragon! The mindless beast gave no pride to his darkscaled breed."

The second low voice was heard again.

"Don't mention that beast! He was only seen in Pearl Forest for a few days, yet he caused a lot of trouble for us! If I ever have the chance, I'd chain him up an' belt his mouth shut. Then I'd take an ice blade and slice off his limbs one by one, starting with the wings. Then I'd finish off by choppin' his muzzle!"

"I've never seen this dragon before, the one that is a darkscale," said the first voice. "I've only heard o' him in stories. He has black scales and his horns have a shade o' brown. Who was he again?"

"The black darkscale," snarled the third voice. "We found him in a ditch near the river. He seemed scared and ran off like a coward. I followed him 'til he found the fairies along the plains. They gave him a map o' some sort. The fairies said the map would guide him to a special treasure. Heh! He had no interest in the treasure."

"Ha! And along the way, the brainless thing caused all your brothers to flee. This allowed him to free the grøls," scoffed the second voice.

"Hold your tongue! The ogres from the swamp found him and were ready to kill him and the dryad that was with him."

"The darkscale suddenly vanished in the swamplands and the ogres still have the nymph," the second voice interrupted. "I remember hearing the news. Where did the darkscaled dragon go?"

"Back to the other world, one of my brothers told me from the word of the ogres. He just vanished!"

Unable to hold back his curiosity, Fenson finally peeked over the sill. He saw two dwarfs sitting behind a table where their horned helmets lay beside large beakers and a melting candle. These dwarfs had little resemblance to himself. He knew they would capture or kill him if they realized he was there. They were both talking to an old

JORDAN B. JOLLEY

goblin. Fenson's heart began to race.

"What if there was a portal somewhere?" the dwarf of the first voice asked. "We could find our way to the other world and find the black dragon."

The second dwarf gave his companion a long, hard look.

"I've heard that there are two dragons, darkscales to be more specific. The other one's dark-red, like our ruler. He is saber-toothed and has four claws on his left foot."

The goblin suddenly burst into laughter.

"Heeheehahahaha-oh-hoho! I know where we can find a portal to the other world! In fact, I already have a plan. A few friends of mine, along with myself, will travel through this portal. We'd have to evade the humans there, but they should be no trouble. Before the darkscales can make their way home, they'll taste our vengeance! Heehee!"

"A plan that is," the first dwarf exclaimed.

The three were going on with their plan when the second dwarf spoke up.

"Would slaying 'em be as simple as we say? I've heard stories o' these darkscales destroying an entire army!"

"Stuff and nonsense," sniffed the first dwarf. "They were the Nibelungs. They didn't even try to win. They deserved to lose."

"It's not just their victory over the Nibelungs that concerns me. They also defeated Triathra. The Sorcerer! Keeper of the three worlds! He was sent to end the rise of the dragon. The new keeper is a wizard I know not of!"

The goblin continued to giggle mischievously.

"Hmhm. Well, we all must take risks, sadly. My plan will go into action in a matter of days."

The two dwarfs guzzled down whatever was left in their beakers. Fenson dropped back below the sill. He could not believe what he had just heard! He had to warn somebody. He had to! Taking several steps back, he waited until he was a good distance away from the house before dashing down the road. He found his horse still grazing and tried to step into the stirrup. The horse took a step back, whinnying.

Fenson tried hard to quiet her, but to no avail. He heard the door to the house break open.

Jumping back to the ground, Fenson quickly led his horse to the closest hiding place he could find. He had no weapon for defense, not even a dagger. He gulped fearfully and took off down the road. He ran as fast as he could. Just when he thought he reached safety, though, he felt a sharp pain strike his foot. He examined the wound only to find that an arrow had grazed the back of his heel. The wound was not critical, but it stopped him from running. He immediately rolled off the road and scooted behind the thick underbrush. Once out of danger, Fenson groped around in the dark. He felt some space beneath the roots of a towering tree and quickly scurried inside. He shivered with fright as he heard the approaching footsteps of his three foes.

"Where is he?" the first dwarf asked.

The goblin sniffed the air. "I smell blood. You hit him."

"But I can't see any footprints in the dark!" the second dwarf whined. "He's not anywhere! This can't be good. Oh, this can't be good! He must have heard us. The plan'll be ruined!"

"Hold yer tongue you drunkard! He doesn't know where the portal is," hissed the goblin. "I'll go now and find our friends. If we are the ones to slay the two dragons, Vesuvius will be pleased."

Fenson did his best not to make a sound. He sat frozen while the goblin continued to search. The footsteps finally moved back to the road, so he slowly squirmed out of the hollow and peeked around the tree. He was startled as he saw the goblin suddenly fall to his knees. Fenson didn't understand what the goblin was doing until he heard him speak.

"Yes, my Great Leader. I have a plan. I will not disappoint you."

Fenson couldn't believe it! Although he could not hear anyone else, he knew that the goblin's leader was speaking: the cruelest leader in all of Elsov! Fenson knew he had to get away. The goblin stood back on his feet and hurried to join the others. Fenson held his breath and scrambled from within the underbrush. He didn't dare take another breath until he knew for sure he was safe. He again found himself under the clear sky, but his horse was gone.

Fenson stood in the cool grass, deep in thought. Something had to be done; he just didn't know what. He wiped tears from his eyes.

"I need help," he murmured.

As he proceeded, alert for danger, he found himself back in the peaceful and lighted part of the woods. The dwarf closed his eyes and covered them with his hands. He could not send the warning alone. Sitting quietly, he heard a voice brush past him like a soft breeze. At first, he didn't hear what the voice had said. He opened his eyes. That was when he saw something that gave him hope. It was a fairy that had come to him. Her blond hair and thin wings flowed in the air. She wore a silk green gown that reached down to her bare feet. Just beyond the glowing trees, Fenson heard singing that created a mysterious yet magical presence in the atmosphere. He didn't know whether it was a second fairy or something else creating the lovely melody. Fenson enjoyed the soothing sound anyhow.

"A fairy is just what I need," he said to the winged being. "Surely you must know how I can spread the warning to the foreign lands."

The fairy descended until she was about a foot above the ground.

"I was nearby when I heard your troubles," she said in a delicate voice. "How may I help you?"

Fenson looked at the wand that the fairy was holding. The wand was an albore, an instrument of magic.

"Tell me, do you know the dark dragons who are of our world?" Fenson told the fairy of his recent experiences before reaching his conclusion. "...and now I'm here and I don't know how to spread this warning. I need help."

The fairy's face went blank. She was silent for a moment. Perhaps she was pondering the problem.

"Travel to the edge of Pearl Forest," she soon said. "Near the swamplands is a colony of dryads. The nymphs will know what to do. Seek then the Keeper of the three worlds when you are there."

"I'm well acquainted with the nymphs. I'm sure they'll help me," said Fenson.

"Find them and continue with your plan."

"Pearl Forest, near the swamplands, is where I will find the nymph colony. A wonderful place last I remembered. Perhaps one of the nymphs there will want to help me."

The fairy pointed in the direction that Fenson should go. She tightened her grip on the handle of her albore, then faded away. Fenson now understood what he must do. Feeling the urgency to leave, he made his way across the hills in search of his horse. There she was, grazing happily as if nothing had happened. Fenson jumped into the saddle and was off.

It took hours for him to ride across the wild hills, on roads that cut into fields, and into meadows. Fenson did not sleep the entire way, nor did he feel the need to.

Morning arrived before he found the place he was seeking on the edge of Pearl Forest, near the swamplands. He was relieved to see small huts on the ground and others hanging atop the towering trees. The nymphs are said to be one with nature, and it was certainly evident in this colony. The early sunlight shone through the leaves, creating a green aura throughout the village. Several people, smaller than Fenson, emerged from their homes and bowed to the dwarf, one of them Fenson recognized as the chieftain of the colony. Fenson responded by dismounting and bowing in return.

"Welcome, friend," said the chieftain. "What has brought you this way?"

Fenson, still shaken from his encounter with the goblin, spoke swift but clear. "My good nymph, I have urgent news. You may remember the black dragon who came not many months ago, the one who was not evil. I know where he is."

Many of the passing nymphs halted their businesses. They all gathered around Fenson, hungry for information. The chieftain became deeply interested when Fenson finished recapping his misadventure from the previous night.

"That darkscale has not been seen since one of our nymphs was captured by the ogres in the swamp," the chieftain explained. "You know where he is? Tell us!"

Fenson sat down on a nearby rock.

"In the human world, the first earth."

A murmur of surprise echoed among the nymphs.

"First earth? How did he travel there?" asked the chieftain. "Has he gone mad? It takes a brave heart, or a loony heart, to go there, let alone strict permission! How would anyone expect to find their way? Any fool who is unprepared would be lost in no time!"

"Indeed," Fenson replied, "but as I've said, I overheard the goblin claiming that he has found a portal to the other world and is leading a small group to seek the black dragon. They're leaving in a few days. I don't know the exact number of those following this goblin, but we must warn the black dragon. I can't do this myself, for I fear I may lose my way, as you've mentioned already. Who will join me?"

As Fenson feared, almost all the nymphs backed down. However, one of them stood up.

"Treetop was my sister. I will free her. I will risk death and travel to the first earth for her freedom."

The chieftain glared at him. "Not in the lifetime of an aged grøl you will not! My son, I will not allow it!"

"Good nymph, someone must go," said Fenson. "Trouble will strike us all if no one does."

The nymph leader buried his face in his hands. Fenson knew he did not want to lose his son as well as his daughter, but he also knew that nothing would be done to save Treetop if the chieftain forbade his son to go.

The nymph took his time in answering.

"I understand... You may go, Bluepond. Fenson, let my son accompany you to the Wizard's castle. Bluepond is kind, though he does like to talk, sometimes more than you want him to."

Bluepond quickly packed some food and other supplies for the journey.

"Let us go," he said. "The sooner we leave, the better."

Fenson was back on his horse while Bluepond chose to walk beside him. Bluepond's father wept as he watched his son leave the colony.

His heart broke at the thought of losing yet another one of his children.
"Goodbye, my child. Free Treetop for me," he said.

⸺◦◦◦⸺

THE CHIEFTAIN RETURNED TO HIS HOME, STRICKEN WITH GRIEF. *Another nymph followed him there.*

"Do not worry. All will be well," the chieftain's acquaintance said quietly.

The chieftain sighed. "I met this dragon. He did not know his name. I hope he has found his way. I believe he has a strong soul, one who will not back down from the fight in what he believes is right. I am quite certain he is valiant among the men of the first earth even as we speak."

CHAPTER 1

THE FINAL DAY

A light shower drizzled over the rolling landscape of Pennsylvania. I was well out of sight of anyone. This gave me freedom to fly around the open range with nothing to worry about. I had no regrets coming here. Clipper and I were waiting in and around the national forests until a new home could be found for us. Being dragons, it was difficult to find a suitable place. Nevertheless, spending most of the summer over the national forests gave me the true freedom I loved.

I was several hundred feet in the air, riding a comfortable thermal. Tiny water droplets tickled my nose, and a cool wind brushed past my black scales. I twirled and spun through the air, enjoying the stunts at great speeds that my friend would never do.

After flying all night, I began to feel tired. I landed back on the protective ground when the gray in the sky grew brighter. The soft grass moistened my paws. Blowing a flame of joy, I took a few steps forward. My ears twitched when I heard an echo of thunder. The sound of distant thunder during a light shower always pleased me. I loved how my eardrums tingled from the peaceful noise. I dropped to the ground and let the patch of white on my underside rest against the wild sward. My final day was here, and I was going to miss this place.

I closed my eyes and began to daydream. Every time I let my imagination loose, I always took myself back to Pearl Forest: a forest not of the first world, but of a world beyond; a world called Elsov.

I remembered my vision well. I didn't know who I was or where I came from then, though I did remember meeting many different and strange creatures; from the tiny, yipping grøls to the helpful fairies and sneaky nymphs. What I remembered most vividly was the blue-ringed planet Alsov in the night sky. Oh, how I longed to return to Elsov! That was my true home. That was where I came from. My parents could be waiting for me there. But the greatest reason why I wanted to return, along with finding my true parents, was to rescue the nymph that was lost in the swamp. If only I had a clue of how to get back, I would let nothing stop me from rescuing that poor nymph and discovering who I really was. I wanted to return. It wasn't because I didn't like the earth where I currently lived. I had much respect for it. I grew up here after all. It was just that Elsov was where I had truly come from, and that was where I was destined to return.

Still lying on the grass, I took a deep breath. A puff of smoke blew out of my nose. My eyes suddenly opened when I heard foot-steps behind me. I stood up and turned around. Another dragon was staring at me. He looked like me except for his crimson scales and sabered teeth that hung below his lower jaw. Each of his paws had five claws except for his hind left foot, which only had four. The other dragon was my best friend, Justin Clipper, who wanted to go back to Elsov just as I did.

"Are we ready to go?" I asked him.

The dark-red dragon nodded.

"We can go to the airfield at any time now," he said.

I blew another small flame. "Well Clipper, I'm going to miss it here. This place was perfect for us. I wish we could stay here longer."

"I wish I could stay too, but I'm sure our seaside home will suit us well. They told us it's in a secluded area. Perfect if we want to be alone, yet close enough to the city to get help if we need it. It'll be a fine place to live while we figure out how to travel to our real home, our home where we were born…"

Taking flight again, I traveled high into the cloudy sky, away from the Allegheny Forest. I reached the airfield and descended to the runway. Clipper landed next to me and groaned with discomfort. Despite being a dragon and his excellence in flight, he still had a touch of acrophobia. Luckily, he seemed to be overcoming it as the weeks went by.

"This one looks bigger than the one we arrived in," I said, setting my eyes on the awaiting plane. "Hopefully we can fit our wings in comfortably without cramming ourselves in. Keeping them folded for hours is a hassle."

"Luxurious ride back to New York," Clipper commented. "It shouldn't take that long for our friends to get ready. When we're all set, we'll take this same plane west."

We boarded the plane and a few minutes later it took off. The pilot welcomed us once we were in the air. He was one of few people who personally knew about me and Clipper.

Gazing out the window, I took one last look at the wild land around me. I was able to hide myself most of the time during my stay here, but I knew I was still spotted occasionally. I found it amusing when Sally told us that many travelers came to these forests in hopes of catching sight of me or Clipper. I felt like the Loch Ness Monster. After what happened in New York, stories about me and Clipper had spread all over the world. I never really minded that. Sometimes for fun I would fly near a town and get the people there all riled up in excitement. Other times I would see hikers looking for me with cameras or binoculars. I would fly into their view for a split second before disappearing (that was my way of saying hello). But for the most part, I loved being alone with one other dragon as a best friend.

About an hour later, the familiar skyline of New York City rose to meet us. When the plane landed, Clipper and I jumped out and stretched our wings and limbs.

"You can go to the dorm rooms," said Clipper, "I've arranged something with… a friend of ours. I'll be with you shortly. Take care and don't attract a lot of attention."

He left me to fly back to the dormitory alone. It was the home where I had lived before I became a dragon. I made sure no one was around when I landed. The courtyard was deserted; typical for summer. I could not remember what the exact date was, though. I guessed it was the latter half of summer, either the end of July or the beginning of August.

Finding the coast clear, I made my way to my old room. The main doors were open, so I walked in. The door to my room had been widened about twice its original size for me to fit through since it had been repaired from my previous damage. I gently clawed on the door. Joshua answered it.

"Jacob! You're here! I can't believe you made it!" he cried. "How was Pennsylvania? I'm glad you're here, oh but I don't think you should've touched the new door. Now it has scratch marks on it. They're very noticeable."

Joshua used to be Clipper's roommate. Ever since Clipper and I found out that we came from Elsov, he had helped us in any way he could.

"They're not too bad," I replied. "Do you know where Sally is?"

"She's at the ice rink, waiting for Clipper. Didn't she visit you last week?"

"She did. I guess she's the friend Clipper mentioned. And they're at the ice rink? Heh, Clipper still has maple leaf blood in him. I never imagined that he could skate the way he does. That was until he showed me before we left. He simply uses his claws as ice skates and slides around. Well, I'll let them play a while before I go get them. I have a favor to ask Sally."

I sat down to relax. A moment later, there was a knock on the door. I stood back up, feeling the strong urge to leave.

"Don't worry your dragon hide, Jacob," laughed Joshua. "It's Sergeant Nelson. He told me he was coming."

My ears flattened in relief as I sat back down. Joshua opened the door and invited the Sergeant inside.

I wriggled my claws as a greeting.

"Sergeant."

"Draco, I hope you had a good summer. Your home is ready now, and as I've said before, don't worry. Where you'll be living is just the place for a dragon like you. How was your stay in Pennsylvania?"

I nodded dreamily. "It was perfect for the summer."

"I would let you stay there, but there's protocol I must follow. Sorry."

"I don't care where we stay just as long as it's out of trouble," I said.

James smiled. "Good. You'll still be in a lonesome place. Yes, you will have a couple of neighbors, but I know them well. And they know very little about you."

"Honestly, I don't care who sees me at this point," I said. "I mean we're here, we're real, and we're friendly."

"Still, I would recommend you stay out of their sight and only go out at night. The reason it's California is because I'll be in Barstow, so you'll have Marine help if you need it. We'll just be an hour or two away. Most of the students at this college and your friends' parents believe that you've simply transferred, that's all. No one else has a connection to you."

"Thanks," I replied. "It sounds like a good place to be, even if I can't fly as freely. I'll miss that."

I waited in the dormitory for an hour after James left. I told Joshua everything about the last few months, except for my personal feelings on Elsov. We had a great time talking about our time apart before I decided to leave.

"Sorry to rush, but I have to see Sally. If there's nothing else, I guess I'll see you later," I told him.

Joshua said one last but quick goodbye. I wriggled out the doorway and took flight once again. Not long later, I took in a hawk's view of the ice arena where I knew Clipper and Sally were playing. After landing in the parking lot, I looked up at the building's marquee.

CLOSED
DO NOT ENTER!

"Closed," I snorted.

Dozens of cars in the street screeched to a halt. Some of the people immediately drove off in fright while most others tried to snap pictures of me. I was used to them behaving like that, so I ignored them.

I opened the unlocked door, crossed the foyer, and then went down into the ice rink. Clipper was there skating in graceful circles around center ice on his claws. A round black puck slid in front of him. Clipper then sped into the attacking zone and held his tail up to the puck. He squinted at the masked figure that was guarding the goal.

"I'll get another one past you," Clipper warned.

The guard remained silent, instead tapping the ice with a stick. Clipper kept his sights on the net beyond the goalie, his tail inching back for the strike. He slapped the puck and sent it racing for the goal. The goalie's padded leg intercepted the puck before it reached the net, causing the black missile to ricochet across the ice. The force caused the goalie to yelp and fall over. Clipper watched grimly as the masked person tried to stand after the fall.

The goalie cheered when she was on her skates again.

"Ha! Not this time! Pathetic shot!"

The goalie removed the protective mask of a vicious monster to reveal Sally Serene's smiling face. Clipper's upper lip lifted to bear his top teeth, particularly his sabered fangs. Feigning anger, he growled and skated over to Sally. He helped keep her balance to show his sportsmanship.

"I finally did it!" Sally hailed.

Clipper grunted after retrieving the puck. "You just blocked it. Simple as that. Ah well, you finally got it after all my other clean shots. Congratulations."

His expression shifted to one of disappointment when I fluttered into the rink and landed next to him and Sally. My feet slid back and forth, but I managed to keep my balance.

"Here you are. I guess I came in at the right time," I said.

Clipper pretended to pout. "No you didn't. I haven't even been here an hour."

"I know, but we're leaving soon." I turned to Sally. "It was nice when you visited us last week. I'll miss you when we leave. It won't be the same without you."

"I'll miss you too," said Sally. "In case you were wondering, Chang and Reno are already in California. It was hard getting used to them not being around. I miss holding little Reno. She was so adorable when we found her. Her scales felt so soft in my hands. I wonder what she's doing right now."

"Not much, I believe," I said. "I remember you telling us about Chang. Since he broke his foot, I assumed he's been house-bound. There can't be much for Reno to do."

"That's the cost of a novice aviation accident," Clipper quipped.

We talked about Chang and Reno for a moment. When I finally had the chance, I told Sally why I was at the rink.

"Sally, I need you to do something. The rest of the potion is in our lab. I want you to hide it so no one will find it. Bury it, lock it up, sit on it, do whatever. Just protect it."

Sally grew concerned. "Jacob, we've been through this before. Are you sure it's a potion and just not the mixture itself? You created it."

"It was a potion," Clipper clarified. "When I had my vision of Elsov, I was told that Jacob and I were both born as dragons, sent here to fight the Monolegions. I have no idea how, but it was only a matter of time before we would have the potion. Jacob and I were in the form of humans. Thus, the potion turned us back into our real selves."

"Our lives are much different than what we had thought," I said. "Now can you please hide the potion, Sally? It shouldn't take too long. We'll wait for you to get back before we leave."

"Fine," Sally sighed.

She brushed back her long brown hair and skated back to the locker room while Clipper and I left the ice rink.

Sally removed the skates from her feet and dressed into her casual clothing. Once finished, she left the arena and headed to the parking lot where her car was waiting.

It was quite some time before she arrived at the empty laboratory outside the city. She still had her key to open the door. Inside the lab, some things had been reorganized and rearranged since the day of the incident, but the empty syringe gun was still aimed at a vacant rat cage. A computer lay lifeless near the wall. Sally searched until she found what she was looking for. The rest of the mixture was stored inside a cabinet in a corner of the room. She took a good long look at the material. It flashed many colors that danced before her eyes.

"What's it doing?" she asked, astounded. "Maybe it *is* a potion."

She picked up the container with the fluid inside. The many colors dazzled her. If anything could be a potion, this was certainly it. Curious to know more, she pulled the cover from a microscope. She turned it on and placed a drop of the potion on a slide. What she saw bound her tongue. She had never seen anything like it! She wanted to know more about the potion. Pulling up a stool, she sat down for a closer look.

Clipper and I anxiously sat in the dormitory room. I gazed at the clock on the wall.

"I feel bad. We have to go and Sally hasn't returned," I said. "I don't want to leave her like this."

"She'll understand," said Clipper. "I feel bad too, but we've got to go."

I knew we had to leave, though I was still worried about Sally. It wasn't like her to be late.

We departed from the dormitory one last time. A drop of emotion fell upon me as I left the campus. It was here where I had lived when I became a dragon. Now I was moving on. This moment felt like a new beginning for me. A few tears crept out of the corners of my eyes. There was no time for deep feelings, however. I turned and left, wondering if I would ever visit the dormitory again.

Joshua took a taxi while Clipper and I flew. I still could not rid myself of my concern for Sally. I hope nothing's happened to her, I thought.

We descended to the ground as we approached the runway, several minutes before Joshua showed up. We were met by the same pilot as before.

"This isn't necessary. I'd rather fly myself," Clipper grumbled.

"I know what you mean," I said. "We could fly ourselves but it's too far. Besides, we don't want to be seen in town after town when there's no reason for it, do we? Plenty of people here have already seen us."

The three of us boarded the plane and it took off.

"I wish Chang could have flown us," said Clipper. "He agreed to pilot us wherever we needed to go. At least he was able to take Reno. I can't wait to see her again. She must miss us as much as we miss her."

Joshua looked over his shoulder toward us.

"And I hope she won't draw attention to herself when she gets rid of the potion. When Sally visited me before she went to find you two, she said that Chang's staying at a hotel. He said he'll join us when our house is completely ready so he doesn't have to unload everything with his bad foot."

The three of us talked and joked for a lengthy time until, after a while, I had to cover a yawn. I felt my eyes become heavy, so I told Clipper to wake me if we were about to land. Before long, I was offered a dream I could not resist.

I WAS FLYING THROUGH THE SWEET-SMELLING AIR. THE SKY WAS *painted a brilliant blue, and the sun touched everything in its reach. I looked down to the ground below. There was green farmland as*

far as the eye could see, almost like the fields where I had lived in Oklahoma. Where was I? I was no longer in an airplane. I was flying alone. Where were Clipper and Joshua? They were nowhere to be seen.

Joy filled my heart when I recognized where I was. It was Elsov! I had returned! Maybe now I could try to find Pearl Forest again.

My spirit felt as light as a balloon. I froze my wings and allowed myself to freefall, only flapping to slow myself as I neared the ground. Once I landed I felt the soft, moist soil; very rich in nutrients. I knew I would come to this world again! I looked up to see that the sun was starting to set over a range of jagged, rocky mountains that frankly weren't that tall.

Feeling uncontrolled and childish, I took flight again to chase after the sun. I wanted to catch it and hold it in my claws. I flew over the sweet land until I came to the rugged mountain range. As I approached the massifs, the bright, welcoming colors of the fields were no longer showing off. Nothing bright was anywhere to be seen. First the fields were there, now they weren't. The sun was obscured by a haze of an unknown pollution. The air was condensed and smoggy.

"It may not be Pearl Forest, but I still love it," I said to myself.

I landed on the flatlands before the mountains and gazed up at the peaks. They were black and covered in ash and smoke. I started to doubt what I had just said. Never had I found dry mountains to be so ugly and unwelcoming. It was no longer a place I loved. Everywhere was bare and desolate. Not even a plant, alive nor dead, was present.

I continued to explore here and there for anything of interest. In between two dull boulders, I found a path that led to what looked like a town beside the mountain. Though the town looked neat, it was completely deserted. I had no feeling of danger, so I went calmly through it. The path was straight for a moment, but soon began winding its way up the mountainside. The string of empty houses and shops followed me up the steep slopes, making this part of the town look like cliff dwellings. I looked up to see where the path ended, but something else caught my eye. Sitting on the tallest peak, glaring down at me, was a huge castle with high walls that ended at the cliffs.

The castle looked impregnable, and I believed that. I felt intimidated upon seeing it.

As I continued forward, I began to feel an intense heat. Feeling uncomfortably hot was a strange sensation for a dragon. An eerie moan from around a bend in the path broke my concentration on the local environment. Someone could be in trouble! I had to help whoever it was. As I rounded the bend, I found a gray-scaled dragon about my size leaning against a boulder. It almost blended completely into the rocks and ash.

"Who are you? What are you doing here?" I asked him.

I was very curious. I never thought I would see another dragon like me or Clipper so soon. Yet here he was, resting in front of me. I came over to greet him. When I offered a paw, he stood up and hissed at me. I was unsure if he was scared or if I should be.

"I can help you," I offered.

"No!" he snarled with a rough accent.

I was a little offended by his impolite behavior.

"Excuse me? I didn't mean to be rude."

"Nethaa!" he hissed.

He blew a large flame at me. I backed away, unharmed. *I wonder why he's so grumpy,* I thought.

"What did you say?" I asked him.

The lonesome dragon unfurled his wings.

"E-saw nethaa! Doss-les or E-viss cendeth ye!"

Strange, it sounded like a bunch of hissing and snarling, but it also sounded like he was saying something to me.

The dragon snapped his jaws and jumped at me with his claws at the ready. I ducked just in time. He jumped past me and I charged at him in defense. But like any dream, my legs suddenly felt as if they were made of lead. There was nothing I could do. Because of my sluggishness, I was pinned beneath him in a matter of seconds. I had to use my hind legs to kick him off me. Luckily, they cooperated this time. He rolled aside then fell over the edge of a steep cliff. My sudden anger turned into utter guilt. I rushed over to the ledge. He was nowhere to be found.

"Who was he?" I murmured under my breath.

I backed away from the cliff. When I did, a small gust of wind came from the face of the mountainside. I turned around to see a large opening like a gate that led inside the peak. Curious once again, I walked inside. The heat grew much more intense. Venturing deeper into the cave, I found many rooms and corridors. It looked like it was part of the castle above.

I found some stairs and began to climb them. The trip was long. I was panting by the time I reached the top. Inside the main part of the castle, I found myself in the great hall. There were two small waterfalls that created narrow rivers on both sides of the room. Between the waterfalls was something I had hoped I would never see in my dreams again. It was the dragon I had dreamt of all summer long. He was wine-red from head to tail. He was far darker than Clipper, almost as dark as me. Even his wings were a murky crimson. He was also much larger than me and had a long spike standing above his nose and many more all over his body. I never thought a real dragon could be so large. He stared at me while sitting on an elevated platform that appeared to be a throne, a throne for a mighty leader. Behind him was a black banner with an orange symbol in the center that somewhat resembled a spider. I remembered seeing that symbol in the Monolegion camp on Komodo Island. I lowered my head in fear from the dragon's devilish auburn eyes.

"Ah, Jacob Draco. Isn't that your name? The brave black dragon is cowering like a hatchling." His voice was fiendish and cunning.

Struck by the insult, I felt my mind beginning its feared transformation. I was aware of my short temper, but I wished it had not come this time. My worries were suddenly blotted out by the need to spill hot, salty blood. Baring my knifed teeth, I lunged at his throne. That turned out to be a costly mistake. With no effort, he lifted a paw and struck me down. I fell back to the floor in front of his throne.

"The Wrath of Vesuvius is now upon you!" he announced. "I am the Wrath of Vesuvius! I am your King! You will have a fate worse than the nymph you lost if you rise against me!"

His remarks echoed in my mind. I hadn't heard him speak in my dreams before. Was he the Wrath of Vesuvius? Was he the one I was warned about? I believed so! I wanted to fight him again, but I remained on the floor, sobbing. I covered my head with my paws, waiting for death to reach me. His tooth-filled mouth lowered to mine and coughed out a stream of smoke.

"Jacob, we're almost there. Wake up!"

I MUST HAVE CRIED OUT WHEN I WOKE. CLIPPER LOOKED AT ME worriedly.

"Jacob, are you all right? You slept through the whole trip. We're almost there. I can see the Pacific Ocean from up here."

I blinked and groaned like a lion.

"Ugh, what a dream. I was back on Elsov, but I saw that large dragon again. There's something about him, Clipper. I know it."

Clipper chuckled, keeping half of his attention out the window.

"Oh, well. Dreams like that happen. It was only a nightmare."

"I know, but this dream was different. This isn't the first time I've dreamt about him. Each time I do, I feel fear. It's nothing how I feel when I'm angry. I wake up startled with my heart racing inside me. Just now, he said he was the Wrath of Vesuvius. He also spoke of Treetop. I'm still worried about her."

Clipper turned back around, his full attention now on me.

"Did you say Vesuvius? The Wrath of Vesuvius? Where have I heard that before...? Monty mentioned that before he died, right?"

"The Wrath of Vesuvius would come upon us is what he said," I clarified. "Do you think there's a connection? Monty said that for a reason. Is Vesuvius this dragon I dream about? And if so, how strong is he?"

Joshua was listening from his seat.

"I would sure hate it if he was a dragon. I don't understand magic like you two do, but if there's a connection with some sort of dragon, I wonder why he would be named after a volcano in Italy. Mt. Vesuvius?"

"I don't know if there's any connection to that or not," I said, puzzled. "The volcano got its name from the Romans. The name means 'the one who lightens' if I remember right. Besides, how can a volcano that had its name for so long have any connection with a dragon from *our* day on a different world?"

"Anything's possible," Clipper concluded.

I was about to reply when the pilot interrupted our conversation.

"I'd like to hear what this magic and Vesuvius is all about, but you'll have to talk about it later. We're starting to descend."

Clipper yawned. "He's right. We can talk about this later. Let's get settled in then try to figure this out. If Vesuvius is a danger to us, I want to be ready. For all we know he could be a lot worse than Monty."

What Clipper said scared me, and it took a lot to scare me. Could he really be worse than Monty? That sorcerer was not easy to defeat.

We were quiet for the next few minutes. I felt an odd sensation under my feet. A few seconds later, I felt the wheels of the plane touch the ground. The plane taxied to a stop and the pilot opened the large cargo door, letting me and my two friends jump out.

My ears perked when I heard the sound of a truck. Clipper's ears perked as well.

"We have company coming. We better go," he said.

Clipper took flight with me close behind.

"See you there, Joshua! We're going to visit Chang! And don't worry, we won't create a fuss!" I called.

As the truck stopped, Joshua opened the trailer door. He thanked the driver and began loading his belongings from the plane to the truck.

SALLY WAS MESMERIZED. THE POTION WAS SO BEAUTIFUL! SHE DID not realize how late it was. She hadn't learned anything new about

JORDAN B. JOLLEY

the potion since her first few observations on it. When she finally glanced up at the clock, she took a deep breath. She had missed the last goodbye to her friends.

She covered her face with her hands, feeling deep shame. They're gone; I need to take this potion away as soon as possible, she thought.

Unsure of the nature of the potion, she decided to take it with her in a canister for safety. Sally knew that in the cabinet where she found the potion was such a canister. Finding it, she quickly placed the container of the mysterious potion inside it. She had difficulty closing the lid but managed to lock it down.

"Now what do I do with this?"

As she prepared to leave, she heard an abnormal hissing coming from the canister. She bent down to investigate the sound when the lid suddenly popped and the canister ruptured. The potion exploded into Sally's face. The sudden fright caused her to slip and fall on the floor. For almost a minute, she was dazed and confused. When she stood back up and her vision readjusted, she looked down. There were only drops of the thick potion inside the canister, nothing more.

"Where did the rest of it go? It's gone!" she gasped.

Dropping on her hands and knees, she searched every inch of the floor, but didn't find another drop of the potion among the shards of glass. Feeling even more guilty, she got to her feet. The potion was nowhere in sight. Certainly it couldn't have just disappeared. As she resumed looking for the potion, she began to feel lightheaded. She sat down in a chair and groaned in despair.

"Oh, where did it go?"

CHAPTER 2

THE WIZARD'S TRUTH

Fenson the dwarf hummed a simple tune to keep himself entertained throughout his long journey. Bluepond, who walked beside Fenson's horse, looked up at him and held a finger to his mouth.

"May I not recommend your music? Lovely as it is, we are in dangerous territory. We do not want any goblins swarming us, now do we?"

Fenson stopped humming, clearing his throat. He kept his pace slow so the little nymph could keep up with him.

"We've been on this path for days," he said to Bluepond. "I know you've said you don't like traveling on horseback, but you must at least have the courtesy to be just a little bit weary. How far are we from this portal or whatever it is?"

"Oh, we are near," said Bluepond, "but we need help from the Keeper of the three worlds. His name is Trihan. The Keeper before him was the Sorcerer Triathra. He was the one who led the dwarf tribes, and for other reasons—"

"I see. I see. In that case, how far are we from this Trihan fellow?"

"His castle is not far. It is a wizard's castle and there is a portal there. We can use that if Trihan will let us. Because of our quest, perhaps he will permit us to travel to the first earth."

The woods soon gave way to an open field. In the center of the field stood a shining, grand structure: the Wizard's castle. Next to the castle's outer walls was a small, empty stable. Fenson dismounted his horse and unsaddled her. After he led her to the stable where he gave her some oats, he and Bluepond looked in awe at the majestic building. They approached the outer gate where Fenson located a clean white rope. He firmly pulled on it. The faint ringing of a bell was heard from the interior of the castle. The wrought iron gates suddenly opened and the two friends stepped through them. They walked along a stone path that led into the courtyard. The yard was lush with healthy grass. A line of young pines, where the songbirds and squirrels played, and colorful flower beds surrounded the path. The two new friends continued around a small, gurgling fountain and stopped before two ornate wooden doors. Fenson grabbed the handles and pushed the doors open. Entering the main hall, they passed over corridors until they found an open door to another room.

"You could have at least waited for an answer," said Bluepond.

Fenson shrugged. "Sorry. I'm used to walking into my friends' homes without knocking. It's a custom where I come from."

"Never mind, it was I who opened the gate when I saw you from my window. Come in, you are welcome."

The dwarf was the first to see the peaceful wizard in a brilliant violet cloak coming from one of the rooms. A smile appeared on Trihan's face as he waved at them.

"And what is it that brings you here?"

Fenson, after introducing himself and Bluepond, gave a quick summary of his recent encounter. He told of his visit to the restaurant and his run-in with the two dwarfs and the goblin.

Trihan nodded after hearing this.

"Hmm... I see. Indeed, this may cause trouble. Is this act of aggression led by the Grün-hære or under Vesuvius' orders?"

"I... believe it was Vesuvius," Fenson stammered, fiddling with his satchel. "I don't know for sure. I believe it'll just be a small group, no real army."

"If this small group is not part of the mighty Grün-hære, I do not want an incident that will attract that nasty bunch," Bluepond stated. "They are a fearful army that should not be bothered with if you do not intend to do so. Trihan, my friend Fenson would like to make a proposal."

Trihan stared down at Fenson. The dwarf gulped, nervous with the Wizard's eyes on him.

"Ehh… I was hoping to help the darkscaled dragons who are our friends. The goblin said his plan will go into action in a matter of days. He must be doing this for Vesuvius."

The Wizard mused. "Ah, King Vesuvius III. A corrupt tyrant, he is. He has worn the crown for some seasons now, being one of the largest and most powerful of dragons. I fear he does intend to harm our dragon friends, him and any Nibelungs who remain. They must be upset with the loss of their sorcerer. Vesuvius' royal lineage founded the Nibelung tribe, and now they're in disorganized bunches. When the two darkscales return to our world, they may be useful to our good cause."

"And they will rescue my sister," Bluepond finished.

"If I may say, the dragons may be lost," said Fenson. "It's possible they have never laid eyes on a goblin before. What they need are experienced allies like myself and Bluepond."

"And this is how you want to help?"

Bluepond bowed his head in respect.

"Yes sir. We wish to help."

Trihan gazed at the two for a moment.

"You must realize that inter-world traveling is highly forbidden under most circumstances. I myself can only do it if absolutely necessary. If another person or creature ventures abroad, there is a risk that he or she will cause trouble. If any person *does* cross the veil elsewhere without permission, he shall stand condemned before me. I should say no… but…" The Wizard hesitated. "These two darkscales you wish to find must return to Elsov. They are the ones born of a different breed in their families. They were born as natural dragons. Before you leave, let me tell you how important Jacob and Clipper are and the nature of their breed."

"Jacob and Clipper? Are those their names?" Bluepond asked.

"Indeed so, they are the ones who were sent to stop the vile Nibelungs. Remember that most dragons come from across the sea. They are darkscales. Over there, dragons are their natural selves: wicked and cruel. But in some lands, dragons are taught wisdom and humility. These dragons have green eyes rather than yellow; they are brightscales, or lightscales, as you may call them. They are small in number compared to the dark and natural dragons. The names of 'dark' and 'light' scales are more symbolic, though. It is a matter if a dragon's heart is light or dark that spawns the breed, not the physical color of its scales. Yes, the color of eyes can indicate his or her heritage, but that explains only so much."

Bluepond's face held an expression of wonder, as if something connected in his mind.

"What are you thinking?" Fenson asked him.

"The black dragon," Bluepond said in a soft voice. "Our colony thought those stories about the two dragons and the Nibelungs were fictitious tales. So, the black dragon who came to our colony those many months ago was one of *those* dragons! It did have eyes of amber. Yes, you mentioned that when you came here, Fenson. We were unsure if the connection was true or not. Now I am sure it is. This is astonishing! I have seen the dragon before, though I did not meet him personally."

"You thought those stories were legends?" said Fenson.

"Popular stories among dwarfs and elves are sometimes viewed in a different way when they reach a nymph's ears. If these dragons were born on our world, how did they reach the first earth in the form of humans?"

"It was not an easy process," said the Wizard. "I will tell you what happened when they were born.

"Many centuries ago, before the spell of the lightscales, one of the good dragons left the human world to assign two hatchlings to take the human form for their first eighteen years and travel to the first world. They would eventually discover a potion that would change them back to their original form. I was there when the two were first born.

"I WAS IN MY NEWLY-BUILT CASTLE. AS EXPECTED FOR MY YOUNG *age, I was excited. It was the home I had always desired. I was inside my study, reading through chemistry and potion-making when it happened. I was preparing to leave for my laboratory when I heard the sound of the bells. I went outside to find a small river nymph. I could tell she had urgent news. She was hopping up and down, unable to speak clearly.*

"'Please calm down before you burst,' I said to her. 'Is there something you need to tell me?'

"The nymph spoke at a pace I could barely handle.

"'A number of eggs were ready to hatch in a nest of the lightscaled dragons,' she said to me. 'I was hoping to watch the hatchlings break from their shells, but the strangest thing had occurred. You are a wizard. Do you know what happened?'

"I patted her head to calm her. 'Please speak slower,' I said. 'Though I may be a wizard, I'm not omnipotent. Now, what sort of something has happened to these dragon eggs?'

"'Oh, Trihan the Great,' she began. 'All the eggs save two had white shells, meaning the hatchlings will be among the good. Two were red, indicating the true, natural dragon: evil. Because you are a wizard, I thought you would know the explanation. Darkscales do not live in our land. Why would this be?'

"I was confused at first. Then I remembered, in my youth, my father had taught me that two darkscales would be sent to the first earth. The teaching was centuries old, and it was finally time. When the two darkscaled dragons were born among the lightscales, they would be sent to the human world to stamp out a rebellious dwarf tribe. I had to witness their birth and send them to the Keeper of the three worlds, for I was not the Keeper at the time.

"'These two eggs, are they in the nests now?' I asked. 'If so, I believe I should see them.'

"The nymph bowed her head. She stopped panting, took a deep breath, and spoke much slower.

"'We believed they were wicked,' she said. 'We had no knowledge of this spell. Though many of the lightscales were heartbroken, they believed it was the necessary thing to do. We could not kill them, so we banished them far away. Two nymphs were sent to complete the task, for the mothers of the red eggs refused to do so. Along the way, they were ambushed by a darkscale who was not native to the land. If the spell you mentioned determined the hatchlings' breed, then the darkscales knew something we did not.'

"After hearing the news, I stood up in despair, yet I kept myself calm. I knew that only one other being besides my family line knew of this spell. I knew that far off in the Eastern Ocean, there was a kingdom led by a dynasty of tyrannical dragons, the darkest the darkscales could be. I guessed that the newly-crowned King would stop at nothing to keep the eggs from our possession. I ordered the nymph to gather one other dragon from the nests and five nymphs.

"'Our little ones have not yet hatched,' I said. 'There is still hope, but we must move fast. Spread the word. I fear that if we lose the hatchlings, trouble may arise. We must get those eggs back to prevent the distant Kingdom from spreading its evil rule. This is urgent.'

"'Is the dark Kingdom truly behind this?' the nymph asked nervously.

"'The one Nibelung tribe of the foreign lands is a branch of the Vesuvian Kingdom,' I said. 'If they hold the dragon eggs that are rightfully ours, the distant Kingdom will rule much more than we, or our friends abroad, can handle. What worries me is the Kingdom's new leader. He is young and unpredictable, as dragons often are. He will show no light to our little ones. They'll have nothing good to learn. Now he is on the highest throne. If he obtains the power he lusts for, a deadly war may arise from his fire.'

"'Who is this new King?' she asked.

"I closed my eyes. His name flowed on my breath. 'King Vesuvius III,' I said.

"I remember gripping the brass handle of my scepter. The power within the living object sank into my flesh. After the small group I had called for was organized, I immediately set out on my mission. It took all day to track down the two dragons, for the one who had stolen the eggs had a companion. They were headed to the sea. If they crossed it, we would lose the eggs for sure. I knew I mustn't let that happen. It was nearly dawn when our lightscale located the thieving dragons.

"'I smell them,' she said, facing south. 'They are just beyond the clear field. I feel sure one of them has the eggs. We must get them back before we lose them forever.'

"Every member of the camp stared at the ground, not knowing how to retrieve the eggs. Dragons are dangerous creatures. Nobody knew how to get past them unharmed.

"'There is no way to bring the eggs back to our possession,' one of the nymphs mourned. 'They know we are here and they will fry us for an early breakfast. We should have never chosen to banish the eggs!'

"Everyone felt hopeless, except for me. I did not feel it was time to quit. I knew that it was a mistake to banish the eggs. We have all made mistakes. I knew the hatchlings would not be lightscales, but they were capable of learning right from wrong. No matter what type of dragon, they were still members of our greater family.

"'Now listen to me,'" I began to say. 'I will try my best to bring them back. I will not let them fall into the enemy's grasp. Now let us stop talking and take action. We need to get the young ones. I especially do not want Vesuvius to force them to the Icy Peaks. They will be much worse there than living in his own Kingdom.'

"The lightscale shed a few tears when we heard the call from one of the thieves. Each of us looked up into the dim sky as the two thieves emerged from their nearby camp. They spotted us and began to flee instead of fight. One of them had a sack hanging from its jaws.

"'There they go! We must pursue them!' a nymph yelled.

"The lightscale in the camp quickly took flight. Her tears turned to steam that floated away as she regained her courage. Holding my scepter high, I summoned one of the spells I had recently learned. A cloud, promising a small storm, materialized over the two thieves. Lightning struck them both. The spell caused a sever ache in my hands and head, but I did not regret casting it. The nymphs of our camp cheered. The storm cloud vanished and the rays of the rising sun relit the morning. I watched our green dragon dive down into the trees and out of sight.

"'I must say that was a clever use of magic,' one of the nymphs told me.

"'I did what I had to do,' I said. I did not think expressing my physical pain was necessary.

"The green lightscale returned with the worn sack hanging from her teeth. She placed the sack on the ground for me to open. The eggs of red were unharmed. I kissed the top of the lightscale's snout.

"'You have done well,' I said. 'I thank you. But next time, please do not banish any eggs. Darkscales or not, these dragons are our family. If we lose them, darkness will fall across the first earth as well as ours.'

"The dragon's ears drooped; her wings fell to the ground. She sorrowfully asked for my forgiveness.

"'I'm not angry with you,' I said. 'Now let us celebrate. We have the eggs back!'

"Our group cheered the moment I said that. But the rejoicing ended very soon when a nymph expressed his desire to leave before the thieves awoke and sought revenge against us.

"I ordered my group to return to the nests as soon as possible. The next day, we returned with our precious cargo. The two mothers were overjoyed yet shocked. I explained to them why their offspring were destined to be born as darkscales. One of the mothers caressed her egg.

"'These eggs should have never been banished, Trihan,' she said, not once taking her eyes off the priceless gift. 'How could I leave it? It is not its fault that it will be born a darkscale. They can live like us. Every dragon, light or dark, has to work extra hard to stay true to our morals.'

"It was not long before we noticed that the egg started shaking. The group of nymphs gathered around. A moment later, a crack appeared. Others formed as the hatchling scratched at the shell. When the cracks parted, a tiny black infant emerged. I could tell it was a male. He had a happy impression of the large world he viewed.

"The second egg soon hatched as well. The second infant was red as the eggshell. He too was male and had two little points for teeth in his upper jaw. Despite the color of their scales, they both seemed excited. They were too weak to stand on their own. They squirmed and wriggled their little wings.

"'Darkness may be the mark of their curse, but it is not the curse itself,' I said. 'They will learn our ways, even if they are not in our presence. We have promised the dragon of old. These two hatchlings will be disguised as humans until they are young adults. They will protect the other world from the Nibelungs before they return home.'

"The mother of the black dragon, with her teeth, carefully transported her new hatchling beside her and set him down. She protested at the idea of leaving her child.

"I promised that her son would be safe. I turned to the mother of the red hatchling. 'Yours will also be safe. Don't worry, you will see them again. They will see Elsov when the right sun rises. I know this is a tremendous sacrifice, but it will be worth it. Trust me, when you see them again, they will not be evil. They will love you as you love them.'

"Another tear formed in the corners of the mothers' eyes. She nuzzled her son's white stomach and began to sing a soft song,

"'Remember the fairy, remember the grøl.
May you find guidance from the dragon of old.
Avoid your temptations, and follow the path;
The path that will lead you through desolation.
This is my song, my song to you.
May we meet again and the old will be new.
Remember the fairy, remember the grøl.
May you find guidance from the dragon of old.'

"*The two heartbroken mothers flew off with their new hatchlings to the Keeper's castle the very next week. Following them was the curious sister of one of the infants; I did not know which. The rest of the dragons of the nest closed their eyes in respect. There was no longer a reason for my presence. I returned to my castle later that day and resumed my business in my laboratory. As I worked, the mother's song echoed in my mind. The hatchlings may have not understood the song, but hopefully they would apply its message.*"

Bluepond nodded thoughtfully at the conclusion of the story.

"The black dragon who visited our colony was very friendly," he said. "I believe his mother and father will be happy when they see him again."

"It is one of the few reasons why a creature is allowed to travel to the other world," replied Trihan. "It is against the rules for anyone to travel to the other world without my permission."

"I'm aware of the law," said Fenson, "but we must stop the goblin's plan."

Trihan began to think long and hard. It was a difficult decision. He rubbed the handle of his scepter, taking a deep breath before answering.

"I would say no, Mr. Katque, but what you wish to do is very important. I know those dragons want to return to Pearl Forest, and they must come home. I will allow it under certain conditions. It is easy for a dwarf to be tempted to fit in with the outside life. First, you must remember that you come from Elsov. Magic is your friend. Second, you are entering near a populated area. You do not have to stay hidden, but you must not draw attention to yourselves. Third, remember that you are on a mission. There is no time to play. Find the dragons and bring them back. You are seeking a portal. You and the dragons are portal seekers."

The Wizard guided the two friends to the portal in an upstairs room. The gray square platform was big enough for Fenson and Bluepond to stand on. Trihan waved his Master Scepter. He turned back to the stone wall opposite the portal. The wall was covered with many different runes and symbols that neither Fenson nor Bluepond could read. Placing his hand on two of the runes, Trihan shut his eyes and began murmuring.

"What's going to happen?" asked Fenson.

"I'm trying to find the man you should seek, so I know where you should go," said Trihan. "Now hush."

He turned back toward the portal a moment later.

"I have seen Jacob and Clipper do many things on the first world. It seems that they are staying in a new home by the Pacific Ocean." Trihan returned to the edge of the portal. "You will be north of the ones you are seeking. Be warned: if you choose to go, you may have trouble coming back."

"What kind of trouble?" Fenson queried nervously.

"There are no active portals on the first earth. You must find the six pieces for the portal to be created."

"The six pieces?" Fenson repeated.

"The last functioning portal on the first world had been taken apart. Throughout the years, the pieces have been scattered. Some of them are buried while others are in the possession of people. When you go to the first earth, travel east and you will find a clue to the guide of the first piece in a forgotten part of town. Sadly, I cannot have my portal take you directly to the seekers."

"A forgotten part of a town," said Bluepond. "I am still lost, but I will catch on. I am ready to go."

"Good luck," said Trihan. "Find the six pieces to return. The pieces will be your keys."

Fenson jumped off the platform so Bluepond could leave. Trihan held his scepter to the portal. A sudden whirlwind materialized over the nymph. Fenson watched it cover his friend. When the whirlwind dissolved, Bluepond was gone. Fenson could not speak.

He bravely returned to the platform with his left hand clutching his satchel in a tight grip. He felt as if his heart was in his mouth. Trihan activated the portal again and Fenson left the castle. He and Bluepond were ready to complete an important task.

CHAPTER 3

THE PACIFIC SHORE

At the Los Angeles International Airport, a liner landed and taxied to the terminal. Passengers emptied from the side and walked up the concourse. Charles Cowley and his thirteen year old son gathered their luggage and left the terminal. The son gawked at the awesome sight of the city as he passed a window. He never imagined that he would be in such a place.

Once everything was in order, Charles and his son left the airport and approached a bus stop where they took seats on a bench. While he was waiting, the boy pulled a book out of his baggage. On the cover of the book was a grand illustration of a green dragon flying over the mystical countryside. It stared into the viewer's eyes, smiling as steam floated from its nose and around its head. A plastic dragon paw of the same color hung on the edge of the book, sealing it shut. The boy took out a small metal key and inserted it inside a hidden keyhole behind the paw. With a click the paw moved up, allowing the boy to open the book and examine the contents. Many of the pages were blank, but the first few had magnificent sketches and drawings of the boy's favorite creatures. The boy was a very talented artist. He had the ability to make any of his drawings appear to jump out of the pages. There were detailed depictions of dragons, some of them infants scurrying out on adventures beyond their nests, some of them adults looking over high ridges; and other fantastic beasts practicing magic.

Charles noticed the open book.

"Not now, Will," he said. "I know I gave you that book for your birthday, but we have to get to the house first."

William Cowley slid the book back in his bag, instead focusing on the city around him. He didn't mind coming to California, but he still wished he was back home on the Isle of Man: a small island off the coast of mainland Britain. He lived in a small house that was not too far from the ruins of an old castle. To William, the Isle of Man would always be his home, welcoming him with ceaseless happiness. William also had a deep love for dragons. He became especially interested in them when he heard stories about the black and red dragons that were sighted in North America as well as Europe and even Britain, which was closer to home.

A few minutes passed by before the large gray bus arrived at the stop. William stepped in as soon as the doorway was clear. When he was comfortable in his seat, he pressed his forehead against the window. He did not say a word the entire trip. The bus sped along a road next to the ocean. William conceded that the ocean was beautiful, being different from the shore at home.

He and his father got off a few hours later when the bus stopped in a smaller town. Walking several blocks, they left behind the neat rows of homes and approached the house where they would be staying. It was a single-floor brick dwelling with a porch sheltered by a layer of green ivy. Sitting about a hundred feet to the north of the house was an empty cabin. To the south was another red-brick home. There were only three houses alto-gether on the elongated street; there were no other buildings and no other people.

William's father proceeded up the front walk and rang the door-bell. A man answered; his wife stood behind him smiling.

"You made it! Come in! Come in!" cried the man. "Oh, I'm so glad you're here, Charles! I'm sorry about your brother. He was a good man."

"He was a good brother, he was. I'm glad to see you too, Frank-lin," said Charles.

William shyly walked in. He noticed a blonde-haired girl about his age standing next to them. To his surprise, the girl was pleasing to him and even a little attractive. The girl had a peculiar twinkle in her hazel eyes. She wore a lime-green shirt, denim shorts, and she held a thick, hardcover book in her hands.

"Hi there, I'm Emily," she said. "You must be William. It's nice to meet you."

"How do you do?" squeaked William, trying not to blush.

"I'm fine, thank you," Emily replied. "I've always wanted to go to Isle of Man. I've heard it's a very beautiful place; all those old ruins, legends of fairies, and even crazy motorcycle races."

Emily's father, Franklin, patted William's back and guided him to his temporary bedroom that faced the side of the cabin.

"New people are moving in there," said Franklin, "but I don't know who they are yet."

"We can meet them as soon as they arrive," William's father told him as he closed the bedroom door.

William unpacked his luggage and began arranging his belongings on the bed. With the window open, he heard the rushing of the ocean on the beach. Though he still missed the whispering of the winds in the pines and willows back home, he began to appreciate his new surroundings. He finished refolding a pair of trousers while feeling the warm breeze enter his room. When all his belongings were organized to his liking, he sat down on the bed and pulled out his book. Unlocking it, he examined the drawing of a dragon sitting on a rock along a shore of sand and seashells next to the large sea.

"This place isn't bad," he said to himself. "If only it was the same shore as this one…"

As he thumbed through his drawings, there was a knock on the door. He quickly closed his book. Answering the door, he found Emily standing there with a shy smile. Her book was still in her arms.

"Eh— hi William," she said, clearing her throat. "I was just wondering if you needed anything."

William kindly shook his head. "I don't need anything, thank you. Your home is very interesting. I love how quiet it is."

"Yes, it's quiet. I love it too. Only a handful of cars drive on our street every day. Our neighbors are nice too, and I'm curious to see who's moving in next door."

William glanced out the window to see the side of the cabin.

"I'm quite sure they'll be great neighbours," he said.

"I'm not worried at all. But what's funny is that that cabin's been empty for years. It just hasn't caught the eye of anyone. It's one of those 'out of the way' places. But a few months ago, some man in the military came and inspected the building. The only words I heard from him was 'this could be the one'. A few weeks ago, he said 'this *is* the one'. By the time he left, we heard that someone was moving in. That's all I know."

"Then I believe you'll soon have other blokes along this seaside road then."

The two laughed for a moment. Then William took a closer look at the book in Emily's arms. He pointed to it.

"What's that?"

Emily glanced at it before holding it out. "It's sort of like a guidebook about elves. It explains who they are and how they live. I know it's not to be taken seriously, but I love reading it anyway. I get this feeling when I read it. It's almost like it's real."

William took in the cover. The illustration depicted an unknown forest in the evening with elves standing amid the trees, holding golden lanterns. Admiring the artwork, he decided to show Emily his sketchbook.

"I've had this book since my last birthday. Would you like to see it?"

Emily picked up his book and opened the unlocked paw. She was amazed the moment she viewed the cover.

"Dragons, I see. I'm into them too. Sometimes I feel about them the same as I do elves, unless they try to eat me first."

William opened the book to show Emily his drawings. For a moment, Emily did not say a word. She did not know how to describe the well-crafted pencil drawings.

"These pictures are incredible, William! You have a great gift. Never before have I seen work like this. How do you do it?"

William's cheeks turned pink as he tried to explain his secret.

"Well, when I want to draw something, I close my eyes and try my best to envision myself in the drawing," he began. "As I think of every little detail, that image travels from my mind to the pencil. When I draw something, I feel I'm in complete control."

After examining a few more drawings, Emily glanced at the clock in the room.

"Well, I hope you'll have a great time staying here," she said. "I have to go help my dad now."

"I'll see you later," said William.

Emily gently closed the door behind her. William continued standing with his book in his hands until he finally locked it and left the bedroom. He passed by his father on his way to the front door.

"Where are you going?" Charles asked.

"I want to explore," said William, opening the front door. "I won't go far. I promise I'll be back soon."

"Just don't take too long and be careful," said Charles. "We'll meet the new neighbours soon."

Once outside, William walked down the sidewalk next to the beach. He marveled at the palm trees towering above him like brown pillars. Looking at the tall trees, he did not watch where he was going. He kept his eyes upward until he suddenly bumped into someone. It was another boy slightly older than William. William took a step back. The boy appeared to be friendly.

"Sorry," the boy said. "I wasn't looking where I was going."

"Don't worry about me. My name is William."

"I'm Henry. Well, that's my western name. My grandparents came from Hong Kong many years ago. It sounds like you're not from around here yourself."

"I'm from the Isle of Man. I'm just visiting here," said William.

"The Isle of Man, that's interesting." Henry eyed the book William was holding. "What's that?"

William held it out for him to see. "This is my sketchbook." He unlocked it and showed Henry the drawings.

"Dragons!" Henry exclaimed. "I like it. I love dragons too." He pulled a medallion from his pocket that had a different sort of dragon carved in it.

William ran his fingernail over the etched image of the serpent-shaped beast. "It's a fine piece of work," he said.

William gave the medallion back when they heard a large vehicle pull up behind them. Both boys turned their heads. They saw an orange truck squeak to a stop outside the cabin. A young man and the driver hopped out.

"They're here!" called Charles.

"You can come with us if you want," William told Henry.

His new friend agreed, and both joined Charles. The three, along with Emily and her parents, made their way to the truck.

"Here it is," the driver said to his younger companion. "You can move your furniture in now."

"Thank you," said Joshua.

As he began to unload the truck, William and Henry walked toward him. William watched the young man set the first items down on the grass and then glance at his watch.

"He seems nervous. Look at that him. He looks like he's waiting for someone," whispered William.

The newcomer noticed the two boys and waved at them.

"Hi there. I'm Joshua. I'm moving in here with a few roommates. Have you seen… anyone else yet?"

"No, sorry," Henry politely answered.

"I must have beaten them here, good." A peculiar look came into Joshua's eyes as he looked at William's sketchbook.

The two new friends walked back to William's current home while the adults greeted Joshua.

"He's an interesting person," said William. "He kept staring at my book."

"He must like it. I'm sure many people do," Henry replied.

SINCE WE WERE USED TO FLYING OVER NEW YORK, A SUBURBAN town did not seem nearly as bad. But any form of civilization was risky enough to fly over, no matter its size. As long as we were about, people would see us nonetheless. As Clipper and I had concluded before, people had to get used to us as well.

We circled over the town until I finally located the hotel that Sally mentioned to us while in Pennsylvania. The window to Chang's room sat just above a section of the roof, perfect for a landing. When our feet made contact, we took a moment to catch our breaths. Clipper then peeked inside a window, hoping it was the right one. From my view beside Clipper, I saw Chang sitting up on his bed, half-startled at our presence. He hopped on one foot to the window and opened it.

"Clipper, Jacob, you made it! You don't know how relieved I am to see you! It's been so long." He pressed his nose against the thin screen in the frame.

"Interesting place," said Clipper. "It's near the ocean. Jacob and I can just fly over the water whenever we want."

"It's been months since we last saw you. You should have visited us when Sally did. Maybe you could've avoided your accident," I said with a deep, dragon chuckle.

Chang pulled up a chair and sat down next to the window. He propped his foot, inside the heavy boot, on the sill.

"The beach will be a good home. That is until we find a way back to Pearl Forest," said Clipper.

While he and Chang conversed for a moment, I gazed around the top of the hotel. My concern grew when I had neither sight nor smell of a third dragon.

"Where's Reno?" I interrupted. "She's not here. Is she by herself?"

"Everything's okay, Jacob," said Chang. "She's at the beach, playing in the water to pass the time. She won't be seen, trust me. You should know how Reno can hide from people really well."

"That doesn't really matter. People catch sightings of us, but they don't believe their eyes," said Clipper. "Some have met us in person or caught a glimpse of us, but nobody believes them. It's hard to convince people."

Chang stared at him. "I'm convinced."

"Well, you personally know us."

I turned to Clipper, waiting for him to finish. "How about I find Reno and take her to the cabin?" I suggested.

"I don't see anything wrong with that," Clipper answered.

Chang agreed. "That's fine, go ahead. It's good to see you, Jacob."

"You too," I said.

Following a quick nod to Clipper and Chang, I made my way to the edge of the roof before taking off into the sky. As I flapped my wings, I took in the warm, Pacific breeze. It felt much different than the cooler New England air. It was a pleasant change. I flew high into the sky, over the ocean where no one could see me with a clear eye. They would possibly mistake me for a bird or something; at least that was what I hoped.

Finding the beach, I descended into a sandstorm formed by the wind of my wings. When everything settled, I looked right to left. I saw short yet firm yellow cliffs sitting in the distance on the right. On the left were no cliffs, but the smooth shore. Off in the distance that way, I could see visitors enjoying the sunny day at the ocean. But where I was, it was a lonely beach. I found that a good name for this place: the lonely beach.

Walking forward, I felt the water brush against my feet before the waves rushed above my elbow blades. The cool, salty water on my scales felt refreshing. I dropped my head below the surface. I had the sudden urge to chase after whatever fish was out there, but I kept my instincts in check. I stepped through the underwater surface until it was deep enough for me to swim. It was not long before I found the young brown-scaled dragon swimming in circles and corkscrews. Reno eventually noticed me and instantly headed for the shore. She shook the salt water off her wings and ran toward me.

"Jacob, you came!" she cried, rubbing her nose on my leg. "I missed you so much! I'm so happy you made it safely! Is Clipper here as well?"

"He'll be at the cabin," I said, looking down at the young dragon about a third of my size. I rubbed the end of my tail between Reno's horns. "Are you ready to see your new home?"

"I am," Reno chirped. "I didn't want to go inside without you. I'm so happy you're here. Oh, I missed you!"

When our wings were dry, we flapped off. They created another sandstorm that was left to settle behind us. We flew several hundred yards to the cabin. As Sergeant Nelson had mentioned, there were two houses south of ours. Nobody was about, so I continued across the yard. I folded my wings to fit through the conjoined set of doors. When I entered the living room, I was impressed with the spaciousness of it. It was big enough to fit at least five dragons! The wooden-beam ceiling rose almost twenty feet from the oak-wood floor. My wings no longer touched both walls when they were stretched out. Joshua was not present. I assumed he went shopping, but I didn't know for sure.

Reno looked around, amazed. "This place is big. Even you and Clipper can fit in here together."

"And I love the décor," I replied.

A china vase stood on a low table, landscape paintings hung on the brown plastered walls, a grandfather clock ticked calmly on one side of a spacious fireplace, while on the other side was a polished bookshelf filled to its capacity with an assortment of old books. On top of the bookshelf stood a globe and a bust of Edgar Allen Poe.

Clipper arrived a few minutes later. Reno was right: the three of us could sit comfortably in the living room. It felt nice for me to relax without feeling the need to tuck in my wings or my tail. The floor had already suffered many white claw-marks, but I didn't care much about that. The three of us continued to explore the house. Going up the stairs, I found a nice spot in front of two bedrooms. I laid there for a moment to test its space. I found it a good napping spot.

But as excited as I was about this new house, I wasn't completely happy. There was something on my mind; something that had a single, simple name: Elsov. It had been months since my vision, but I remembered it vividly. I remembered the fairies giving me the strange map. I remembered my unclear past. I remembered freeing the funny grøls. I remembered confronting the nasty goblins. My joyfulness of the day turned into sadness of the evening. A tear ran down my eye as I longed to go home. There were so many reasons why I had to find Elsov again. It wasn't only because I wanted to. It was also because I had to.

CHAPTER 4

LOST IN A NEW LAND

Gray clouds loomed overhead the next day, showering the town with heavy rain. The thick water droplets thumped on roofs like tapping fingers on a table. Fortunately, the storm helped clear any pollution in the air. Fenson and Bluepond awakened in the precipitation to find themselves on the side of a road. They both rose to their feet, lightheaded, and eyed the world around them.

"Ah, we are here on the first earth! Splendid!" Bluepond's exclamation was a mixture of excitement and fear.

Fenson didn't say anything right off. He was distracted by the skinny, towering tree that stood to his right. It was the loftiest he had ever seen.

"'Tis such a sight," he said.

The dwarf approached the round trunk and continued looking up. He saw the flat green leaves dancing in the mild wind.

"I've never seen a tree like this before."

"That is because you have never been in the climate where they grow," Bluepond explained. "Those are palm trees. They grow in warmer regions, unlike the land where we live."

"And how do you know what they are?" Fenson asked.

"I am a dryad; a *wood* nymph. My spirit belongs to the true children of the earth: the trees. I know each and every tree in existence."

He and Fenson looked around once more, both unsure of the new world. They at least knew there was an ocean nearby.

"Take in the view of this location and have it in your memory," said Bluepond, "that way we can know where we are when we come back."

"Trihan said we are north of the portal seekers and west of the first clue. If we know the correct direction and head south, we can get closer to whom we seek. But these people may not be able to help us if they don't know of the dragons living nearby."

"Right. It may take days, so we must not doddle. If we are to help the portal seekers, we must find them before our foes do." Bluepond looked up at the morning sky. He could see the rising sun's glow from behind the cumulus clouds. He then looked along the ground. Next to the row of palm trees was a busy street. "Here," he pointed out, "I see a footpath next to this road. Some of the town's folk are walking on it. We can use it too."

Fenson took a step on the sidewalk and watched the cars whiz by on the road.

"Phew! I feel a little dizzy from all this. These machines are something I've never seen before. They're a work of art, I must say."

Bluepond didn't reply. He looked back up at the dim sunlight and navigated himself southward. "We will go this way. There must be a clue for us somewhere."

Before long, the nymph proved his excellence in navigation.

Fenson scratched his head after they ventured into town. "Let's look around for a moment," he said. "We must learn where to go from here."

They began exploring different places: shops, grocers, offices, the library, and the sort. After visiting several establishments, one after another in their tireless search, Bluepond began to doubt himself.

"I am an expert at traveling in wooded terrain. When I am in any sort of populous settlement, I must confess I am not as skilled."

Fenson laughed. "Ha-ha! I guess now it's my turn to lead the way! I have been to many cites. Our towns appear to be similar with rectangular streets and whatnot. If we can just adapt to these rash changes in the environment, I believe we can find where we need to go."

Fenson took the point. They continued onward, making their way south. Again, they visited several places, but found nothing. Eventually discovering a small alleyway, they decided to rest there. They sat down against a dirty wall.

"Do you know where we are?" Bluepond asked doubtfully.

Fenson shook his head, frowning. "I suppose I can't lead us through a town like this either. Perhaps I'm more used to traveling like you."

"What are you saying?"

"I'm saying I have no experience either. We're lost. And all I've brought in my satchel is a spoon and three pennies that I'm sure are worthless on this world."

"We will find the portal seekers," said Bluepond. "Do not worry. Look! There is someone coming towards us! Maybe he can guide us to where we must go. A dragon cannot hide himself so easily, especially in a town like this."

Fenson thought Bluepond's idea was worth a try. They approached the gentleman, who was dressed in a fine black suit. The man held a coffee mug in one hand, a newspaper in the other, and was hurrying down the street in a stressful state. Fenson tried the best he could to pretend he was a local citizen.

"Eh, good day," the dwarf stammered. "Have you seen two dragons about?"

The man stopped. He stared with disbelieving eyes at the short, brawny bloke.

"Dragons? What do you mean? I don't have time for that. Now if you'll excuse me, I don't mean to be rude, but I'm late for an important meeting."

Before Fenson could utter another word, the man left in a hurry. Bluepond sat back down against the wall.

"So much for that," he said. "I guess we must realize these people cannot help us. They believe dragons are myth since the creatures have not set foot on this earth for many ages. Besides, who would trust us? We certainly stand out, especially me. We need to somehow blend in with this town."

Fenson spat on his boots and wiped them with his wrist. "How do we blend in? I'm a dwarf. You're a nymph. This environment is new to us. You may know about palm trees, but you have never been here before, and neither have I. And besides, you're right. How can we find the dragons if nobody knows they are here?"

"We knew this quest would be difficult before we came, my friend," said Bluepond. "Now enough with the questions we cannot answer. Let us continue." The nymph looked down at his rustic clothing. "With much regret, I have to say we must find the portal seekers by ourselves. We may, should I say, eavesdrop on conversations if they are of interest, but do not raise suspicion. We do not know if there are enemies about yet, and we do not want them to find us."

WILLIAM WAS OUT ON THE SHELTERED PORCH, LISTENING TO THE waves rushing onto the lonely beach. After meeting Emily and Henry, he felt glad that he had found such good friends so quickly. Now he sat alone, studying his drawings. He created his images with the shading of his pencil.

"Oh, I wish you were real," he said to his newly created dragon. "I wish."

Henry spotted him from the sidewalk and ran to the porch to get out of the rain. "Hi William, how are you? Don't mind me, I know the Wilcox's." He kept his eyes away from the book to keep William's new work private. "You know this place can be very nice. If only the dragons and other creatures in your book could enjoy it too."

"I know how you feel," said William. "I sometimes wish they could come out of my book."

Henry pulled out the medallion from his pocket, squeezing it in his hand.

"If they existed, I wonder how different our lives would be," William said thoughtfully, eyeing the shining bronze metal in Henry's hand.

"Who knows?" said his friend.

There was a brief moment of silence. Neither of them knew what to say next. The silence was broken when they heard a door close in the distance. William leaned from behind the vine-covered lattice to find Joshua on the front porch of the cabin. He saw Joshua take a step then turn to open the door again.

"Hey, Clipper," he called. "I'm going to get something for a homecoming dinner. Do you want anything?"

William heard a low, monstrous growl, followed by a rough voice.

"Fish! You know that's my favorite."

"I *was* going to get fish," said Joshua. "Anything else? Does raw beef sound appetizing? Never mind. I don't know what you and Jacob like to eat anymore."

"Fish sounds good, but anything else you want to get is fine by me."

William was confused. The voice sounded like it belonged to some sort of monster. He scratched his head when he heard a second voice that sounded much younger.

"Can I come? I'm small enough. I can find a way to go with you."

"All right, Reno," said Joshua. "My windows are tinted. But if you come with me, you'll have to stay in the car. Just remember, you must stay out of sight."

Joshua looked left and right. William and Henry shielded themselves with the trailing ivy over the porch.

"Reno, stay on the ground and get in the car," Joshua said. "We've got to be careful."

"Oh, you're no fun," the oddly feminine yet raspy voice replied.

William heard the car door close and the engine start. As Joshua drove away, he and Henry looked at each other with puzzled frowns.

The neighboring cabin appeared to be empty, but William sensed there was something else in there.

"Something strange is going on," said Henry. "Did you hear those other voices?"

"Let's not assume anything," said William. "My bedroom window looks directly at that house. If I find anything new, I'll tell you."

Henry took a deep breath. "Fair enough." The rain started falling again after a brief respite. "There's no need to get wet. I better head home," he said.

William said goodbye. He returned to his bedroom with his sketchbook unlocked. Opening to a fresh page, he began drawing the images of his dreams. He drew the trees and the bright sunny sky he saw the day before. He then created a young dragon watching the sky. As he did so, Joshua's conversation with whatever was inside the cabin echoed in his mind. William continued moving his pencil back and forth, shading and drawing, when the door to his room opened. It was Charles. He examined his son's work.

"Your art is lovely," he said. "I know how much you wish for them to be real."

"I do," said William. "It doesn't hurt to dream, does it?"

His father smiled. "You're right, it doesn't hurt. Anything is possible."

As Charles left the room, William closed his book and laid back on his bed.

"Anything is possible.

CHAPTER 5

THE STRANGE VISITOR

A goods truck just crossed the state border. It was a long trip for the driver. All he wanted to do was deliver his load then spend a long week resting. When he left Nevada, he was in the heart of the Mojave Desert. The signs of civilization became more common with each mile of traveling. He knew he was getting close to his destination.

Almost there, he thought. When I make it, I'm going to get the sleep I need.

The deeper he ventured into town, the more intersections he came to, which meant more frequent stops. One of the traffic lights turned green, so he allowed the truck to move forward. Just as he was about to accelerate, though, he caught sight of someone standing in the road. Thanks to his quick nature, the driver pressed his foot on the brake just in time. As the truck screeched to a halt, he pulled down the rope that activated his air horn. The pedestrian continued to walk casually across the road, paying no attention to the warning call.

"The idiot! I almost killed him," muttered the driver angrily.

As the person mindlessly and slowly cleared his path, the driver continued on his way.

"These canned goods will soon go where they belong," he said, trying to calm himself.

The driver started on his way again. All seemed well until he heard a tremendous bang from inside the trailer.

"Now what?" he griped.

The ruckus became louder by the minute. The driver hoped he could make it to the distribution center before he had to stop. He continued to ignore it until, in the reflection of his mirror, he saw the trailer starting to tip. It leaned from side to side before crashing into the opposite lane. The truck itself snapped onto its side as well. Several cars passing in the other lane slid off the road to avoid the impending hazard. The truck driver, horrified but not harmed, freed himself from his seatbelt and climbed out of the cab to see what had caused the accident. As the banging continued, he noticed several dents bulging from the roof. The driver stopped dead in his tracks.

"What's in there?" a nervous bystander asked.

"I don't know, but it's scaring the children," the bystander's wife replied. "I don't want our nice vacation to be ruined by this."

"I think you should move back," the driver suggested. "I'm going to open it and see what it is. If it's something dangerous, I don't want you or your family to get hurt."

The spooked family moved back a considerable distance. The driver approached the overturned trailer. It felt like an eternity before he reached the rear end of it. He lifted his shaking hands up to the lever. Pulling it back just a few inches, he peeked inside. All was dark when he heard a deafening roar from inside. The doors were suddenly ripped from their thick hinges. The driver was forced flat on his back, the wind knocked out of him. A large blue creature stepped out of the darkness, baring its blood-hungry teeth. Without a second to spare, it caught sight of the winded driver and spat out a fiery storm. The beast then spread its broad wings and took off into the cloudy sky. The driver was shielded from the worst of the intense blaze by the broken door, though small flames licked at his clothing. In panic, he ran to a nearby yard and rolled in the grass that was still wet from the rain. After the flames were out, the driver, gasping for air, sat dazed in the middle of the lawn. An older man and his wife rushed out of their house in terror.

"What was that thing?" the wife wept.

The blue dragon was already off, but the terror had just begun. The driver watched other vehicles stop on the road and the passengers look up. The dragon flew off beyond the foothills, to the west.

I WAS LYING IN THE MIDDLE OF THE FLOOR WHEN JOSHUA CAME home. He joined me in the living room.

"Hi," I said lazily.

"Hi Jacob. Reno just went to the beach with Clipper. I rented a movie while I was in town, and I was wondering if I could watch it now."

"Go right ahead, I won't mind."

Joshua turned on the television set then sat down with the remote in his hand.

"I haven't seen this movie yet," he said. "It's about a knight seeking to slay a dragon. I hope that's all right with you."

I rested my head back down on the floor, smirking. "Sounds like a good movie, to be honest. Don't worry about me."

Joshua relaxed on the couch as the film began. I couldn't help but look at the screen out of curiosity. I watched the wicked dragon hiding in his cave, preparing to burn the lonesome knight. Its amber eyes bore a close resemblance to my own. I simply blinked before placing my head back onto the floor. I closed my eyes, attempting to sleep when the vision of Vesuvius reentered my mind. I believed he was more evil and nasty than that fictional monster on the screen. In my opinion, the two dragons had similar features. They were both the same creature I was, they were both terrifying, and they were both as evil as could be.

If I ever confront Vesuvius, I'll show him my true wrath, I thought. I would never cower down like I did in my last dream.

My ears perked up when I heard the telephone ring. The sounds of the movie ceased as Joshua answered it. A worried look crossed his face.

"What is it?" I asked when he hung up the phone.

"Chang just called. There's something going on. We need to watch the news."

Joshua turned the channel to a news broadcast where the reporter was speaking in a frightful tone. I read the headline scrolling at the bottom, *Creature Terrorizing the Santa Ana Area*.

An invisible weight pressed down on my chest. My eyes were glued to the screen that displayed many buildings and trees up in smoke. The reporter continued her story over the melee, *"I'm across the street from a bakery. The animal has already set it on fire along with many establishments in and around several communities, and then…! The roof of the bakery has just collapsed! There's smoke everywhere! The whole area is ablaze! I just heard something screech in the distance! It's not safe and I've just been asked to leave…"*

The broadcast switched to another scene. I stood up and stretched my legs just as Clipper and Reno came inside. Reno, struggling to stay awake, went upstairs to take a nap.

"Reno had a great time," Clipper said. "Are you finally watching TV after all this time, Jacob?"

Joshua explained to him what was happening. Clipper looked at the screen, then at me with a dumbstruck expression. He blinked in confusion.

"Where did *this* fellow come from? Is it after us?" he asked, concerned.

I took a deep breath before answering. "I'm not sure, but I think we should do something about it before any more damage is done. For all we know, this dragon may have come from Elsov. I don't want anybody getting hurt."

"Do you think it's really from Elsov?" Clipper bared his fangs in anxiety.

"I don't know, but we should find out."

Joshua opened the double doors for us. I jumped into the air with Clipper following close behind me. It didn't take long for us to reach Santa Ana. High above the buildings, we could see the police and firemen on the streets below.

"The people themselves shouldn't have anything to do with this if this dragon's after us," I said to Clipper. "This is dragon's business and we have to take care of it ourselves. They don't know what they're dealing with."

I landed on the roof of a restaurant and sniffed the air. My strong sense of smell did not pick up food. There was an obvious odor of something else. Clipper landed next to me and sniffed as well.

"It smells like… another dragon," he said.

My heart started to race. I observed the area around us. "I know. We must be getting near. We'll find him very soon. Be prepared to fight. And don't forget to keep an eye open."

The sky, which was clearing from the storm, was again darkened from the smoke of the many fires all over the city. Someone was causing all this chaos, but who? I looked at a fresh tower of smoke. I could hear the beating of my heart inside my ears, but I still couldn't see anything.

Clipper chirped in alarm. His wings moved up and down as he pointed with his muzzle.

"Over there! I saw something orange flash in the air, something fiery! It's… It's *him*! He's here!"

I followed Clipper's gaze, but saw no dragon.

"Where did you see him?" I asked, squinting.

"Over there. He's gone now."

I kept my ears erect. I knew for sure the creature was nearby. Just as I turned around, the mysterious dragon suddenly swooped down from above my head. I caught sight of it just in time to duck. It landed and immediately charged at us. It crashed into Clipper, sending him head-over-tail off the edge of the roof. The strange dragon leapt after him. I heard a roar, and the savage enemy jumped back onto the roof, facing me. I stared at it. Emerald-green eyes returned my hard glare. With sky-blue colored scales and a body a little smaller than mine, I realized that my foe was a female. And I could tell she was about to pounce on me! I did my best to avoid a fight.

"I don't want to hurt you," I said. "I have a bad temper, you know. If you would please calm down, we can talk."

The dragon did not answer. She started to charge again; I backed up. She made another monstrous growl then jumped at me with her claws at the ready. I dropped down and rolled to the side. The blue dragon missed me by inches. She halted, turned sideways, and again charged with her white horns ready to strike. With a painful blow to my side, I hurled off the roof and landed on the grass with a force that shook me up. The dragon stayed at the top where she let out a nasty flame. As expected, it didn't harm me. In the middle of the fire, I stood up and shook away burnt grass. The dragon closed her mouth and lunged at me once again. This time it was a successful jump. We were locked in an intense battle. There was scratching, biting, charging, and fire coming from the both of us. In the middle of the fight, I made the mistake of moving into a position that got me pinned under the dragon's paws.

"Don't make me angry. You don't want to taste my wrath," I warned again. I could already feel unbridled anger pulsing in my veins.

The dragon screeched. She aimed a paw full of claws at my snout. That was the tipping point for me. But just as I was about to unleash my worst, a rock came flying from behind the dragon and struck her between the wings. She bounded off me, staring at Clipper. Growling, she charged at him. Clipper spat venom in defense, which only splattered on her chin. She snarled and continued her charge. Had she still focused on me, I would have succumbed to my fury.

"I don't think that was a good idea, Clipper," I said, trying to calm myself.

Clipper jumped to the side. "I don't think so either. I think we've made it angrier."

As the dragon cast more fire at Clipper, I jolted back up with more anger building inside me. A car parked against a curb gave me a quick idea. Running around it, I lowered my horns and ran forward with an involuntary roar. With brutal, dragon strength, supported by my fury,

I bashed into the car with extreme force. It twirled weightlessly through the air, as if in a tornado, and landed right in front of my target. She turned, ready to attack me again. I let out an instinctive flame, which didn't do any good. Unexpectedly, she ejected a stream of her own venom at me. A sharp sting flooded across my eyes as it struck me. The world around me suddenly began to spin. I started to envision disoriented flashes and false, abstract images. The sounds around me became distorted as if coming from a broken music player. Feeling sick to the stomach, I fell flat on my face. I was no longer a threat to the dragon. She walked up to my suffering body, ready to unleash her own fury. But before she could lay any more harm, a metal disk struck the back of her head. The blow was so hard that she fell next to me, dazed. Clipper stepped forward and pressed the dragon down with his front paws. The dragon was too stunned to fight back. Clipper examined my battle wounds once I scraped the venom away from my eyes.

"Are you okay?" he asked.

I stood back up, snarling as the world returned to normal.

"I'll be fine," I said. "That stupid dragon deserved what she got."

My tail brushed over the creature's spiny back. She tried to squirm under Clipper's weight but had little strength. The whack on her head must have really knocked her senseless.

"I'll show this jerk what real pain is," I hissed.

Clipper held a paw to my chest before I could advance. "Easy, Jacob. Let's not lose ourselves. When it… I mean *she* wakes, let's try to talk to her. That is if she knows how to speak."

I released another cloud of smoke. My head pulsed with rage, but I took a few deep breaths.

"Okay. We'll give it a try," I answered, sighing.

We were trying to decide what to do next when a man in a military uniform ran up to us.

"Draco! Clipper! I was sent by Sergeant Nelson! What do you know about this new dragon?"

"We don't know anything yet," Clipper replied. "Can you help hide this strange visitor?"

"We need to do something before she comes out of it," I said. "We should find some sort of holding cell until we can get some information. This dragon was quite aggressive."

Other soldiers arrived. They bound the dragon's legs and belted her snout shut, then carefully transported her to an isolated building outside the city. The structure was old, but with the proper guards, the dragon would not escape from her small red-brick jail. An hour later, she woke up on a concrete floor covered in soft wet straw. The straw was kept moist so she would not start a fire. It made the inside of the building smell a little musky. The dim, enclosed room had no windows, but there were two overhanging lights on either side of the walls. She looked up at me standing in front of her.

"If you're calm, we can get this done quickly," I said to her. "I'm going to take the belt off. You can't hurt me with fire and I have a few questions to ask you. Don't you *dare* snap at me. And don't even *think* about using venom on me again."

With caution, I loosened the belt and tossed it aside. The dragon wanted to fight back, but she did not have the energy. She had to have had a huge headache. She still seemed somewhat dazed.

"Let's begin," I said. "First of all, I must ask if you are you from Elsov. Speak up please. Why did you come? Were you specifically after me and Clipper or is there something else I'm not aware of?"

The dragon turned her livid face away from me, silent as a mouse.

"Okay," I continued, "if you don't want to answer that, so be it. But I must ask, how did you get here? It'll help if you tell us *how* you came here."

I started to become impatient at her lack of response. If she did come from Elsov, she might know a way back.

She remained silent, but I continued the interrogation.

"It's kind of a coincidence how you crossed paths with us, isn't it? Now let me ask again, did you have knowledge of us, or were you sent to kill us maybe?"

The dragon finally reacted. She turned at me and hissed. I bared my teeth and hissed in return, telling her to stand down. Sensing no progress, I folded my wings and moved to an iron barred door. My tail slithered behind me in disappointment.

"She needs more time. Put the belt back on her and keep her here," I called to the other side.

I gave her one last long look as I walked through the door. I crossed a small hallway before reaching the second door to the outside. With the free space, I stretched my wings. Clipper was sitting there waiting for me.

"So this dragon's a girl," he said.

"She is," I replied. "I realized that before we started fighting. Also when she hissed at me, I could easily tell what gender she was."

"Great, now I kind of regret hitting her with the manhole cover."

NIGHT HAD FALLEN. THE STORM CLOUDS HAD CLEARED, BUT THE smoke from the battle still haunted the city. William had remained in his room all that evening. The desk light was on and his book was open. He was engrossed in another sketch. This time he took a different approach. He drew a dragon lurking inside a bamboo forest, inspired by Henry's medallion. When he locked his book for the night, he turned off the lamp, then stared out the open window, into the darkness. He gazed at the distant house while he changed into his pajamas. As he finished changing, he heard one of the cabin doors open. The familiar growling returned.

"Ugh, this is door creaks terribly."

"We've had a long day," a second voice answered. "I'm ready for a good night's sleep. Fighting one of our own kind wears me out."

William became confused. The voices did not sound human. They sounded lower, slightly louder, and rougher than normal. He also wondered what "our own kind" meant. He moved back over to the window. Before he could hear anything more, though, the neighboring door closed.

William's curiosity was aroused. He remembered when Joshua hesitated when he asked William if he saw anyone else before the truck came. William *knew* somebody was staying with Joshua, but he did not know who, or what.

I've got to find out what's going on, he thought. Tomorrow I'll see if Henry can help me. When Joshua leaves, I'll try to find out who's there.

After climbing into bed, he closed his eyes; though it took him a while to fall asleep. He woke up early next morning and went to the front porch. He wanted to work on his first sketch of the beach in the sunrise. While he drew, he noticed Henry walking down the street. William decided he should express his intentions to him. He left his book on the porch and ran up to the sidewalk.

"Hi William, it's nice to see you again." It did not take long before Henry noticed William had his eyes on the cabin. "Is something wrong?" he asked.

William swallowed hard. "I think so. Something's going on in the house next door. Last night, I heard… strange voices. They were talking about 'fighting their own kind.'"

"You could be on to something," said Henry when William finished. "I've been hearing voices like that too sometimes when I'm outside."

"I don't care if I get into trouble or not. When Joshua leaves, I'll enter the other house."

Henry shook his head. "Don't! Even if you're able to get in there without anyone watching, that strange something may be more than what you bargained for. What if they're part of something horrible? Then you'd *really* be in trouble."

"I'll be careful," said William. "I simply must see; just for a few seconds, anyway. When Joshua leaves, I'll—"

He stopped speaking when he heard Joshua leaving his house. William's eyes lit up.

"Now's my chance. He's getting into his car. I can go see whatever is in there."

Henry had his hand in his pocket, fingering the medallion. "Well, if you're going in there, good luck."

He moved to the sandy beach across the street, keeping a solid eye on William. The young man approached the door and knocked. There was no answer. He looked left and right to make sure he was alone, then he placed his hand on the doorknob. It was certainly not locked. He opened the door and stepped in.

RENO WAS SLEEPING ALONE ON A BED IN THE UPSTAIRS ROOM. HER belly rubbed on the soft blankets while her wings hung down both sides. Her tail was curled up to her body when she slowly woke up. She rubbed her eyes with the back of her paws, jumped off the bed, and headed for the stairway. From the top step, she barely saw William moving about the house. Reno's eyes narrowed. She resisted the strong urge to attack him for breaking into her home, but she remembered the warning not to show herself to anyone. William wandered around the living room, looking at the bookshelf. This gave Reno the perfect opportunity to sneak downstairs and duck into the kitchen. She held her claws upward to avoid making any clicking noises on the hardwood floor. When she was close enough, she jumped onto the table. William remained oblivious to her presence.

Reno was about to move when she heard William moving closer to the kitchen. She had mistakenly believed that the intruder would have moved upstairs before going into the kitchen. She had to think fast! She was going to get caught! She had only a few seconds before William would see her. Just as the boy entered the kitchen, a single and quick idea came to Reno's mind. She froze in a sitting position with her eyes closed. She fought to keep her tail from twitching. William walked in. Reno heard him stop.

"What have we here?" William approached the little brown dragon with an air of excitement. "This is an interesting statue. It looks very real. I should have brought my sketchbook."

Reno, holding her breath, ignored his remarks. William leaned closer to her.

"You don't look like a typical statue. You look real… but you are… the voices… but I…"

Reno did not react. All was going well, but just as she was least expecting it, she felt a sweaty hand touch her head. She felt his soft fingers run over her rough scales and dangerous spikes. Being touched by human hands, except for Sally's, was something Reno did not like one bit. After feeling the sharp ends of Reno's horns, William left to search the rest of the house. When the coast was clear, Reno opened her eyes. Looking around, she noticed her empty water dish beside her. She decided use the dish to scare William away. She bumped the dish with her tail, and immediately resumed her original position.

Just as she had hoped for, William panicked at the noise and ran for the front door. He opened it and raced off. Reno jumped off the table, running to the door to close it.

"I don't think he's dangerous. He was only a young human," she said.

She retrieved her water dish with her jaws and jumped onto the counter next to the sink. She lifted the handle with her claw, jolting back when water came running out. She then pushed the dish into the sink with her nose. When the dish was filled with water, she pulled down the handle and placed her dish back onto the counter. After her thirst was quenched, she returned to the bed upstairs. A cloud of smoke escaped from her nose as she lay back down. There was no need to worry now that the strange visitor was gone.

WILLIAM SLOWED DOWN WHEN HE REACHED HENRY.

"What happened? You look spooked!" Henry exclaimed.

"Someone was at the back door. I had to leave," William said, panting hard. "I didn't see anything suspicious, but I did see something interesting. There was a statue of a brown dragon on the table. It looked very convincing! As I examined it, I questioned whether it was real or not. I couldn't resist; I had to touch this statue. Whoever made that dragon must be talented. I was almost convinced that it was real."

"It sounds like an interesting statue indeed," said Henry. "Now I wish I could have seen it for myself. Maybe you can put it in your book."

"That's exactly what I'm going to do for my next project."

Henry wished him luck on it. When William returned to the porch, he opened his book. With the image of the dragon fresh on his mind, he finished the final touches of the previous two drawings before starting the sketch of the brown dragon. He was well-engaged in it until his father called him to breakfast. The statue was on his mind all morning. Was it even a statue? That was William's only explanation. It couldn't have been a real dragon, because dragons didn't exist; at least in the reasonable side of his mind. The other side wasn't so sure.

CHAPTER 6

Loose Ends Meet

Fenson and Bluepond headed farther south. The following morning, they agreed that they had to try again and ask for help. They visited various public places, but their plans were cut short yesterday when they heard about the blue dragon.

"We must find the darkscales as soon as possible," said Bluepond later that morning.

"We've been a'lookin' throughout this entire town," Fenson complained. "We have searched all day. I need sleep, my stomach is ready to dissolve, and the invasion the goblin spoke of could take place at any time, especially if that other dragon is about. I still feel confident that our help will be valued or we would not have been allowed to come. But even if we *do* find the dragons, what do we do next? In a deep corner of my mind, I fear they may still harbor a bit of evil in their hearts."

"I do not think these dragons will be against us in any way if they know who we are," said Bluepond. "They will put up a good fight against our foes, but I too have doubts they will be victorious without our aid. I know Trihan had said they once fought a tribe of dwarfs and a sorcerer, and I must say it takes much bravery and power to defeat them. The Sorcerer with his scepter? That is impressive! But can he stand against Vesuvius? I do not know. Even with these fears, we must find the dragons. I did not come here for nothing, and I believe you did not come here for nothing either. I am not going to bend on my knees and surrender just because things are not going perfectly for us. I am doing this for my sister, Treetop. She will be freed on the rightful day. The black dragon came across our colony and I know he and his said friend are not evil."

Fenson sensed Bluepond's heartache for his sister. "I understand. It was my idea to come here, anyway. I won't give up either."

The two continued on their way. Late in the morning, they stopped in front of a spacious hotel.

"We haven't visited this place yet," said Fenson, pointing to it.

They were somewhat unsure if they should go inside. They stood for a moment, watching the clientele coming and going. A taxicab came to a stop at the front doors. Two well-dressed gentlemen, deep in conversation, climbed out of it.

"I'm telling you, it's the very dragon," one of the men said with emphasis, "same as on the east coast earlier this year. Before we know it, the events that happened in New York will happen here."

"That's just too much of a coincidence, wouldn't you say?" the second replied.

Fenson and Bluepond looked at each other, their interests stirred. They followed the two men through the doors of the hotel, keeping a discreet distance behind them. They followed them up a stairway, around a corner, and up another set of stairs. Finally, the men entered a hallway some floors up and approached their adjoining rooms. From around the corner, Fenson and Bluepond watched as one of the men unlocked his door. While doing so, a younger man limped by on crutches. A brief exchange ensued among them, as if the younger one was giving directions. They then shook hands before the first man retired to his room. Fenson and Bluepond approached as the young man unlocked his own door.

"Greetings," said Bluepond. "We are but travelers who would like to ask you a question. It appears your foot is injured. Please, return to your resting quarters while we gain our information."

The young man hesitated. His eyes squinted before he nodded slowly. He kept his eyes on the dwarf as he limped into his room. He pushed the door wide enough for Fenson and Bluepond to enter.

"You can come in," he said. "You came at the right time. I'm leaving for home soon. My name is Chang, by the way."

Chang propped his crutches against the wall and sat on his bed. He picked up a glass of juice from the nightstand to take a sip.

"What was it you wanted to ask me?"

Bluepond performed a small bow. "Beg pardon, sir, but have you seen two dragons recently? Forgive the unusual inquiry, but we are on an important mission."

Chang nearly spat juice out of his nose in surprise. He immediately turned away. Fenson and Bluepond glanced at one another. Of all the locals they had questioned, Chang seemed to behave differently. He had to be hiding something.

"Why do you ask?" Chang questioned. "Many have never seen a dragon in their lives. Why did you come to me?"

Bluepond felt that the young man had spoken with a strange tone. He began to believe Chang was the turning point in their search. Was he was testing them?

"Sir," said Bluepond, "have you heard of the recent news? Many say there was a fight of three creatures described as dragons."

Chang nodded. "I've heard. My friends Jacob and Clipper have the situation under control."

Fenson listened closely. Chang was clearly testing them.

"Jacob?" repeated the dwarf. He suspected that Chang had revealed an important clue, for he had heard the two names from Trihan.

"Jacob's just a friend," said Chang casually.

"Is this Jacob... a dragon?" asked Bluepond. He whispered to Fenson, "Trihan mentioned that one of the portal seeker's names was Jacob."

"I never said he was a dragon," Chang said, his voice calm.

The dwarf and the nymph both knew that Chang held the information they needed. It was time for them to state the reason for their presence. Fenson took a deep breath.

"Mr. Chang, I must inform you that I am a dwarf. I come from a lovely forest on the world of Elsov..."

Chang looked up, wincing from the ache in his foot. "Did you say Elsov?" He sighed in a suspicious manner. "Who are you? Don't lie to me. I've met people like you before. They tried to kill me and my friends."

Bluepond puffed out his chest in courage. "I am a wood nymph. My name is Bluepond. And yes, my friend here is a dwarf. His name is Fenson. We have traveled here to the first earth to warn the two dragons. Trihan told us their names were Jacob and Clipper. Perhaps we may let them travel back with us, but it will not be easy. There could be an upcoming attack led by hostile forces. Also, in order for us to travel back, we must collect the six pieces to make up the portal."

Chang kept his eyes on Fenson. "Last time I met a dwarf, he was a Monolegion. You're dressed differently, no horned helmet or Norse look, but you still caught my eye with what you're wearing."

"I am indeed a dwarf, as we've told you," said Fenson, "and I have been told about the Monolegions. They were evil dwarfs, Nibelungs to be specific, on this earth. I'm not your enemy. I would fight the Nibelungs and any others who wish to harm your friends. I'm your ally 'til the very end."

Chang's suspicions seemed to have melted. He remained silent for a moment.

"Sorry I misjudged you. I'm quite surprised the two of you are here, actually. You can be very helpful. As I've told you, I'm going home soon. Come with me and I'll take you to Jacob and Clipper. But tell me, why did you come to this hotel to look for them?"

"We'll no longer need to search for the dragons!" Fenson cheered, ignoring Chang's question.

Bluepond told Chang about the goblin's plans and what was yet to come.

Chang frowned at the mention of goblins. "I'm glad you came. You can help my friends find Elsov. Goblins… It's good to know some of the obstacles we may cross. I'll help you and my friends get back to Elsov. The good dragons, the portal seekers you called them, are searching for a way home."

Fenson and Bluepond were astonished, ready for action, scared, and excited all at the same time. The three of them became one alliance.

I SAT IN THE DINING ROOM WITH CLIPPER, RENO, AND JOSHUA THAT evening. We finally had time for our homecoming feast. And oh, what a feast it was! The topic of our conversation would change time and time again until it finally revolved back to my vision of Elsov.

"I have faith I'll return," I said.

"I have faith as well," Clipper added. "I feel that we'll be able to leave this world. When I dream, I can practically see Pearl Forest before me."

With our dishes filled with grape juice, I lapped the drink until it was almost empty. (I didn't want to know what alcohol did to a dragon's mind. Besides, I wasn't one to drink alcohol anyway.) Clipper too drank most of what was in his dish. Our teeth and tongues were purple. A feeling of contentment wrapped us in its cocoon as we enjoyed our meal and each other's company. Humming to myself off and on, words began forming in my mind. I cleared my throat and began to recite the lyrics off the top of my head,

> *"Though the sun may shine in the sky*
> *While we taste our bread of rye,*
> *Evil is a 'lurkin'*
> *And dragons are on the prowl.*
> *But Goodness is emerging from the den!*
> *Though this dragon began as bad,*
> *He may soon turn to good!*
> *Like me, for evil once I stood.*
> *I turned to light,*
> *Saying goodbye to dark!"*

Clipper cackled in laughter. "For a poem you recited off the top of your head, it doesn't sound that bad."

He and I started laughing and chattering. Reno blew a joyful stream of smoke. I felt at peace as we continued eating our meal. Joshua ate politely with a knife and fork while I picked up an entire raw herring with my teeth and chewed it into delicious mush, bones and all. I swallowed it whole and scooped up another morsel. Clipper picked up a semi-frozen herring of his own and tossed it in the air. He caught it in his mouth with no trouble, swallowing without chewing.

Joshua looked at us in disgust. "You two really need to learn some manners. And your breath is foul! I can smell it from here."

"Sorry," I said. I lowered my head, slightly embarrassed.

I suddenly felt a bubble of air coming from my stomach. I belched gently, but a small flame escaped. My eyes widened as I hiccupped a cloud of smoke.

"Sorry about that as well."

Joshua shook his head with a hand on his forehead. "At least the smoke alarms are disconnected."

"I feel excited in a strange way," Reno said. "I know how Jacob and Clipper feel. Sally told me about the time they saw their home. I don't remember it at all, but I feel it must be my home as well. I want to go there myself. I don't like to keep hiding. I just want to stretch my wings and let myself be free."

Joshua petted Reno's head. "Don't worry. I'll do whatever I can to help you."

"I shouldn't say it'll be easy to find a way back, but we'll try our hardest," I told her.

Joshua smiled at her. She, Clipper, and I were going to find a way to Elsov somehow. All was quiet when there was a knock on the door. Joshua quickly stood up.

"Somebody's at the door, you three better take cover."

Reno chirped and trotted under the dining room table while Clipper and I made our way upstairs. The knock was heard again.

Joshua answered it when all of us were hidden. Annoyed, I heard an unfamiliar voice.

"Greetings, friend. Lovely home this is during a day of beauty. Is this the abode of one Jacob Draco or Justin Clipper?"

Like me, Joshua must have not expected to hear my name.

"…Why do you ask?"

Chang's voice came from behind the stranger. "Joshua, you can let him in. This is someone that the others might want to meet. Don't worry, I'll tell you who they are."

The two strangers walked through the door. Chang, wielding his crutches, clumped in behind them. He heaved a sigh of relief as he sat down on the couch.

"I'm glad you made it home, Chang," said Joshua.

Chang sounded as if he was a part of our excitement at the dinner table.

"You won't believe it!" he said to Joshua. "We did it! Jacob, Clipper, and Reno can go home! Where are they? I want to give them the good news."

"Jacob and Clipper are upstairs. Just how is it you think they can go home?" asked Joshua, eying the two newcomers. "Wouldn't you like to introduce your friends first?"

Chang did not have to. The first stranger stood up and shook Joshua's hand.

"My name is Fenson Katque, good sir," the dwarf said. "The nymph is Bluepond, a brother of Treetop. Treetop once followed the black-scaled dragon, Jacob."

"He and Clipper will want to hear this," said Chang.

Somewhat skeptical, Joshua approached the bottom of the stairs and called to us. I heard every word spoken, though. My heart began to race at the mention of Treetop. From the top of the stairs, I leapt over the railing and landed on the floor below. Clipper followed suit. The two visitors gasped in surprise. Neither me nor Clipper spoke, but rather looked directly at their faces. Fenson cleared his throat. He was a dwarf with apparel that looked as if he were from another time. If I had ever imagined a cowering stranger, it would be him.

"Eh— Good evening— kind dragon," he gulped. "My name is Fenson and I am from the world you seek."

Chang couldn't contain himself any longer. "Jacob, Fenson is a dwarf; not a Nibelung that we're used to. He wants to help us. The other one is a nymph from Pearl Forest. He's from the village you visited."

My ears rose. "So you're a brother of Treetop? I can't ever forget what happened to her. Do you know where she is?"

Joshua rubbed his own ears at the uncomfortable volume of my voice. "Reno said she felt a strange excitement," he said. "She was right. Jacob and Clipper were, too."

Reno had been listening from her spot under the table. At the mention of her name, she peeked around the corner. She eyed Fenson and Bluepond nervously. She decided there was no reason for her to hide, so she stepped out into the open.

"I haven't seen you before," said Fenson. "You must be a friend of the others."

Reno was too shy to reply.

"Her name is Reno," Chang said for her. "She was the emblem to Triathra. We rescued her as an infant."

"She is still in her youth, I see," Bluepond pointed out.

"And she's going home with Jacob and Clipper," said Chang.

"That makes all of us," Fenson laughed. "All we need is to find the six pieces, that's all. Simple as that!"

"I have a few questions about all this," said Joshua. "Jacob and Clipper told me a little about Elsov. What is it exactly?"

"The second world," Bluepond answered. "Elsov is its official name. We dryads treasure the beauty of the land and the natural life she sustains. Elsov is a truly beautiful world with mountains, deserts, forests, and plains."

"It must be as wonderful as Jacob and Clipper say it is," said Joshua. "What are these six pieces you mentioned?"

Fenson told us about his visit with Trihan, how he and Blue-pond had come to our world, and the six pieces to build the portal back to Elsov.

"Finding the pieces sounds like it should be no trouble," the nymph said, glancing at me and Clipper. "But I am afraid that brings us to the reason why Fenson and I are here. Fenson overheard a goblin and two evil dwarfs planning to travel here. They may be a threat, along with surviving Nibelungs. I cannot tell what may come." He looked at Reno. "I do not mean to frighten any of you."

Clipper looked down at the floor. "That *could* connect to the blue dragon that attacked us."

"We have heard of this beast. It may have very well been sent by our enemy," said Bluepond.

I gave a sharp glance at the nymph, then at Fenson. I had no doubt they were who they said they were and where they were from.

"I will risk my life to help you. The new Keeper of the three has said you may be the key to ending a plague over all of us," said Fenson.

"You are the black dragon," Bluepond added. "I remember when you came to my colony. My father spoke with you. My sister Treetop was with you when you were captured by ogres."

My throat became tense.

"Your name is Jacob. You did not know your name when you visited my colony."

I didn't know what to say. Bluepond was *there* when I had visited his colony! *He* was the brother of my lost friend!

Chang broke the brief silence. "Jacob and Clipper told me about Elsov, their true home. We're so glad you're here to help us."

"Yes, we've come to help. And you're right about the most important reason. We came here to warn you," said Fenson.

The dwarf went on to explain to us about Vesuvius and exactly how he stumbled upon the goblin's plan. What he told us about Vesuvius, along with what Bluepond had said about Treetop, stiffened my joints. From what I remembered about goblins, they were worse than the Nibelungs. And even then, there could be remaining Nibelungs still about, seeking vengeance for their downfall.

"King Vesuvius, I'm right! He haunts my dreams," I cried. "He's a dragon like me. He has scales like Clipper. There's so much in common. What scares me is that I think he knows me. It's possible he knows what I've done. If I stopped his attack on this world, he may not be too happy with me. His wrath could possibly even destroy me. That's what bothers me."

"He *could* know us," Clipper emphasized. "Those were just dreams. But now we know about him. Vesuvius or not, we're going back to Pearl Forest. The more we know about him and Elsov, maybe the stronger we can stand up against him."

My breath shortened as I blew smoke out of my nose. "Hhh… You're right. I'm glad you've come here, Fenson. You too, Bluepond. Now we'll know what's to come."

"We can leave soon," said Chang. "My foot is getting better every day. Even Sergeant Nelson is nearby if we need his help. We should go as soon as possible once we know where to go. If any goblin or monster comes our way, we can defeat them. We'll be the ones who will be feared."

"I think we can and should start tomorrow," Clipper suggested, "but we need to stay alert. Someone can keep an eye out until we do start."

Reno finally spoke up. "Maybe I can do that. I'm small, so I can stay on the roof overnight without trouble. If anything out of the ordinary happens, I can tell you."

Fenson smiled at Reno. "I believe that may work."

We discussed our new adventure for the rest of the evening. The clock tolled one by the time we finished our long conversation. Clipper and I stayed downstairs while Joshua took the others upstairs to the bedrooms to sleep. Reno, however, stayed awake on the roof all night, keeping watch. As I fell asleep, I felt very pleased to have met Fenson and Bluepond. I realized that returning to Elsov wasn't only a wish, it was an actual possibility.

CHAPTER 7

Plans Unfold

The mountain range stood at the southern end of the island with fields of thriving crops surrounding it. Near the foothills and along the central portion of the island was a busy town. Everywhere else on the mountains was covered in ash. In the same world where Pearl Forest gave beauty and light, the contrary was found on the volcanic isle so far away from the peaceful realm. The desolate island itself was about fifty miles from the nearest mainland shore.

In a shipyard along the coastline, a small caravel sailed from the horizon to the docks. A passenger left the ship in the hands of the crew once she was anchored. This passenger was a goblin, the same goblin that Fenson had discovered in the old house several nights before. The dragon lord himself knew of his arrival.

The goblin took a deep breath, eying the town along the base of the mountains. The foothills themselves were about a mile away. The bitter goblin began the walk down a well-maintained boulevard when something appeared to fly out of the massive, castle-like palace that sat atop the highest peak. The gray spot in the sky circled around one of the lower peaks before flying straight to the goblin in the middle of the busy road. The passing people; humans, dwarfs, goblins, and the like; reverently stepped aside. The gray-scaled dragon was the one who guarded the entrance to the palace. He was a darkscale, born and bred, from internal to external. The flapping of his wings caused dust to waft in the air. He hovered then landed in front of the goblin. The darkscale's head stood higher than the goblin's by a good foot-and-a-half. The dragon spat a small flame off to the side, flicked his forked tongue, and spoke with a grim voice in the goblin's language.

"The master 'imself told me ta meet ya. State yer name an' state yer business."

"My name is Mallutin if that is what you're asking. My business? Our Leader is expecting me. My business is with him. If you will please let me pass, there will be no trouble between you and me. How does that sound, o' wise and noble dragon? Hah!"

The gray darkscale exposed his deadly fangs, hissing. Saliva dripped from between them; his breath held the stench of a burnt carcass.

"Very well. Enter at the front gate. 'e's waitin' fer ya."

"That's what I wanted to hear," responded Mallutin, grinning like a naughty child.

The dragon took flight back to where he had come from, leaving Mallutin to walk the extra distance by himself. Through the mountainous slopes were walls and guard-towers that blended with their surroundings, as if the mountains were a natural fortress. When Mallutin reached the base of the tallest peak, the gloomy path led to the entrance that he wished to enter. He traveled up to find two dwarfs standing guard at the palace's upper gate. Not twenty feet away, without a railing, was the edge of a high, sheer cliff. The well-decorated dwarf guards nodded to the visiting goblin and then opened the gates for him. Mallutin entered the great hall, the largest chamber in the keep. There were lines of giant marble pillars going down the hall with statues of men and monsters carved at the top of each one. In between the pillars were banners of purple, brass, wine-red, and auburn that hung with national pride. Along the ceiling were several lit chandeliers made from the bones of animals. As Mallutin crossed the first half of the great hall, he was met by two steaming rivers, one on each side and both teeming with slimy vinery. The other half of the hall revealed entrances to other places in the keep. Mallutin approached that end of the hall, the humidity of the hot water causing him to sweat immensely. The rivers were formed from artificial waterfalls along the stone wall. In between them at the end of the hall, the goblin stopped. There he stood before Vesuvius, the most vile dragon of all, the one whom Triathra had once served. Mallutin bowed in respect. Straightening afterward, he eyed the tyrannical King sitting on the elevated platform of gold: a comfortable throne for such a mighty creature. Sitting in a silver-trimmed and scarlet-satin chair on the right of the King's throne was a sorcerer. He wore a black cloak with bright orange on the hood and sleeves. Sewn into the cloak's chest, also in orange, was the Kingdom's symbol, called the Inhĕt, which represented strength and unity.

The Sorcerer tapped his scepter on the floor, signaling Mallutin to come forth. Vesuvius growled to clear his throat before speaking in a voice of thunder, "With the help of the Heitspel the Sorcerer and his scepter, I spoke to you in your mind not long ago. I assume this is the reason you're here?"

Mallutin lost his giddy mood. "Indeed it is: the two dragons."

"Do you remember what happened early in my reign? My servants stole two eggs from the nests of the lightscales. As the ancient spell came over the eggs, their colors turned dark. Despite that, they are still enemies to us. They are traitors to my sovereignty! What is this plan you propose? Answer me!"

Mallutin gulped. "If you would please, o' King, inform the warlock of ice, Glaciem, to help us. I also have a trained Minotaur and Unitaur." He realized how small and squeaky his voice was compared to his leader. "They are called Wildhorn and Bloodgutt. As you know, those dumb creatures rely on us for their survival. If you could simply—"

Vesuvius roared to silence him.

"I have no need to inform Glaciem! He is already on the first earth; his ice dragons are at the ready. But you have requested the use of Minotaurs. I can see use in them. You want Bloodgutt and Wildhorn, do you? I can arrange that. You will take them both and find the dragon traitors. There will be no risk of a war if you personally kill them. If they die before they leave the wretched world, I will reward you. If you do not succeed, don't fret. Your health will be of no consequence to me. I will simply return to my original plan."

Mallutin saluted his master, thanking him for his merciful promise. He held his right fist over his left shoulder then stretched it outward, performing the Vesuvian salute.

"I will do that, your Majesty. You have a portal in this keep. I will use that to travel to the human settlement. I'll slay the two traitors with an ice blade. Dragons are deadly beasts. With the necessary help, I will be victorious!"

An eerie howl echoed from other monsters throughout the keep. This satisfied Mallutin. He waited in Vesuvius' presence until his two large animals were summoned. The animals looked much like the traditional Greek depiction of the Minotaur, save for the females (the Unitaurs) who have a single horn above their noses. Their thick, dirty fur of muddy-brown blended in with the threatening environment. Each held a large mallet that they used to destroy anything they desired. Bloodgutt, the Unitaur, was the first to arrive, only seconds before Wildhorn, the Minotaur. They did not speak to anyone who was not of their species, and they could only understand a few commands given to them.

"Be sure you keep them in order while in my palace," said Vesuvius. "As you can see, I hate messes."

"They will be in order, Sire," said Mallutin. "With the help of Glaciem and the Minotaurs, you will find the traitors dead under our feet. You are a great and clever leader."

"Of course I am!" bellowed Vesuvius. He was already used to many compliments, and was therefore not that flattered with Mallutin's.

Bloodgutt and Wildhorn snarled like freight trains as they swung their mallets through the air.

"Let's slay ourselves some traitorous dragons, shall we?" Mallutin said to them with a giggle.

The goblin left the great hall. He made his way to a room several floors above. The Sorcerer, Heitspel, followed him. Mallutin stood on the square-shaped, stone platform of the portal. He waited there for Heitspel to cast his spell.

"When you reach the first earth, you must immediately search for the dragon traitors," the Sorcerer ordered. "You may be a few hours north of them. Be sure to keep Bloodgutt and Wildhorn under your control. We do not want the foreign people to find you and overpower you. Vesuvius will use my power to know of your progress, so make your journey an efficient one." To Mallutin's delight, Heitspel pointed to a sword and a knife that rested on a table on the other side of the room. "Take this sword. Use it to slay them," Heitspel directed.

Mallutin stepped off the portal and approached the table. The sword had a blue blade and a shining silver handle. It was an ice blade. Beside it was a shining dagger. The Sorcerer also gave Mallutin a thick leather tunic and a belt. Mallutin fitted the tunic over his chest then tied the belt around his waist. To thank him for the weapons, he saluted Heitspel in the same fashion as he had Vesuvius. He felt the power coming to him when the two Mino-taurs came barreling into the room. Heitspel shook his head at the damage they had already created. The table was destroyed, and a few propaganda engravings lay in ruin. The floor, the walls, and the door were scratched and gouged. Heitspel didn't worry about it for the moment. Holding his scepter tight, the jewel on top began to glow. The portal under Mallutin's feet started to feel as if it were wobbling. Wind brushed around him and the goblin disappeared from Heitspel's sight.

Second's later, Mallutin found himself lying on a bed of cool sand. The Minotaurs arrived shortly thereafter. The goblin stood up and examined the new world. He was on the sandy shore next to the midnight ocean. Surrounding the beach were black cliffs that pointed to the dark, cloudy sky. The air was warm, but nowhere near as humid as the great hall within Vesuvius' keep, but pleasurable all the same. Bloodgutt and Wildhorn were both overwhelmed by the sudden change to their new environment. They glared at Mallutin, again lifting their mallets in the air. They began smashing them into the sand. The ground shook with each impact. Mallutin clicked his tongue, signaling the Minotaurs to lower their mallets.

"Hmmhmm. What obedient beasts you are," he said. "Not a single human is present at this late hour, I see. Haha! As much as I want to slay the miserable beings, we must not be seen. If these humans send an army against us, we may not survive. We've been sent here to do a task. If we are to receive our reward, we must move now. Heitspel said we are north of our enemies. If we start moving now along this shore, we may make it to their location by sunrise."

The Minotaurs did not understand a word Mallutin had said. They showed their urge to destroy by smashing their mallets into the sand again.

"Yes. Yes. I see what you want." Mallutin raised the ice blade high over his head. "We will walk the long journey and kill those traitors. Now let's go!"

The Minotaurs bellowed in return. They followed the giggling goblin southward.

WILLIAM WAS DEEP INTO HIS NEXT SKETCH IN THE MIDDLE OF THE night. He recalled the brown dragon he had seen the day before. He was still impressed at how real the statue appeared. It didn't look like a statue at all, but a real dragon! He would have been convinced it was real had his mind been a little more open. After another hour, he closed and locked his book. He changed into his pajamas, turned off the lamp, and stood next to his bed where he had a clear view out the window. He gazed into the night sky, trying to catch a peek of the waxing crescent moon that would show its face after the mild storm. It hung next to a pattern of twinkling stars, just the way William loved it. His eyes then wandered over everything else outside the window. He was about to turn away when he saw something in the moonlight, sitting atop the mysterious cabin.

"What's the statue doing up there? That's funny."

He peered harder into the darkness. His attention was glued to the little brown figure. Suddenly, William noticed something. Did its ear just twitch? William stared at the creature, not even blinking. What happened next made him jump. A car was heard on the remote road. It drove past the houses and then out of sight. William saw its head turn to the road. He blinked and rubbed his eyes. This had to be a dream!

As he gazed out the window again, he saw it move, trying to keep out of the porch light. At first William could only stare in disbelief. He was scared, not knowing what was happening. The only answer to this was to investigate, he decided. He quietly opened the door and left his room. Tiptoeing down the hall, he took each step with care to prevent awaking his father and the others. He slipped out the front door and onto the porch. Once he was on the lawn, he moved to the property next door.

William tried to get another look at the dragon on the roof. From that angle, he could not see anything, but he heard footsteps; not human footsteps for that matter, but from some creature with claws. William was overjoyed, not thinking about what he was doing. He placed his hand behind his ear. He could hear a soft breathing that was not his own. William picked up a pebble from the ground and tossed it up on the roof. He heard it bounce off something. Then he heard a strange, low growl. William wanted to respond, but didn't have the courage yet. He was almost hyperventilating from the fact that the creatures he loved, the creatures he drew in his sketchbook, were real! He had seen the living dragon up close with his own eyes without even knowing it!

Not able to bear it any longer, he uttered, "D— don't be afraid, little dragon." William assumed the creature feared him. "I know you're up there. I won't hurt you. Come on, little dragon, you can come down."

A few seconds of silence filled the air. Then Reno suddenly glided from the roof. She landed in front of William, baring her sharp teeth in defense.

"Don't tell anybody about this," she hissed. "I'm not allowed to show myself to anyone!"

"I promise I won't tell anyone," said William, startled when Reno spoke to him. "But… you're here! I thought you were only legend. How I have wished you were real, and here you are!"

Reno snapped her jaws, causing William to jump back in fright.

"I know you," she said. "You're the one who broke into my house the other day. Who do you think you are you little thief?"

"I'm no thief," said William. "I'm a very curious person. If I see something out of the ordinary, I like to find an answer." His excitement started to become fear the longer he gazed a Reno's teeth.

"You're wasting my time," the brown dragon growled. "Go back to where you came from and don't speak of this to anyone."

Before William could say anything else, she spread her wings and fluttered back to the roof. All William could do was watch as she disappeared from his view. He started back to his house when he heard something whistling behind him. Before he could turn around, something struck his head. He was out like a light before he even touched the ground. Reno glided back down from the roof. She picked up the baseball-sized rock and tossed it aside. Gently using her teeth, she dragged William to the house where he was supposed to be. Reno was smaller than William, but she had plenty of strength to move the boy's dozing body. She dropped him on the porch then returned to her post on top of the roof.

WILLIAM WOKE ON THE PORCH WITH A LUMP ON THE BACK OF HIS head. He slowly stood up in the bright sunlight and looked down. His pajamas were riddled with small tears. The throb in his head was difficult to bear. He tried to remember what had happened the previous night. When his memory did return, he educed from his mind the dragon glaring at him, bearing its fangs. William gazed back up to the cabin roof. Nothing was there. He concluded that meeting the dragon was only a dream. Something else had to have struck him. As he rubbed the back of his head, his father appeared in the doorway.

"There you are, William, enjoying the early morning. Would you like some breakfast? There are blueberry pancakes if you're hungry."

William sighed before answering. "That sounds fine."

Charles raised an eyebrow as he noticed William's pajamas. "What happened to your clothes? They're all torn up!"

William shook away the throbbing. "I don't know what happened to me. My head hurts. Maybe I was walking in my sleep, but I can eat breakfast."

As he followed his father inside, he was still puzzled. Was he really sleepwalking? He had never done so before. That was the only reasonable explanation, however. But the dream! The little brown creature spoke to him. He could not dismiss it so easily. Could it have been real?

Unable to answer his questions, he changed his clothes and joined the others for breakfast. His head continued to throb in painful pulses all morning.

CHAPTER 8

THE FACE OF THE ENEMY

The blue dragon sulked in her small prison. Several guards, stationed outside, kept her secure. All she could do was sit with the layer of wet straw for comfort. Her paws were still tied and her muzzle was tightly re-belted. She sat in the middle of the windowless room with the barred door in the center of one wall. As she twisted herself to a new position, she took a deep breath. A cloud of smoke puffed out of her nose. With her mind now cleared, the smoke gave her an idea. She knew the mouth was not the only source where a dragon could exhale fire. She could blow small streaming flames from her nostrils as well.

The dragon looked down at the rope around her feet. She breathed in, then let out a flame just large enough to incinerate the rope. When she heard the snap, a sense of freedom washed over her. First she scratched a bad itch on the back of her neck, then she used her claws to slice the belt off her snout. She stretched her jaws and yawned. Looking down at her feet, she noticed that they were different from the last time she had seen them. She stared at her five-fingered paws with deadly sharp claws coming from the ends. Lifting her front two paws, she placed them on top of her head. She felt two smooth horns, sharper and stronger than her claws, and spikes that ran down her back. The dragon placed her paws back down on the damp straw before dropping her head in shame. The recent error was barely comprehendible. Before she could shed a tear, however, the desire to leave the prison overcame her. She did not like the confinement one bit.

Stepping up to the door, she started beating it with her horns. She shrieked and roared to make herself heard. Just as she had hoped, one of the guards outside opened the thick fire door just beyond the bars. The dragon turned to a far corner, waiting for the right moment. The nervous guard stepped down the hall until he reached the iron bars that separated him and the dangerous creature.

The dragon turned her head and spat venom from deep within her throat. The venom flew between the bars and struck the guard in his eyes. With a cry, he held his hands over his face. The dragon whirled around and charged into the barred door. The remaining guards appeared in the hallway as she broke through. Shrieking once more, the dragon let fire escape from within her lungs. The guards jumped aside to avoid the heat. The beast moved through her flames with no trouble and crashed through the fire door. She ran away from the building without looking back.

Once the prison was for sure out of sight, she sat down to catch her breath. Her tail slithered back and forth as she panted; her mind was filled with regret. As she sniffed mucus back into her nose, the vivid memory of her friends brought her to her feet. Perhaps if she could find them, they would know what to do! She beat her wings and took to the sky in a desperate search.

I SAT IMPATIENTLY IN THE HOUSE WITH CLIPPER AND RENO, WAITING for Chang to finish his visit to the doctor. Fenson and Bluepond were waiting with us also. They reminded me and Clipper of the warning and the six pieces.

"Didn't you say the first piece is only a few miles from here?" Clipper asked them. "That doesn't seem so hard."

"It is not the first piece that is nearby," said Bluepond, "but rather a clue to help us find the pieces. These six pieces differ from one another. They work together to make up the portal, but they are scattered all over."

I cleared my throat in a deep rumble. "*Ahem…* If I may ask, how did these pieces get scattered so far and wide? These are magical relics we're trying to find."

"Most people know nothing of Elsovian magic," said Clipper. "The last time the portal was used must've been a very long time ago. When it was taken apart, the pieces could have been lost and fallen into many hands. Maybe those who had the pieces didn't know what they actually had. Who knows, maybe they're being held by people who know about us?"

"I think your first guess is right," I said. "Hopefully when we find our clue, we can be on our way. I'm sure Fenson and Bluepond will be a tremendous help." I turned and winked at them. "Thank you both. I appreciate what you've done. It had to have been hard coming here."

"It was difficult for sure," Fenson chuckled, "and we still have to keep our eyes open. This is going to be more than just a stroll near the pond. This journey will be very dangerous. We won't know what monsters will be coming until they do come. They could attack us at any time. Whether it's a minor skirmish or a full invasion, we have to be prepared. Battling these monsters will be difficult and unexpected, like the blue dragon you fought nay too long ago."

"I'm not certain, but I believe she might have been one of them," I said.

I blinked my eyes, trying to stay awake. Earlier that morning, Joshua had told me that when Chang finished his doctor visit, he would call him over the telephone. Joshua was in town, but we expected him to come back before the call. We all sat there quietly, thinking about the upcoming events. Fenson and Bluepond retired to an upstairs bedroom to rest before our long and unpredictable journey.

Reno stretched her legs. She tried to create a conversation to pass the time.

"Is Joshua going to stay here?"

"He has to," Clipper answered, "and Chang too unless we need him to pilot us anywhere. We can't put any other people in danger. Besides, Joshua and Chang need to keep this place in check *and* they will be restarting school soon. If we fail to get the six pieces, we'll have to come back here."

"I can barely stand it here," I huffed. "I'll do whatever it takes to get back to Elsov. There are so many reasons why. I appreciate Sergeant Nelson for providing this house. It's a good place to stay for the time being. But all these memories of Pearl Forest won't go away."

"I don't remember Elsov at all," said Reno. "I've spent all my life here, but I really want to go home, too."

"You may have spent most of your life here, but you were born on Elsov just like us. The only difference is you weren't in the form of a human," Clipper reminded her.

"I was the emblem," she recalled.

Silence fell over the room again. We all felt that there would be a lot of traveling, a lot of searching, a lot of fighting, and, possibly, a lot of sacrifices. We knew this journey would be life-changing, maybe more-so than our war against the Nibelungs.

I soon felt the urge to move my muscles. I was too anxious to sit still in one place for so long. My joints felt relaxed as I stretched and stood up.

"Where are you going?" Clipper asked.

"Just outside for a minute," I yawned. "I'll be in the back. Come tell me when we're ready."

I stepped through the dining room, into the kitchen, and out the back door. Behind the house was a picket-fenced backyard. I laid there for a moment. My white stomach rubbed on the grass, giving me a sense of ease.

Soon this will be Elsov ground, I thought. I will never accept defeat. I *will* find the six pieces. No remaining Nibelung dwarf or any sort of monster will stop me, not even Vesuvius, wherever he is.

With my eyes closed, I allowed the vision of Alsov to enter my mind. I imagined myself sitting in a sparkling pond near a village of grøls. If I ever found Pearl Forest, I planned to search for the swamps. That would be the first thing I would do.

I remained on the grass, deep in thought, when I felt a strong breeze blow over the rooftop. I stood up to see a shadow on the cabin roof. Turning around, a familiar scent came back to me. I rolled my eyes. There wasn't any time for another battle! I unfolded my wings and lifted myself to the roof where I found the blue dragon. The heat in my lungs began to build.

"The blue dragon has escaped from the prison," I hissed. "How did you find me? Answer me!"

I lowered my horns, growling once more. But just before I attacked, I noticed the dragon had tears in her eyes. She was not in any sort of defensive stance. I didn't know if she was distressed or if she was trying to trick me. Still, without the urgent need to fight for the moment, I took notice of her distinct scales. I hadn't taken the time to worry about them before. Her scales were not dark like mine. Maybe she was not as naturally aggressive as I was. I fought my strong instincts to attack; instead I tried to talk to her.

"It seems you were confused before. You must miss your home. I know this world is different from what you're used to. I'm from Elsov too. You may have been sent here because of me in the first place."

The blue dragon lifted her head. She looked deep into my eyes.

"J… Jacob. I'm not from El… Elsov. Do you r… recognize me?"

I looked back at her in shock when she spoke my name. My jaw dropped. I was unfamiliar with her voice, but I instantly knew who she was.

"Sally? Is that you?"

She nodded sadly. "Oh, Jacob! It… It was an accident. I tried to secure the potion inside a capsule. It ruptured and somehow I absorbed it. When I left the lab, I realized what had happened. By the end of the day, I didn't feel well, as did you before you transformed." She practiced a few more words before continuing. "I was still aware enough to recognize that what had happened to you and Clipper was happening to me. I thought that if I found you, maybe you could help me. I climbed into a truck that I found was going to southern California. I knew what was going to happen, so I sat alone in the dark. I thought an enclosed space would be fitting for me so I wouldn't hurt anyone. I was alone for hours. The last thing I remembered was feeling my skin. It turned scaly. Then I fell asleep. This morning I found myself tied up with straw at my nose. I'm sorry if this causes any trouble, truly I am." Another tear slid down her snout.

I coughed out a cinder in despair. "Ah, Sally! I told you to be careful!"

"Jacob, I didn't want to do this. It was an accident. Now I have to deal with the consequence for the rest of my life. Please forgive me. I was examining the potion for myself. That's why I didn't get to see you off. I lost track of time."

"But look at you!" I barked. "You're something you shouldn't be! I know Clipper and I transformed ourselves, but that's because we're from Elsov. It had to be done. You, however, were born a human. You have a life on this world. You still have a family that loves you! How do you think they'll react? Now the potion's gone. There's no way to change you back."

I was about to scold her more when she started crying. Her tears dripped onto the shingles and flowed over the edge.

"I'm… I'm sorry, Jacob. I didn't mean to do this. My… my life is ruined and it's all my fault!"

As she wept, I realized her heart was truly broken. She didn't want to be a dragon. I knew it was an accident. Feeling sorry for her, I walked up and sat next to her; my tail coiled around the wrist of one of her forepaws.

"Oh, Sally," I said gently as I rubbed my nose against hers. "I'm sorry I yelled at you. I know it was an accident. You know, I have an idea that may work. Do you want to travel with us to find the pieces of the portal?"

Sally looked back at me. "What portal?"

"We're going on a journey to find the six pieces to make a portal to Elsov. We have a dwarf and a nymph inside right now. They're from Elsov. They came here to help us. I won't let you be alone in this world, Sally, I won't. When we go home, you can come with us. Remember how Monty was the Keeper of the three worlds? The dwarf told me that the Keeper is now a wizard, not a sorcerer. Maybe he can help you turn back into your true self and then come back here."

Sally stopped crying. "Is... Is that possible?"

"I'm not sure, but it's worth a try," I said. "If we can't find a potion, you can live with us. We'll find a way for you to be in touch with your family. Don't worry, Sally, you're my friend. Friends stick together and help each other. When you followed us to the Guarded Forest, you showed how much you cared for us. You were worried so you tried to help us any way you could. You're a true friend, Sally. You've helped me before. Now I'll help you."

I took a step forward and again rubbed my nose against hers. We then glided from the roof to the front door.

"By the way, how did you find me here?" I asked her.

Sally paused for a moment. "I think I... smelled you."

"Oh right," I muttered.

I walked inside first to tell Clipper what had happened. I didn't want to startle him and have him fight Sally out of instinct. He was already agitated and on his feet. He must have heard the noises on the roof.

"Clipper, do you remember the blue dragon we fought?" I asked as I walked in. I tried not to sound nervous.

Clipper turned his head away. "Don't mention her! I'm trying to forget about that."

"Well— that's going to be hard for you," I said, swallowing. "I found out who she is. You may not believe me, but it's Sally. It's Sally! She accidentally gave herself the potion!"

Clipper turned back to me, gaping. "That was Sally? She's a dragon? How did she take the potion? You know she's going to complicate things. Oh, I can't believe this!"

Clipper huffed as Sally walked in. She folded her wings to fit through the doorway. At that point, she stared innocently at Clipper, who glared at her in return. Sally was pleased that Clipper was not too angry. She spread her wings again in delight.

"I'm not going to complicate things," she said. "I promise I'll help you, not get in your way. Jacob and I thought of a solution that may work. Please just let me come with you."

It took a moment for Clipper to calm down.

"Hhh… You can come with us," he sighed. "I'm sorry, Sally. I didn't mean to sound so angry."

"That's what I wanted to hear," I replied.

Reno flapped her wings. She chirped joyfully when she realized who the blue dragon was.

"Sally! Is it really you? I missed you so much! You're a dragon like me now!"

Sally lowered her head to Reno's eye level. "Oh, Reno! I haven't seen you for so long! Jacob was right about the potion. Don't worry, I won't be like this forever. I'll be the woman I was again."

"I don't care about that. You're here! You get to be with us!" Reno turned to me and Clipper. "If Sally's here, that means there are four of us, plus the dwarf and the nymph. Oh, I'm so happy you're here, Sally!"

As with me, Sally rubbed noses with Reno in the natural way of greeting. Sally was overjoyed to see Reno again, but she was not paying attention to where her tail was. I took a step back when it pushed over the fine-wood table, shattering the china vase. Sally turned around and gasped. Fire spewed out of her mouth as she exhaled. I quickly stamped on the fire until it was nothing but a cloud of smoke.

"Sorry," Sally gulped.

I unfolded one of my wings, which did not touch a single piece of furniture.

"Don't worry, Sally," I said. "Clipper and I were clumsy on our new feet. Before you know it, your size and shape won't stop you from going anywhere."

Reno jumped onto Sally's back, ignoring the damage. "You'll help us find the six pieces, won't you? I want you to be with us."

Sally nodded. Her eyes shined with happiness. Fenson and Bluepond, having heard the noise, came downstairs. They both stopped when they saw Sally inspecting the broken vase.

"Who is this lightscale and how did she get here?" asked Bluepond. "Is this the blue dragon you mentioned, Jacob?"

Sally's ears stood up. I could tell she was surprised to see a nymph for the first time. She kept her emerald-green eyes on the little man in his native clothing.

"So, you must be the dwarf and the nymph," Sally said slowly and carefully. "Don't be afraid. My name is Sally. I'm the one who fought Jacob and Clipper recently, but I'm not their enemy. It's quite a long story how I got here."

Bluepond descended the stairs. "I am not afraid of her. She is welcome to join us if she wants to. Sally, my name is Bluepond. I live in Pearl Forest near the swamplands. My companion's name is Fenson Katque. We have come to help Jacob and Clipper. The reason why we—"

"There could be dangerous enemies after us already," Fenson interrupted. "We must be prepared for anything."

As Bluepond remained silent, I headed for the door.

"This is a big group, like one huge circus," I said. "Well, the more the merrier. This will give us the upper hand if and when we must fight. It's getting crowded in here, though. I'm going back outside if you don't mind."

"I think we should be out here when Joshua comes home so we can tell him about Sally," said Clipper, following me to the door.

I stepped out into the backyard. Clipper was right; it would be a good idea to tell Joshua about Sally so he wouldn't be frightened. Reno passed Clipper and trotted beside me.

"I'm coming with you. I'm getting bored," she said.

"You'll soon forget the definition of boredom," I promised. "What is yet to come will be very important."

"We're going home. I can't wait," Reno responded with excitement.

Some minutes later, Joshua's car pulled up in the driveway. I made a light chirp to beckon him to the backyard. He came toward us with dry lips and shaking hands.

"Hi everyone. Chang hasn't called yet, right?

"Yes," said Clipper.

Joshua sighed. "Oh good, I haven't missed it. All this waiting is driving me crazy."

"I feel the same way," I huffed.

Joshua sat down on the patio bench and began tapping his knee.

"I hope there won't be much trouble," he said. "We still need to be on the lookout. I don't know why I'm as anxious as I am. I'm not even going with you."

I puffed a cloud of smoke out my nose as I told Joshua about Sally. Joshua was left speechless when I mentioned that she was inside. At least it gave him something to think about other than waiting. He asked me if Sally could come out.

"All right," I replied. "I think we'll hear the phone when it rings. Come on Reno, let's go get her."

Reno did not want to go back inside. "I can't take it any longer!" she croaked. "Why is he taking so long? Is something wrong?"

I placed a paw on her head. "Nothing's wrong, Reno. You just have to be patient. Chang's reliable. Think positive and before you know it, we'll be searching for the six pieces and building our grand portal. You'll see Pearl Forest in no time. I'll even take you to see the fairies. You'll love them."

The very second the telephone rang, Joshua jumped up and ran inside to answer it. I heard him warmly greet Sally whilst speaking to Chang at the same time. A few minutes later, he, along with everyone else, came bursting out the door.

"Jacob! Clipper!" yelled Joshua. "He called! He said his appointment is over! He's on his way home!"

"Now we are ready to go," Bluepond said in relief.

Reno chortled while flying in a helix. "We can leave! We can leave!"

I brought up my rear foot to scratch my ear again. "Let's hurry and tell the rest. We'll go there and— hold on." I placed my foot back on the ground. I sniffed the air. A strange scent filled the atmosphere, yet I heard nothing but the warm, pacific breeze.

Reno sniffed as well. "What's that smell? I don't like it."

CHAPTER 9

DAVID & GOLIATH

"What do you smell?" asked Joshua. "I don't smell anything. Can you just ignore it? I thought we were eager to leave."

I wasn't listening to Joshua. This scent was something I could *not* ignore. I moved across the lawn to the road. There I stood alone. There was no sign of anyone except for my friends. I didn't hear anything, but I knew something was near; something dreadful, something that did not come from the first earth. I bared my sharp teeth, though nothing happened. I was about to turn around when I heard something whizzing through the air. I turned my head and looked up. Something flew straight at me, pounding me between my wings and straight into my spikes. Reno screeched in horror and raced back to the doors of the house.

"What just happened? Jacob, are you hurt?" she cried.

I stood back up, my legs quaking. I realized I had been struck by a large brown mallet that had been flung by something from a great distance. With anger feeding off my pain, I batted the mallet to the side with my horns. I roared at the massive beast that approached me, caring not if the neighbors heard me or not.

My heart jumped when I heard Reno scream again.

"Help! He's got me!"

Turning around, we all saw a green creature holding Reno to the ground by her neck. With his free hand, he drew a glowing blue sword. The unknown person had characteristics similar to that of a human; except he had sharp, unclean nails on the ends of his fingers and dry gray hair on his head. His green skin alone told me he was an outsider. He was a goblin.

Sally spared no time. She blew a stream of fire at this newest foe. The hideous being released Reno and rolled to the side to escape the flames.

"Joshua! Get back inside!" she roared.

The goblin smiled evilly as he picked up his weapon. Clipper could not believe what he saw. His bravery appeared to have vanished. He was almost killed the last time he came across a blue blade.

"It's the sword. It's the sword!" he cried.

He took a step back. I knew he was having a flashback of his near-fatal injury. He wanted to use more fire for defense, but the goblin was standing right next to the cabin.

"What sword are you talking about?" Sally asked.

"When we were fighting Monty, he had some sort of sword with him," Clipper explained in fear. "It looked like that one."

"You mean the sword that almost killed you?"

"Yes! It can impale a dragon!"

The goblin wielded his weapon and advanced on Clipper. He was too close. If Clipper tried to use fire, the goblin would still have time to react.

"Indeed, it can impale any creature!" the goblin sneered. "The ice blade can kill any living thing at the possessor's disposal, especially you. There are swords, daggers, and even arrowheads made from the ice spell! I am Mallutin. I was sent by his Majesty the King, King Vesuvius III!"

Clipper attempted to spit venom at the goblin, but missed. He forgot that the green creatures were incredibly swift. Clipper's shivering joints did not help either.

From the road, I rushed to aid my friends. The strange odor became more potent when I did so. Halfway there I heard the large monster charging at me from the side. I felt something long and sharp strike me before I could turn. The great force caused me to roll painfully while accidentally destroying a part of the road.

"Heeheehee! Bloodgutt will be the death of you, blacksmoke, or Wildhorn, when he comes," laughed Mallutin. "You'll die no matter who you fight. Hahahahaha!"

The monster who had gored me was the one Mallutin called Bloodgutt. As the animal glared at me, she took a step sideways to retrieve her mallet; then she charged again. This time I did something I had never tried before. I jumped several feet into the air and flapped my wings as hard as I could. Hovering in mid-flight, a minor sandstorm arose from the beach. Bloodgutt covered her eyes, spinning in confusion before losing her balance. She leapt back to her feet, bellowing. I ignored her loud bellows and flapped my wings even harder; the sand again swirled in a blinding storm. The Unitaur banged her mallet on the ground, causing more of the road to shatter like glass. I gained about forty feet of altitude then dove straight down toward Bloodgutt. I latched onto her back with my claws and bit into her gritty-furred shoulder. Bloodgutt stood up, waving her mallet through the air like a baseball bat. I tried the best I could to keep my grip on her as Clipper rushed over to assist me. He was not watching when Mallutin raised his ice blade and slashed at Clipper's hindquarters. Clipper roared from the assault. Blood was visible.

Before Sally could help him, she saw another strange occurrence. Several drops of Clipper's blood landed on the goblin's feet. Mallutin reacted as if the blood was hot oil. He frantically wiped it off with his other sandal. At that moment Reno jumped onto his head, casting fire and snapping at his ears.

"Reno, don't!" Sally cried.

Mallutin jolted the ice blade over his head. Reno ducked then shifted herself, avoiding every swing. She jumped off his head to the ground beside him where she blew a brief flame at his feet. Mallutin jumped away from the concentrated fire. This gave Clipper and Sally the perfect chance to advance. It seemed as if Mallutin was ready to flee. He couldn't take on three dragons at once with one ice blade. He was trapped. That was until Wildhorn arrived. The

Minotaur came barreling through, charging into the north half of the cabin. Most of the front face of the house was demolished by his horns and mallet. Both Sally and Reno were covered in rubble. Reno stopped her fire in fear of it spreading to the cabin.

Mallutin, slightly bemused, got to his feet. He looked through the opening in the wall where Fenson and Bluepond stared back at him from the upstairs balcony.

"Ah, you dwarf!" Mallutin growled. "I believe you're the one who spied on me, am I right? So this is where you've been hiding! Hmmhmm."

Bluepond was unarmed. All Fenson had was the spoon he carried in his satchel, which was obviously useless in battle.

"I should have asked Trihan if I could borrow an albore," Fenson groaned.

"It would have been a great use to us. But it is too late now," said Bluepond. "We need to find another solution."

Mallutin entered what was left of the house and ran up the exposed stairway, leering as if he was Satan himself ready to drag poor souls down to the bowels of Hell. Fenson was already at the top, waiting for Mallutin's head to appear in front of him. When it did appear, Fenson kicked the goblin's head hard with his boot. Mallutin tumbled back down the stairs. Bluepond slid down the railing to where his injured foe lay bruised and bleeding. He picked up the ice blade while Mallutin was still on the floor. With both hands, he held the point above the goblin's black heart.

Fenson hurried down the stairs, stopping behind the nymph. "What are you going to do to him?"

"I must slay him," said Bluepond.

Mallutin squirmed for one last attempt to retrieve his ice blade. Bluepond lifted his foot and pressed him back down. The blade hovered over the exhausted goblin, who made a face that asked for mercy.

"Eh, heh-heh. Well, it seems you caught me at a disadvantage, wood nymph. I know your kind hates folk like me. Perhaps you can surprise me by… hmm… not killing me, eh? Does that sound reasonable?"

"You are evil," Bluepond declared. "I may be small compared to you, but I will never let the likes of you, with your filthy ways, roam free."

He used the blade, the same type of blade that had nearly killed Clipper, and thrust it into Mallutin's chest. The goblin shrieked and squirmed before he lay motionless. Fenson placed two fingers on the body's neck to check for a pulse.

"He's dead."

"As much as I dislike killing, it had to be done," Bluepond said.

Fenson had to agree. Mallutin would have possibly killed them if he was left alive. Now that he was dead, the dwarf shifted his attention to the commotion outside. He and Bluepond knew they still had the Minotaurs to deal with.

Dealing with one Minotaur was difficult enough, but dealing with two was definitely a challenge. They reminded me of the Persian immortals in a way: when one fell, the other took its place. The damage from their mallets transformed the lonely beach into the site of a war-torn battlefield. I clung tightly to Wildhorn while keeping Bloodgutt away with fire. After a few grueling minutes, Wildhorn finally collapsed and rolled onto his back. His body, larger and heavier than mine, squashed me like a fly; at least that was what it felt like. He stood back up and smashed his mallet on the side of the road. Moving back a considerable distance, he charged at me with his horns lowered to my level. I stumbled back up on my feet, gasping for air. Wildhorn had more than enough time to make his move. His grimy yellow horns scooped me up from the ground and sent me through the air. This time I crashed into the house next to our cabin. The front door and its outer frame were completely destroyed. The family inside appeared to have been hiding from the ongoing fight. All except one retreated to the basement without looking back. From the corner of my eye, I saw a frightened boy peek his head up from the stairway.

"What just happened?" the boy shivered.

As scared as he must have been, he had to have known the real danger was outside. He saw Wildhorn charging at the house. The boy rushed over to me.

"Stand up! He's going to kill you!" he cried.

By the sound of his voice, I could tell he was not sure if he should speak to me. His extra boost got me back on my feet, though. I harmlessly bumped him aside with my wing, then got into my own charging stance. I ran out the destroyed doorway.

It was dragon against Minotaur. Black scales against brown fur. David against Goliath. I was running at my full speed while he was running at his full speed. Time itself seemed to have fled the scene. I was waiting for the bullhorns to clash with my own set. As each second passed, it seemed as if nothing happened.

At last, in the center of the front yard, everything mashed together. Wildhorn's bulk gave him the advantage to halt my progression. My advantage was the sharpness of my horns and my firm stamina. I slid backward, my claws digging into the mud. I felt my enemy slow drastically until we were at a complete stop. He backed up with his body quaking. Two bloody horn marks were on his face. The collision must have taken everything he had. As I was about to engulf him in fire, Clipper jumped onto his chest. The bull was in no shape for fighting a second dragon. Clipper's sudden attack helped much more than I expected. One of his elbow blades, sharp as it was, slid across Wildhorn's right horn. The tip of it flew clean off. Blood dribbled out from the center. Wildhorn shrieked in agony.

Now it was my turn again to fight him. I continued as planned and let the fire free itself from within my lungs. The heat was too much for Wildhorn. With his fur charred black, he turned toward the low tide coast. As he tromped into the water, Sally followed him. She grabbed him by the scruff and started swimming farther out to sea. She had to have guessed that Minotaurs were never known to be graceful swimmers. Sally paddled effortlessly underwater while keeping a firm grip on Wildhorn's scruff. Wildhorn panicked for air, wriggling in vain until he was not moving at all. Sally had drowned him. She let go of his carcass, letting it sink to the ocean floor. When she was free, she swam back up to the surface.

With two dead, the four of us focused on the final monster. Bloodgutt knew she had lost the battle when all in my group surrounded her. She quickly stomped off down the seashore toward the cliffs. I wanted to pursue her, but Clipper stopped me.

"There's no need," he said. "We can't throw away our chance to find the six pieces because of that thing. Let Nelson or some other force take care of her."

Sally got up from her serpentine crawl to a neutral stance. All of us, including Joshua, who had emerged from the cabin, and our Elsovian friends viewed the damage. Rubble littered the street, which was coated with a layer of sand. I realized how destructive the battle had been when my anger subsided.

"This place is a mess," Sally said in disgust.

Clipper groaned as he felt the minor wound in his hindquarters. "I don't like those blue swords. This isn't serious, but it gives me an ugly memory from before. Now two different homes are damaged and the road is torn up. Jacob, when you flapped your wings like that, you sure made the sand fly everywhere. It covered everything."

"Those poor excuses for monsters were Minotaurs," said Fenson. "I'm sorry to say your home is in pieces because of them. However, I am pleased with your actions, Jacob. The wind that a dragon can produce with his wings can be very great. Several autumns ago, a friend of mine was ambushed by a darkscale when he traveled afar. He said when its wings started moving, he felt as if he was in a whirlwind. He was lucky he escaped with his life. After that, I warned him not to wander too far from home by himself. Nasty vermin, darkscales are. I mean no offence to the two of you."

I was thoughtful for a moment after Fenson finished his story.

"You said that Sally is a lightscale, right?" I said. "That means she's a different breed. What about me, or Clipper and Reno? Does that mean we're darkscales?"

"A darkscale is typically born with a dark soul," Bluepond explained. "A lightscale or a brightscale, call it either, is born into a better society. But that is not always the case. Color only shows origin. Most lightscales are born into good. In your case, there is an exception. You were born under a spell that is centuries old."

I listened closely. "I figured that it was a spell, but I'm still fuzzy on the details."

"Jacob, we don't have time. Just have him explain on the way to Chang," said Clipper.

"I know there's a lot of damage and Chang is waiting for us, but I'm curious. We won't be long," I said.

The nymph waited until we were silent before he began to explain. He told us Trihan's story of when Clipper and I were born. The shells of our eggs were red instead of white. Bluepond continued to talk about the recovery of our eggs. I felt my shrinking anger turn into sadness when he mentioned my mother. I knew she loved me as a hatchling, before I was taken to the first earth. If my parents were still on Elsov, they had to be waiting for me. In any case, it was quite fascinating to hear about my birth. Bluepond then explained about the lightscales' spell and how Clipper and I were sent away because we were darkscales.

"You two were supposed to end the rising threat of the Nibelungs on this world. If the thieves took you away, you could have been taken to Glaciem and be turned into ice dragons."

Sally stopped Bluepond before he could finish.

"Ice dragons?" she asked.

Clipper huffed, but Bluepond did not attempt to shorten his explanation. "Glaciem is an ice warlock. He is an ally of Vesuvius, despite one being of ice and one of fire. And your heart will break when I tell you about the young ice dragons. Glaciem kidnaps the young of your kind, those who are as young as Reno right now. He would rob their bodies. Their souls were reduced to ashes. Their scales would turn to a color of blue ice. They do not breathe fire. They breathe icy air, and they will stop at nothing to see their victims dead. They kill everything within their path. No matter how many you destroy, they will not run. They become soulless servants to do only as Glaciem bids."

"That's horrible!" Sally exclaimed, her wings drooping.

"And remember the blue sword? That is called an ice blade. Many weapons are made from the enchanted material. Yestooth and claw can cut dragon scales, but the ice blade does it more efficiently."

"That's why it hurt me so badly," said Clipper, trying to finish the conversation.

"Well, now we know more," I said. "Our time has come. The Nibelungs have fallen. Let's go find Chang and we'll be ready to go. Sorry Clipper, I just needed some things to be cleared up."

I was about to leave when I saw the boy standing in the open doorway to his house. He had his wide, frightened eyes glued on me. I quietly hissed, wishing he would leave.

Clipper closed his eyes in frustration. "Oh, great."

"What are we going to do about him?" Reno asked in a shy voice.

I did not say anything. I decided to leave instead. The rest of my friends followed me on foot except for Bluepond. The nymph, holding the ice blade gingerly by the handle, looked at it in derision.

"This is a cursed weapon," he said forlornly. "I will not take it with me." He went around back and returned shortly, empty-handed.

I assumed that leaving with no word would be best for the boy. Besides, after what Bluepond had told me, I wanted to leave as soon as possible.

WILLIAM COULD BARELY CATCH HIS BREATH. HE GLANCED LEFT AND right before returning to his house. His father, along with the others, emerged from the basement.

"Oh, no!" Franklin cried in horror. "What happened?"

"Nothing like this has ever happened before," said Emily. "Our front door is gone! Our home is damaged. And what was that outside? I saw something very big!"

"William, you're not harmed, thank goodness," said Charles. "Why didn't you come with us? You could've been hurt."

William wanted to explain what he saw, but he did not think anybody would believe him. He talked about it anyway.

"You should have seen it! There was a black dragon fighting a giant Minotaur! I— I can hardly believe it myself!"

His father stepped outside, noticing the sand all over the road. "William, it must have been your imagination. What you may have seen must have been something that really wasn't there. I'm sorry to say that. I'm just happy you're safe."

Emily seemed more convinced than Charles. "You saw a black dragon fighting a Minotaur? I remember hearing about the black dragon during that incident in Santa Ana the other day..."

"I've heard of this black dragon too, along with the red one," said William. "I don't really know much about them, but I did see the black one use its wings to blow sand everywhere. Both creatures then locked horns in a brutal fight. I know this sounds strange, but I really wanted to help the dragon. He looked straight at me after the battle ended and flew off!"

Charles appeared to be fascinated by his son's story. "No matter what you saw, I think you should see a doctor. You could have been hurt or possibly killed."

William thought visiting a doctor was a good idea, though he knew what he saw and could not deny it. At the hospital, the doctor diagnosed William with a concussion, with the point of impact being on the back of his head. William was sure it was from last night, since he hadn't been hit during the fight. After the visit, he and his father returned to the lonely beach where Emily's parents were discussing the repairs needed on their home.

"Did you really see a dragon?" Emily asked William.

"I did," he replied. "They were residing in the house next door! I knew there was something mysterious going on over there."

Charles overheard them. "William, you must calm yourself. You will learn what you need to know when the time is right."

William could not tell exactly what his father was thinking, but Charles seemed as if he wanted to believe his son's story.

CHAPTER 10

WRITTEN ON A CLOTH

Chang was shocked to see the newest member of our group. I had to explain to him, as I had Clipper, about Sally and her accident. Once Chang understood, he took note of our weary appearances.

"You took quite a while to get here, even if Sally joined us as a dragon," he said. "You all look terrible. What happened?"

It took me a moment to find a way to answer. "That? Oh, right… Remember how Fenson and Bluepond warned us about upcoming attacks? I know this sounds strange, but a goblin and two 'Minotaurs' attacked us. The goblin and one of those bulls are dead. The other ran off. We don't know where it is."

Chang cringed. "Oh no, what's the damage?"

I let my eyes travel away from his. "Oh… not much. The front of our house is in pieces and the street's all cracked up."

Chang slammed one of his crutches on the asphalt. "What? Our house is destroyed? And how did the street get all cracked up? Better yet, how did these monsters find you?"

"It's… a long story," I stammered, thinking of the painful experience.

Fenson stepped in between us. "We can talk about this later, Mr. Chang. Now let us find the spot where Bluepond and I arrived. The first clue is not far from there. We just have to head east once we get there."

"Go to the spot where you arrived and head east," said Chang. "If you say so."

"Dragons, a nymph, and a dwarf," said Clipper. "What a group we are! Let's be careful where we go. The less trouble the better."

Fenson and Bluepond rode with Chang while Clipper and Reno flew above them. I was not too far behind, flying with Sally since she was still a little slow on her new wings. It was not long before I saw Chang's car turn right; Fenson and Bluepond must have found their landing spot. We're making good time, not far now, I thought.

While heading east, I hardly noticed any other car on the road besides Chang's. It felt like we were the only beings on earth. We did not realize we were indeed being watched by someone. In fact, we were being watched by many. The fairies, wanting to offer any help, monitored our progress. The same went for one of the Sorcerers who served the King himself.

We started circling above Chang like vultures once Sally caught up to Clipper and Reno. The four of us patrolled the area, watching for enemies. It was Sally who first noticed something was wrong.

"Jacob! Is it just me or is it getting dark?"

She was right. Though the sun was still well above the horizon, the sky was darkening.

"I don't know what it is," I called back.

Moments later, a dark fog, black as my scales, loomed around us. Daylight disappeared entirely. It was even more dark than night itself.

"What's going on?" Reno asked nervously.

"I don't know, but I don't like it either," said Clipper.

Down below, Chang turned on his headlights. I then heard him honk three times, signaling those of us in the sky to land.

"Did you find anything?" I asked as I reached the ground.

"Nothing yet," said Bluepond, "but this black fog has me worried. This may very well be the product of sorcery. Someone may have found our trail. This fog could be a sign or a signal."

"If that's the case, let us open our ears and you dragons open your noses," said Fenson. "Let's keep looking for the clue, but be careful. We could be walking into a trap."

Clipper huffed out a flame that temporarily illuminated the street. "I'll stay sharp for sure," he said.

We began our search immediately. The darkened sky and eerie silence wrapped themselves around us in an icy blanket, creating a haunting environment. While investigating, I crested a small rise and, with Reno beside me, walked back downhill. We found ourselves in the middle of what appeared to be an abandoned town. The scent of people was fresh, but I could neither see nor hear them. Other than the smell, this place felt like a ghost town.

"Where are we?" Reno asked.

Chang looked around with his flashlight. "I don't know. This place looks deserted."

"It seems that everything here is over a century old," I said thoughtfully as I examined a nearby shack.

"It just adds to the creepiness," said Clipper.

"Creepy" was the exact word to describe our surroundings. There was no sound, not a soul was to be seen, the buildings were aged (some were in very poor condition), and the fog continued to hang over our heads; yet we searched tirelessly, exploring different offices, houses, parks, and the like. Time passed before Clipper's voice broke the silence.

"Over here! I found something!"

We all turned around and joined him.

"He has something in his teeth," said Reno.

Clipper had a piece of cloth hanging from his mouth, dangling between his fangs. He carefully dropped it and laid it out for the rest of us to see.

"There's writing on this," he said.

Chang shined his light on the cloth. He may have needed it, but I didn't.

I read the text on the cloth,

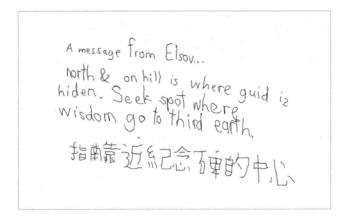

A message from Elsov...

north & on hill is where guid iz
hiden. Seek spot where
wisdom go to third earth.

指南靠近紀念碑的中心

The last line was a language I could not read. "I think it's Chinese," I said. "I can't make it out. Maybe Chang can."

Chang leaned forward to read the inscription and translate it. "The guide is near the center of monument," he said.

"Great, this whole thing is another riddle," I huffed. "I've seen these before."

"Even with the entire riddle in English, it's still confusing," said Reno.

We all took a moment to try to decipher the meaning of the message. It took some hard thinking, but I soon had an idea of what it meant.

"This message was intended for us," I told everyone. "We are aware that this world is the first earth, Elsov is the second, and the spirit world is the third. Maybe this riddle ties in with death."

"Right," said Clipper. "We're looking for a place where those who rest search for the third earth. Could it be a graveyard or cemetery? I can't think of anything else."

Reno sat down and scratched her neck. "Are we looking for a graveyard? That's odd. And if so, which one?"

"North and on a hill," I said brightly. "A cemetery must be nearby. We should look around."

"I assume there must be a monument in the center of this cemetery?" asked Fenson.

"A monument in the center of a cemetery that is north of here, on a hill. Makes sense to me," said Clipper.

"So how far are we from this cemetery?" Sally wondered. "Hopefully the guidance to the first piece is not that far away."

I took a deep, smoky breath. "There are a few things that are confusing me. This doesn't lead us to the first piece, but just to the guide; and I'm sure anyone who lives nearby is unaware of the other worlds. But the cloth looks as if it's as old as this town. Besides, who on Elsov knows about the geography of the land around here?"

Clipper reread the message. "Well, whoever wrote this knows Chinese, even if his penmanship is bad. And with it talking about the cemetery and a monument in the center of it... it's as if they've been there themselves. How would anyone from Elsov know all this?" He gently rubbed the curves of his claws across the cloth.

"We know it's from elsewhere and they have knowledge of this place, but it's still the clue nonetheless," said Sally.

"You're right. No matter where it came from, it's still the clue," I said. "We're trying to find the guide to the first piece. So, I guess it's at the cemetery; north of here."

I jumped into the darkness and spread my wings with the others close behind me. We again flew in circular motions instead of in a straight line, this time so Chang would not lose sight of us through the fog. We now had the first clue and were on our way.

CHAPTER 11

THE VIEWING RING

I was relieved when the fog lifted not long after we took off. The sky became a welcoming blue once again. The air was much cleaner and brighter. Nothing serious yet, I thought. After only a few miles, Chang's car made its way to a little green hill that was home to the cemetery we were looking for. Clipper, Sally, Reno, and I were already there. We discovered an iron fence that surrounded evergreens and many headstones. In the corner of the cemetery, a family appeared to be visiting a loved one's grave. They were unaware of our presence.

"Is there some sort of funeral or memorial going on here?" Clipper asked quietly.

"I hope not," I answered.

"How can we search for the monument?" asked Chang after he got out of his car. "I don't think anyone would appreciate me scavenging nearby."

"Not to mention the rest of us," I added.

From where we sat, we saw another group of people coming in through the entrance of the cemetery. Luckily the trees gave us extra protection. I was about to jump over the fence when I felt something land gently on my head then flutter to the ground. Chang picked it up. It was a piece of paper.

"Where did that come from?" asked Bluepond.

"There's something written on it," Fenson pointed out. He read the brief note aloud,

"The fairies are watching you. Though you cannot see them, they will provide you with good help.

—Trihan"

"The Wizard sent us a message?" Reno questioned. "How can the fairies help us if they're not in our presence? And how would this wizard know where we are?"

"Trihan is the Keeper, you must remember," Bluepond explained. "He does not see us, but I suspect the fairies may inform him of our actions. We do not see them, but that does not mean they are not there."

"It's good to know someone is on our side," I said. "Right now we have to find what the fairies call the guide. Just remember to keep a low profile."

Chang, Fenson, and Bluepond entered the cemetery using the main gate while we dragon-folk hopped over the fence. After I thudded onto the ground within the cemetery, I saw Chang limp to the entrance with his crutches tight in his hands. They headed for us once they were inside.

"I'm glad the darkness in the sky is gone," said Reno. "This place would be even spookier than where we found the clue."

Clipper looked up at the sun. "Yes, but there's only a few more hours of daylight left."

I looked around for a spot where I could see the monument. Searching along rows of granite headstones, I found the trunk of a tree. I leaned next to it and sat down. Nothing caught my eye.

"May I recommend we split up?" Fenson suggested when his group reached mine. "The monument must be here somewhere if we are near the center. But with as many of us as there are, we may appear suspicious to others who are here."

"He is right," said Bluepond. "We should form separate groups."

I took another cautious scan. "That's a good idea, Fenson. That way if one of us gets caught, the others can escape. Now let me see... Fenson and Bluepond can go together.

"I can take Reno one way," said Clipper.

"All right, Sally and I can go our own separate ways. And just remember, be discrete. I know it's hard for a dragon, but we must do so. Having that kid see us still bothers me."

"Sounds good to me," Clipper replied.

We wasted no time. I quickly jumped over to another row of headstones. Before long, I was alone. I dropped to the ground after a quick glance. Folding in my wings as tightly as possible, I started crawling forward. Many muddy claw-marks formed in the smooth grass. I lifted myself only a few inches while I crept quietly until I found an open, shaded area. I could see the family standing over a grave. I sat in my hiding place and waited for them to be on their way. When they finally left, I continued forward. As I reached the shaded area, I stopped again. Still, I could not see the monument. Huffing with annoyance, I continued onward. I soon found myself on a narrow pathway at the end of the row. I stayed still when Clipper and Reno rejoined me.

"Sally's just ahead of us," Clipper whispered. "She can see the monument. Unfortunately, there's a group of people there. It looks like some sort of ceremony."

"Did anyone see her?" I asked in concern.

Clipper shook his head. "No. She's doing just fine. She's on the opposite end of the monument, behind a tree. Reno and I found her and she sent us to find you. If only we can get those people out of there, Sally can make her way to the monument and search for the guide."

"How are we going to make those people leave?" Reno asked, jumping up and down.

"That's a good question. I don't know," Clipper huffed.

"If you can take me to the monument, I'll think of something," I said.

Clipper stood back up, telling Reno to wait for a moment. "It's just ahead, beyond that stand of trees," he told me.

I followed him silently. He halted between two trunks and sat down. I peeked over to see the people he was talking about. Peculiar... a group of twelve men were standing in a perfect semicircle. Each person wore a long robe, standing motionless like statues.

I kept my eyes on the organized men. "Seems like an interesting ceremony," I remarked.

"As I've said, Sally's just on the other side of the monument," said Clipper, arching his head to get a better view of the men.

Looking beyond the group, I found Sally staring back at me from the distance. I nodded noticeably to signal her. Pausing, I thought of an idea. I sighed with doubt, though. Looking at the monument again, I could see a marble statue of an angel in the center of a round flower garden. Behind it was a small but grand structure, also made of marble. The colorful windowpane just below the triangular roof told me that it was some sort of tomb. According to the clue, if the guide was anywhere, it should be somewhere near that monument. It might even be in the tomb. All I had to do was get that sect (or whatever it was) out of there.

Clipper studied my face. He guessed what I was thinking. "Jacob, we don't know how they'll react if they see us. You said that—"

"Clipper, you know that a second's glance doesn't convince anyone that easily. If we find some way to scatter them, we can quickly search for the guide. If somebody is still there... maybe they should get a taste of venom."

Clipper shook his head. "No! Venom should only be used for defense. Why would you think about hurting innocent people; those who are mourning the dead no-less?"

I stretched out my wing in an effort to push Clipper aside. Clipper resisted and pushed my wing back.

"We have to do this," I said. "It's the only way to find the guide. The only pain they'll feel is a slight sting in the eyes. Trust me, I know. It's not a pleasant experience with the hallucinations, but it's not that bad."

I stepped out into the clearing. Clipper huffed again and followed me. With their backs to us, the robed men did not see us. I folded my wings as Clipper spoke softly, "If you think this ridiculous plan will work, how will you slip past them unnoticed?"

"We need to get them away from the monument," I whispered. "And speak a little more quietly. We're louder than we might think."

Clipper did his best to keep his low, dragon voice quieter. "Sorry, but how will we get them to scatter? And think fast, we don't have any cover out here."

I lifted my head, looking everywhere for a source of a distraction. I searched until I found a thick evergreen standing a considerable distance away.

"What if we set fire to that tree? That should bring them over here. If you can set fire to that tree, Sally and I will search around the monument."

Clipper looked at me doubtfully.

I said nothing else and returned to the row of headstones, leaving Clipper alone. He hissed at me then turned to the tree, tapping one of his fangs. "If this is the best way to get the guide, so be it," he huffed.

He took flight down the shallow incline, landing near the tree. He then checked to see if anyone was around. I was in his sight. From where I was, I could also see Fenson and Bluepond moving along the perimeter fence of the cemetery. Clipper looked up at the branches, inhaled, then blew out a flame that engulfed the bottom branches. The fire spread higher and higher until the whole evergreen was burning. Clipper did not hesitate to fly off for cover.

From my hiding spot, only a few rows away from Reno, I saw a man in the line turn around. He pointed to the tower of smoke above the tree.

"Fire! Help! There's a fire!"

The other men turned around. The majority of them ran down the gentle hill in panic. Three of them watched from the safety of the monument. Reno hopped over the row of headstones and landed on my back. "They're not all gone," she said. "Will you show yourself now?"

"In a way," I replied. "We can't have them stop us from finding the guide. We're too close."

"I'll help you," she promised.

She took flight from my back and flew straight to the angel. I wanted to stop her, but I knew I was going to expose myself anyway. I did not spread my wings, but rather ran up the path. Reno hovered and landed on the head of the angel. Each of the men turned around. Not one of them spoke. They stood like ice, staring at Reno in horror. I came up from behind. Two of them turned around and slowly backed away from me. I quickly spat a stream of venom into the nearest one's eyes. As he fell on his hands and knees, his mind consumed by false images, the second man turned and ran down the path, out of sight. The third man of the group gazed at me and then Reno. He simply fainted, overwhelmed by our presence.

"Take care of these people while I go look for the guide," I told Reno.

Reno jumped off the angel, staring at the fainted man before carefully climbing onto his stomach. Keeping her claws up, she wrapped her tail around the man's right wrist. "Sorry about all the trouble. We just need to find something," she said soothingly.

I left Reno to her duty. I circled the garden, looking for anything that might lead me to the guide. I had found nothing when Sally joined me.

"Sally, go tell Clipper to find Fenson and Bluepond," I said. "The guide is somewhere around here, I'm sure of it."

"I'll look for him," said Sally.

She turned around in search for Clipper. I continued sniffing around the edge of the garden. When I reached the spot where I had started, I lifted my head. The guide had to be somewhere nearby! If it came from Elsov, surely I would recognize it. I soon came to the conclusion that it was neither near the angel nor the garden. My attention turned to the tomb behind me. Walking up to the heavy paneled double-doors, I bumped them with my horns. They were obviously locked. Bumping them harder, the lock broke and the doors squeaked open.

Inside the tomb, the sunlight, streaming through the window, painted the cold marble floor with beautiful, dancing colors. Along a flat surface next to the far wall was a polished wooden casket. It was neither the colors nor the casket that caught my interest, however. I smelled something out of the ordinary. It was a scent that seemed familiar, something that brought back the vision of the fairies. This smell was very similar, like the scent of blooming flowers on a bright spring day.

Searching along the side walls, I found something lying in the far corner. It was some sort of ring. I picked it up with my claws as carefully as possible. It looked as if I could fit a claw through it, maybe three fingers if I was still a human. The silver-coated rim was covered with a thin layer of dust. Instinct told me this was it. This was the guide! It must have been sitting here in the tomb for a long time! I gave a light puff of air over the ring; the dust lifted from the strange object. I would think the dust would do nothing, but I felt the tiny particles tickling my nose. No ordinary dust had the strength to do that. I felt it travel up my nostrils and into my sinuses. With my eyes starting to itch and water, I saw something appear before me. Above the glass pane, a white cloud materialized. It floated right above me. The cloud then opened to reveal the place I had sought for months, Pearl Forest! It was as if that world was right in front of me! The sunlight smiled down through the trees. A bright stream flowed in peace down a smooth riverbed. It was my home. I assumed the dust was some sort of potion, for I knew this was just an image.

While I enjoyed the vision, I noticed dark, greenish clouds looming above the forest. The clouds did not look friendly at all. Bolts of lightning flashed, followed by claps of thunder. The wind around me began to pick up, causing the tree boughs to whip and flail about. The stream started to overrun its banks. My feelings of peace vanished. Pearl Forest suddenly became a place I wanted to leave. As I took a sorrowful breath, a thick snowflake landed at my feet. It was snowing? It was quite unusual for a thunderstorm to spawn snow.

The falling flakes became thicker and thicker. I felt a sharp pain in my throat, as if I had swallowed a shard of glass. Coughing out the flake, I noticed it was not snow that was falling. It was ash. This was no storm; it was an eruption! I stared into the sky in disbelief. I saw a flash of orange. I could not take it any longer. I wanted to leave. In my mind, I heard a faint voice. It was a dark voice that was similar to mine. It was the voice of Vesuvius from my dreams.

"I am coming for you, Jacob Draco!"

I closed my eyes, waiting for the vision to end. The wind stopped blowing. The ash stopped falling. The river stopped flooding. I opened my eyes to find myself back in the tomb. The ring lay on the floor between my paws. This was a special ring. It *was* the guide. It would help us find the six pieces and our way back home. I did not know how just yet.

"We've got it," I said. "I won't let anything stand in my way. Vesuvius doesn't scare me now—"

The two doors to the tomb suddenly burst open. Startled, I turned around and growled.

"Whoever you are you aren't going to stop me!"

"Jacob, calm yourself. It's only me."

I quickly recognized the dwarf. My wings unfolded and dropped to the ground. My ears and tail followed suit. "Oh, sorry Fenson. You scared me."

"Not to worry," he said. "Clipper told me and Bluepond where you were. The other dragons were searching too when they had to leave. Firemen have just arrived. They brought much water to douse the fire that Clipper created."

I picked up the ring and gave it to Fenson. "This is what I found in the corner here. Do you know what it is?"

The dwarf held it up to his eye. "Hmmmm… I have seen something like this only once before. I believe it is a viewing ring. When determination affects the body, the viewing ring will be activated.

That's my understanding, at least. When you know what you are seeking, this will help you find it."

"It uses magic?" I asked.

"Yes, but the only sort of magic I've ever used up until today has come from an albore, I must confess."

"I can see why we would be given a viewing ring," I said. "It'll make it much easier to find the six pieces."

"Most certainly. Viewing rings are made by fairies, hence the note we received earlier. I have only met a handful of fairies in my lifetime. Still, they have blessed and helped me and my state in many ways."

I stared at the viewing ring in Fenson's hand. It was a fine piece of work. I was amazed that something so small and simple could do much more than it appeared it could do. As astonished as I was, I was still full of questions. "So how does it guide you?" I asked.

"You look through it."

Fenson shut one eye. He used the other to look through the hole. A smile formed on his face. "Ah! You *do* look through it. You will be surprised at what you see."

He took a step closer to me. I lowered my head so he could hold the viewing ring up to my eye. Everything around me turned green. The color pattern on the floor was no longer visible.

"That *is* interesting," I said. "So how does it guide you to whatever you're seeking?"

"As I have said before, I'm not certain exactly how it works. I have never used a viewing ring in all my days until now. If I may guess, there is a change to the color that occurs."

"Well, we may not know exactly how it works, but we know it does work. We found it! Now we can look for the first piece!"

Fenson had to cover his ears from my roar of satisfaction. Placing the viewing ring in a pocket of his shirt, he walked out of the tomb. I followed him to Bluepond, who was waiting at the garden. The man who got my venom was gone; the other was still fainted on the ground.

"Did you find the guide?" asked the nymph.

Fenson patted the pocket over his left breast. "We found a viewing ring. Hopefully it will help us find the six pieces."

Bluepond snapped his fingers. I could tell he was eager to leave. "I am excited. Truly I am, but I cannot express it right now. Other people are coming. The alarms I hear are very loud. We should leave this moment if we are not to be discovered face to face. The rest of our group separated when the commotion started. We must bring them back together immediately and show them the guide."

Bluepond said no more. He scurried off into another group of trees away from the fire. I followed him to the edge of the large cemetery. My dragon friends were nowhere to be seen, but I could smell them nearby. I had to wait for Fenson to catch up before I could help him and Bluepond over the fence. My anxiety did not help while I sat. When Fenson reached the fence, I lowered my head close to the grass. Bluepond placed a foot between my horns, in front of my spikes. His hands grabbed hold of the black metal bars. Lifting my head, Bluepond ascended to the top of the fence. He quickly scrambled over the top and dropped to the other side, landing perfectly on both feet. Lowering my head again, I did the same for Fenson. I lifted him to the top. As he scrambled over, he fell, landing flat on his back.

"Are you hurt?" Bluepond asked.

Fenson shook his joints as he stood up. "When you fall as much as I do, you no longer notice the pain."

They both fell silent as I jumped cleanly over the fence, not even using my wings. I landed neatly on all fours.

"Now that we're out, I can go back to the car," I said. "I know how this sounds, but between us, you two are the least likely to draw attention. I think the others are out of the cemetery as well. Do you think you two can round them up?"

Fenson and Bluepond complied. Once they left me, I took a low flight beside the fence, avoiding the commotion the best I could. Luckily the car was not too far away. Chang was already there, sitting in the passenger seat with his broken foot resting on the driver's seat. The door was open.

"I couldn't walk around for so long. My foot is very sore right now," he said when I arrived.

"Don't worry," I replied. "We found the guide. It's what Fenson calls a viewing ring. It's used to find any piece or clue."

"Great! But I have to ask, was it you that started the fire? I saw the smoke and a fire truck went by a few minutes ago."

"Oh, that was Clipper. We had to distract the people from the monument. It actually worked!"

Chang patted one of my horns. "That's great, Jacob. We have the guide now!"

"All we need to do is wait for Fenson and Bluepond to find the rest of the group," I said.

"You're one step closer," said Chang. "It surprises me how there is interference from Elsov and nobody knows that except us. I'm pretty sure that darkness earlier was a spell of some sort."

"If it was a spell," I began, "then what was it for? It didn't help us."

Chang ran through various possible answers. "If it wasn't intended for us, it might have been for someone else who would have known what the message meant." He paused, looking distressed. "Could it have been a warning or signal? What if there are monsters tracking us down? That fog of darkness was their signal. They might be nearby."

I thought about what he said. He could be right.

"Chang, close the car door and lock it. Don't get out or open it until Fenson and Bluepond come," I ordered.

Chang did not hesitate. I hopped back over the fence and sniffed the air again. It did not smell like the flowers and trees as it had earlier. It was more of a musky odor, something I had smelled before. Just then, the ghostly sound of an ancient trumpet was heard in the distance. I knew my friends were in danger. I took another step forward when what I feared emerged from behind headstones and tree trunks. Before I knew it, I was surrounded by unknown dwarfs. They must have sneaked in while I was talking to Chang. Their horned helmets alone told that they may have once been Nibelungs. Their tribe may have lost their power since Triathra's fall, but I knew they were not all gone. This bunch must have known we would be here for the ring. Just looking at them gave me ugly memories of my recent past. Anger started coursing through my veins.

"You made a grave mistake coming here," I growled to them. "There's no reason for you to be here except to meet your end. What's your business?"

I gave a threatening roar, causing one of the dwarfs to finally speak up, "Do you want to know why we are here? We are after you! You call yourself a hero when you forced our women and children from our homes in the Guarded Forest? They now live rotten lives. They have no one to lead them as Triathra's great authority did. Heitspel the Sorcerer created the black fog as a signal. Now you will get what you've paid for, dragon traitors!"

I took a step back before charging through the circle of enemies. I turned around and sprayed a wave of fire in their direction. Most saw it coming and jumped for cover. Many trees nearby fed the fire. I headed for the fence while my enemies were distracted. In a matter of seconds, the dwarfs were after me again. As I reached the path, I ran into Clipper. We both fell onto the hard path.

"Jacob, thank goodness you're here," Clipper said as he stood back up. "There are dwarfs nearby, I just saw them."

"There are a few behind me," I warned. "I was defending myself and my flames spread into the trees. Now there's a second fire."

We stood tail to tail, both of us prepared to fight. Our enemies reached the path and approached us with weapons drawn. There were daggers, crossbows, and a few swords. It surprised me that none had firearms, since their people had used them on us before. Whether this band had them or not, however, nothing they currently had looked lethal. They may have believed that too, for many of them appeared frightened rather than determined. Some even had tears in their eyes. It was possibly their rash changes in their lives that were driving them to attack us in such a manner.

"I believe there are more of you lurking about," one of the dwarfs said.

Clipper did not listen to him. He began fleeing down the path. With the entire band after him, this gave me the perfect opportunity to charge from behind. The power of my horns caused most of the dwarfs to fly off the path. Some of them turned back around and advanced on me, caring not of the presence of my claws or fire. They readied their own charge like Viking bezerkers. I exhaled a small flame to ward them off the best I could without spreading any more uncontrolled fire. But the closer they came, the more my fury grew. In a matter of seconds, I would become the most powerful bezerker out of all of them, and I say that with shame.

"Jacob! The other fire is attracting the firemen!" Clipper called.

His words barely processed in my brain. The firemen would spot us no matter what we did. I had to find a way to make the dwarfs retreat, thinking they may attack the other people. Suddenly, the concern for the people no longer became a problem... because I snapped. Nothing mattered to me except for spilt blood on my claws at this point. For a short while, I had no feelings or morals. All that was on my mind was death to my enemies. I roared, blew more fire, and, I regret to say, tore a few dwarfs into shreds by tooth and claw.

"Jacob! Stop! They're running away now!" Clipper tried to hold me back.

I refused his request by simply roaring again. Clipper then made the poor mistake of biting my foot to stop me. I instantly turned around and jumped on him, trying to rip open his neck.

"Jacob! Snap out of it!" Clipper wailed.

Before I could lay any more harm on my best friend, I caught my breath. I yelped in horror and jumped off his back.

"Oh Clipper, I'm so sorry. I... I just couldn't..." I didn't finish my sentence after seeing the damage I had done. My heart started to ache. The results of my rage led to quite a disgusting scene. How could I have caused all this? The Nibelungs did not see me as the mere enemy. They saw me as a monster, and they were right! I closed my eyes so I would not see my atrocities any longer.

"My fury…" I gasped. "My fury… I can't control myself when I'm like this."

Clipper led me away from the site, speaking softly. "It wasn't you, Jacob. The darkscale did this, not you. You were only defending yourself in the most civil way you could."

I wiped away a few tears. "I'm sorry, Clipper. It's just that when I get upset like that, I'm not me anymore. I hate when this happens, I really do."

Clipper placed his paw over mine. "You'll overcome it, I promise. The rest of the Nibelungs won't hurt us. There's no need to fight. Let's just go."

"Right, go," I said, trying to cheer myself up.

Clipper was right. When I attacked those dwarfs, I was not myself. Jacob Draco knows better and does not kill in such a savage way. Jacob Draco strove to do what was right. The darkscale within me was what caused the atrocities.

To this day, that battle in the cemetery is one instance I wish I could forget. But it's the things we wish to forget that we remember the most, and with good reason. We must remember the dark side of life to treasure the good and to not repeat the bad. With that concluded in my mind, I felt a sour-sweet pull at my heart. Sadly, this was just the beginning of my internal pain. It would only be a matter of time before something else would happen that would test my very conscience. A battle inside me would commence, and either Jacob Draco or the evil darkscale was going to take full control of this scaly creature. I would be on the edge of the bridge, either hanging on or about to fall into the cavern of eternal doom.

Now, back to the cemetery…

It felt wonderful getting a burst of fresh air after taking off. But the battle wasn't over yet.

"Slayer!" one of the surviving Nibelungs yelled. "He's in the sky! Archer, ready and fire an arrow now!"

Down below, I saw a dwarf load a crossbow. He fired an arrow straight for me. The arrowhead struck me in the right wing, embedding itself. That was it... I had to take care of him fair and square in Jacob Draco's way, not the darkscale's. I landed in front of the archer. With the arrow in my wing, I stepped closer to him. He shot two more arrows at my breast. Both shafts snapped, yet each sent me a surge of sharp pain through my chest.

The dwarf dropped his crossbow and curled up on the ground, crying.

This time, I did not roar. Instead, I said gently, "Listen, I don't want to go through what just happened again. What I did was wrong. I'm sorry I destroyed your tribe, but there was sorcery that had to be stopped. I will let you and the rest go, as long as you live honest lives. Never speak of Triathra again. This is the best option for you and I recommend you take it."

The archer looked up at me. Knowing I was serious, he scrambled up and ran away as fast as he could.

"Regroup!" he shouted. "Regroup! Let us leave this cursed carnage behind us! The fighting is done!"

I watched as the rest of the tribe climbed over the fence and ran out of sight, never to be seen again. That felt much better, I thought. If only every conflict could be solved that way.

In the distance, I saw the firemen approaching the fire that I had caused. Water gushed from the hoses and drowned the flames. Clipper and I silently made our way back to Chang's car. The rest of our friends were there, all unharmed.

"We saw what happened," Sally said. "Are you all right?"

I groaned from the entire experience. "Yes, we are."

Sally noticed the arrow in my wing that I could not reach. She lifted her paw and grabbed the shaft. I yelped from the sudden sting when she plucked it out of my wing. A trickle of blood ran down it.

"It's okay, the wound looks minor. It'll heal as soon as it stops bleeding," she said.

I stretched that wing to ease the nipping pain. Clipper looked at my wing, then at the ground. "Did anyone find the guide?" he asked.

Fenson pulled the viewing ring out of his pocket. "Here it is," he said cheerfully. "Jacob found it near the monument just as the clue had said, in a tomb to be more precise."

Reno jumped onto the roof of Chang's car to get a better look at the guide. Her tail swayed slowly as she gazed at it. "So, this will help us find the pieces," she said. "We've got a start now!"

Bluepond took the ring from Fenson's hand. He closed one eye to have a clear look through it.

"Ah! It is a viewing ring for sure! The young one is right: we have a start. I am pleased that it did not fall into the hands of our enemies. There were many of our foes who advanced upon Jacob and Clipper. Our friends can be very dangerous if provoked, I have come to find out."

"I do have a tendency to act without thinking when I'm angry," I said, ashamed. "Every dragon has his poor temper, but they're at different levels. Clipper's temper seems a bit milder than mine."

"What you are saying sounds like something any of us experience," said Bluepond. "In every one of us, we have the ability to choose between good and evil. Whatever we choose is expressed within us while the other is fighting for dominance. As dragons are evil creatures, they can be bad tempered."

I winced at that last sentence. "I'm doing my best," I said. "Right now, I suggest we build this portal and go home. The sooner we do it the better for everyone."

Chang tapped his crutches in the ground. "I don't want to be here if there are others after us. This seemed like a small group that attacked. There may be more. Jacob's right, let's get to it."

Bluepond moved over to Chang and gave him the viewing ring. "I trust you can hold this in the meantime," said the nymph.

Chang held the viewing ring up to his eye. "That's interesting," he said, turning his head around. "The whole world just turned green. That is except for a dot of red off in the distance."

"I think the red is what we're supposed to find," Fenson explained.

"That's good, we don't have to search blindly," Sally said happily, "and hopefully the pieces are not in well-known or populated places."

Clipper brushed his wing over Sally's face. "That's the spirit, Sally."

"I'm just glad Sergeant Nelson sent us here, close to the ring," I said. "We were so close to the guide and the first clue. But who knows? We may have to venture far and wide."

"We're ready," said Chang. "I think we should get out of here now."

"Perfect," I huffed, "let's get going."

"We'll regroup at your home. Eh... what's left of it anyway," said Fenson.

Once again, we were in the sky while Chang drove with Fenson and Bluepond as his passengers.

WE LEFT MINUTES BEFORE THE STATE POLICE ARRIVED. THEY swarmed the cemetery in search of any evidence. Captain Larson, leader of the bevy of officers, started questioning one of the men who had attended the ceremony at the monument.

"When did you notice something was out of the ordinary?" the Captain asked.

The man thought for a moment before answering. "I wasn't paying attention behind me. We were all worried when the sky darkened... I was standing at the angel's garden when I heard the roar of the fire. As I turned around and found the tree in flames... and the black mist earlier... it... it... just seemed... supernatural! But as I inspected what had happened, from the corner of my eye I saw a something move within the trees to my left. All I saw was a blue creature of some sort. A few minutes later, all kinds of terrible noises echoed around me. I could not bare it!"

Larson nodded. "Thank you. I know you're scared, but we have this under control now."

After patting the man's back, Larson asked another one of the men the same question.

The second man gulped. "Well... I... I... I don't know how to say this. When members of our group rushed over to where all the fuss was, I stayed still along with two of my colleagues. As I waited anxiously, some... beast came and attacked me!"

The man started heaving for breath as if there was a brick on his chest. Larson tried to comfort him. "Now don't worry. This creature is not here anymore. How did it attack you?"

"I got a good look at it just before it spat at me with its vile saliva. This beast was as black as night and had long brown wings. When the spit landed in my eyes, I saw flashes of color and grotesque images everywhere. I was ready to lose sanity when I luckily passed out! You wouldn't believe what I've been through!"

Larson gave the man a cup of hot cocoa. "Well you're safe now. If this is some sort of beast as you say, we'll take care of it."

Larson left the second man to sip on his beverage. He was jotting down notes when one of the officers rushed up to him.

"Captain, we have found bodies near the monument. It's quite a mess, but something funny is going on. These bodies are wearing some sort of aged, Viking clothing. We are unable to identify them."

Larson snorted. "Hm! Beasts with wings. Strange men lying dead. Dragons squabbling with dwarfs. I was told something like this may happen. I have never dealt with anything like this before."

The officer cleared his throat. "Ahem, with all due respect, sir, will you please be serious?"

"Oh I am," Larson replied. "A few weeks ago, I received word from Sergeant Nelson about two... dragons who were seeking a new home. These dragons were once normal people like us. But I think the Sergeant is hiding something else. It must be classified information."

"Did you say dragons?" the officer squeaked. The hair on his arms began to rise.

Another policeman came to Larson. "We found strange weapons near the second fire, sir. Older-style weapons."

The officer handed one of the swords to him. The Captain noticed the old steel and the unreadable runes that ran up and down the blade. As he reached his finger over to touch it, he felt the smooth handle with a gem on the very end.

"Something doesn't seem right," he finally said. "I remember the Sergeant mentioning a rebellious tribe of dwarfish-like folk. He told me how the dragons defeated them, but what about the blue one that was found in Santa Ana earlier? And what about the witness who claimed he was attacked by the black dragon? I think they may be more dangerous than anticipated." He took a deep breath before making his decision. "These dragons are a grave threat to us all. Sergeant Nelson must have underestimated them. They are running free, not even under the Sergeant's order. They have to be under some sort of control. They must surrender, or if necessary, we should exterminate them."

Larson dropped the sword into a large plastic bag. He organized his own force. Traveling back to the station, each member was provided with a special gun. Each gun fired a powerful poison. Larson was aware that a bullet could inflict pain but not kill a dragon. However, a tiny needle could slip between the scales. When every member of Larson's force prepared themselves, they began their search for us.

CHAPTER 12

LARSON'S ATTACK

W e all returned to the lonely beach just as the sun dipped below the watery horizon, setting the ocean on fire with flames of gold. We stood in our front yard, gazing at the ruined cabin which was draped with tarps across the front face.

Joshua walked from behind the house to greet us. "You made it back. Did you find anything?" he asked anxiously.

Fenson showed him the guide. "'Tis a viewing ring. It will help us well."

We all went to the back yard to go inside the house. Fenson explained to Joshua how the viewing ring worked. As he finished, he held it up to his eye. A surprised expression came over the dwarf's face.

"As I look through it right now, it seems that we are very close to what we seek. The red is very bright!"

"Does it show us where we need to go?" Reno asked, standing on her hind feet to sniff at the viewing ring.

"It's just over there." Fenson pointed.

"I'll go see what it is," said Joshua. He returned to the kitchen and went out the back door. I peeked out from behind a tarp to see where he was going. I saw William jump off his porch and wave at him.

"Good evening, Joshua," William said in a nervous tone. "I have something to say… I want to say this straight out; I know who lives in your house. I saw them when that giant beast attacked."

To my surprise, Joshua remained calm. He did not sigh, groan, or put his hand on his forehead. He simply nodded.

"I should have known you'd find out," he said. "But you must *not* tell anyone about this. This is dangerous business and you could put other people's lives at risk if you say anything."

At that moment, Henry stepped into the yard to inspect the damaged homes. The medallion hung around his neck, glowing with a bronze patina.

"William!" he cried. "What happened here?"

"Didn't you see?" asked William.

"No, my parents and I just got home. We spent the entire day away."

William was trying to figure out what to say when Chang limped toward Joshua. "Sorry for the interruption," he said. He hesitated as he looked at the two boys. "Joshua, Fenson said what he was seeing through the ring seems to have been moving." He looked down, noticing Henry's medallion with the Asian dragon engraved in it. "Mind if I see that?" he asked.

Henry didn't think much about Chang's interest and handed the medallion to him. Chang eyed it in fascination, rubbing his fingers lightly over the surface. He turned it over and examined the back.

"This side feels strange." He took a closer look. "There's something carved here."

Henry looked at the engravings on his medallion. "Those? I thought they were just old scratches. My great-grandfather gave this to me when I was young."

Joshua and Chang looked at each other in disbelief.

"It could be the clue to the first piece," Chang said. He sighed, knowing he had to tell Henry the truth. He grabbed the two boys by their arms. "I know Joshua told you not to tell anyone. He's right. If you inform others, you could put yourselves and them in serious danger. Now I'm afraid there's something you need to know." He took a deep breath. "The residents living in the cabin with me are dragons, darkscales to be specific."

Henry's jaw dropped. As fascinated as he was with dragons, it still had to have been hard to believe. The realization made him speechless.

"He's right, Henry," said William. "That statue I saw wasn't actually a statue. It was a real, living, breathing dragon! And there's more than one." Henry shook his head in disbelief while William continued, "A black dragon was battling a Minotaur earlier today. I couldn't believe it myself, but I saw them with my own eyes. I've never been so scared!"

Henry gulped, not saying anything.

"I guess we'll show you," said Joshua reluctantly. "Reno, come out here! Don't worry, it's okay!"

In a matter of seconds, the small brown dragon ran past me, taking flight when she was in the yard. She landed in front of Chang to find William and Henry staring down at her. She looked as if she wanted to leave. Joshua reached over and touched one of her horns.

"It's okay," he said again. "They won't hurt you. Why don't you go keep watch by the main road, Reno? There may be… visitors from the cemetery who may want to meet us again."

Reno cast a nervous glance at the two boys before leaving without a word. Her wings created a small wind that made Henry take a step back.

"I started a drawing of a dragon like her," said William. "Since that previous night, I knew she had to be real. She was too real to be a statue."

What Henry saw left him with an open mouth and wide eyes. He began to sweat. "William. I… I don't know what to say."

From where I was, I listened closely as William and Chang tried to calm Henry. I approached them from my hiding spot behind the tarp. Everyone else in the cabin followed me. I could tell Henry was frightened. His face blanched; tears began forming in the corner of his eyes.

"M—more of them?" he quivered. "How can they be so close by?"

"Do not be afraid," said Bluepond. "We are friends."

Clipper and I focused more on where the viewing ring was pointing. We knew William had seen us already, but my primary focus was not to introduce myself to him and Henry. My heart felt heavy introducing myself, anyway. I thought it was a little funny to be shy, since I never had been up to this point. I, the big black dragon, felt awkward at the presence of juveniles. To help myself, I turned my eyes to the medallion.

"Is that it?" I asked.

Chang flipped the medallion around to its back, showing me what looked like scratches. "There's something carved here," he told me.

I sniffed the medallion, studying it carefully. It took me a second before I had an idea how to bring out whatever was etched there.

"Chang, give me your finger," I said.

"What are you doing?" he asked.

I held a sharp claw to the end of his forefinger. Painless and swift, I pricked his flesh. A few drops of blood came oozing out. Chang understood what I was thinking and he held the medallion under his finger. He allowed the blood to drop onto it, then he spread it over the entire back side. The blood brought out small, faint words.

Chang read the message, "It says it's from the second earth, Elsov I presume. It says the first official piece of the portal lies in a cave in the Sevier Valley. 'Seek the mountains of the Dixie.'"

"How did *that* get on my medallion?" exclaimed Henry.

"I don't really know about that," I said. "It's just as mysterious as that old man back in Atlanta. He had knowledge of Elsov even before Clipper and I knew about it."

I was not at all worried about how the riddle came to be on the medallion; we were all puzzled by the riddle itself. By the mention of *Dixie*, I believed it meant somewhere in the south. Did we have to go all the way back to Georgia?

Chang started snapping his fingers. "Sevier. Sevier. Where have I heard that before? I remember, I think, reading it somewhere. It was during the time after that fight and… wait here."

All of us were silently confused as Chang limped back to the cabin. He came back out a few minutes later, holding a dusty map.

"The Sevier River," he said. "When we were tracking Monty in Utah, I picked up this map. Look here." The map presented the state of Utah, all right. He pointed in the south-central region. "There it is, the Sevier River. And look at this county here. It's named Sevier, too. This region is also called Dixie."

"I guess we go back to Utah then?" I pondered aloud.

"We won't have to hide a lot if we're in an isolated part of Utah," Sally said in relief. "It'd be nice to roam free again."

"Now we know where to go," said Clipper. "Can we go back home now? Don't you think we've been seen by enough people today? If all goes well, we can leave tomorrow night so we don't have to travel during the day. The day itself has been so long."

Bluepond looked around. "The road is damaged. I do not believe anyone will pass this way tonight. I doubt that we must hide this very minute."

"Good," I said. "That'll help us. It seems we have learned a lot on how to hide these past few months."

Clipper looked down at his paws. "We've learned a lot. When I first discovered that I was a dragon, I hated it. Life as a dragon was hard for me, especially with my acrophobia. But when I saw Elsov, I felt something change inside me. I know who I am and what I'm supposed to do. It's like there's something lost in my memory that has bubbled to the surface."

"Is this Elsov where you live?" asked William.

"Indeed it is," Bluepond answered. "I live just along the border inside Pearl Forest. Sometimes a wizard will come and visit us. We are occasionally gifted with albores. They are magical tools that we love to use, but we have to use them with responsibility."

A moment of silence fell as we each pondered our path home. I knew it was not going to be an easy journey, especially since we had to travel hundreds of miles just to get to the first piece. A sense of eagerness seemed to have come over us. The memory of the beautiful oaks of Pearl Forest hovered in my mind.

The warm feeling suddenly shut down when I felt a sudden gust of wind. Reno landed beside me, staring at me in horror.

"They found us! They're coming *here*!" she cried.

"Who?" asked Sally.

"Those who came to the cemetery just as we were leaving. They know where we are! They're coming for us!"

Clipper looked around. "The Nibelungs?"

"No, the police! I heard their captain say to take care of these rabid animals. They're going to kill us!"

The fear in her eyes was real and clear.

"What did he mean by 'take care of these rabid animals'?" I said. "I don't like that." I turned to the boys. "You two better go home. Tell the rest of your family to stay locked up someplace. Go there and stay there. And give as little information about us as possible. Hurry!"

"Bluepond and I will help you any way we can," Fenson said to me.

"You two can sneak out of here," I told them. "I understand nymphs are good at hiding and sneaking around and the like. Umm— go north... and... no, go north-*west* until we meet up with you. That way if we get separated, you'll be far from danger and we'll know where you're going. If you don't see us soon, keep going. Don't stop. I don't care how far you go. One of us can find your scent. Now go!"

Chang gave the medallion to Henry and the two boys ran back to their homes. Fenson and Bluepond disappeared while Joshua returned to our house. The rest of us remained in our yard just as a group of armored men approached on the crumpled street. Each man held a specialized weapon in his hands.

Captain Larson came into view. He spoke to us from a safe distance, "Because of the people you have harmed, you must come with us or we will be forced to take extreme measures. The darts we will fire contain a fatal poison and I highly recommend you do not try to fight. We don't want any trouble. I hope you feel the same way."

"What do you mean?" I responded. "We may have caused a disturbance, but we haven't harmed any *innocent* people." A jolt of shame zapped me when I thought of the Nibelungs I had killed. I again reminded myself it was the darkscale, not me. "I used venom on one man to protect him. The less he knows the better. The others we fought in…" I felt a second jolt. "…fought in self-defense. This is a misunderstanding. Talk to Sergeant James Nelson, he knows us personally."

Larson gave Sally a sharp look. "This blue dragon caused widespread panic. It set fire to many buildings and risked many lives. That one certainly intended harm."

"That happened to us too," Clipper argued. "That happened to me and Jacob in New York when we became dragons ourselves. Sergeant Nelson came after us then. But when we told him who we really are, he became our friend. Sally just went through the same thing. She's not a monster."

"You've killed several men in the cemetery," Larson said. "You are dangerous creatures who should not be allowed to roam free. Don't you even think about blowing fire or whatever you do! One sudden move and we'll have to kill you. Your fire or venomous spit can't save you now. So what's your decision?"

Reno stepped back, whimpering in fear.

Larson moved his eyes over to Chang. "Is your name Lewis Chang?"

"I am," he replied.

"You are friends with these creatures, aren't you? You must leave them immediately."

Chang took a step forward on his good foot, but did not go any farther. Some of the officers aimed their guns at him. Chang was in a dangerous and difficult spot. I knew he would never leave us, his friends. But if he stayed with us, he could be considered an enemy to Captain Larson. He did not take long to answer.

"I promised my friends I would help them. I'm not going leave them. If this means I'm against you, so be it. I made a promise and

I intend to keep it. I'm sorry."

"As you wish," said Larson. He turned his attention back to me. "Listen, black dragon, the blue one has not only destroyed a costly amount of property, but has also put many people in danger; and you're protecting it!"

"*Her!*" I growled. "Not *it!*"

"You dragons cannot be trusted. You must surrender yourselves or face death," Larson ordered.

The Captain's stubborn attitude was starting to get to me. My heart pumped faster and faster. My yellow eyes began to glow.

"Jacob, remember," Clipper whispered to me.

I remembered for sure. I took a few deep breaths to keep my temper under control. The breathing helped, but I was still upset with Larson.

"Listen, you… captain… whoever you are! I may not be like you. My home may be elsewhere, but that changes nothing. I have choices. I have agency. You are taking that away from me. Now I know you're scared. I'm a dangerous beast, but my power doesn't mean I'm your enemy. Just let us go and nobody will get hurt."

Everyone who heard my voice must have noticed I was fighting intense anger. Chang took a few limps away from me.

"What are you talking about?" Clipper asked me.

I snorted in return. "You need to leave, Captain. Of course I'm a dragon. You see, you've never met dragons or nymphs or grøls or other types of people or creatures. I know you don't know what I'm talking about, and I don't care. But I do care if you imprison me or my friends."

"You are a dragon and you're dangerous!" the Captain yelled. "You don't know what you're talking about!"

Clipper stepped in front of me. He spoke calmly and clearly, "Captain, listen to Jacob. If you want to fight us, go ahead. But be warned, if you choose to fight, we *will* fight back. Please listen to us. We don't want to hurt anyone."

Larson did not even ponder Clipper's warning. "I am not falling for that." He waved his arm. "Troops, prepare yourselves!"

Reno sobbed in fright. "Sally, Clipper, somebody! Make it stop! I don't want to die! I want to find Elsov!"

Sally stood between Reno and Larson's men. "Don't worry, Reno," she said. "You'll be okay."

Larson ordered his men to raise their weapons. That was when I felt the strong urge to retaliate. Luckily it wasn't the same fury as before, possibly because these officers were innocent. Anyhow, I would not let them hurt my friends. Before anyone could fire a poisoned dart at me, I spread my wings and leapt from the ground with my hind legs. My wings surged. Just as I expected, sand and even some pieces of the cracked road were blown into the air. Every single man, including Larson and Chang, were momentarily blinded. When the sand settled, a few of Larson's men scrambled to their feet. Clipper seized the opportunity to take to the air as well.

Larson wobbled to his feet, determined to continue the fight. "Don't let them escape! Take the young one alive!"

Reno heard that. They were going after *her* now! I saw her frozen in fear. Her eyes were filled with tears. Sally fiercely protected her while keeping her sight on the armed officers.

Swooping down from above, I cast a firestorm below as a distraction. I didn't aim at anyone in particular. Before any darts were fired, my attackers dove for cover. Some of the stray flames caught one of the trucks by accident. It spread until the entire vehicle was burning, lighting up the starry night like an enormous torch. The people inside escaped just in time.

I believed Larson knew that going after only one target was not safe. He ordered some of his men to fire at me and Clipper while the others went after Sally and Reno. Five of the attackers moved closer toward Reno. Sally growled, urging them back. As one attacker prepared to fire a dart at her, she spat a harmless yet effective globule of venom into his eyes. With four remaining, Sally blew whips of fire from her nose as a warning. The attackers did not stand down. They were all preparing to fire on Sally, who seemed to be in an impossible situation. Would she hold ground and let herself be killed? Or would she jump to safety and let Reno fall into the hands of Larson?

Reno fled, disappearing under the tarp that protected the faceless front of the cabin. Sally knew there was no reason for her to stay anymore. She started pumping her wings up and down, disorienting the officers. As they aimed into the night sky, blind from their target, darts were fired into the air. All of them missed. Sally gained altitude until she was out of range. She then shifted her flight to join me and Clipper.

Down below, Larson was not in any position to be giving any more orders. We swooped from all over, spraying more fire around the officers. I felt glad that I wasn't trying to hurt them.

Larson shook his head. "Regroup! Regroup!" he called.

As Larson's men started returning to where they had come from, we remained in the sky. They were no longer after us. We circled the beach next to the road, satisfied with our easy victory.

INSIDE THE HOUSE, RENO FRANTICALLY SEARCHED FOR A PLACE TO hide. She could see one of Larson's men moving about. His face was covered with a mask and he held a container filled with a strong gas. He found Reno cowering beneath the dining room table. Reno hissed in defense, though she did not dare use fire inside the cabin. Her venom would be of no use either because of the mask.

The officer threw the container, which landed next to the little brown dragon. He turned around when the vapor started to rise. Reno could not bear the gas. Her eyes itched in pain. The officer, quick to leave as well, located Reno. Producing a rope and a belt from a bag, he bound her snout and legs. Again, another one of us had been belted. He picked up Reno by the torso with her claws pointed away from his body. Reno wriggled in the man's arms, but the gas made her tired and weak. The officer took her away.

CHAPTER 13

THE SPYING DRAGON

Tension rose over the island as the news spread of Mallutin's death spread. Vesuvius, unlike most of his people, remained calm. He was never one to let minor setbacks upset him.

"Jacob and Clipper have defeated him," he said. "My followers have underestimated them. At least those who have fallen have given me some valuable information." He turned his eyes to address those who were in his sight. "I will return to my original plan now that the traitors are again roaming free!"

Vesuvius summoned one of his servants. A loyal human, decorated in high-class attire, stood before his throne and performed the Vesuvian salute. "What is it you require?" he asked in deepest respect.

The red King puffed out a cloud of black smoke. He slowly stepped off his pedestal. "Triathra has fallen. Those whom I have sent have fallen. My first idea shall now come to pass. Bring in General Visatrice."

The obedient servant saluted again before leaving to do his master's bidding. Vesuvius began pacing between the steaming rivers in the great hall, reflecting his mood. He then decided to take care of other matters involving his growing nation. A few hours later, General Visatrice arrived at the palace. The goblin was dressed in ragged furs, and his pale face had twisted stripes painted in black. Regardless, Vesuvius saw him as an influential creature. Visatrice's army was not a large one, though it had several divisions. Vesuvius had plans to expand his own military power in the near future.

"O' King," said Visatrice ingratiatingly. "You have summoned me. Are there foreign foes whose power I need to demolish for you?"

"It seems that wretch-ranked Mallutin has failed," Vesuvius told him. "The traitors are still walking on the first earth. Now is the time for a much stronger force to execute my original plan. Under your decision, *your* decision, I emphasize, I recommend you organize a portion of the Grün-hære. Keep the number of soldiers small, but big enough to be an army to fear."

Visatrice grinned in a fiendish fashion. "The Grün-hære will be the perfect force to prevent unnecessary rushes in your race for dominance, my King. What have you in mind?"

Vesuvius roared. He stood on his hind feet and cast his eyes about the great hall. "Look upon my Kingdom!"

Visatrice tilted his head upward, gazing around the enormous hall. The smooth gray stone walls rose straight to the ceiling with the height of a good ninety feet. Visatrice could also see large bat-like monsters hanging from the rough top and bony chandeliers.

"My Kingdom has remained dormant for many years," said Vesuvius. "Soon I will expand, erupting with my mighty forces. When my prophecy is fulfilled, all will bow to me. Order shall be re-established."

"I look forward to that day, great Leader. But I must ask, why do you wish for me to seek the dragons that have stopped Triathra? They have little knowledge of you."

"The dragon traitors are seeking the pieces of a portal that will bring them back to this earth. They could be useful to us if they are witnesses to my power on that filthy world. This could aid in the return of the Nibelung power, something that must be reborn in due time."

Visatrice agreed. "We will travel to the first earth. Excellent choice, your Majesty. How will we return?"

Vesuvius spat a ball of fire from his mouth that vanished into smoke. "You leave the first earth either through Mt. Ellen or by death. You must let our enemies know that *I* will soon be Leader of all. Leave the dragon traitors alive, but kill anyone they care for, friends or family alike. When it is time for my arrival, those who see my face shall burn! When you finish your task, there will be a portal that my advisor Heitspel will open. It will be on the slopes of Mt. Ellen. Don't worry; you will know where once you get there." He roared one last time before Visatrice could leave. "One more thing, General. This conversation between us never happened. Any action will be on your shoulders, not mine. Don't speak of this to anyone. Do I make myself clear?"

Visatrice winked and saluted again. "I will gather *my* army immediately, o' King I know not of."

Visatrice left the great palace. The dancing nebula was difficult to see from the heavens due to the smoke in the air. Since Alsov was only a slim crescent at this point, the only light Visatrice could use was from a lantern. Near the gate, protected by human guards, was an ancient wooden chest covered in silicone dust. Visatrice opened the lid and pulled out a messaging trumpet. He held it up to his lips and blew as hard as he could. The sound of war reverberated beyond the gate, signaling any living thing within the trumpet's range. A second trumpet was heard in the distance, followed by a third that was farther away. The chain of trumpets echoed like sirens across the range.

In a matter of hours, other goblins, dwarfs, and a few darkscales arrived at the great hall of the palace. Their numbers were not great, just about a hundred. Visatrice stood at the front of the crowd and spoke among the group,

"Listen well, servants of Vesuvius! The bell has tolled! The hour to dominate has arrived! By the power vested in our Majesty the King, we will prepare for war on the other world! The dragon traitors will fear our great Leader, and those alongside them will be at our mercy! We will turn the skies as red as their blood! We will organize an army and attack the dragon traitors!" One of the darkscales roared as Visatrice continued. "Glaciem and his ice dragons are standing by! Now it will be our turn to show our dominance of

Elsov in North America! We will not back down until our enemies cower before us!"

Howls and cries met Visatrice's ears. He began to organize his troops. Other goblins joined him; each wore thick leather armor for protection. The royalist dwarfs, trained for battle, wore horned helmets on their heads and fur around their shoulders. Swords, battle-axes, and a few pistols were handed out, along with food rations and extra armor for the privileged. This group of goblins and dwarfs were among the fabled Grün-hære.

Three lilinges arrived as well. The lilinges, in the opinions of many, were the worst of all. Other than their dark-red eyes, their black-winged bodies resembled those of enormous bats.

Although this portion of the Grün-hære was not massive, nor was it under Vesuvius' main command (at least that was what they wanted everyone to believe), they supported Vesuvius' sovereignty. The terror they inflicted gave them a strong advantage. The Grün-hære would have made Triathra's dwarfs shrink back in utmost respect.

"We will conquer the traitors and spread the reign of our King!" Visatrice yelled.

The other monsters joined in with their eerie shrieks that echoed throughout the mountains around the palace. It was a terrible sight, beyond a nightmare. The Grün-hære, entering the palace, formed several lines in the great hall. In a militaristic fashion, they all stood before their master and raised their weapons above their heads. Some chanted, *"Hail King Vesuvius! Hail King Vesuvius!"*

Vesuvius lifted a prideful paw high in the air. The Grün-hære cheered.

"Darkness will fall over our enemies, just how we like it!" Visatrice cried. "Now move out!"

Ghostly laughter filled the hall as the army marched off.

"To have our plan work, we must hurry!" said Visatrice. "Heitspel the Sorcerer has informed me that the traitors are about to leave! Now let us go! And let us conquer!"

One by one, each soldier made his way to Heitspel's portal room. The wicked King hummed in a low rumble. With everything going his way, he flew back up to his throne and sat down once again. He smiled like a devil as he anticipated his army's attack. All seemed well; that was until a familiar scent reached his nose. The last time he smelled this particular odor was when he had kidnapped a young lightscale and offered her to Glaciem. The smell had come from her parents. Vesuvius felt certain this was the scent of a spy.

NEAR A BACK GATE OF THE PALACE, A BRIGHT ORANGE LIGHTSCALE gazed up at the outer walls. He knew he had been discovered, so he backed away from the entrance until he had enough room to spread his wings. Leaping off the cliff, he caught the air. But just as he thought escape was probable, he heard the faint creak of the iron gates. Looking back, he saw Vesuvius taking flight after him. The young lightscale knew he was no match for a dragon the size of Vesuvius. There was no way he could defend himself! His only hope for survival was to escape, which now seemed far less probable. The lightscale lifted higher into the sky. Vesuvius had much bigger wings than his own, and therefore could fly much faster than the lightscale ever could.

The lightscale soared over the fields. He remembered the sea was not far from the mountains. If he could only find some way to slow his pursuer, he could dive and swim underwater. He did not know how well Vesuvius could swim, but it was the only chance he had… that is if he even made it to the sea. Improvising, the lightscale glided to the ground, waiting for Vesuvius. The giant red dragon was only seconds behind him.

When the King dove down to snatch him, the lightscale rolled backwards. It was not a smooth summersault, though. The joints in his wings stretched far beyond comfort, and his tail bent at an awkward angle. He yelped in pain, but watched as Vesuvius crashed into the ground, destroying several acres of crops. The lightscale realized he had a chance that was one in a million!

"My escape has come!" he cried.

He stood up in the soft soil, groaning from the ache in his wings. Despite the pain, he again took flight until he was over the sea. He then pulled his wings close to his body and barrel-rolled with beauty into the water with a splash. Taking the fortunate chance, he swam off into the night.

The sun rose over the horizon hours later. The lightscale whirled up to the surface where he realized that he was far from the dangers of the treacherous island. His joints were stiff, but he paddled on. He took several deep breaths at the surface, the salty water immediately steaming off his snout. He looked up to find some rocky fjords with green vegetation covering the tops of the cliffs. He sighed in relief; he had reached the mainland. Now I must spread my message, he thought.

He could not fly straight out of the water, so he paddled to the mouth of a river until he was between two cliffs. His wings were too sore to fly, anyway; but he had climbed the fjords before. Despite his bitter fatigue, he knew he could do it again. With each claw grabbing hold of a jagged rock, he took his time to make it to the top. He was relieved to find a great abundance of poplars, wavy grass, and wild daisies smiling at him. He also heard the gurgling of a nearby stream. The lightscale's sharp teeth revealed a smile of relief. He knew he was far from the gloomy isle. He was safe.

He pressed on through the forest, feeling at peace. After venturing inland for some time, he approached a particular chestnut tree. The lightscale knew that just beyond that tree was a little wooden cottage surrounded by a white picket fence. When he got there, rays of morning sunshine reached through the gaps of the leaves where they rested upon the thatched roof. The outer walls of the cottage had healthy vines climbing up, down, and all around the sides. Respectfully, the lightscale opened the front gate and walked up the footpath. The front yard was home to a tulip garden and some ornamental woodland creatures. One such ornament was a grinning squirrel that held a sign which read "KARI-GILA" (translated as "WELCOME" or "COME IN"). The lightscale lifted his paw, gently tapping on the door with a claw. There was no answer.

"Losdir, are you in there?" he called.

No smoke rose from the stubby chimney. The lightscale pressed his paw on the door and pushed it open. The house was empty. He shook his head and smiled.

He's gone again, he thought. He usually is this time of morning. He will be back soon.

The lightscale wandered around the house for a moment, then went back outside. Since nobody was around, he curled up next to the door. There he anxiously waited for his friend. However, before he could close his eyes, his ears lifted. The dragon knew someone was coming. Opening the gate was a figure that was barely taller than a dwarf. The owner of the house was skinny, had slightly pointed ears, and had short brown hair. He wore freshly washed clothing over his smooth skin.

"Ah, Auben! Mae hana we les sa mizi. I thought you were an intruder," the person laughed. "I'm pleased to see you once again."

Auben stood back up, shaking blades of grass off his scales. "Losdir, you have returned."

Losdir ran his fingers over Auben's head. He was an elf; more specifically a Kuslan. Unlike many kinds of elves who were often mischievous twerps, Kuslans were quite friendly. They loved to sing, dance, and play when necessary; but were usually devoted to work. Kuslans were never slothful and were always productive. It was indeed rare for one to quarrel with a lightscale.

Auben had been friends with Losdir since he left the protection of his eggshell. Throughout Auben's life, he frequently visited Losdir's house near the fjords. Losdir loved every living creature, although he preferred to live isolated from the condensed Kuslan city.

Auben looked into the eyes of his trusted acquaintance. "My good friend, do you remember many years ago, before I was born, the day when two hatchlings were born of dark among the bright?"

Losdir nodded. "I was quite young then. A friend of mine informed me of the news."

"Well, I have recently been inside the Kingdom of Vesuvius. With the help of a sorcerer, they have been watching the black dragon. They have sent their own darkscales, goblins, and even a Minotaur and Unitaur to find him! *And* they have begun to organize a part of the Grün-hære!"

The elf took a step back in surprise. "What ever possessed you to go to that King's keep? You could have been killed! I have only heard of the darkscales on the first earth, but I have never met them. How would you be able to help them? Going within Vesuvius' borders is dangerous enough."

"But we must do something to help them!" Auben said, shaking in anxiety. "I would like to help you organize a militia of our own and stop the Grün-hære. It won't be an official war since the Grün-hære is not under Vesuvius' direct rule. A militia is quite possible to organize. And, before I traveled to Vesuvius' isle, a nymph told me that Trihan the Keeper has opened a portal in his castle. We need to persuade the Wizard to let us use the portal."

Losdir's tongue nearly knotted itself. "I'm afraid I don't know how to respond to this, Auben. Why would the Keeper let us go to the first earth? It takes a highly valid reason for someone to travel there. That world is dangerous for us."

"You haven't even met the people from that world," said Auben.

"No, I haven't. But when I was a child, my father used to read bedtime stories to me about the other world. The way of life in that distant realm enchants me, especially to this day! Is it even possible the Keeper would ever grant us permission?"

"It is to help the friendly darkscales," said Auben. "We may not know them personally, but they need our help. The Grün-hære, the Horde, is after them!"

Losdir took a deep breath. Auben's proposal was something he had never dreamt of hearing, yet he knew Auben was serious.

"This is a difficult decision, my friend," he said. "I accept. I will go, despite my fears. I will spread the word once I pass through Kusla. You go to the Wizard's castle while I find help."

"It may take me a while," said Auben. "I have injured my wings and I'm forced to travel on foot."

Losdir went inside his home to gather tools and supplies. "Never mind that," he told Auben, who remained outside. "We will stop Vesuvius' terrible advance. Our victory will be for the good of every creature."

After wishes of luck to one another, the two went their separate ways. Auben moved on foot until he found a trail that would lead him to the Wizard's castle. Losdir began his search for potential comrades to join him on the unexpected quest.

CHAPTER 14

DISCOVERY IN THE JUNCTION

Another blanket of gray clouds covered the sky by morning. After searching for what felt like ages, we found we were near a railway junction. The area was rich with the sounds of shunting engines and air horns. We concealed ourselves behind an abandoned warehouse to steer clear of the workmen who were all about the yard. Encountering someone face-to-face was the last thing I wanted, though a simple sighting was nothing new at this point.

Clipper and Sally were behind me. We were all immensely worried. Reno had been missing for a whole day; there was no sign of her anywhere. We searched high and low all night but found no trace of the little brown dragon. Also, the first piece, hidden somewhere in the north-west, had to be found before any more unwelcome visitors could find us, or so I desired.

Sally finally huffed with apprehension. "Ugh! We've searched everywhere. I don't have Reno's scent and there's no clue as to where she is. I'm very worried."

"I think our good friend the Captain is behind this," growled Clipper. "If he is, he better not do anything to her, or so help me I'd lose my own temper."

We crept discretely along rough gravel next to the rails when Clipper suddenly lifted his head. I listened as well with my ears twitching in the soft wind.

"I think I hear someone coming. We've got to hide!" Clipper whispered.

We each looked left and right for refuge.

"Quick, come around here." Sally had her eyes on an empty freight car.

We scrambled behind the lonesome yellow vehicle, making sure our wings did not kick up any loose gravel. From our hiding spot, there was no smell of man. All I could smell was dust, diesel, and metal. The footsteps came closer, followed by grunts of pain.

"Jacob? Clipper? Are you here?"

I peeked around the corner of the car to find Chang slowly shuffling beside the rails. When I did so, his scent reached my nostrils.

"Chang!" Clipper called as he emerged from our hiding spot. "How did you get here?"

"Joshua dropped me off," Chang said. "I did the best I could to avoid calling attention to myself. I'm not being hunted down or anything, but I'm not on good terms with Captain Larson either; that's his name, just so you know. I've felt a little edgy since our confrontation last night. Joshua told me where you were going, so I came looking for you. Your voices *are* easy to hear, you know."

"Now we know where everybody is except for Reno," Sally hummed sorrowfully.

"What about Fenson and Bluepond?" asked Chang. "Didn't you tell them to go somewhere, Jacob?"

"I told them to leave before Larson came," I said. "They're heading north and they won't stop until we meet up with them."

"Maybe Reno is with them," Clipper said hopefully.

Chang soberly shook his head. "Joshua and I know where Reno is. She's been captured, being held in a cell. Joshua found out it's the same place where Sally was held before. If that's true, I'll bet they're making sure there won't be another escape. She's not going anywhere."

Sally groaned in despair. "Reno's been captured? We have to rescue her!"

"We won't find the six pieces without her," said Clipper. "We're not going back to Elsov without our little Reno."

"I agree," I said. "We'll get her back. She's our emblem and we have to protect her." I was not sure what might happen to Reno. For all I knew she was being treated humanely, but I was determined to rescue her all the same.

"I've got an idea," said Chang. "If all of us go after her, the chances of us being seen by enemies might increase. What if we split into two groups? One goes to find Reno while the other heads to the airfield. I know the manager there, but he won't ever know about you. Still, we'll have a plane ready for us, one big enough to fit all of you. This airfield is about a hundred miles north of here, the most isolated one I could find that wasn't too far away. That group can also look out for Fenson and Bluepond."

"Clipper and I can stick to the main line that goes out of this junction," I said.

"I'm going with you, Chang," said Sally. "I've been there already. That should be to our advantage. And you're right, Jacob, you and Clipper can head to the airfield. It may take a while, but we'll eventually regroup. And like Chang said, you may find Fenson and Bluepond."

Clipper beat his wings a few times. "I'm for that. Let's do this now; the sooner the better."

With a brief farewell to one another, we went our separate ways. I felt a little better now that I knew where Reno was. I did not think Larson was a monster. He was more than likely scared of us, and he had good reason to be.

Sally stayed aground next to Chang. Both were alert.

"So what kind of prison is this?" Chang asked.

"It's not really a prison," explained Sally. "It's more of a single cell. It's actually only a few miles away from here. On the outside, it looks sort of like an old storehouse. Inside, there's a hallway just wide enough for someone about my size in this form to fit through.

Down the hall is a confined room. No windows, just a cell door. But they must have improved security around it since I escaped there already."

"Great, a few miles away you said?" Chang muttered, looking down at his crutches. "I don't know how I'll get there. I don't have my car, and I can't go home to get it now that I'm on the wrong side with Larson. I don't want to appear suspicious."

"And you are *not* riding on me," Sally assured him. "Jacob told me that carrying a passenger is not as easy as it seems." She stood up on her hind legs. Her head was about a meter above Chang's. "I'm bigger than you, but I'm not a giant. Since flying isn't an option, I don't know what we'll do— Hey! What about Joshua? He can help us, right?"

"You're right, I think he can help," said Chang.

"Good, we need all the help we can get."

They had just left the junction when Clipper unexpectedly descended from the sky, landing between them.

"Clipper!" Sally exclaimed. "What are you doing here? You're supposed to be with Jacob."

Clipper coughed and stuttered. "Eh... I— Sally. Jacob said somethin'— eh... something strange is going on and I should tell you."

Sally rolled her eyes. "What is it now?"

"He said he can smell other monsters in the area. They might even have been sent by Vesuvius himself. I fear we're being hunted. They were sent along with an— a horde of goblins. They're going to kill all of us. We can't let that happen if we want to go to Elsov."

Sally squinted. "So, they *could* be sent by Vesuvius? And you think there's a horde of goblins after us? Did you see them? And speaking of smell, you don't smell the same, Clipper. Are you all right?"

Sally was puzzled. Clipper barely opened his jaw while he spoke, as if there was something on his tongue. Also, when he mentioned Vesuvius, he didn't seem at all worried. He sounded more like he was giving a casual report.

"I'm just nervous," Clipper replied.

"And you don't sound concerned at all knowing that enemies are nearby," Sally continued. "You two were heckling about Vesuvius so much before you went to Pennsylvania for the summer. I thought you'd be more worried about this."

"Oh, we are!" Clipper answered. "We are! I mean… look at my paws. They're quaking like… never mind. Oh, and by the way, Jacob wanted me to stick with you. He preferred to go by himself."

Sally stared at Clipper, more confused than ever.

Chang could not believe what he had heard either. "I usually have to pry you two apart," he said. "Now you're splitting up? What about these goblins?"

"Jacob can fight them off," said Clipper. "I know he can take care of himself."

Sally huffed. "Oh well, come on Clipper. Let's go free Reno. But I hope leaving Jacob alone isn't a bad idea, especially if there's danger nearby."

"Jacob will be fine. Now let's go find Reno! For freedom on Elsov!"

Sally wondered what was wrong with Clipper. He did not seem like himself. He was acting strange, and his smell kept bothering her.

It was not easy locating the directions of the various lines in the railway junction from the ground. I figured locating the north-western line from the air was necessary, even though I knew I was risking exposure. I circled around for a while until I found an old-fashioned passenger train ready to pull out. It was the train's position that had caught my eye. I didn't know if it was on a special branch line or not. However, it rested on a north-facing track that pointed straight out of the junction. The glossy black steam engine, with the numbers 1-9-4-5 painted in yellow on the tender, idled with four red coaches lined up neatly behind it. Yes, the train was going to pull out at any minute! I could use it to find a line that could guide me to Utah and hopefully to Sevier County!

I dropped down onto the roof of the first coach, bringing my wings close to my body. From where I was, I could hear the voice of someone speaking from inside the engine's cab.

"Yes. I've got to get out of here soon. The people had a great time, especially the kids, and now I'm taking the empty coaches back. They loved the classic ride. I'm warming up the engine and I'll be on my way... No, don't worry about that... Yes... I'll be aware of that, thank you. I'll see you in Reno, bye."

I assumed the driver must have been talking to someone by radio. I turned my attention back to the line as I jumped off the coach. There was limited space for me on the ground, so I searched for a clear spot.

"Hey, Clipper! I think I found it! There's a train going north." I called in no particular direction.

Clipper appeared from behind a freight car a few seconds after my shout.

"Are you talking about the steam train?" he asked.

"That's it."

"That's fine, but I think we've got trouble coming."

I bared my teeth. "More? What is it now?"

"Take a sniff in the air... and keep your voice down."

I sat on my haunches and sniffed. Clipper was right, something was wrong. I heard only the ambient sounds of the junction, but I could sense that there was some sort of threat nearby.

"Do you smell that?" asked Clipper, concerned. "The funny thing is that there's someone snooping around here. He was short and stubby and wore suspicious clothing. He also had a sword in a scabbard. It might be an ice blade."

"Did he look like Fenson?" I asked.

"No, I searched for those two. Fenson and Bluepond are long gone. I guess you're right about nymphs 'disappearing'. Not only that, I also saw someone wearing some sort of black hooded cloak, but not like a sorcerer's. He did a good job hiding his face, though I managed to catch a glimpse of his green skin."

I hissed. "Green skin? Great, more goblins and dwarfs lurking about. We need to keep our eyes open. Maybe if we leave in peace, they'll get lost and eventually caught by authorities. Hopefully that will convince Larson to leave us alone. Either that or I'll tear them to shreds."

"Jacob, don't say things like that. Remember the cemetery?"

My reply was interrupted by the passenger train's whistle. The sudden screech caused me to jump in fright. Clipper did not even flinch.

"Jacob, relax. It's just the train," he said.

I opened my mouth, coughing out a small flame. The whistle aggravated me a little: it was the effect of an instinct I wished I did not have at the moment.

Clipper held a claw over his mouth. "Jacob, keep quiet. We don't want to be heard. Get a grip on yourself."

"Get a grip?" I barked. "If you're getting scared, why don't you just sick me on them? I can be dangerous if I have no control. You should remember that."

"Will you please stop talking?" Clipper hissed. "I don't want to fight these monsters in a train junction. Just calm yourself. Here, do what I do. I want you to relax." He sat down on the rubble, his tail swaying behind him. He took a deep breath. A cloud of smoke encircled his snout after his exhale. "Okay, Jacob. Now you try."

I followed suit, taking a deep breath. As I breathed out, a bright flame left my lungs and covered my friend. Clipper sat in the smoky cloud and moaned.

"You see what I mean? Don't breathe fire."

He repeated his soothing exercise. Calming myself down, I released no flames in my next exhale.

"Good job. Maybe we try that later," Clipper said. "In the meantime, let's follow this train. It's starting to pull out. I suggest that—"

Before Clipper could finish, I noticed a dark figure emerge from around the freight car. It lunged at him like a shadowy phantom.

"Clipper, lookout!" I roared.

With the sudden warning, Clipper had no choice but to act out of reflex. He spun around with his claws out and allowed a small flame to escape his jaws. The figure was forced back, the blue sword he carried flying out of his hand. Clipper tore the cloak away from the figure, discovering a short, messy coward.

"Forgive me," the man squeaked.

"Dwarf!" Clipper growled. "You've made a bad mistake coming here!"

As I watched the scene between Clipper and the dwarf unfold, I heard an ugly cackle behind me. I turned around to find a sickly-looking goblin (actually, most goblins looked sickly in my opinion) who was also armed with an ice blade. When he thrust his weapon toward my eyes, I ducked; then, with my horns already lowered, I charged. My momentum was weak due to the short distance, but there was enough to get the job done. I butted the monster clear across three sets of rails. Landing in the rough gravel, he held one hand over his disfigured leg and the other over a deep gash in his shoulder. This time I approached him with an involuntary laugh, taking a deep breath in while doing so. Any thoughts of Clipper's calm breathing did not feel applicable at the moment. The goblin's eyes widened as I prepared a flame. He scrambled up and tried to limp away. I cast my fire before he could do anything else. The goblin had just enough time to escape with his cloak singed and smoking. Parts of his skin were blackened and bubbled with burns. During his retreat, the steam engine next to him started to move. The whistle blew again in sets of long bursts, followed by the ringing of a small brass bell near the engine's dome. The startled goblin covered his ears; a cloud of hot, hissing steam engulfed him. The only way he could escape me now was through the stairway of the first coach. Crawling up the steps in agony, he disappeared on the other side. I began trotting alongside the train. The sound of the brass bell was almost drowned out by the hissing steam. When I reached the side of the cab, I heard the driver yell in fright.

"What in the devil's name are you?" I heard him cry with a quiver in his voice.

At first I thought he was talking to me, but then I noticed he was not even facing me.

"Move rat! You stand in my way!"

Peering inside, I watched as another goblin lifted a dagger into the air. The steel blade was about to come down into the driver's heart. The driver, at the last second, jumped out the opposite side of the cab. He barely escaped the blade that struck the floor instead. The goblin was about to pursue him, but then he saw me. He wrapped his fingers around a lever to lift himself to his feet. The lever jerked before he maintained balance. Another cloud of steam burst forth and the engine jumped forward. The goblin tumbled back to the floor. He quickly righted himself, keeping his eyes on me. By then the train was gaining speed.

"Kill me if you must, you traitor!" he yelled to me. "There are many more of us here and beyond! The Grün-hære will find you!"

I lost sight of the goblin. Instead, I was met by the passing coaches. I realized the train was moving with no one at the helm! The goblin did not how to control it. I flew to the roof of the nearest coach and looked back, just in time to see Clipper run into view.

"Clipper!" I cried. "The train's out of control and there's a goblin in it! This train's a runaway! We've got to stop it!"

Clipper could not respond. The train was moving faster than he was. His captive remained behind, staring in bewilderment. Clipper glared at the dwarf then reluctantly spat venom into his eyes. The dwarf yelped and fell onto his back once again. I watched as Clipper began to catch up to the train.

"What's going on?" he yelled over the roaring of the engine.

"We've got to stop the train!" I replied.

Clipper flew to the roof of the next coach. "How?"

I desperately tried to think of a solution, but not for long. Something terrifyingly familiar appeared in the sky. I gazed up at them in terror.

"Clipper, do you see what I see?"

Clipper shuttered. "What are those things?"

"They look like... bats... and... dragons! Darkscales! They're after us! Not only that, but we have a runaway train on our hands!"

It was clear this was the beginning of a messy situation.

RENO HAD BEEN IN THE CELL SINCE HER CAPTURE THE PREVIOUS night. Her feet were bound together while she lay on her side. She stared at the wet straw around the floor with nothing better to do. Tears coursed down her muzzle. For the third time in her young life, she was being held as a captive.

She was still crying when she heard the cell door open. Captain Larson was standing before her. The man frowned down at the little dragon.

"I had them take the belt off your mouth," he said. "Don't be scared."

Reno did her best to speak peacefully. "Please, sir. I don't like having my muzzle belted. I promise I won't breathe any fire. I didn't do anything bad. Please let me go."

"I see you are crying," said Larson. "Is this an act?"

"Of course not," Reno wept. "Jacob told me we're free until we go home. Why are you keeping me here?"

Larson chuckled. "Isn't it obvious? Look at you. What are you?"

Reno did not answer.

"Exactly, you're an animal. There's no need to be sad. You're protected now."

"I know I'm not like you," said Reno, "but I'm speaking to you in your own language. I can blow fire at you at any moment. But I won't because I've been taught right from wrong. Please speak to the sergeant that's our friend. He understands."

Larson shook his head. "No need. Dragons are known to be violent, you know. Have you read any books lately?"

"I'm still learning how to read," Reno murmured.

"Then you'll get an idea of what dragons are like. After the blue dragon attacked, and seeing the carnage at the cemetery, I knew you were dangerous creatures."

"I was told that too. I am naturally evil. Look at my scales. They are dark brown. I was born as a bad breed, but I was raised differently. My descendants will be lightscales, I know it."

"Lightscales?" Larson asked in confusion. "I think you're making this up. I'm afraid you have to stay here for a while. Don't worry, we'll take good care of you."

Larson turned and left the cell. Reno squirmed with her feet still tied. "No, please! Let me out!" She started sobbing again. Thoughts whirled through her head. Was anyone coming to rescue her? Would she ever get out?

CHANG'S FOOT WAS BEGINNING TO BOTHER HIM, SO HE DECIDED TO stop and rest. Sally agreed to go on with Clipper and find Reno. Chang told Sally to meet him at a particular abandoned storefront once Reno was free. He would get there by public transportation.

Near the small jail, Sally stayed on the ground to remain hidden. She was getting more annoyed with Clipper. He constantly wandered off and did not seem to be serious about the rescue mission.

"Look, Clipper, why don't you go back to Jacob?" Sally suggested. "I'm pretty sure he needs your help more than I do. I can handle this."

"Jacob's fine. He doesn't need me," replied Clipper. "Now let's go get Reno. Come now, let's go."

Sally stared at him, shaking her head. "Clipper, I'm a little worried."

"I'm fine," he said, almost harsh in his voice. "You don't need to worry about me, or Jacob."

Sally blew a small flame. Her thoughts returned to Reno. With her enhanced senses, she was sure something was amiss. When she finally caught sight of the jail, she lifted her ears.

"Clipper, over here. We're close."

"You found the prison, great job," said Clipper.

The two continued toward the jail. Sally was becoming increasingly suspicious. Clipper was acting very odd. His voice sounded a bit lower than normal, and the strange odor he was emitting only added to the evidence that he was not who he seemed. He began walking in front of Sally to their destination. Sally looked down at Clipper's feet. Her eyes widened. Clipper had five claws on both footpaws! He was supposed to be missing a toe on his left foot! Now Sally knew something was wrong.

"Why are you looking at my feet?" Clipper asked when he noticed her expression.

Sally did not answer, but her eyes narrowed as she glared at the imposter. At that point, the red darkscale knew his cover was blown. It was not Clipper at all! He looked nearly identical to her friend, which fooled her. The darkscale bared his sabered fangs and roared. For the first time, Sally saw the inside of his mouth. No wonder he did not show his tongue, it was forked!

"So, ya figured it out, huh? Yer time 'as come, dragon traitor!"

Without warning, he lunged at Sally, snapping his jaws at her. Sally tried her best to fight back. "You're not Clipper!" she said, gritting her teeth. "You're no friend of mine!"

The darkscale roared again and tried to claw at Sally's face. In defense, Sally spat the venom she could bring to her throat before casting a wave of fire. The darkscale did the exact same thing.

Thinking of Reno, Sally fought with all her energy, determined to protect the emblem she so dearly loved. She recalled the cute infant who was always energetic and curious. Even though Reno's horns and claws had become longer and sharper over time, Sally still saw her as the adorable hatchling that was found inside a box in the Guarded Forest.

Sally refused to give up the fight. Instead, she grew more aggressive against the deceiving darkscale. She never thought she would be in such barbaric combat. The darkscale cast more fire and charged forward. He jerked his horns up and struck Sally in the chest. Both tumbled through the jail wall where Sally found herself in the hallway. Three men were inside, but not for long. The two guards bolted away in fright. The darkscale ran behind the third man, who happened to be Larson. The Captain remained still. The darkscale dug his claws into Larson's shoulder, making him groan.

"Let him go," Sally growled. "Now!"

"And I thought it was yer precious Reno you were worried about. Surrender now or this 'elpless man dies under my claws!"

Larson was unable to move, a hostage at the mercy of the dragon. Sally was in a bad spot too when a simple idea came to her. She used her venom once again. It flew past Larson and landed square in the face of her enemy. Backing away, the darkscale slid his claws across Larson's arm, taking him down. Sally picked up one of the bricks from the damaged wall and threw it as hard as she could. The brick broke into several pieces on the darkscale's head. That only made him angrier. Sally grabbed another brick and clubbed him between his horns. The brick disintegrated into dust. Before her dazed enemy could return to his senses, Sally clubbed him with a second, third, and fourth brick. Each one crumbled dust on the darkscale's head. He finally fell unconscious after a fifth brick. Sally took a deep, smoky breath when she knew she had won the fight. She was overjoyed when she heard a familiar voice coming from inside the cell. She dropped her sixth brick and turned around.

"Sally! It's you! You've come to rescue me!" Reno cried.

Sally burst through the barred door and tore away Reno's chains. Once she was free, Reno climbed onto Sally's back.

Larson got to his feet, rubbing his arm. His clothes were tattered and torn, and he had a bad cut on his shoulder. He watched as Sally and Reno rubbed noses. There was nothing he could do. Sally glared at him. The Captain took the warning and left.

"Why, Sally? Why did they imprison me?" Reno asked when they were alone.

"They were scared of you," said Sally. "People are not used to creatures like you roaming about. They just don't understand, that's all."

"That's silly," said Reno. She started to whimper again. "I... I don't like humans! I don't trust them! I want to go to Pearl Forest like Jacob and Clipper promised!"

"Reno, you shouldn't say that about humans. I was born a human, but I'm a dragon for now. I have to deal with it until I can find a way to turn back. Here, let's find the six pieces. We'll make it to Pearl Forest with the portal we will build. Don't worry, everything will be fine."

Reno nodded and rubbed her face with Sally's one more time. "I'll never trust humans again," she snorted.

"You don't really mean that," said Sally. "Of course, people are selfish at times, but you must forgive. You really don't want to be the bad one, do you?"

Reno blew a small cloud of smoke. "I still want to go to Elsov."

"And that's okay. Don't worry, Reno. You'll go home."

Sally wanted Reno to forgive Larson for what he had done to her. But she also knew that deep inside, Reno held a strong grudge against humans. It would take a lot of work to change that.

CHAPTER 15

'To Shiloh's Pass, We Bid Thee Farewell'

Auben was elated upon finding the Wizard's castle. He had departed from the fjords early that morning, and it was well past midday when he arrived at his destination. After passing a small pond, Auben stood at the front gates of Trihan's home. He took a second to stretch his stiff wings before pulling on the white rope with his paw. He waited uncomplainingly for the Wizard to answer the bell. Looking up at an open window on the second floor, he saw Trihan staring down at him.

"You may enter, friend!" the Wizard called.

Auben squinted. He saw Trihan holding out his scepter. When the amber-yellow jewel was glowing like a beacon, an invisible force unlocked the gate. Auben carefully tapped the gate open with his horns. Not even the faintest screech was heard from the well-oiled hinges. Auben passed the lines of young trees and the small fountain. The landscape left Auben with a sense of ease, especially after his close call the previous night.

Trihan opened the front doors. He held his hands out in a welcoming gesture. "Hello, I sense that you come as friend and not a foe. What brings you to my home?"

Auben folded his wings so he could fit through the doorway. "Forgive my size. I will be careful in your humble abode. You must be Trihan, Keeper of the Three."

"'Tis me indeed," said Trihan, "I am the Keeper. What can I do for you?"

"I feel foolish, sir," Auben sighed, "but I have grave news and I need your help."

Trihan chuckled at Auben's innocence. "And just why would you be feeling foolish?"

The Wizard watched as Auben paced back and forth in the foyer. Trihan understood that Auben was a dragon with something on his mind.

"A few days ago, I had to fight off a band of ruthless monsters in my homeland. I wondered why they were there, so I decided to follow them back to where they had come from. They spoke of a plan conceived by Vesuvius himself, so I traveled to the isle that is home of the King. As I spied on the evil dragon, I overheard his plan. One of the goblins began organizing a small army. Vesuvius supported the idea to send the Grün-hære! Goblins, other darkscales, and even lilinges! They have gone through the Sorcerer's portal and are searching for the two dragons. They are seeking revenge for the destruction of the Nibelungs. They want their revenge before the two dragons can return to Elsov."

"Heavens!" exclaimed Trihan. "I received a pixie's telegram that told me about the Grün-hære on the first earth, and now I know why. Jacob and Clipper are not prepared for something like that. They have battled Nibelungs, but not goblins and lilinges. Those creatures belong to a league that Jacob and Clipper are not yet prepared for, especially if that league involves hostile darkscales."

"I too understand why the Grün-hære was sent," said Auben. "If Vesuvius used his official army, a major war would be born between his nation and our allies."

"Hmm, I see. Sending the Grün-hære will prevent a major civil incident, yes. I see what Vesuvius is thinking."

"I wonder how the two dragons will fight them," said Auben.

"I wonder as well, my friend. When I was elected Keeper, I kept a watchful eye on Jacob and Clipper. They have resided in Pennsylvania over the course of the summer. Just recently, they traveled to California. They are now searching for the six pieces to create a portal back to Elsov."

"I want to help them!" Auben pleaded. "My elven friend Losdir is organizing a militia of nymphs and dwarfs. We can fight the Grün-hære!"

Trihan held up a hand. "Young dragon, you must know that that is against my better judgment. I have already sent a dwarf and a nymph to help Jacob and Clipper."

Auben's ears drooped. "Please, sir. I want to help. The Grün-hære will kill them. Vesuvius is evil, and I will do what I can to foil his plans. I promise I will follow every regulation you have. Please let us go, please!"

Trihan saw the twinkle in Auben's green eyes. He took a deep breath and stared into the yellow jewel on top of the Master Scepter. He debated with himself. Auben waited silently yet anxiously.

"You live in a world with magic all around you," Trihan said after a minute or so. "You will be going to a world with a different sort of magic. You must know that if you try to attack the Grün-hære by yourself, you will be in a very bad situation. But...as much as I know I will soon regret this, I will allow you to go *only* under strict regulations. You must find a human named Lewis Chang. He is traveling with Jacob and Clipper; visit none other. I will explain my laws when your friend Losdir arrives. The portal is in my upper quarters; only one must go in at a time. Do not enter the upper quarters of this castle until you and your elven friend are ready. Is that clear?"

Auben felt exasperated. Without saying more, Trihan went back to his previous duties. He left Auben alone in the hall. The young lightscale paced back and forth again, huffing in distress.

"I want to help them," he muttered to himself. "He told me to stay here until Losdir comes. But I can't wait that long! I must find the Grün-hære as soon as possible. I'll fight them even if I die."

Looking left and right, he found that Trihan was nowhere to

be seen. He was unsure where the Wizard had gone. He knew he was supposed to stay put until Losdir came, but the urge to leave was too overwhelming. All Auben had to do was find the portal upstairs. He would be on the first earth in no time! Taking a deep, smoky breath, he flew up the stairs as quietly as possible. When he reached the top, he began searching for the correct room. Opening a strangely carved, wooden door, he found the portal next to the opposite wall of the room. Auben entered the room and stepped onto the platform. Nothing happened. He was confused at first, but then he realized what he was missing.

"I need the Master Scepter," he huffed.

Before he was able to leave the square platform, Trihan stepped into the room and gave Auben a stern stare.

"You were not in the hall, so I knew you were up here. I told you already, you mustn't go alone."

"Please! I want to help!" Auben begged.

"I can't allow it," said Trihan. He cast a spell that pushed Auben off the platform.

Auben could no longer hold in his emotions. He growled in frustration and hurled an unintentional breath of fire over the platform. Trihan quickly cast another spell that doused the flames.

"Young dragon, you *must* listen to me. I know you're upset."

Auben clenched his forepaws, tearing shreds in the violet rug. "Please sir! Losdir and his army can fight the Grün-hære! But I over-heard Vesuvius! This is urgent!" He was about to growl in despair when an idea came to him. "What if you send Losdir to the Grün-hære while I go find the two dragons? We can be prepared from both sides. Please, Trihan. Please!" He started pacing once again.

Trihan clapped his scepter onto the floor. "Calm yourself, young dragon! You must listen to me."

Auben stopped pacing. He sat down and took a deep breath. Trihan lowered his scepter to Auben's nose.

"Young dragon, your strategy does sound reasonable. But you have shown your tendency to act before you think. You may wander into serious danger if you are not careful. Now I could help Jacob and Clipper myself, but I am bound to stay on Elsov. It's a serious violation for a wizard to leave here without a proper reason. Triathra the Sorcerer ignored this and he is suffering the penalty. I do not want to face the same consequence. If you want to help the two dragons, you must promise to behave."

Auben gave a quick nod. He climbed back upon the platform. "Yes, I promise, good wizard. Please let me go."

Trihan held up his hand. "I will send you to a land that is much like your home. A piece of the portal is not far from where you will be. Wait there until you meet the two dragons. Remember, do not speak to anyone else unless it is a young man named Chang. Maybe I can send your friend Losdir to where he may meet up with Fenson and Bluepond. They were heading far north last I knew. Just remember, *only* talk to Chang. Promise me."

Auben sighed. "I promise."

The Wizard waved his scepter, which activated the portal. "Take care of yourself," he said.

A small whirlwind formed around the portal. Auben felt the power of the wind grow. Feeling nervous, he kept his eyes closed.

"I will be obedient," he promised.

Trihan left the portal room once it was quiet. He was already beginning to regret sending Auben alone. He wondered if the elf was actually coming, or if the young dragon had lied to him.

LOSDIR LOADED A SACK WITH APPLES, NUTS, AND OTHER FOOD-stuffs. He did not know how long he would be away from home, so he prepared in such a manner. After the sack was filled with food, utensils, and a few small tools, he grabbed an empty canteen and a carving knife that both attached to his belt. Everything was now together. Losdir crossed the meadow where he found the stream. He knelt down with the canteen open and filled it with fresh water.

Checking his supplies one more time, Losdir locked the front and back doors to his house and then set off on his journey. He began on the road to the nearest city in the land of Kusla: Fjordsby.

On his way to Fjordsby, he hummed a light tune to keep his spirits lifted. An hour or so later, he came upon a cobblestone road. Along the shoulders were unlit streetlamps. Losdir continued down the road, greeting humans, dwarfs, and other elves as they passed by. It was not long before he arrived at the city gates. Inside, structures of wood, stone, and granite became more prevalent. Near the city hall and courthouse was a fountain that spouted glistening, clear water. A young elf-maid dressed in red sat on the edge of the fountain's base where she played a wood-carved fife. Trees and ferns grew in designated places. There were markets, banks, and a library along the streets. There were no horses or mules; those who were transporting big loads did so with handcarts. Large animals were not allowed in the city so the streets could remain neat and clean. Nearly every office building was covered in fresh, healthy vines, and had a flower garden or shrubbery near its entrance. Some of the city's citizens waved at Losdir with heart-felt greetings. This was the life in a city of honest-working Kuslans.

"Kusi jena, Losdir!" an elf called from across the street.

Losdir waved back. "And a good day to you as well!"

The fellow Kuslan crossed the street and walked beside Losdir. "So what matter of business brings you here, Losdir?" he inquired. "You never seem to come to Fjordsby unless you are on an errand. Is it the public garden? Do you need vegetables to ease your hunger? Or are you simply in the mood to meet others?"

"I'm satisfied with the food I have, thank you," Losdir said, holding up his sack. "I'm currently a traveler, just passing through."

"Ah! If it's not food, are you seeking furniture for your home? Or a lovely new linen outfit? Or… or…"

"I am just passing through," Losdir repeated gently.

"If that is so, where is this 'passing through' taking you?"

Losdir paused. He did not want to give away any unnecessary details. "I'm leaving Kusla and I don't know how long I'll be absent.

I am going to attend a serious matter, that's all."

"I see," said the Kuslan with a shallow bow of his head. "In that case, my prayers and best wishes will be upon you, Losdir. I will miss your presence and await your return. Travel safely."

The two elves shook hands and then parted ways. Losdir rubbed his forehead when he was alone. He found some elven customs quite odd at times.

"I will return if I can, though I can't promise that," he murmured.

Losdir's journey took him on a western course. In the span of a day, he was able to recruit various nymphs from various colonies; namely: dryads, malaises, naiads, and thirads. Many of these nymphs, especially the dryads and the malaises, had precious medical training. They brought herbs and medicines and the like. Losdir saw the beginnings of a very good army. He now had one more stop to make.

It was late afternoon by the time he and the nymphs entered the land of the Free States. Within the woods, Losdir found the very mountain that he sought for. It had a green, welcoming base and a jagged, rocky tip that impaled the low clouds. Losdir knew of several confederations of dwarfs in the region who had a variety of economic advantages. Although dwarfs are commonly associated with mining (which is still an important factor to their state-wide economy), it was far from the only occupation available to them. During the daylight hours, some of them would farm, others would collect lumber, some had white-collar desk jobs, and still others would either work in the mines or fight the savage monsters within them; which included, but was not limited to, cave goblins and lilinges.

Losdir knew the miners were the best of fighters among the dwarf state, and those were the people he was searching for. He had traveled to the grand peak only once before and knew the region was home to a friendly yet fierce people. He knew that every morning for six days a week, many of the men-folk would travel up the mountains. They would bring axes, pickaxes, brushes, lanterns, kegs of gunpowder, and, just in case, pistols. They used these tools throughout the day, and then they would come home in the evening to a fine supper and plenty of rest. This was a routine the families of the miners had grown accustomed to.

Losdir held up a hand as his assembly stopped just outside the town. It was not Sunday, so the people he was looking for were still out on their jobs.

"Stay here and rest," he told the nymphs. "I will find those who will join us."

The nymphs seated themselves in the trees, talking amongst each other. Losdir walked on alone in search of the leader's home in the town of Shiloh's Pass. He believed that the leader, called the konmester, would support him with reliable soldiers. The largest house in Shiloh's Pass was next to the town hall. Losdir assumed it was the konmester's house, so he gave a firm knock on the door. A dwarfess answered it. The moment she laid eyes on the Kuslan, her eyes filled with concern.

"'Tis rare for one of your type to be here," she said. "My husband the Konmester and his workers will be here by the even. What brings an elf to our village, if I may ask? An elf does not often show his face here unless there is something extraordinary about."

"Not to be rude, madam," replied Losdir, "but I would like to explain my presence when your husband returns. I am searching for those whom I may recruit for a very important mission."

The dwarfess folded her arms. "Mission? What sort of mission?"

"I cannot answer that for the moment," Losdir said in a respectful tone.

The Konmester's wife remained silent for a moment, as if she were debating whether or not to let Losdir in. At last she stated her decision, "You may rest here until he returns." She turned and left after shaking his hand. Losdir decided to return to the Konmester's house at eventide. He gathered his nymphs in a camp just outside Shiloh's Pass.

TRAHERN WAS NOT ONLY KONMESTER OF HIS STATE; HE WAS ALSO owner and boss of the local mining company. He was looking forward to a warm supper when the day had ended, but his love for food did not show on his body. He was a muscular and very strict dwarf, yet he was kind and fair to his people. He had just crossed a highland field between mineshafts when one of his workers approached him.

"Sir, we found a group of cave goblins in shaft six. We scrubbed them clean with one minor wound to the shoulder at our cost."

Trahern stroked his short red beard. He smiled, as he often did. "Keep the wounded man home for the next three days in case there are signs of infection," he said. "There's no need to worry. We have not lost a soul yet this season. We have been very fortunate thus far."

"It seems we have not crossed paths with a lilinge in a while," said the worker.

The smile faded from Trahern's face. "And that I'm grateful for. The last time one of us encountered a lilinge, he became one of them… a sad moment indeed. But that was ages ago. We have not seen a lilinge since, and I'm glad the cave goblins are not very bright. We flush out at least a few every day. Soon enough, the mines will be clear and we will no longer worry about losing precious lives to them."

The worker looked at one young dwarf in particular, off to Trahern's side. "How is your son doing on this fine and productive day?" he asked.

Trahern slapped the worker on the shoulder. "Ha-ha! Need you ask? Twenty is a very productive age, I've noticed. I'm still full from his birthday dinner yesterday. Now we are on our way home for yet another fine supper."

At the cry of the work whistle, the other dwarfs returned their gear to the sheds and joined Trahern on the downward road. The mined ores and minerals were taken down by wagon trains to the storehouses where they would wait for exportation. As the dwarfs marched down the mountainside road, they began singing their evening songs of thanksgiving as they drove their horses and donkeys down the road.

> *"Hard days linger upon me;*
> *Their cries sing in my ears,*
> *And my feet are weary and sore.*
> *But in my heart I shall thank thee*
> *And love as well as fear*
> *Oh, my loving and gracious Lord.*

> *"We will sing and share our reverence,*
> *Our thanks shall be forever more.*
> *All our prayers have been answered:*
> *Our feet shall ache no more,*
> *Thanks to our merciful Lord."*

There were many verses to the song and the dwarfs all continued singing them happily. Trahern was the only exception. His mind was elsewhere as he thought of his son Brenus, who looked fatigued but satisfied.

"Another day has come to an end," said Trahern when his son joined him on the trek. "Since you were a boy, playing with your friends, you would pretend to fight the goblins under the earth with a stick as a sword. Now you are working along with the rest of my fine workers. I have even received word that you had to fight a few monsters. Is this true?"

"Yes, father," said Brenus. "All my preparing and training has paid off. I'm glad I can work with you."

He and Trahern hugged.

"I'm proud of you, son. It is pleasing to see that you are enjoying yourself. Now let us go home and surrender ourselves to a delicious supper. Tomorrow brings another big day."

The workforce soon returned to Shiloh's Pass. They were

greeted warmly by the children. Each and every dwarf retired to his personal home. Trahern and Brenus returned to their house as well. The two were surprised to see the elf sitting on their couch.

"Never once have I seen a… elf? Is that what you are?" questioned Brenus.

Losdir removed his scarlet cap. "Indeed, I am Kuslan." He turned to Trahern. "You must be Konmester of this lovely state. I noticed you have conquered that mighty peak. You must have great warriors."

"Mighty we are," said Trahern with a hint of pride. "And what does a Kuslan desire in my state?"

"You say you are mighty, which brings me to the purpose of my visit," said Losdir. "I have something serious to discuss with you."

Before he could speak further, a knock was heard. Trahern answered the door to find many of his people accompanied by Losdir's nymphs. All of the dwarfs began speaking at once. Trahern scratched his head in confusion and turned to Losdir. "What's happening?" he asked.

Everyone had their eyes on Losdir. Losdir did not know how to begin. He knew his request was going to be difficult. He swallowed hard as he addressed the people.

"I have knowledge of your bravery against the horrors on the slopes and in the mineshafts. You fight the goblins so that you yourselves might live. I must say, I am looking for some of you to join me on a very important mission."

The moment he finished speaking, the dwarfs exchanged looks with each other.

"You praise us with words so you can persuade us to follow you," one of them said. "So where will you take us?"

Trahern beamed and patted his son's back. "If we choose to leave, I will lead my followers. My wife the First Lady can administer in my stead until I return."

A murmur of agreement echoed among the dwarfs.

Losdir raised his hands high in the air. "Kemin! Kemin! Quiet please! My friends, you may have heard of the legend of the black dragon?"

The murmur changed tone.

"We are all aware that not long ago, in the nest of our dragon allies, two eggs bore the colors of the darkscale. This was spoken of by our forefathers. The dragons were placed under a spell and sent to the first earth in the form of humans."

"I have heard of this legend. Are you sure it is true?" asked one of the dwarfs.

"If this legend is true, are they here on Elsov?" another asked.

"Are they dangerous?" called still another.

"Listen to me!" said Losdir. "They are our friends. They are not enemies despite their vicious breed. And sadly, no, they are not on Elsov. But there is trouble. A friend of mine has informed me that King Vesuvius has attacked our two friends by means of the Grün-hære. Everybody listen, for our friends are in danger; we must gather an army of our own and help them! We must stop the Grün-hære's advance before they reach our friends!"

Trahern frowned. It took a moment for him to stutter in response, "D—do you mean—?"

"Yes," answered Losdir, knowing what the Konmester was going to ask. "I must say this straight and forward… I mean we must go to the other world. I believe the Keeper will allow it."

"We must travel to the first earth?" several of the dwarfs asked.

"I will not allow anyone to join until you know what you are about to encounter," said Losdir. "The world itself is an enigma. It is like our own world in many ways, but it is also very different."

"Surely it has land and sea much like we have here," the nearest dwarf said.

"I have heard the people there create interesting tools from within the earth," another mentioned. "They gather resources like we do, but use them to build objects and weapons we have no knowledge of. Their magic differs from what we know."

Losdir took note of the remarks. "I can only state truth. Those who follow me will have their lives changed forever."

More of the dwarfs began speaking their minds.

"Indeed, the first earth can be different in many ways, but I have also heard of its many beautiful lands. It has lovely mountains and forests just like Elsov."

"Of course, there are many of our race who are evil. Humans are like that as well. There is war and contention."

Some of the children murmured in utter confusion.

"I know some of you may be afraid. Do not be ashamed, for I fear this quest myself," continued Losdir. "If you do not want to come with me, I understand. But we have friends; *friends* who are trapped on the other world. We must help them so they may return to Elsov! This is their home as much as it is ours!"

Losdir's eyes roamed over the people. Some backed away in fear while others were determined to help. He continued speaking.

"Listen, you may see similarities; you may see differences. Take a look at yourselves. You are dwarfs. I am an elf. We are different in many ways, yet we have something in common: we oppose Vesuvius' Kingship. However, dwarfs like yourselves have a culture to fight for what is right. I come from a culture that prefers peace and diplomacy. We as Kuslans love to make friends, but will fight if we must. All the creatures of Elsov are different. As we travel to the first earth, we will see a whole new brand of cultures."

Silence fell among the dwarfs. Losdir could tell they knew the importance of the mission, but they were scared all the same. They remained still until Trahern spoke up.

"This may be dangerous, but it is for the better. I will go, even if I die to save us all."

His wife rushed over and grabbed his arm. "No! It will be too dangerous! If you go, you may never come back!"

Trahern rubbed his wife's hand. "If I don't go, our friends may be slain." He turned to his followers. "We are dwarfs! We are powerful fighters! This elf came here because he trusts us! He believes we are good fighters! I will show him what a true dwarf is! Who is with me?"

A dwarf from the crowd leapt to his feet. "I will go!"

"I will go," said another.

"So will I."

"I will as well."

Several more dwarfs volunteered as well. Trahern was pleased to see that so many of his people were eager to help him.

"It is official, then. Enough is said," he exclaimed. "Rosemary, my wife and First Lady, will you be Konmestress in my absence?"

Rosemary gave a courageous nod. "I will, Trahern. Everything will be in order under my temporary administration."

"It is your state now," said Trahern.

The rest of the dwarfs cheered.

"You will not regret your decision," said Losdir. "We will fight and save our friends."

The crowd stamped their feet.

"We will do this to free Elsov from the terror of Vesuvius!" a dwarf cried.

Losdir waited for Trahern's volunteers to prepare themselves. It had been ages since the shed of defense (as it was called) was last opened; and now once again its doors were unlocked for the sake of war. Inside the shed were rifles, crossbows, extra pistols, and ammunition. The dwarfs gathered their old weapons, along with some spare bows and arrows for the nymphs. From another shed, they distributed camping tools amongst each other, along with buckets, a few musical instruments… and some shovels.

Losdir's Militia was formed. All the families in Shiloh's Pass had one last meal together that night, followed by lamenting goodbyes from the wives and families the next morning. Brenus opted to stay behind to take care of the mines with the rest of the workers who chose not to go.

Losdir had no magic to take the Militia directly to Trihan, so the entire army had to travel either by wagon or on foot. Losdir concluded it was good training for the new recruits, anyway. Before the Militia left Trahern's land, the dwarfs sang their song of departure,

"Oh, great Shiloh's Pass, we bid thee farewell.
Thou art our lovely mountain home.
We may leave thee now, for how long? we cannot tell;
But we promise to return so thou shalt never be alone.

"To Shiloh's Pass, we bid thee farewell,
Thy birds and beasts and people too.
Fate has led us away, for how long? we cannot tell.
We know not when we shall see thy skies of eternal blue."

They reached the Keeper's castle early the next day. Trihan, who was expecting them, was waiting at the front entrance.

"So, the young dragon has succeeded in finding help," he said as the Militia arrived. "I assume you know what you will face? Are you prepared?"

Every member of the Militia answered with a loud "yes".

"They have spoken. We are ready," said Losdir. "Is Auben waiting for us?"

"I'm sorry to say this, but no," replied Trihan. "He is already gone."

Losdir felt goose bumps on his arms. "Auben went to the other world alone?"

"I understand how you feel, but he suggested that your Militia should follow the Grün-hære. Your friend Auben will find the other dragons and their friends and warn them."

"That is a reasonable suggestion for one so young," said Losdir.

Trahern clapped his hands. "I believe the two dragons have the best of help. Now it is time for us to do our part." He turned around and addressed the Militia. "We will fight the goblins and dwarfs who shame our race! Beware of darkscaled dragons and lilinges. They will regret leaving our world!"

The Militia cheered, but their voices had fear mixed in with it. Trihan escorted them inside the castle, up the stairs, and to the door of the portal room.

"One at a time," he directed. "The portal only works for one being, but you will arrive at the same location. The Grün-hære lies to the south of where you will land. Keep a watchful eye on human settlements and do not create trouble."

"We will leave the humans in peace," said Trahern. "We just need to show our kindness and not mention our place of origin."

Losdir and Trahern waited for their army to travel to the first earth.

"This is will be a perilous adventure, but one that is necessary," Losdir said to his co-commander. "We will bring back the lost dragons. They must come home."

Trihan tapped the scepter on the floor. "Just remember, most are not aware of the second earth, our magic, or our sorcery. Only a few are aware of our existence. The Grün-hære knows this and will likely not bother them as well. If at all possible, this is something that we should deal with ourselves."

"Little help. That is a shame," said a nymph who was in line. "May I suggest that we find the Horde quickly once we get there? I want to return home as soon as possible."

The other nymphs agreed.

"Plan with intelligence," Trihan advised. "Now please listen to my instructions: you will likely meet up with a fellow dwarf named Fenson and a dryad named Bluepond. They both left when the two dragons were first attacked. If you find them, guide them to the one they call Chang."

He beckoned one of the nymphs to step onto the platform with a wave of his scepter. The dwarfs out in the hall raised their weapons high as a symbol good luck as the nymph was transported away. A second nymph stepped onto the platform, pledging victory before she left. A nervous dwarf was third. He entered the room while hugging his rifle as if it were a teddy bear. Trihan urged him forward. The sweating dwarf took a deep breath and stepped onto the platform. Trihan again activated the portal and sent him away. One by one, each member of the Militia stepped onto the platform. All had finally departed except for Losdir and Trahern. As they stepped inside the room, Trihan stopped them with the end of his scepter.

"Remember what you must do," he said, pointing a stern finger at Losdir. "You are not going to destroy the Grün-hære, but you must stop them with all your might. Even if the portal seekers never see you at all, they will be grateful for your service. Keep this task in mind."

Trihan went to a table next to the window. On the table were two sword cases. The Wizard opened them and presented the swords to Losdir and Trahern. The swords were not special, nor were they enchanted; but they had a beautiful glimmer in the sunlight with their clean steel blades and cocked-hat hilts.

"I prepared these for you both," said Trihan. "These weapons will mark your leadership. Use them well."

"We will, Keeper," said Losdir. "But I am worried. Auben… are you sure he is safe? We have known each other since we were young. If he dies… I do not know what I will do."

"Unfortunately, I cannot guarantee that. Do what you must and you may meet him again."

Losdir shook hands with the Wizard before stepping onto the portal. Trihan motioned his scepter and it was activated. Losdir shut his eyes as he waited for the strong wind to calm. It was only a matter of seconds before he opened his eyes again. He was surrounded by fir trees at the base of a slope to a steep mountain, steeper than the ranges in Trahern's State. The ground was cold. Clouds filled the sky. As Losdir explored the landing site, he found the rest of the Militia grouping together. They stood on wobbly legs. Some had green faces. Trahern soon emerged from a small whirlwind.

"We made it, and we are in a lovely forest," a nymph said happily.

"The air brings a chill. This is a place I certainly will enjoy," a dwarf added. "Oh, how I love firs! You can really smell the fresh air."

Once the Militia regrouped, they all fell silent. Losdir listened to the wind brush past the needles on the branches and the songs of birds and insects near and far. Some members of the small army started plucking the strings of the lutes they brought. A nymph joined in with a smooth, wooden fife.

"We are here," said Losdir. "Sadly, we cannot enjoy the peace here. We need to hunt down the Horde. We are not inexperienced woodsmen who band together and hunt supper, we are soldiers. We may sing and dance later."

Lifting his new sword, he waved it in front of everyone.

"I organized this militia. Konmester Trahern will carry out orders with my approval. I will lead the way. Dwarfs line up front while nymphs line in the back. Keep your weapons out and stay alert."

Trahern yelled like a drill sergeant at his dwarfs to line in order. He stood next to Losdir and watched the nymphs fall in line as well.

"What is your plan if we are attacked?" Trahern asked Losdir.

"Whatever happens, we cannot have your troops charge like greenhorns," said Losdir. "If we do, we will have many graves to fill. We will use the terrain to our advantage. Forests like this one may be our best battlefield. If the enemy charges up front, the nymphs will act first. They will fire a storm of arrows. As they reload, we will take your troops and charge while keeping the front line strong. They will retreat when the nymphs fire again."

"That is a good plan for a frontal assault," said Trahern, "but what about the rear?"

Losdir paused to think. "I don't know yet, but I will know soon. In the meantime, we should move out. Time is not our ally here."

Trahern felt the sensation of war. He turned around and yelled at the Militia, "You heard what he said, you lazy group of swine! Move out!"

Each soldier stood in a loose line and began marching out of order. Many started singing while others fooled around. Losdir and Trahern did not approve of that. They knew they needed to train their soldiers for what was yet to come. They figured the second verse of "Hard Days Linger Upon Me" would be necessary to sing, but only once, to create a marching rhythm. Trahern led them off,

> *"My good lady awaits*
> *My daily homecoming,*
> *And my child awaits my loving hugs;*
> *Because my family is grateful*
> *For all my days mining,*
> *I will pass my woes with a shrug."*
> *The dwarfs raised a crescendo for the chorus.*
> *"We will sing and share our reverence,*
> *Our thanks shall be forever more.*
> *All our prayers have been answered:*
> *Our feet shall ache no more,*
> *Thanks to our merciful Lord."*

CHAPTER 16

CHASE OF THE DARKSCALES

We lost hope the moment we saw the three darkscales, and the train was not slowing down. The engine's fire must still be hot, I thought. It sounded like the roar of a dragon accompanied by wild, angry huffs. The side rods over the wheels spun faster and faster. The train itself gained momentum with each passing second, forcing me to cling onto the coach with my claws. Clipper, on the other hand, jumped off and took flight.

"Jacob! Get off the train!" he yelled. "We need to fight off these darkscales!"

"All right," I called back, "but keep the train in sight! I think I'll—"

A black shadow obscured my vision. Just as I was about to open my wings, something latched onto me, throwing me off the coach. After hitting the ground, I rolled several excruciating yards. Despite my pain, I quickly stood up. Clipper landed to confront the beast that had attacked me, only to stop and blink. He must have been as surprised as I was. The shadow belonged to another black dragon, who was female. She bore a great resemblance to me, only she was slightly smaller and more slender, like Sally.

Clipper did not hesitate any longer. But as he charged, the darkscale dodged him, then pounced on his back and pressed his wings down.

"My name's Syntare," she hissed, flicking her forked tongue over Clipper's ear. "Yer at my mercy. Now ya mus' pay the penalty, ya filthy traitor."

My temper worsened upon seeing my friend down. I charged at Syntare. She saw me coming and lowered her horns. I did manage to push her off Clipper, but our horns locked; which drastically slowed my momentum. I knew she was going to be a tough opponent when she growled at me. In return, I cast a blazing flame at her. She roared before attacking within my fire. I remembered being told that black darkscales were the worst tempered of all dragons. Syntare was clearly no exception.

While I was occupied, the next best thing Clipper could do was follow the runaway train. We both knew tragedy would strike if neither of us did anything about it. Taking flight, I attempted to follow while Syntare pursued close behind me. Fire erupted. Dragon calls rang through the air. There was now a storm of hostile creatures surrounding us. I watched as Clipper circled over the train. The other two darkscales following him landed on the rear coach.

CLIPPER KNEW HE SHOULDN'T USE FIRE OVER THE COACHES. INSTEAD, he tucked his wings and descended from the air. As he spiraled down closer to the train, the darkscales prepared for his coming. Clipper was descending faster but suddenly veered off, much to the surprise of his enemies. He could see the darkscales looking at each other in confusion.

"Where'd 'e go?" the first asked.

"'e flew off, the coward. 'e mus' not like flyin' through the air," said the second.

Clipper did not bother with their comments. He was sick to his stomach, though he did manage to get a good look at his enemies. One had copper-colored scales while the other had blackish-violet scales and sabered fangs. Both of them looked like true darkscales, not because of their forked tongues, rough accents, or any of their physical appearances; it was the darkness in their hearts that presented them as true darkscales.

Clipper knew he had to overcome his acrophobia. Flying back to the train, the two darkscales raced after him. Clipper landed on the engine's boiler where he hung onto the dome. He felt secure there until he saw something beyond the cloud of steam that made him shudder. It was a level crossing in the distance. What made matters worse was that a small white car lay over the rails. It looked like it was broken down. Clipper could also see the driver attending to the smoking vehicle. He appeared unaware of the train barreling toward him. Clipper could not fit inside the cab and blow the whistle. Besides, he had the darkscales to worry about. Luckily the man turned his head. With wide eyes, he franticly climbed inside his car and tried to start it. Failing to do so, he climbed back out and ran down the road. He had just reached safety when the train collided with the car. The small vehicle twirled, smashing against a signal. The signal tumbled into a nearby ditch. Clipper slipped off the boiler after the impact. He reopened his wings and retreated back into the sky. The two darkscales followed him. Clipper looped back to the engine where he waited for them. He was not sure if he was ready for a battle against other dragons or not.

I tried my best to catch up with the train, but Syntare made sure I didn't. She clamped down on my tail with her jaws. I roared in agony before losing control. I took another hard fall to the ground. Syntare landed next to me and laughed.

"You be the one named Jacob Draco, eh? Yer a black 'un like me. Yer supposed ta be the most deadly o' dragons, yet here ya are lettin' me destroy ya."

She butted me onto my back with my wings sprawled out on the ground. She pressed her front claws into my chest. Even with my armored scales, her claws felt like knife points ready to impale me.

"Ya think movin' to the other side makes ya more powerful, huh?" she taunted. "Look at ya. Yer little machine's rollin' away an' yer friend can't stop it."

I said nothing, but growled instead. Syntare growled back.

"Ya think I'm goin' ta kill ya, is that it? I only will if ya refuse ta come with me. If ya pledge allegiance to Vesuvius, I'll never dream o' killin' you."

I continued to hold my tongue. It was as if Syntare wanted to tempt me to go down to Hell with her. I could not let that happen. I had a mission I needed to complete and I was determined to not allow Syntare to stop me. I tried to free myself, only to feel her claws digging deeper into my chest. I wanted her out of the way; but for some reason, I felt a soft spot for her. She had said she didn't want to kill me, but rather have me turn to her side. I expressed my answer by remaining silent.

"So ya won't speak, eh? I guess ya need some battle scars."

Before she could lay any more harm on me, I decided to speak up.

"Sorry to disappoint you, but you can't hold me."

I spun on my back, tossing Syntare aside; then I spat venom into her eyes. The next step to keep her down required brutal action, but I refrained when I saw her hallucinating. She shrilled and cried, wanting her agony to end. I felt no wrath. I felt sorry for her. That feeling in such a situation was alien to me. However, since she was incapacitated, I took back to the sky. Had she been a dwarf or a goblin, I would have been much harder on her. Maybe it was easier to hold myself back because Syntare was a female of my kind and breed.

When I reached the train again, I could see that the other two dragons had gone after Clipper. From the sky, I noticed the railway line meandered through a small town. Another level crossing lay in the distance. This one was much busier than the previous crossing. It bothered me that no shunter or signalman had set any switches yet for this runaway train. There was no clear way to send an alarm. Clearly, the goblin inside the cab wasn't going to blow the whistle. My heart began to race when I saw a long tractor-trailer full of logs roll slowly over the crossing. It was futile. Clipper and I watched helplessly as the engine crashed into the tail-end of the trailer. Splinters of wood showered all around. I cringed at the destruction that lay everywhere. The engine's cowcatcher was badly damaged at this point. But despite all that, the train still raced along like an angry bull. I was thinking of ways to stop it when I heard Clipper calling desperately for assistance.

"Jacob, help!"

The two darkscales descended on Clipper, both casting flames over him. Some of the flames caught on the roof of the front coach. Not a moment later, the entire roof was ablaze. Other bits of flame simmered in the ground by the ditches. The fire on the coaches rapidly grew. I had to distract the darkscales before they could cast anymore fire. I landed on the rear coach, ran and jumped to the next, then flew through the smoke that came from the first. Even as a dragon, I almost choked in the thick black cloud. When I was past the burning coach, I flew around the white cloud of steam coming from the funnel. I saw the two darkscales diving toward Clipper, who growled back with a snarl. The darkscales did not realize I was below them. I sank my fangs into the copper's left wing. We both tumbled through the air and took a rough landing. Clipper turned to engage the violet. They both collided in the air. With his sabers, Clipper bit down on the violet as hard as he could. His enemy lost grip and tumbled to the ground, blood gushing above his forepaw. I managed to fly off before the copper could spread any more fire. There were no more dragons for the moment, but there was no time to celebrate.

Clipper and I landed back on the roof of the engine's cab.

"Jacob, we need to find a way to stop this train," said Clipper.

"We've gone I don't know how far and we've had trouble at two different crossings," I huffed. "Do you have any ideas on how to stop it?"

"I don't."

I would have scrambled for ideas had another monster not shown up. I felt something as gentle as a feather land on the back of my neck. I turned my head to find something straight out of my nightmares. The creature looked like a large bat, but with a devilish face. Yellow saliva dripped from its upper fangs as they rose to bite me. I did not know what the effect would be if its teeth touched me.

"Jacob, look out!"

Clipper quickly blew a small flame at me. The creature jumped off my neck and flew off as quickly as it came. It disappeared into the smoke above the coaches. By now the roofs of all three were burning.

"What was that thing?" I asked.

"I don't know, but at least it's gone. Now what should we do about this train?"

JOSHUA SAT ALONE ON THE COUCH IN THE CABIN. HE HAD FLED the contention the previous night, and Captain Larson seemed uninterested in him. All was quiet in the house, but Joshua was not at peace. Many thoughts crossed his mind. He knew nothing of the train at the time, or that Reno had been freed. All he did know was that plans had changed since Larson's attack. Everything seemed to be going awry.

My friends are finding their way back home, Joshua thought. I wish they could stay here, but how? They're dragons, and they need to go home. If it weren't for the Monolegions, I would never have known them.

His thoughts were cut short at the sound of the telephone. Joshua answered it, hoping for good news. Much to his excitement, he heard Chang's voice.

"Chang, I'm so glad to hear from you!" Joshua cried. "How's everything going?"

Chang told him about Reno's capture and the dangers lurking nearby.

"I see," said Joshua. "This doesn't sound good. Tell me where you are and I'll meet up with you… Don't worry about me… Okay, I'll see you in a few minutes."

After Chang told Joshua where he was, Joshua hung up. He wiped his forehead.

"Goblins! What more could there be?"

He gathered his wallet and keys and was about to leave when the doorbell rang. Grunting, Joshua opened the door. A dark-haired man stood in front of him.

"Good day, sir," the man said. "If you will please, I'd like to have a word with you."

Joshua started to feel anxious. "Eh— sure. Come on in."

The man stepped inside, followed by William, who had his sketchbook in his hands.

"Hi William," Joshua said when he saw the boy.

"Hullo Joshua," said William's father. "My name is Mr. Cowley. Call me Charles. My son William and I need to discuss something that may seem… rather unusual."

"Go ahead," said Joshua, sweating.

Charles hesitated a moment. "I believe you have something in your home that has caught William's attention. He says there are dragons here."

Joshua couldn't believe what he had heard.

"I didn't say anything," William said to him. "He already knows about them."

"Already knows?" asked Joshua.

"My son is right," said Charles. "I know of these dragons. I know they seek Elsov. And I know Triathra has fallen."

Joshua took a deep breath. Charles knew about Elsov! He knew! Joshua wasn't sure what to do next. William gazed wide-eyed at his father, surprised as well.

"Sorry, sir, I wasn't expecting that," said Joshua. "How do you know all this?"

"I'm a historian," said Charles. "I have studied folklore for twenty-six years now, and I can tell you this: Elsov has its references in folklore from all around the world, including the Isle of Man where William and I live. But these references are not obvious. It takes time to decipher their meanings and fit them together with other folklore across various cultures. I, however, have done just that, and I am not the only one who has. I also know these legends are true. I knew the rise of the dragon had come when I heard about the first incident in New York City. That is the real reason why I have come here, knowing the dragons would be here. My late brother and his close friend Franklin know of this as well."

"If that's true, how did Franklin wind up here?" Joshua questioned. "He was here before my friends and I came. Nobody knew Jacob and Clipper were coming to California except me and a few others."

"A man has his sources," said Charles, smiling.

Joshua was at a loss for words. Charles looked down at his son.

"And you say your new friend has seen these dragons, too?"

"Yes. I can bring him here right now," said William.

It turned out that William did not have to go anywhere. The doorbell rang again. Joshua answered it to find Henry and his parents standing on the front step. Joshua was overwhelmed by the company.

"You see," Henry's father said to his son, "there's nothing here. I must tell you again, what you saw had to be your imagination."

Charles greeted them before Joshua did.

"How do you do? I am Mr. Cowley, William's father. I must tell you you're wrong. When my son William and his friend here were outside last night before the police came, the two boys *and* the dragons were talking to each other." He pointed to Joshua. "Even you were there."

Henry pulled the medallion from his pocket, showing his father the writing on the back. Chang's blood was faded to the point that the writing was barely visible.

"Here's the inscription that talked about the dragons," Henry explained. "And like I said, I never noticed it until last night."

"But that doesn't prove anything," said Henry's mother. "It could just be an old poem."

"Mom, I saw the dragons with my own two eyes," said Henry. "And this writing directed the dragons to Sevier County. That's in Utah. It can't be that old."

"It's a clue to something the dragons are searching for," Charles clarified. He said nothing more.

"Where are they now?" asked Henry's father. "I would like to see them."

Joshua rubbed his chin again. "Maybe you can all help me. I can take you somewhere to see them, but we have to hurry."

He escorted the two families back outside. Charles and William followed him to his car. Henry's parents promised to follow.

Charles sat next to his son in the back seat. "You have had your sketchbook since your last birthday," he said. "All this time and you didn't know."

"You always told me dragons were myth," said William.

Charles placed a hand on his son's shoulder. "What I know can be risky for all of us. I don't give information away easily. I'm sorry if I upset you, William. You must understand what I'm trying to do."

"Don't be sorry. I understand," said William.

Joshua put the car in gear. He and the two families headed to town. Not a soul spoke from then on as they passed the short cliffs on the shore. When they were in town, Joshua turned onto a smaller street. He pointed out his window.

"Look, there's Chang."

He honked the horn and parked to the side of a curb. Chang shuffled to them on his crutches. Henry's family arrived soon after and parked behind Joshua.

"Are you crazy?" Chang whispered to Joshua. "I don't want to draw attention to myself. Here, there's an empty storefront behind me. Sally said it would be a good enough place to hide."

"How are Sally and Reno?" Joshua asked.

"They're all right. Sally told me she had to fight off a darkscale who impersonated Clipper. She said it almost killed Larson."

Joshua and the families gasped in unbelief.

"A darkscale impersonated Clipper and attacked Sally?" Joshua repeated.

"There are dragons out there that don't like us," said Henry. "That's a scary thought."

"They managed to escape safely, but Reno's not acting like herself," said Chang. "She growled at me and crawled under Sally's legs. She's behaving like I kicked her."

Chang opened the door to the storefront and invited the others in. Joshua let the families go in first.

"Are you ready to meet two of them?" Joshua asked the parents.

"Despite my knowledge, I don't think I will ever be ready," said Charles. "You must know that I've never seen a dragon face to face before."

William looked around. "Reno's here? I like her the best."

The two families stepped inside. Charles seemed excited while Henry's parents seemed terribly afraid. They simply had to trust Chang and Joshua. The interior of the building was dark. The only light came from the sun that peeked through a few small windows. The group followed Chang as he made his way to the back corner of the storefront. Sally's dragon voice caused the families to jump.

"Chang, you're back. I see Joshua brought the boys and their parents."

Sally stepped out from the shadows with Reno beside her. The adults froze. Cold sweat ran down their foreheads. William and Henry, on the other hand, were happy.

"You see? I told you they were real," said Henry.

His parents did not answer.

"Well… hello," Sally stammered. "I'm sure you never thought you would be in a position like this."

Charles looked down at Reno. "I see what you were saying, William. She's lovely."

He bent down to pet Reno's head. Despite Chang's warning, he was surprised when she hissed and backed away under Sally's tail.

"I wonder what is wrong with her," he said.

"She's been like that since we rescued her," Sally explained. "She's not very fond of humans right now."

"She won't even talk to me," said Chang.

Charles and William looked at each other. It was clear Charles still had a lot to learn about dragons.

Sally suspected they were trying to guess Reno's age. "She'll be a year old in a few months," she informed them.

"You see? She's a fast learner. Just look at her. She's not even a year old yet and she can speak," said Henry.

Reno glared at him, keeping a safe distance.

William scratched his head. "This blue one can speak but the young one *won't*? I think I remember hearing her speak that one night when she was on the roof."

"Oh, she can talk for sure," Chang assured him.

William bent down to get a better look at Reno. "Look at her. I don't care where she comes from. I love her."

Reno growled and took off into the darkness. Sally stood up and followed her.

"What is it?" she asked in a comforting tone.

"*Them*," Reno huffed angrily. "I don't like them… humans."

"Reno, you don't mean that," Sally replied. "I know it was awful when Larson turned on us, but what about Chang or Joshua? They're humans. They are our friends. They love us and care for us. I'm still a human, remember?"

"Care for us? I thought the Sergeant helped us. If he did, why did the other one try to kill us? Why did they hold me captive like I was a mad dog? I don't like it here. I want to go home. I'll never trust humans again."

"Stop that, Reno, right now," Sally snapped. "I get what you are saying. I know how selfish people can be. But think about it, we all do bad things. We should hate the bad thing, not the one who did it. Everyone has done bad things at least once in their lives. You've got to believe that, Reno. I've done bad things in my life, and you will too. We aren't bad ourselves, though."

Reno grunted. She was in no mood for arguing. "Fine. I'll help Chang and Joshua. But that's it! I don't even know why you brought the others here. They're going to be trouble. I know they are."

"They found us and want to help us. You see? There are others who want to help you."

"Well, I don't trust them. I'll only join *these* people to help us find the six pieces of the portal and get back to Elsov."

Sally rubbed her nose with Reno's. "Okay, if you allow them to help us, I'll leave you alone about all this. Pretty soon you'll give up your grudge, you'll see."

The two stepped back into the light where the group was waiting. Joshua and the others heard the entire conversation.

"You… are human?" Henry's father stuttered.

"Yeah, it's a long story." Sally didn't want to talk about it yet, so she changed the subject. "Chang, didn't you say something about Jacob and Clipper following a railway line?"

"I did," said Chang. "I don't want to say this, but they're gone. I don't like being split up like this. It's going to be harder to find the pieces now. Luckily I still have our little viewing device."

He pulled the viewing ring from his pocket and looked through it, groaning.

"Nothing but vivid green. If only the dragons can go one way while the rest of us go the other, maybe we can straighten this mess out."

"I have an idea now that William and Henry are here," said Sally. "Reno and I can go find Jacob and Clipper. Chang, being a pilot, can meet us in Sevier. He can follow our reported sightings or use the viewing ring. The boys and their families can see if Sergeant Nelson can help us. Captain Larson doesn't empathize well right now and we need to let him know we're not against him."

"That's a good idea. I can fill them in on what's going on," said Joshua. He explained to the boys' parents while Chang and Sally made their own plans.

Chang pointed at Reno as he spoke. "Sally, take Reno. You two can fly out of here. Head for Sevier County; that's north-west of here. I know it might take days, maybe weeks before we're back together. It should only take me about a day or two to go north, though it may take a little longer to find you and the others. I'll use the ring if I must. I have friends at the airfield that might help me anyway."

Sally sighed. She did not want to be separated any more than Chang did. The fact that finding the first piece could take at least a month felt exhausting. But she could not think of an alternative solution. As much as she was not looking forward to a long journey, it was one she knew she had to take.

"Go ahead, Chang. And good luck," she said.

Chang hugged Sally, avoiding her spikes. "Good luck to you too. You and Reno will need it more than I do. I'll see you soon."

Joshua hugged Sally as well. They spent a few minutes saying their farewells.

"We have to hurry. Let's go, Reno," Sally said when they finished.

They immediately left the deserted store and took off into the sky. Henry and William, along with their parents, stood in awe as they watched them fly away.

Joshua was now pleased that there was a good plan to find the pieces, rather than not knowing what would come next. Things seemed to be going well.

THE TWO DARKSCALES SOON RETURNED, BUT SYNTARE DIDN'T. NO matter, I was already trying to think of a way to stop the train. It was slowing down a little, meaning the fire that fueled it was dying. But even with the train slowing, it was still going at a dangerous speed, and I had to deal with the darkscales one way or another.

"Clipper, they're after us again!" I called. "Get ready!"

I was flying parallel to the train while Clipper clung to the engine's boiler. "We crashed into another car," he reported. "This cowcatcher is next to useless with all its damage. More crossings are bound to come. There's no way to stop this train ourselves."

Clipper had good reason to be concerned. A long row of houses was in sight. If the train derailed in that area, people could be in harm's way. Derailment was something I had to prevent at all cost! I encircled the coaches to lure the darkscales away from Clipper. I was satisfied when it worked, for they flew after me now. Clipper was clear, but now I wasn't. I flew past the train, going much faster than it was. I was approaching the houses when the copper darkscale caught up to me. He blew a flame that temporarily blocked my vision, forcing me to land. The joints in my wings ached terribly at this point. When my vision cleared, I returned to the tracks. The train was not in sight, but I could hear it coming.

Next to the row of houses was a siding that was occupied by several freight cars. There was a risk that the train may be on the same line as the cars. I had to warn Clipper! I was unable fly back to him since the copper was spiraling down toward me. He landed between the rails in front of me. Behind his head, I could see the giant tower of steam and smoke. The train was getting nearer and nearer. My fears were confirmed: the train *was* on the same line as the freight cars! It was going to hit them! The black engine rounded a bend and came into view, approaching peril. Clipper watched from the front of the funnel. We both saw the disaster that lay ahead. Clipper was yelling something to me, but I could not make it out over the roar of the engine.

At that moment the violet darkscale swooped down, striking Clipper. They both fell into a ditch off to the side. Clipper was out of the way. I was too close. I started to panic. The copper would not let me off the tracks. He roared and struck me in the face with his claws. That was it... I could hold back the pressure no longer. I let out an even louder roar and bit down on the copper's neck. I clamped harder until I could taste the satisfying reward of blood. The copper screeched and un-pawed me as he tried to squirm away. I had no mercy left. It almost felt relieving having my pressure burst.

The copper finally slid out of my grasp and tried to fly off. I pursued him. I didn't care who saw me or heard me. I cast a massive fire at the copper. Many houses started to burn, but I ignored that. I ignored the screaming and wailing below me altogether. When I caught up with the copper, I bit down on his tail, the same way Syntare had done to me. With him in my grasp, I flew back to the siding just behind the stored cars. I was not going to let the copper live. My fuse had blown, and it was time for him to pay. I took another hard bite in his neck until I knew for sure I struck the vital spot. I would have bitten him again, but my inner darkscale at least had the decency to consider my own survival.

The startling hiss of steam rang in my ears. I jumped out of the way just in time. The dying darkscale, trying to scramble to safety, collapsed into the ditch. Then came the worst. It was a terrible sound, but the darkscale inside me enjoyed every second of it.

The front of the engine collided with the cars. The intense thunder of the collision drowned out any hiss of steam. The copper darkscale disappeared under the wreckage. On my right, I saw the burning coaches derailing. I leapt out of the way just in time. Debris was tossed in every direction, fire spread rapidly. The coaches collapsed while still traveling at their great speed. The houses nearby suffered from fire and debris, not including the ones I had already destroyed myself.

The earsplitting noise of the crash came to an abrupt end. The sudden sound of silence shook me back to my senses. All I heard now was the haunting rumble of the monstrous fire. The darkscaled dragons were no longer a threat, but the damage was done. The column of smoke was now four times the size of what it originally was. Many homes were gone. In the distance, I heard people calling for loved ones or weeping in despair.

"What have I done?" I moaned.

I realized that I was the one who made the goblin run into the train. I was the one who first set fire to the houses. *I* was the one who brutally slaughtered the copper. This whole tragedy was *my* fault!

I was sitting within a small group of trees when Clipper found me. He shook off the rubble and coughed many times. He had several open wounds in his wings; the blood ran in small rivers to the edges. He too was shocked at the scene of destruction, but not nearly as much as I was. The train lay derailed, the front wheels rotating slowly in the air. It was terrible sight. Clipper, wincing from the pain in his wings, shook his body one more time.

"Jacob. Jacob. Answer me, please," he said, nudging me with his horns.

He kept a sharp eye out for any of the three darkscales. There was no sign of them, so Clipper turned back to me.

"Jacob, say something," he pleaded.

I pressed my horns on the trunk of a tree. "I'm okay," I mumbled.

Clipper took a deep breath. He was relieved that I was all right, but also concerned. "Jacob, what's wrong? I'm okay. You don't have to worry about me."

"Clipper, look what happened," I said. "Look at the damage I caused. *I* caused the accident. *I* did all this. The darkscale inside me… this monster… me… Look what I've done!"

"You didn't do this," said Clipper. "It's not your fault. You jumped out of the way, I saw you. You couldn't do anything about it."

"Clipper, look at me!" I wailed. I opened my mouth to show him the blood on my teeth. "I didn't know what I was doing… the darkscale… *me*… doing such a thing… Augh! Now look at this! Fenson was right, we are evil beasts." I couldn't stand looking at my paws. The black scales horrified me. "Why was I born like this?" I asked myself. "I can't stay here or something else will happen."

"It was an accident," said Clipper. "Remember what we said when those dwarfs found us? It's not you, it's the darkscale. Stop blaming yourself. Like you said after we became dragons, you can't change the past."

"That's just the thing. I can't."

Clipper was about to say something else when he heard a moan behind him. The copper darkscale was lying in the wet ditch by the train in very bad condition. Clipper rushed over to him. He now knew what I was talking about. The wounds in the copper's neck nearly made Clipper throw up.

The darkscale looked at him and gave a weak hiss. "Mas-thleass viss nae ye thleass. Me death'll be yer death," he said on his last breath.

With Clipper's tail to me, I silently took flight. I could not live with the fact that I was responsible for such a tragedy. Little did I know a small part of my heart allowed some of the darkscale to seep inside. The blackness would only continue to grow there. The darkscale began to take over my body.

Away I went, and I did not stop. I flew at a speed I never thought possible. Before I knew it, I was far from that dreadful place.

POLICE AND PARAMEDICS ARRIVED AT THE SCENE IN NO TIME. THE officers and other workers were everywhere, searching for answers. A detective was examining the damage when his partner arrived at his side.

"The locomotive itself can be repaired, even if the coaches are destroyed," said the detective. "Did you find anything, Geoffrey?"

"We found another body in the wreckage," the detective's partner replied. "The body is in pretty poor condition. Like the first one we found, it's hard to identify. The funny thing was that the skin, or what was left of it, appeared to be green."

The detective searched methodically in the wreckage. "Whatever the case may be, I think the dragons had more than a little involvement in this."

"Dragons are myth, aren't they?" asked Geoffrey.

"Well, remember the excitement in Pennsylvania over the past few months? The sightings are now happening here on the west coast. Most people deny their existence, but I know there's something out there, dragon or no dragon. I remember hearing about some residents in Utah who 'swore' they saw them. That and the events in New York happened earlier this year."

An officer rushed up to the detective when he finished speaking. "Sir, you've got to come see this."

The detective shrugged and followed his comrade to the scene. Much to his astonishment, there it was. He bent down and examined the desecrated carcass. "See this animal?" he said. "It's dark yellow in color. It looks like a real mess around its neck."

"So it *is* some animal," Geoffrey assured.

"But I thought it was the black one that had no sabered teeth. This one isn't black."

"I see it doesn't have sabered teeth either," said Geoffrey. He took a deep breath, running his hand through his hair. "Excuse me."

He moved toward the trees, holding his stomach. He could not believe what he had just seen.

"Dragons," he said to himself. "I'm not sure. They can't be. It has to be something else. But— what was that?"

He felt something whoosh over his head. He stared up at the sky. There was nothing around. Shaking his head, he continued pondering the evidence.

"So if dragons have been real all along, then why are we only now finding evidence?"

He heard the faint whoosh again and looked around in frustration. There was not a living soul in sight. Geoffrey continued muttering under his breath.

"So, these fire-breathing creatures are real. If the non-sabered one's supposed to be black and this one's yellow, then I guess there may be more than the two we found— Who's there?"

Something was definitely nearby.

CLIPPER WAS NOT FAR FROM THE DETECTIVE'S PARTNER. HE STAYED where he was, watching Geoffrey's inner turmoil. He didn't want to fly until the bleeding in his wings ceased. Luckily they were healing quickly.

Geoffrey did not know Clipper was nearby. He continued talking to himself.

"This must be— why do I keep hearing that noise? Is anyone here? Show yourself. This isn't funny."

Clipper kept quiet. He thought he was the one making the noise. He sat motionless and did not make a sound, not even did he breathe. He saw Geoffrey looking into the trees. Clipper was puzzled. He was not even in the trees. What could Geoffrey be hearing? Clipper continued to watch the detective's partner when something dropped silently out of the sky. It landed on the man's left shoulder. Clipper recognized the creature. That's the thing that almost bit Jacob, he thought.

The monster opened its jaws and sank its teeth into the man's soft neck. Geoffrey grunted and shooed the monster away. The lilinge made an odd clicking sound before flapping off.

Clipper was spooked. He was unsure what the lilinge had done. Geoffrey looked around, rubbing his bite wound. He was about to walk away when he started coughing and groaning. Clipper was worried enough that he no longer cared about his cover. He stood before the victim of the lilinge. To Clipper's horror, the detective's face grew pale. The white in his eyes dilated into a blood-red. Foam dripped from his mouth. Even more to Clipper's surprise, the man began to change. Short brownish-black fur began to sprout on his body, his ears became pointed as an elf's, and he began to shrink in size. Clipper blinked, believing his eyes had deceived him. The man's arms became wings. In a matter of minutes, he became a lilinge himself! The newly formed creature lifted its head and squeaked. The noise echoed back and forth among the trees. The new lilinge took flight over the crowd of officers at the site of the crash.

Clipper could see that the detective in charge was worried about his partner. Seconds later, Clipper looked on in fright as two lilinges, one of which had been the partner, landed on two other officers. At first the paramedics thought the officers had been exposed to a sickness after they started coughing and drooling. The paramedics screamed, backing away after the two officers also became lilinges. Some of the other officers in the area stood frozen. A few grabbed the creatures before they could bite them, but some were still overcome. Clipper knew he should not let the people fall under the curse of the lilinge's bite. He ran into the melee. The only way he could think of to get rid of the lilinges all at once was to use fire. He opened his mouth and completed his task. The swarm of lilinges burned under the sudden flames. The surviving officers pointed at him.

"There's one of the dragons!" one of them shouted. The others pulled out their weapons.

Clipper had no desire to battle them after his experience with the lilinges. He dashed off into the trees before taking flight. His wings seared in pain, but he did not care. The sight of the giant bats rattled his mind to the point where he cried. Innocent people were no longer innocent! When he landed, he heard the people at the scene of the wreckage in commotion over the catastrophe.

"I don't believe it," Clipper wept, trying to keep his mind calm after what he had seen.

He took flight and landed again a few miles away, feeling utterly hopeless at the recent tragedies.

"Everything's falling apart! Jacob… those people…What more can there be?"

Clipper shut his eyes, trying to rid himself from the stress. He was out of breath and the air stung his nostrils. His sense of smell was temporarily weakened.

Syntare watched Clipper from a distance downwind, grinning.

"Our plan's a workin'," she mumbled. "If Clipper follows Jacob, the Grün-hære'll be upon 'em in a matter o' days."

She jumped into the air and hovered over Clipper. She began to empower the wind with her wings. Clipper opened his eyes just as Syntare flew out of sight. He was again alone. He placed his head on the ground, crying.

"Someone needs to help us! Reno's been locked up, Fenson and Bluepond are gone, now I don't even know where my best friend is. Our group is scattered like broken glass. If only someone could give me a clue on how to get everyone back together, then we can be on our way like we should."

Clipper had never felt so alone in his life.

PART 2

THE SEARCH FOR THE SIX PIECES

CHAPTER 17

Help on the Way

Fenson and Bluepond were unaware of the recent happenings. Over the next several days, they traveled in the direction they had planned to go, hoping to reunite with us soon. A day prior, they were helped by a kind man who saw them walking on the side of a highway. The man said he was on his way to Moab. He took Fenson and Bluepond as far as Monticello: a town near the forest of Manti-La Sal. They had no idea Sevier now lay to the west.

Late one afternoon, two weeks after leaving the lonely beach, they wound up on a trail through Manti-La Sal. They intended to do this so Bluepond could take advantage of his expertise of Mother Earth. The forest, covering the land around several snow-capped peaks, provided the dryad with the land he was born to be a part of. It also made it easier for Fenson too, for he was also an expert woodsman.

He and Bluepond stepped through long, soft grass and over large rocks. There was the occasional sound of a snapping twig under their feet, but the swish of the greensward was the most common sound about. Despite the protection of the evergreen conifers, Bluepond felt something peculiar in the air. He tested the balance of a stick that he had found and carved into a spear. He, as nymphs often do, wanted to confront his enemies rather than run. He knew, however, that a small, pointy stick would not be the best weapon if they were attacked by a large animal or, worse, an Elsovian monster that may have followed them.

Fenson scratched his beard, which had grown long and shaggy over the last two weeks. "When will Jacob and Clipper find us? It's been so long. We've traveled so far, yet there's been no sign of them. Maybe we should stop and wait here."

"Be calm," said Bluepond. "Jacob told us to keep moving in case we are being followed."

"I just hope our friends are out of danger," sighed Fenson nervously.

"No need to worry. We have seen them fight already. They have survived the Minotaurs' wrath. Sally also proved herself a friend and good fighter. When she first fell under her curse—" Bluepond suddenly halted.

Fenson looked around, swallowing. "What is it?"

"I smell something, like food cooking over a fire," Bluepond whispered. "We must be careful. If the goblin was able to follow through with his plan, they may be after us by now."

"I thought the goblin's plan was to attack us with the two Minotaurs. The smell has to be from an innocent campground."

Bluepond picked up a flat rock and used it to sharpen his makeshift spear. "That could very well be, Mr. Katque, but I make no assumption." He tapped his thumb on the spear's point. "I pray that Jacob and Clipper and the others are safe. We fled when the city's police arrived. We came to warn the dragons, but it seems it was all in vain."

"We had to leave before they caught us," Fenson reminded him. "I think it was a good idea to do so. If we were caught, we might have been forced to expose who we really are. They would learn that you are a dryad and I am a dwarf. Trihan warned us against revealing our identities."

"Nevertheless, if our enemies are nearby, we will have to fight. And I do not think we can claim victory with only a dead stick."

"Think good thoughts, we will make it to the next breakfast," said Fenson.

Bluepond swished his fingers, warning Fenson to keep quiet.

The nymph tightened his grip on the weapon in his hand. Step by step, they followed the appetizing smell. They soon heard shouting nearby. Bluepond quickly ran up a fir, leaving Fenson alone on the ground.

"Where am I supposed to hide?" Fenson complained.

Taking a step sideways, he continued to make his way forward. But before he could turn back around, someone sprang out from behind the trunk of fir. The surprise visitor had an arrow in her bow that was aimed at Fenson's heart.

"Move an inch and I will give you this to your breast!" yelled the stranger.

Fenson, eyes wide, held his hands up. He kept still while holding his breath. It was surprising yet relieving for him to meet another nymph, even if it wasn't a dryad. He tried to give a friendly nod, though he did not know how successful it was.

"I am a dwarf. I mean no harm," he said, remaining calm.

"You are not of our militia! How can I be certain you are not lying?" the nymph inquired.

"You must trust me. I have a nymph like you as a companion. My name is Fenson Katque. I come with no intentions of hostility."

The nymph cautiously relieved some tension on her bow. "You are Fenson? Trihan mentioned you. You were supposed to warn those whom we are seeking. How do I know you are the true Fenson? Where is your companion, Bluepond?"

Fenson looked to his left and up one of the trees. He saw Bluepond jump down from a low branch then land hard on the ground. He waved at the other nymph.

"My respects to you. I am Bluepond. We mean you no harm. The dwarf is telling the truth. He is Fenson."

The nymph finally lowered her bow. She replaced the arrow in the quiver on her back before holding out her hand. "I see the dwarf is honest. I mean no harm to you as well, now that I know who you are. I am Jasmine, a maliae scout. It is a pleasure to meet you, Bluepond."

Bluepond shook her hand. "And a pleasure to you too, madam. I must ask, though, why are you here? I believed Fenson and I were the only ones sent by Trihan."

"Trihan sent the Militia to distract and hopefully detour the Grün-hære who lurks about these lands," said Jasmine.

Fenson snapped his fingers. "There *was* more to that goblin's plan after all! I feared this would happen. Now the Horde is here! You said you are here to distract them with a militia?"

"Yes," said Jasmine, flicking the string on her bow. "We are here to aid our dragon friends, the portal seekers. If the Grün-hære finds them, it will certainly complicate matters, especially with innocent people around here. We as a militia were sent under Kuslan Losdir's invitation to find the Horde. If they battle us, the seekers may have a chance. If we are successful, our friends can escape the Horde. These dragons who have defeated the Nibelungs may be useful against evil forces on Elsov."

"Indeed clever," said Bluepond. "When the time comes, we can find them and we can all return to Elsov together. Now I must ask, who is this Kuslan, Losdir? Fenson and I would like to meet him."

Jasmine started up the trail, beckoning to them. "Come. I will take you to our camp, but please do not step on any flowers along the way. You can meet Losdir. Another man in authority is Konmester Trahern."

Fenson and Bluepond were close behind Jasmine as she led them off the trail to their hidden camp. It was not long before they came to a clear meadow. The appetizing smell came from a rabbit roasting over a fire. As they crossed the main site, they met up with Losdir. The elf was standing next to Trahern, who was commanding a line of five other dwarfs.

"Now keep your position! Draw your arms!" Trahern yelled.

The dwarfs pulled out their guns as quickly as they could. Trahern stamped his foot.

"That was better, but not perfect! Needs improvement!"

Losdir tapped his shoulder. Trahern turned to see the two new faces.

"At ease!" he called. He approached Fenson, Bluepond, and then Jasmine. "You must have crossed paths with them on your post. Who are they?"

"They are the ones whom Trihan mentioned," said Jasmine. "They are Fenson and Bluepond."

Upon hearing the names, Losdir bowed his head in respect. "So, you are Fenson and Bluepond. You must have traveled far if you came from the far south. Bless you for your bravery. I assume the maliae has informed you of our reason for being here?"

Fenson nodded. "Of course, I was hiding from the goblin and his two companions when he told them of his plan to come to this world. I had to find some way to protect those who completed their mission. I never imagined the Grün-hære would ever be here."

"It's our job to keep them occupied," said Losdir.

"Well then, it seems then we have the same task on different ends," Fenson chuckled.

Losdir looked up at the sky with hope in his eyes, as if he were searching for something. "Are the dragons here?" he asked hopefully.

"No. Our group was separated and we had to leave. Bluepond and I were told to travel north-west. A kind man offered to transport us as far the town near this forest. We decided to cut through here when we stumbled upon Jasmine."

"If you know where your friends will be, we can find them when our work here is done," said Losdir, bowing his head. "We will be pleased if you joined us. If the Horde is after them, we will follow. It will help us if we know the Horde's path."

"It would be an honor," said Bluepond.

Trahern heartily patted Fenson's back. "Wonderful! You two can lead the way! I think we should move out now, if you don't mind. If you are right, Fenson, we could stand in front of the Grün-hære as they come along."

The Konmester ordered a dwarf with a wooden bucket to fetch some water from the stream. With the fire doused, Trahern held his hand next to his mouth.

"At-ten-tion!" he yelled, long and loud.

Each member of the Militia joined his or her rank in a timely fashion.

"Your skills are improving, my comrades," said Losdir. "Our new friends, Fenson and Bluepond have discovered our camp." He paused for a moment as the Militia applauded. "They know the land around here. If we intercept the Horde, then they will have more to worry about than tracking down our dragon friends. Fenson and Bluepond will guide us with my and Konmester Trahern's permission."

The dwarfs raised their firearms high as a welcome to Fenson and Bluepond. The two waved in return.

"About an hour ago, our nymph scouts spotted the Horde's camp to the south-east," Losdir reported to Fenson. "It looks like you must have walked right past them. You and Bluepond are lucky, indeed."

"Then south we shall go," said Fenson. "There has been no sign of Jacob and Clipper yet. If they discover the Grün-hære and this militia, they may find us anyhow."

"Then let us move before the Horde does," Bluepond suggested, "and be on the lookout for enemy scouts."

Losdir pointed his sword forward. As he began marching, the rest followed to the sound of a war drum. Since Fenson and Bluepond were present, Trahern did not mind marching with the rest of the dwarfs. The Militia moved slowly through the forest.

About an hour passed when Losdir spoke up, "We have traveled for some distance. Let us stop and rest before we continue."

"Our soldiers will need all their energy when the fight comes. We can rest," said Trahern.

Some of the dwarfs and nymphs sat down while others leaned on tree trunks. Fenson and Bluepond found a boulder on a smooth slope and shared a seat. Losdir offered them his canteen. Without hesitating, Fenson took it and gulped down half of the refreshing water.

"Ah, thank you," he said, wiping his mouth.

"We have made good time, so we should be all the more cautious," said Losdir. "We must be getting close to the Grün-hære."

Fenson scratched behind his ear. "I fear the beginning of our business with the Horde."

"Each one of us fears the upcoming events," said Bluepond. "But we must use this fear to drive our courage."

Fenson pulled a map out from his belt and unfolded it. He laid it on his lap. He explained to Losdir that the man who had driven him and Bluepond had also given him the map. Losdir inspected the many features.

"Despite the unusual shape of the continent, this world looks similar to Elsov, land and sea alike," he said. "Very useful to have a map if I may say so."

Fenson pointed out their location. "We are here in the state of Utah, in the west." He ran his finger up and over where they were. "Jacob and Clipper have to cross over this region here to this mountain range. The forest we are in is Manti-La Sal, a name in which I believe is a foreign tongue." He ran his finger to the left. "Over here is where the first piece is believed to be."

"How long will it take for Jacob and Clipper to fly here and search this land?" asked Losdir. "We could run our rations empty if they don't come in time, and we still must battle the Grün-hære."

"That will not be the case," said Fenson. "We will finish this task and soon go home to a nice meal."

Losdir examined the map again. "I have no doubt this will be a complex plan. There is no promise that the dragons or their friends will meet us, but we must have faith. We will stick to the plan and stand by. There are goblins, royalist dwarfs, a number of darkscales, and maybe a few lilinges. That is if I remember the Grün-hære's formation correctly."

"Lilinges, eah!" Fenson cringed. "Nasty vermin those beasts are. One bite and you become one of them. I had a distant cousin who fell victim to them on his way home from a merchant's trip."

"I'm terribly sorry," said Losdir. "That explains why we must clear them out. But we have not lost all hope. A lightscaled dragon who is a friend of mine is somewhere on this world, destined to meet the other dragons."

"We'll do what we must here and they will do what they must there," Fenson promised. "The biggest problem, I believe, are the lilinges. They may be worse than the darkscales. We must avoid their bite at all cost."

"Losdir is a trustworthy Kuslan. I trust him with all my heart," said Bluepond. "I will do whatever it takes to free our darkscaled friends and stop the Grün-hære."

Fenson took a nervous breath. "So be it. Lilinge or no, they will not pass us and live."

"Fight we must," said Losdir. "If all goes well, you will be home in no time, far from those devil creatures." He patted Fenson's back before ordering the troops to rise and move out. The army of Elsovians returned to their formal lines. The march continued.

The hours passed and soon it was late noon. Losdir led the way next to Fenson and Bluepond.

"We must be reaching the edge of this forest," said Bluepond. "There is sure to be a village or a town nearby."

"How will the folk react to us if we all descend upon them at once?" asked Losdir. "Trihan recommends we avoid that."

"He told me and Mr. Katque the same thing when we began the search for the dragons ourselves," said Fenson. "Many stared at us but seemed unworried. Our clothing differs from theirs. The dragons had to stay hidden, of course, but Bluepond and I did not. If we are to enter this town, we better send only a few."

Losdir was thinking about how to enter the town when Trahern approached him from the dwarf lines.

"Sir, the dwarfs are complaining of hunger. Some of the nymphs are too."

"Our rations are limited and we have to eat sparingly," said Losdir. "We are unable to gather more food."

"I told them to wait 'til supper," added Trahern.

Losdir pondered the dilemma. The Militia continued down the wooded slope until the thick forest cleared into a small open field. Just as Fenson expected, a small town was seen down below.

Losdir eyed the settlement. "Maybe we can go there and ask the townsmen for food. We can gather some for ourselves so we don't have to starve."

"I see there's a town," said Trahern. "As you have said before, Fenson, send a few. I don't want to scare the townsmen silly."

"The nymph scouts are on the lookout," said Losdir. "They know where we are and they will know if the Horde is coming. We'll be safe."

"Fenson has experienced the culture here. He can tell us what to do and how to obtain food," said a dwarf in the line.

Everyone in the Militia listened closely to the conversation. Fenson felt nervous with all the attention on him.

"Ehh… Two of us can go to the village and obtain food. Perhaps we can find a market or a grocer. While Bluepond and I were on the road, the kind gentlemen who brought us here gave us some money; fifty dollars to be exact. We will not need water if we can refill the canteens at the streams."

"Fifty dollars," Losdir repeated. "I will go with you to the town, Fenson. I'd like to gain some social experience while I'm here."

Bluepond found nothing wrong with that and decided to join the nymph scouts. With everything arranged, Trahern ordered the troops to halt and rest. The dwarfs and nymphs began making merry while Fenson and Losdir continued down the mountainside toward Monticello. They soon stood near the first houses that formed the outskirts of the town. Losdir dusted down his surcoat, licked his fingers, and straightened his eyebrows.

"Do I look presentable?" he asked Fenson.

Fenson squinted at him before pointing to the elf's cap. Losdir understood his concern and pulled the edges of the cap over his ears. Fenson sloppily combed his own hair with his fingers. "Now we are ready," he said.

"Will these fifty dollars be enough to purchase plenty of food?" asked Losdir.

"I hope so," said Fenson. "Just in case, maybe we can find an honest way to get more money."

The elf and the dwarf found a line of streetlamps and began to follow them. The small cluster of houses became more condensed until various stores appeared. Losdir was impressed with how sophisticated the town was. In a way, it reminded him of Fjordsby.

"Look alive. Here comes someone," Fenson whispered to him.

From around the corner came a young man who looked to be in his twenties.

"How do you do?" Fenson said to the man.

The man gave a quick but friendly nod at the two strangers. Losdir expected him to look at his clothes in an awkward manner, but the man did no such gesture. He only kept his eyes on Losdir as if he were a next-door neighbor.

Fenson sunk his hands into his pockets. "We have traveled from a far land and we are in search of food. Could you aid two harmless travelers?"

The man frowned, patting his pocket. "I'm sorry, but I don't have a dime on me right now."

Losdir remained silent, allowing Fenson to talk for him. He gently tugged at his cap to make sure his disguise was secure. The man finally wished them luck and left. Fenson and Losdir continued their search. Soon they saw a middle-aged woman walking her dog. Fenson chuckled with delight.

"Here comes another stranger. How about you talk to her, eh?"

"I'll try," said Losdir. "I don't want to make a mistake. If she discovers who we are, there is no telling if the Horde can benefit from that."

"The Horde won't know of this. You must try to talk to her. I know Kuslans are adept at socializing. This will be no trouble for you."

Losdir cleared his throat and wiped his perspiring forehead. He pulled his cap down once again.

"Good day to you, madam."

Like the young man, the woman took no notice of Losdir's clothing. She only smiled while pulling back the dog's leash. "Hi there. Don't mind my dog, he's just curious. He won't bite. Down Winston! Down!" She patted the dog's head.

Losdir tried to speak again, but began to stutter, "Err... my name is... eh... I was going to ask if... if..."

The woman stood patiently while Fenson filled in. "My friend and I are new here. We have traveled far and wide. We are just asking for a small donation of money to take care of our needs, if you would please."

Fenson winked at Losdir. The woman happily obliged and reached into her purse. "I can give you something. I hope it helps," she said as she gave them the money that she had fished from her wallet.

The elf bowed in respect as he accepted the bills. "I thank you for your kindness. May good luck and fortune bless you."

"Why thank you," said the woman in return. Her dog continued whining and sniffing Losdir's leg as she continued on her walk.

"Funny dog," Fenson whispered to Losdir when the woman left. "They are smaller and much different on this earth. I'm sorry for interrupting you."

"Never mind that," said Losdir. "It looks like she gave us a total of twenty dollars. That makes seventy altogether. Now where can we purchase food with this money? There has to be a grocer here."

The two walked on until Fenson pointed out one of the stores. "This here is a market. I believe I can see fruit for sale."

Carefully watching the street, they crossed to the other side and stood in front of the store. Baskets of peaches, apples, and plums beckoned them. Inside, Fenson and Losdir examined everything on sale. No adults took in their appearances, but the children, however, pointed at them and asked their parents who "those funny people" were, followed by the parent disciplining the child. Losdir ignored them. He instead pretended he was a returning customer.

A lone, aging clerk wearing a white apron came from the back room with an empty peach basket in his hands.

"Hello. How may I help you?" he asked the nervous elf.

Losdir decided again to start the conversation. "My pleasure to meet you. I am— searching for something to fill the bellies of my people and I'm willing to pay for the food."

The clerk set the basket on the counter and pulled out a small notebook and pencil.

"And what will you like?"

"Enough to feed a small army, if you know what I mean." Losdir hoped he hadn't said too much.

The clerk arched his bushy white eyebrows and wrote something in the notebook. He placed the pencil back in his pocket when he was done. Losdir started picking out different foods that he was familiar with. The clerk pulled out several bags and filled them with what was ordered. Walking over to the front counter, he placed the bags one by one on a scale. Counting and adding the weight, he punched in the amount on the cash register.

"With this much, that will be seventy-two dollars and thirty-four cents," the clerk said. "That's a lot of food. You must have a lot of hungry people on your hands."

"This is all we have, I'm afraid," said Fenson, placing the money on the counter.

The clerk counted each bill. "Seventy dollars even, I see. I'll accept it. I'm glad to help you out."

He pressed a button on the cash register that opened the drawer on the bottom. He placed the money inside and closed it again.

Fenson gathered half of the bags while Losdir grabbed the other half and the receipt. There were a lot of bags, but Fenson and Losdir handled them well.

"You have helped us tremendously. My thanks," Losdir told the clerk.

"I need to ask you one question, if you don't mind," the clerk said before they left. "Where are you from? I'm just curious."

Losdir swallowed. He made sure his cap still covered his ears. "We have come from very far away," he answered vaguely.

"I see," replied the clerk. "I don't mean to appear suspicious. I'm just asking because everyone around here is scared right now."

"And why is that?" asked Losdir.

"There've been more sightings of these dragons or whatever they are. This county hasn't seen any around here before, but it's happening now. One has been seen this morning, in fact! Some ranchers have lost a few of their cows, too. Most think it's something like coyotes, but there are some who really believe there's a dragon out there. Do you believe that by any chance?"

"I don't know, but I understand their fears," said Losdir. "I wish you well, sir."

He and Fenson left the store after one more thank you and then started on their way back to the camp with the food.

"It seems this was a productive venture," said Fenson. "I'm more than pleased at how well we were treated. We were given money and now we have food for your soldiers."

Losdir set his bags down and readjusted his cap so his ears could be out again. "This was good experience. I wonder why nobody stared at me except for the children. I thought we would certainly stand out. But they did talk about a dragon. I hope this dragon, darkscale I presume, does not attack this town. I don't believe it is Jacob or Clipper."

Fenson and Losdir decided not to talk about the darkscale anymore. They soon returned to the mountain slopes. They found it much more difficult to climb with all the bags they lugged along. In the camp, some of the dwarfs were playing their banjos and dancing lively while others prepared a deer they had killed for extra rations. The nymphs were about doing their own business.

"There they are!" Bluepond called out. "You see? I knew all would be well!"

Losdir placed his bags of food in front of Trahern. The Konmester fished out a fresh red apple. He took a bite and chewed, letting the juice run down his chin.

"Ah! A tasty little fruit, this apple is," he said. "It seems as if you've gathered a nutritious supper for us. That should balance out the animals we hunt. Besides, the thirad nymphs won't eat meat anyway." As he took another bite, the entire army surged to the bags of fruit and vegetables. Trahern held his hands out. "One at a time! One at a time! Haven't you learned to form a line? Just for that, the ones up front will pace across the camp until I say you can eat! Now run!"

A portion of the dwarfs and a few desperate nymphs sighed and began running slowly. The others formed a straight line, patiently waiting for their turn.

Trahern clapped his hands at the runners. "Go faster, you pigs! That's much better. After we eat, prepare to march again 'til sundown."

He allowed the obedient soldiers to take three of either plums or grapes, three leaves of lettuce, an apple, an orange, and an optional slice of fresh venison. Trahern picked a plum and dropped it in his mouth, spitting out the pit. "A fine supper this is before we approach what lies ahead," he said to Losdir.

"What lies ahead will be no easy task," Losdir replied as he finished his apple.

Some of the dwarfs cringed when they mistakenly ate the peel of the oranges, having never seen them before. Others grinned like children when they tasted the inside. The peaceful evening suddenly turned sour when the troops heard the call of a warning horn.

"They are coming! They have spotted us!" cried a nymph scout.

The leaders dropped their food into the bags and drew their arms. Jasmine the maliae rushed into the camp.

"The Grün-hære! One of our scouts has spotted them! They are approaching us!"

The rest of the Militia searched urgently for their weapons. Nymphs grabbed their bows and vanished in the branches of strategically positioned trees while the dwarfs distributed their firearms amongst each other.

"Now's not the time to panic, troops," said Trahern. "You must keep calm!"

"How can I keep calm?" yelled a nymph in the trees. "These are not cave goblins or ogres that the dwarfs fight! They are much bigger and heavily armored! And I think a darkscaled dragon is with them!"

Chaos and panic prevailed at the mention of a darkscale. Trahern picked up the wooden bucket of water and tossed it over the fire. "Keep calm or we won't live!" he bellowed. "We have been trained for this! Now quit whining and prepare for battle! We all knew this was coming!"

Arrows were loaded into bows while bullets were loaded into guns. In the distance, they heard another eerie trumpet.

"Here they come! I can see them!" Jasmine called from her spot in a tree.

Losdir and Trahern quickly ordered their troops to line up.

"Fenson, you and Bluepond go to the rear. We need you two to guide us after this battle," said Trahern.

Fenson and Bluepond did as they were told. In a matter of minutes, they heard the shouting of goblins and royalists. The enemy army marched into view in an experienced military fashion, much more experienced than the Militia. Without words of reasoning with Trahern or Losdir, they charged with spears and rusted blades. The Militia may have had more advanced weapons, but they were heavily outnumbered. The plan of attack was clear as day in Losdir's mind. He moved forward until he was right below the nymphs. The dwarfs advanced in front of them, each had a face of aggression. Trahern held his gifted sword high above his head and stood in the center of the frontlines. The closest line of goblins was about fifty yards away. Forty. Thirty. Twenty. Their howl echoed across the forest. Trahern's resolve wavered when he had a clear view of the goblins. Their green faces were painted with red and black, the lines detailed like dancing demons. Trahern knew that if the Militia was to be victorious, he himself had to overcome the goblins' fearful appearance.

What Trahern heard next certainly lowered his morale. He could hear the screech from the sky. It was too quiet to be a dragon's roar, but it was something. Despite his fears, he waited for the nymphs to fire before he would lead his followers into the first battle against the Grün-hære.

CHAPTER 18

SORROW

Several days had passed since the tragic incident. Not once did I rest. The feeling that I was responsible for the terrible disaster weighed down upon my heavy heart. I didn't care if my friends were worried about me or not. I was sure they would be better off without me. I was thoroughly convinced I was a monster, and I did not want my friends to get hurt because of me.

As I traveled over the empty desert, dark, wet clouds became my constant companion. The storm seemed to have a mind of its own. It felt like it was deliberately trying to worsen my mood. Not only that, but I felt as if the entire world was against me. I remembered being eager to find the first piece to the portal. I had made no progress since then. First, I was thought of as aggressive by Larson, then I was ambushed at the junction, and it all ended with the devastating train wreck that I believed *I* was responsible for.

I was filled with more sorrow than I could handle, and I flew on throughout the night, out into the wilderness. I had never before flown such a distance alone. Eventually, my wings grew tired. I knew I needed to rest soon, so I landed on a hill somewhere in Nevada. (Or was it Arizona? Who cared anyway?) As I came to the ground, I was met with the strong scent of sagebrush. The coming of autumn was a little more noticeable here. The change in the temperature only worsened my mood. At the lonely beach, it was warmer. Thinking of it reminded me of the humidity in Vesuvius' keep that I had felt in my dreams. I still wanted to go back to Pearl

Forest, but Vesuvius stood in the way. There seemed to be no way to get past that. I wanted no more of Vesuvius.

After curling up under the branches of a cottonwood, the desire came back to me. I wanted to live in Pearl Forest, *alone*. My home was calling to me once again. I was eager to take flight to find the other pieces, but I was too tired. I yawned as I looked at the dark outline of the mountainous landscape. It was as dark as my saddened soul.

IT SEEMED AS IF I HAD BARELY CLOSED MY EYES WHEN I OPENED *them again. I was back in a familiar forest, not like the one in Pennsylvania, though. Surrounding me were various species of trees. I suddenly felt a mist of fairy's magic brush past me. It was a good magic, not evil sorcery. I stared up at the sky. Stars and the mighty planet Alsov hung in the heavens. I remembered my first encounter here when I had lost my memory. The little grøl had told me about the beautiful blue planet. A stream of tears rolled down my snout. I stood up and wandered around my home world. And home it was!*

I started down a path that I had found when the atmosphere changed in an instant. It still felt like Elsov, but somewhere far from Pearl Forest. It was a place where sorcery prevailed. I stood on ashy ground in front of a large mountain castle. I examined some of the rock at my feet. The evidence of my location did not seem hopeful. Every time I dreamt of Elsov, I came here. A sudden explosion erupted from the castle's tallest spire. A large dragon flew out of the opening and directly to me. He was much bigger than me. It was Vesuvius, no question about it.

"What do you want?" I asked firmly but fearfully.

"Oh, Jacob Draco!" Vesuvius laughed. "You wonder why you have visions of me."

"That's my problem, not yours," I said. "You're not even here. This is all in my head." (It was quite confusing with this lucid dream effect.)

"I know your progression," Vesuvius sneered. "Heitspel informs me. We may not be together physically right now, but I'm no dream. You are mistaken if you think you can find the diamond without me harassing you just a little bit. I can find you and destroy you at any time, but I won't because I'm offering you a choice."

I grew concerned when he said he was no dream. He was right; this was something else. Vesuvius knew my progress, contrary to what I had first believed. This was a serious matter.

"What choice did you have in mind?" I asked him.

"Right to the point, good," he said. "I remember when you defeated Triathra. Using cold against him, I must admit that was clever. Here is my offer: become who you truly are; simple as that! Look at yourself. You're a darkscale. Your literal dark scales mean nothing, but your technical breed says otherwise. The reason for your sorrow is because you are fighting back the nature of the dragon within you. Let your savagery run free."

"I was told by the spirit of an ancient dragon that my natural self is evil," I said. "He gave me great influence and freedom, and he won't be the last one to do this. I've been told about you. I know what you're trying to do to me."

"Your stubbornness will be your downfall," Vesuvius hissed. "The Grün-hære is looking for you. If they do not stop you, I will. Any progress you make will be futile."

Before I could say anything else, Vesuvius faded like a ghost from my vision. I was left alone. I was now aware that something terrible was coming for me, much worse than the Monolegions. I was lost and confused. I did not know what to do next.

I FOUND MYSELF BACK ON THE HILL UNDER THE COTTONWOOD. I lowered my head back to the ground, thinking about the vision. It reminded me of who I was. On the outside, I was a terrible beast. But then I remembered when the spirit of the dragon of old was with me, I knew right from wrong. Maybe he could help me out of these sour emotions! I waited for the ancient spirit to come to me. The only way I could hear him was in my heart in times of need. I expected his voice to come, for this was certainly a time of need. I sat there the entire morning. Not once did I hear his voice.

"Why aren't you coming?" I asked, looking into the sky.

I growled, closing my eyes. Fresh tears formed.

"I don't know what to do," I mourned.

No matter how much I wanted the ancient dragon's voice to come, it never did. I wondered why he was not helping me. I started to weep again. Life was hopeless! I had not felt this much heartache since I first turned into a dragon. In fact, I felt much worse. The memory of Treetop and her fate suddenly started to bother me again. I tried to ignore it, but that only made the thoughts grow stronger. They did not allow any peace for me from my guilt and pain. With a sigh of despair, smoke came out of my nose and surrounded my head like ethereal clouds before floating away.

I tried to sleep again when I smelled something out of the ordinary. My ears perked up in full alert. I also heard footsteps nearby, not human footsteps for that matter. I sniffed the air again. There was danger nearby. I stood up and planted my claws into the ground when two darkscales approached me. They found me and trapped me between them and the cottonwood. The first was the violet dragon from the train incident. The other looked almost exactly like Clipper, even though I knew it was not him. Both had sabered teeth. I shook away my tears in embarrassment.

"Seems Visatrice sen' us in the right direction," the violet one said. "Four o' us join the 'orde and one dies. But three live. We get sen' 'ere and look who we find, tha blacksmoke. The sabred 'un mus' not be too far away. Aw, 'e's a-cryin' too! What's eatin' ya, blacksmoke? Findin' the pieces to the portal too 'ard?"

I did not answer, though I did take a good look at the two of my breed. The second darkscale, the red one, cackled. "I 'eard that blacksmokes are the fiercest o' fighters. This un's cryin' like an 'atchling who's lost on the trail. I guess that things did not turn out as 'e planned."

"What are you doing here?" I finally growled.

"I'm a dragon like yerself," said the violet. "I could've been like a traitorous lightscale, but I'm not. Ya may be a blacksmoke but yer actin' like a lightscale. Ya live like yer eyes are green."

"Relax yerself," the red darkscale said to me. "We're not like that, an' neither are you. Yer a *black dragon*! We won't slay ya if ya join us."

"I've already made up my mind, no!" I barked.

"Ya don't see what we're sayin'," said the violet. "'eitspel and Visatrice are right. The goblin gen'ral said you'd might be a-runnin' round 'ere. Now they're right about which side yer on."

I sniffed threatening mucus back in my nose. "You know what I mean. I may be responsible for the train crash, but that doesn't mean I'll come with you. I'm alone and that's final!"

The violet gave me a sly grin. "But look! Ya said you'd be alone. Yer actin' like a fool but thinkin' yer wise by denyin' us."

"Leave now!" I growled. "My friends may not be here, but they're safe and far away. I don't need them."

"Careful what ya say," said the red. "Yer either with us or against us."

Before I knew it, my sadness transformed into a sudden anger that had a mind of its own. I spat venom into the red darkscale's face. I did not quite get his eyes, but he still jumped back, yelping.

"I'll never be loyal to anyone!" I roared.

"So be it," said the violet.

He readied and cast a breath of fire. I left the flames to burn the cottonwood behind me. I charged at him, lowering my horns and springing toward him. The darkscale, slightly smaller than me, was sent tumbling backward. He screeched from the awkward landing on his wings. I was about to jump on him when I felt the red pounce on my back. He held on to me as his tail wrapped around my leg. The violet stood back up, blowing a puff of smoke in my face. His nose almost touched mine.

"You'll regret yer decision, traitor! You'll feel much more pain than this if ya ever reach Elsov!"

Snarling, he clouted me with a set of claws. I shrieked and kicked the red off me. I bit his forepaw then struck him with my own claws before spitting more venom at the violet. This time it got him in the eyes. With both dragons on the ground, I took flight and circled back. My fury was too active to leave the darkscales be. I landed on the ground and attacked them once again. I bit and scratched until both were nauseated and exhausted. With any sympathy I had left, I flew away, leaving them to nurse their wounds. This time I did not fly northward but eastward. As I left them, I began to regret what I had done. I was unable to control myself again! It seemed that everything I did was wrong. I could not bear to meet anybody else, friend or foe. I believed that whoever I would meet would either get hurt or killed. I was a monster; nothing was going to change that.

CHAPTER 19

THE TREE & THE ABYSS

Clipper was determined not to give up. He had been flying for days with minimal rest, searching everywhere for a clue as to where I could be. His wings, on the brink of exhaustion, felt like they were being pricked by hundreds of tiny needles. He occasionally backed-tracked and flew in circles to make sure he did not miss a cold scent. He was tired and sore, but the memory of my grief haunted his mind. He did not want to rest, despite his growing fatigue. Atop of that, the warm summer days were on their way out and the temperature was dropping the farther north he flew. Clouds filled the sky. An icy rain began to fall. Clipper blew a small flame into the night air and let the heat brush past his face.

"I won't let you go, Jacob. I won't," he said for the umpteenth time.

The night dragged on. Clipper felt like he was going nowhere. He groaned in pain as he landed on the shore of a small, pristine lake for a brief rest. Some of the wounds in his wings he had acquired during the train incident were still bleeding. Clipper knew his wings needed a short break if he were to continue searching affectively. When the stinging somewhat subsided, Clipper sat down and took note of his surroundings.

"I should be in Nevada somewhere," he said, "but there's still no sign of Jacob. Where did he go? The train crash wasn't his fault; he needs to know that. But where is he? I've been his best friend for years and now's the time to show it."

Heat left his nostrils as he exhaled. No matter how hard he thought, he had no ideas.

"If I could find just one hint as to where he is, then— I don't know! I'm lost, I'm hungry, and I haven't slept in days. I want to find him, but how?"

"Don't worry Clipper. All will be made right."

Clipper lifted his head. There was no one around. Curious, he asked the air. "Who's speaking to me? Are you the dragon of old?"

"Indeed, I am," the calm voice answered. *"I have not spoken to you in a long while. I know that your friend Jacob is blaming himself. You need to find him as quickly as possible."*

"I've been searching for him, but I don't know where he is," said Clipper. "He could be anywhere."

"I suppose by now you have learned of Vesuvius?"

"Yes. I had a dream about him. He's red like me, but he's much bigger, and he has an enormous spike on his nose. Could anyone possibly defeat him?"

"Clipper, you must be aware that your friend Jacob is in danger. He is falling into darkness, even if he denies it. You must save him."

"What do you mean darkness?"

"I knew you would ask that. I will show you; close your eyes, Clipper."

Clipper gulped, uncertain of what the spirit would do. But doing as he was told, he shut his eyes and waited for the spirit to connect to his mind.

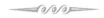

Instead of falling asleep, Clipper's mind opened to an unsettling vision. *He found himself standing on top of a sheer, rocky cliff that looked down upon a river far below. The river had white rapids surging against large rocks while wood and other debris tumbled helplessly down the waterway. Clipper gazed down the chasm doubtfully until he caught a glimpse of the other side. The flat, open land there*

was home to tall grass and an abundance of delicate wildflowers. In the distance, he saw massive trees spread out far and wide. Clipper then gazed at his own side of the canyon, which was brown and empty. Nothing in the dull wasteland gave him reason to stay. He was sure that if he was on the other side, he would feel much better. He took a step forward and again peeked down over the high cliff, into the dark abyss.

Clipper decided that a quick flight was the best decision. He spread his wings and prepared to take off. But just as he lifted his feet, a strong force pressed him back to the ground. After a failed second try, Clipper understood what was happening: he wasn't allowed to fly here! He had to find some other way to reach the other side. Looking around, he discovered something that offered a valid alternative to flight. Not too far from where he stood were a man and a woman approaching a narrow land-bridge. Looking back at the other side, Clipper found the bridge provided easy access to the land he sought. That must be the only way to cross, he presumed.

Clipper made his way to the bridge. Reaching its starting point, he saw the man and woman keeping to the center of the smooth top. He noticed they refused to look left or right, but rather had their eyes focused at the end. A moment later, they successfully reached the other side. They immediately ran toward the shade of a tree and sat down, sharing what looked like food they had found there. Clipper guessed that if he crossed the bridge in a similar manner, he could make it there just as easily. Sucking in as much air as possible, he again looked down at the dark river below. His stomach started to twist.

"How can I go over this without my fear of heights getting in the way?" he groaned to himself.

Clipper sat down, pondering his situation. He noticed that the bridge was narrow. If he stayed the middle and did not look down, maybe his phobia would be less severe. With an anxious huff, he got to his feet. He took one brave step forward. Breathing deeply, he took a second step, followed by a third, and then a fourth. He kept his eyes at the end of the long bridge just as the man and woman had done.

Even though he refrained from looking down, however, he could still see the long drops in his peripheral vision. Taking another few steps forward, he felt the height catching up to him; he dared not wander any closer to either edge. He continued moving with his feet staying in the center. When he was about half-way across, a high wind suddenly formed and began pushing on his left side. As he continued creeping forward, the wind grew stronger. Clipper folded his wings and kept his tail straight to stabilize his balance.

"I can do this...I can do this...I may not be able to fly right now, but I have flown before. Heights— heights don't scare me anymore. I can do this."

Clipper thought about what he was saying. He had flown before. He just couldn't at the moment. Keeping his wings folded tight against his body, he took more steps. The mighty wind gained even more strength. Clipper knew the wind was there for a reason. It was trying to blow him off the bridge! Feeling tempted, Clipper took a peek down the side. He saw the river crashing down its course, heeding no mercy. The whole world felt like it was spinning! Clipper gulped and turned away with a dizzy head.

"That's such a long way down, but I'm almost there. Just a few more feet..."

One step after another, he came closer to the end. He had only a yard left. The wind suddenly blew stronger than before. Clipper dropped to the ground, keeping his claws anchored as firmly as possible. The force of the wind was hard to bear, yet he was so close!

I can't move in all this wind! he thought.

He did not know what to do. The wind kept screaming in his ears. Holding as tightly as possible, he felt his wings unfold in the force. In his terror, his wings acted like sails. He felt himself being dragged even closer to the edge, his claws sliding in the rock as he moved. Clipper didn't think there was any way out of this. But as he kept his eyes forward, he realized he was right at the other end of the bridge. He could not reach it with ease, though, for the wind was far too strong. He knew the only way to safety was to jump. If he didn't, he would be swept off the bridge and into the abyss. He had to jump now before it was too late! Blowing a flame from his nose, he took the desperate leap. The wind blew him away from the bridge. Before he fell into oblivion, he grabbed the top of the cliff with his claws. Clipper hung on the side for dear life. Luckily, he managed to keep his courage. He used his rear feet to lift himself and scramble up until he was able to lean forward, away from the cliff.

The gale of fear became a current of relief. He no longer heard the screaming wind in his ears. He was instead met with bright sunlight over dewed grass. He had crossed the slender bridge without plunging into the canyon! He had overcome his fear and made his way to the other side! A tree, one of many, welcomed him with branches covered with lush green leaves. Clipper walked up to it. The tree stood strong while he rubbed his nose against the trunk. He felt the brown wood tickle his nostrils, causing him to sneeze. Fire spewed from his nose, but it did not spread. After he sneezed, he noticed something in the corner of his eye, something small and red nearly hidden in the tall grass. Curious, he went over to see what it was. It looked like a mushroom. He poked it with a claw. It smelled like fruit.

"Hmm, this isn't fish. It may not be my favorite, but I'm willing to try it."

Opening his jaws, he ripped the mushroom out of the ground with his smaller yet sharp teeth. He sat back down, chewing the outer layer of the strange fungus. An explosion of tasty flavor danced upon his tongue. His eyes lit up with pleasure. The fruity taste was so delicious, even for a carnivorous dragon! It must have been a mushroom that the man and woman were sharing in the shade. They were still under that tree, smiling and waving at Clipper. Clipper waved back. It was nice to meet friendly people who didn't fear him. Looking around the lovely place, he took another glance back at the unpromising bridge. His way of handling the high bridge had worked: keeping to the center had saved him. Doing so led him to the rewarding side of the canyon. Clipper picked another red mushroom and took it near the cliff to eat it. As he chewed, he peered over the canyon. Little light came from below, but Clipper could still see the rapids in the river. Listening carefully, he also heard the rapids crashing over rocks. The world around him started to spin again.

It must be a whirlpool down there, he thought. It has to be at least a mile-long drop to the bottom. And that nasty wind almost pushed me off! Well, it's all over now. With this good food and that friendly couple, it can't get any better.

Clipper listened to the river as he searched for more mushrooms to eat. But as he looked back, he noticed another man atop the other side of the canyon, looking down the bridge with clear confidence. Again, Clipper did not recognize the man, but he knew he would face vertigo and the wind. Clipper ran over to the end of the bridge, blowing a small flame to grab the traveler's attention.

"Mister, be careful!" he called. "Stay in the center! Don't go near the edges! There's a bad wind that'll try to blow you off!"

The traveler answered back in a grim voice, "I don't need to do that."

The man began to casually walk over the bridge. Clipper felt the wind pick up again. He blew another small flame, but the man ignored him. Clipper did not want to witness the fall. He turned his head away and shut his eyes. The man's scream was devastating to hear.

A COOL NIP IN THE AIR CAUSED CLIPPER TO OPEN HIS EYES. HE WAS back in the desert in the middle of the night. The cold air posed no threat to him, though he could feel it biting his nose.

"Why didn't he listen to me?" Clipper asked the spirit. "He should've listened to me. I was on the other side. I experienced everything he was about to encounter."

"*He was ashamed of himself,*" the spirit replied. "*We are all free to choose happiness or misery. We can choose to follow and learn from the guidance of those who have wisdom, or go our own way, which can often lead to peril.*"

Clipper thought about the statement for a moment. "So we can choose to be safe and cross the bridge with caution or not and fall."

"*We can choose,*" said the spirit. "*But you must realize this: dragons are usually ones who fall. Remember how you could not fly to the other side? When I was in my mortal life, lightscales did not exist. Dragons were almost always lost in the dark abyss, hence the name* darkscale. *Dark* hearts *is a more appropriate name in my opinion. It was when I refused to fall that I discovered who I wanted to be. Because of that, my descendants have a brighter path if they chose to follow it. Under a magic spell, they became the lightscales you now know; lightscales because they are under the light of good.*"

"I was born into evilness on Elsov. I was lost," said Clipper.

"*Not necessarily. Before you were born, your egg was supposed to be that of a darkscale. You were the one, along with Jacob, who had to come to this world until you were ready. I followed through with my idea. You would be raised by good people who taught you Good from Evil. When you were ready, you were given a potion that transformed you back into who you really are.*"

"A dragon," said Clipper. "The important thing now is that I find Jacob and get the other pieces. I'm anxious to go back to Elsov because I want to meet my parents, but I'm worried about Jacob. I can't find him. I don't want anything bad to happen to him."

"*I know how you feel. After visiting this world myself in my mortal life, I was eager to return to Elsov. Don't worry, Clipper, I will help you along the way. Before you can find the first piece in the land of Utah, you have a very important task to accomplish.*"

"Find Jacob."

"*Find him. The vision you received was a warning. Remember the lost soul who fell? Jacob is near the edge of the bridge. He cannot make it to the other side if he falls. In his heart, he does not want to fall. He wants to hang on. The natural darkscale inside of him and his own guilt are causing him to slip. He could lose his grip and fall. I cannot speak to him through his inner darkness right now. You must find him yourself.*"

Clipper grew worried. "What will happen to Jacob if he remains this way?"

"*He will turn to his evil ways. He will fall into the abyss and it will be difficult for him to climb back out. He does not realize it, but he may become as evil as Vesuvius himself, maybe worse. You know how ill-tempered the black dragon is.*"

Clipper pawed at the ground. "Jacob! No! He has to hold on! Hold on! Spirit, do you know where he is? I have to find him immediately!"

"*Jacob is not as far away as you think. Go north.*"

Clipper wasted no time. He was back in the sky in a matter of seconds.

"Oh, thank you, spirit! If I fly without stopping, perhaps I can catch up to him!"

"*Careful, Clipper,*" said the spirit. "*Someone else is following Jacob. Remember the other black darkscale that attacked him? She is now ahead of you. I know what she will do; darkscales do this often. She does not want to kill him, but rather tempt him to join her.*"

Clipper flew as fast as he could, much faster than he ever had before. "Is it possible Jacob will fall for her?"

"*Yes. And if I am right, she will coax and tempt him with all her power. If he happens to not comply, she will fight him until one or the other dies.*"

"He's already on the edge," said Clipper. "I have to save him!"

The spirit stayed with Clipper as he continued on all night. Clipper was aware of the distance he had to cover, but in the state of urgency, he easily made up for lost time.

"Jacob, I'm coming to save you!" he roared to the crescent moon. "You aren't going to fall! I'm here! I'm here!"

CHAPTER 20

The Commencing Fight

Trahern ordered his dwarfs to take a defensive position. The screech that was heard was less of a worry since no dragon was spotted. If it were a lilinge, Trahern knew it would not fly in direct sunlight and would therefore be no threat at the moment. Nevertheless, he and his men were in true danger. The Grün-hære charged at the Militia with spears, shields, and a hunger for killing.

The dryads did what they do best: they hid in the trees and prepared to fire a volley of arrows. They had little experience in official combat, but they had enough training in archery within the branches. Before the goblins reached the fortified dwarfs, arrows rained down from the treetops. With a few exceptions, most of them struck shields. Three enemy dwarfs fell; two were only wounded. Most took cover after the first volley. When they advanced again, Trahern's dwarfs took action. The dwarfs were shorter than their green enemies, but their muscular builds showed no signs of disappointment. With their guns at the ready, they fired. The forest suddenly came alive with thunderous *bangs!* and cries of the wounded. Everywhere, birds and mammals flew about in mad frenzies, trying to escape the terrible noise. Many of the goblins were still able to reach the dwarf lines. Pistols replaced rifles, but not all could stop the oncoming storm of spears and axes. The battle grew intense as Losdir joined the bloody brouhaha. Soldiers fell from both sides. The nymphs remained the kings of the forest, thus giving the Militia a precious advantage. But despite the alliance with Trahern's men, the battle between the Horde and the Militia dwarfs was locked in a brutal stalemate. Occasionally a dwarf was able to reload his rifle and fire again, but did not have much time to reload after that. Soon enough Trahern ordered his troops to fall back as the next barrage from the nymphs was ready. The dwarfs took this short time to reload efficiently.

"How many have we lost?" Losdir asked Trahern, catching his breath.

"Six dwarfs and two nymphs," Trahern tallied. "'Tis a bloody battle for sure, but we mustn't surrender. Sadly, we haven't fought with such brutality in years and I myself can hardly bear it! One loss for us is heartbreaking enough."

"We are holding our own for the moment," said Losdir. "Keep your head up and never allow defeat upon yourself. Keep with the plan and we shall not be defeated!"

"Let us hope so," Trahern responded.

The Militia was struggling, but their casualty count was small compared to their adversaries, thanks to ranged weaponry. Losdir thought he could see victory in sight, but he was unaware of a common Grün-hære strategy. Losdir and Trahern mainly focused on what was in front of them. The nymphs were the first to notice the flank coming from behind. They immediately opened fire on the surprise foes.

"Goblins from behind! Goblins from behind!" they shouted.

Losdir turned around to find goblins and royalists coming from every direction.

"We are surrounded!" yelled one of Trahern's dwarfs.

Losdir was determined not to be defeated. He raised his sword high and attacked two goblins at once. He fought with valiance despite the losses in his army. One of Trahern's dwarfs observed Losdir's aggression and, taking heart, did his best to match his leader's valor. Losdir did not realize that the young dwarf was in a bad position. Fighting bravely with only the butt of his empty rifle, the dwarf stopped when he realized there were far more goblins than before. Members of the Horde attacked him left and right. Losdir first thought the dwarf could fight his way out, but soon had second thoughts.

"I need some assistance please!" the dwarf cried.

Before Losdir could respond, two of his allies quickly jumped in to help. They too were overwhelmed. They fought the best they could; but before long, one of the two friends fell under the blade.

Losdir was horrified and rushed into action. He would have reached the helpless dwarfs had he not been overwhelmed himself. He was unable to kill any of his enemies, but he did manage to hold them back. He still could not clear his way to rescue his comrades, though. He watched as General Visatrice killed the other helper and approached the first dwarf, grinning with chiseled teeth linking into each other. Visatrice said something to the dwarf that Losdir did not understand. From the sound of his voice, the childish General was more than likely gloating.

Losdir lunged at one of his enemies to get to Visatrice, but he did not even wound his attacker. Another goblin charged at him. When Losdir fought the goblin back, he saw something that nearly killed him on the inside. With a wicked cackle, Visatrice thrust his favorite weapon, a rusty iron sword, into the helpless dwarf's chest. Wailing from the pain for a split second, the dwarf fell lifeless on the ground. Visatrice pulled out his sword once he knew for sure his victim was dead. Losdir finally heard him say something in an understandable language,

"My weapon of choice is simple yet effective. Its rust delights my fingers each time I rub the blade, especially if there's blood on it."

The scene of atrocity before Losdir's eyes sent a burst of vengeance throughout his body. There was no reasoning with someone so terrible. When he spotted an enemy dwarf advancing on him, Losdir quickly lifted his sword took care of his opponent. He then finished off another dwarf and a goblin. In about a minute, he cleared his way out and returned to Trahern.

Losdir knew the image of the rusty sword would forever haunt his memories. As a result, he transported that image to his own weapon and then to whatever goblin or royalist he crossed paths with. Losdir hated killing, and he knew he would never feel otherwise. He only did what was best for the sustainment of peace and freedom. He, Trahern, and the rest of the Militia soon began their advance into hostile ground. Shots continued to roar throughout the usually quiet forest.

CHAPTER 21

BRIDGING THE GAP

The sun was not yet shining, but the stars that hovered over the earth were beginning to fade. The first bit of daylight turned the snowy ground to a deep, dark blue. During my flight, I had passed over various towns and dormant farming communities. Oh, how I wanted to just land at a house and beg for food! My stomach felt like it was ready to digest itself! The last thing I had eaten was an open-ranged bull several days before. Despite my hunger, I did my best to avoid any living soul; for I was convinced I would do something awful to whoever saw me. They would see the claws and spikes all over my body and run in fright. I worried I would lose my temper and hurt them. Since my last encounter with the two darkscales, I had not uttered a single word to anyone, not even to myself.

I continued to fly until my wings could take no more. My claws sank into a sheet of snow when I landed. The air seemed unusually cold for early autumn, but I was too fatigued to care that much. I lay on my side and felt the soft white blanket touch my scales, which somewhat soothed my tormented heart. I closed my eyes in anticipation for a relaxing sleep. I waited there in the frigid wind for several minutes, but I was not any closer to proper rest. I opened my eyes, glancing left and right. I saw nothing that would prevent me from falling asleep, so I closed my eyes once more. Again, nothing changed. I was too anguished to sleep, yet I couldn't continue in my weariness. So there I lay. Another sluggish hour slipped by on the freezing breeze. The dark blue world soon became brighter and much more colorful. The tree trunks became their usual brown while the needles became a rich green. The snow glistened white and the sky became alive. I remained motionless in my spot, slowly regaining my energy.

CLIPPER, ON THE OTHER HAND, WAS FULL OF ENERGY. MOST OF IT came from the urgency of his search. He flew everywhere, trying to find a familiar scent. He finally rested in a field for a few hours before flying over the Nevada-Utah border. After finding a clear spot of land, he swooped to the ground. He looked around to make sure he was alone.

"Oh, where are you, Jacob?" he huffed.

He kept his eyes on the landscape and sniffed the air while thinking to himself,

Jacob has to stop eventually. If I travel straight, perhaps I can intercept his path. There's no cold scent anywhere. It's a long shot, but I'm not giving up. I'll make sure I find him, and then we'll—

Clipper's thoughts cut short as he lifted his ears. He couldn't smell anything of interest, but he heard the familiar sound of flapping wings. He then saw who was coming toward him from above.

"It can't be! It's—"

He heard the faint voice high in the air. "Clipper! I see you! Stay there, I'm coming down!"

Clipper looked up at the little brown dragon high in the sky. "Reno!" he called. "You're free! I can't believe it!"

It took a moment for Reno to reach him. She and Clipper rubbed noses.

"Reno! Reno. I'm so happy you're okay. How did you find me here?"

"Chang told me where you were going," said Reno. "He said that I should follow you. Sally is right behind me."

A few minutes later, Sally came into view from among the conifers. She landed nearby and ran to Clipper. "My guess was right," she said. "I knew I'd find you around here." She took notice of Clipper's battered wings. "Are you all right?" she asked. "You look hurt."

"My wings are fine for now," said Clipper.

Sally looked around. "Where's Jacob?"

Clipper stammered. "Oh… It's hard to say right now." He caught them up on all that had happened since his and Sally's departure in the railway junction, sadly telling them of the train incident. "… Jacob got a little carried away with his enemies after succumbing to dragon-wrath. He accidentally set a few houses on fire during the fight. It was quite a nasty sight after it was all over. Jacob really took it hard."

Sally gasped. "Is Jacob hurt? Is he okay?"

"He's not hurt, but he's blaming himself for the incident. He wouldn't talk to me and instead flew off. I haven't seen him since. Right now, I believe he's somewhere north of here. I'm trying to pick up his scent."

"Do you really think we can find him today?" Reno asked with doubt in her voice.

"I have hope," said Clipper, "but we better keep going. I don't know how much time we have. I need to talk to him before it's too late."

"I want to leave now, but I'm so tired and thirsty," Reno said, fighting back a yawn.

"We can rest, but not for too long," said Clipper. "There are others following him, too. If we cross a freshwater lake or river, Reno can take a drink and maybe have something to eat."

I stayed where I was all that day and throughout the night, until early the next morning. I pressed my head on a soft bank of snow.

"Why can't I get to sleep?" I moaned.

My muddled mind remained awake. I had not slept in days, and I certainly was not going to sleep in this snow patch. No matter how much I tried to think about something else, my thoughts did not leave the incident. I tore the darkscale's throat over and over again in my mind. I could not get that "satisfying" taste of salty blood off my savage tongue. At least nobody was in danger, I decided. Being so far away from civilization offered a little comfort.

I was about to place my head back on the ground when I felt my stomach rumble. I needed to eat something soon. The thought of anything edible from the water came to mind and made me drool. Finally, something that might distract me from my pain! I had to find some sort of water source or I would have to search for land prey. I stretched once I got to my feet. My stiff joints popped and twisted. I flapped my wings a few times to loosen them, making the snow flurry around me. Following a yawn, I jumped into the air where I scanned the land below. I soon found a semi-frozen, highland pond. I landed on its bank. Taking a step closer, I dipped my paw into what would have been freezing water. I knew my internal heat kept me warm, so I dropped my head underwater and searched for anything appetizing. Steam and bubbles came from my open mouth. I looked everywhere, but found nothing worth eating. I lifted my head back out of the pond. My stomach hurt even more, and the cold water caused my sense of smell to temporarily weaken. I sat down in discouragement.

"I'm very hungry. I wish the fairies were with me. They would get me out of this slump," I murmured.

"I'm no fairy but I'm 'ere," a serpentine voice replied.

The sudden arrival caused me to jump. I slipped awkwardly into the pond. Huffing, I quickly crawled back out and shook off the water. I crouched in defense when I realized who had spoken to me.

"Syntare, what are you doing here?"

The black darkscale snickered. "Oh, ya don't need ta prepare fer a fight, Jacob. Look at yerself, yer sta'tled like a li'l grøl. Yer still livin' on this first earth, I see. Ya know nothin' what it's like on the second." Despite her hideous voice, it almost sounded sweet in my ears when she wasn't threatening me.

Syntare moved to the pond where she stared at her reflection. She appeared to think that I was no threat to her at all. Recalling how aggressively she had fought before, I never thought she could be so subdued.

"Quiet day it is," she said serenely.

"I know why you're here," I said. "You're trying to stop me from finding the six pieces. You followed me here because you don't want me to return to Elsov. That's why all those goblins and dwarfs are here as well."

"Yer assumption's quite accurate," Syntare assured me, "but there's more. I've told ya this before. D'ya 'ave fish tails in yer ears or somethin'?" She took a step closer to me. There was a funny twinkle in her eyes. "Ya'd die if ya don't b'come yer da'k self. Look at ya. Yer a da'kscale! Ya look almost exactly like me. We 'ave much in common, but I can give ya pain that'd make ya wish for an ice blade." I growled, but Syntare went on. "I've encountered ya before. I fought with li'l effort and ya faced trouble despite. If ya jus' let yer natural-self fly out, ya'd be invincible! Right now, ya can't 'urt me. I assume ya 'ave a bad temper? So do I. I believe yer sorrow's in control now."

"Quiet!" I snapped.

Syntare responded by making a feminine giggle. "Haha! I can teach ya 'ow ta change it back. Let me say it again, yer a da'kscale. Tell ya the truth, I was quite impressed by the way ya 'andled my comrade by the neck before the iron beast fell. Yes, my comrade's dead, but that's no matter ta me. Why don't ya fight me like yer true self? I know ya 'ave a fever inside ya. I can see it. Yer eyes are glowin', I see."

She was right. I could feel my anger starting to grow when she mentioned the train incident and mocked my weakness. I knew I had a bad temper, and I knew she was aware of that as well.

"Never mention that incident again!" I barked. "Why would you be happy that lives have been lost? I won't follow your ways even if I die under your claws!"

"Ya don't mean that, sweet Jacob," she said, smiling innocently.

I bared my teeth and hissed. "I told you, I won't follow your ways and you know it! Now leave me alone!"

At first, Syntare began to whimper as if I had hurt her feelings. She turned her head away and said something I could not understand. I heard her mutter and snivel. I was beginning to feel bad. Not once had I expected to hurt her in such a way.

She then turned her head back to me and snarled.

"I warned ya!"

She suddenly lowered her horns and struck me down. I quickly got back to my feet and let out a small flame at her. With my claws ready to fight, I knew my fury was definitely rising. I jumped forward and swiped my claws. Just as I expected, she fought back with a similar level of rage; or possibly she had more. We both roared and screeched as we fought. The sound echoed over the mountainside. A giant mist of snow blew into the air. Junipers, cottonwoods, and other kinds of trees were knocked to the ground. Sagebrush was crushed beneath our feet.

Call it fate or simple lack of experience, but my little uprising was brief. She again pinned me down on the exposed layer of mud. Her rear feet kept my wings down while her front paws kept my back in place.

"Oh, Jacob," she laughed. "Ya fight like a coward."

"Why don't you just kill me right now?" I retorted.

"Oh, sweet Jacob," she said. "I'll let ya live 'cause I like ya, but right now I'd like ta show ya what happens ta grøls or dwarfs when I get 'em under my claws."

She exposed her sharp teeth when she finished speaking. But before she could lay any real harm on me, she lifted her head like a fox that heard the bay of a hound. Her eyes squinted in anger. From behind, I heard another voice.

"Get off him!"

The pressure lifted off my back. Syntare yapped before getting struck off me. Breaking a fir trunk as she tumbled, it tore away from its stump and fell over her back. She remained stuck underneath the tree, dazed from the blow. I stood back up and turned around to find another darkscale. This time it was someone I trusted.

"Clipper, when did you get here?" I asked.

Clipper's mouth was wide open, his tail mobile in his excitement. "Jacob! I knew I'd find you! Thank goodness you're safe!"

He rushed over and playfully butted me with his horns. He was filled with happiness, quite the opposite of my sickened feelings.

"I said when did you find me?" I asked again.

"I was following you. I'm not getting the six pieces alone," he said.

"I'm not letting you come with me," I told him. It was firm reply that was even a little harsh.

Clipper's tail drooped in confusion. "What do you mean? I'll always help you. We're best friends, Jacob. As a matter of fact, Sally and Reno are here as well. Why do you want to go alone? You know that I'm dying to go home as much as you are."

"Something bad will happen," I said. "Save yourself while you can. Those who are with me will get hurt. You should know that by now."

"That's not true," said Clipper. "The spirit's right, you've gone to the edge, Jacob. You need to fight to the finish or you'll fall."

I glared at him. "What are you talking about?"

"A few days ago, the dragon of old spoke to me. He gave me a vision. I had to cross a narrow land-bridge over a deep canyon to get to a beautiful green land. The food that I found on the ground was strange but delicious. Metaphorically speaking, if you want to cross this dark canyon, you have to stay straight and true to the center or you'll fall into the raging river below. In my dream, someone else tried to cross the bridge without keeping to the center. He didn't make it."

I didn't listen at first, but I started paying attention after he mentioned the last part. "Are you saying I'm the one about to fall off this bridge?"

"Yeah, but I'm going to help you back up."

"Something will happen," I said, "I just know it. I don't want to take you down with me. This must be why I had to fight Syntare. I'm drowning and if you come, you'll drown too."

Before Clipper could say anything else, I spread my wings and left him alone with Syntare. Clipper watched me fly off into the distance. I landed at the base of a small hill several miles away.

"I HEARD WHAT HAPPENED," SAID SALLY WHEN CLIPPER RETURNED. "He doesn't sound well. Did he just fight another dragon?"

"Yes, but she'll be down for a while. I've got to find a way to get closer to Jacob. I won't let him go, no matter what happens to me. He's not falling into the abyss while I'm alive."

"Maybe *I* can talk to him," said Sally. "You two are close friends, but I'm also his friend. I know we occasionally disagree on some things, but two heads are better than one."

Clipper blew some smoke out his nostrils. "Maybe you're right."

They prepared to leave when Sally heard Syntare make some chattering noise.

"Can we find him now?" Reno pleaded. "I don't want to be here when the other one is nearby."

The three looked in the direction of Syntare's noises. They all prepared to fight when they saw Syntare take to the air. But instead of attacking them, she snorted and flew away in the other direction.

"Why did she do that?' asked Reno.

"I don't know," said Clipper, confused.

"Well, we don't need to worry about her for now, I guess," said Sally. "I'm going to look for Jacob."

Reno moved over and sat next to Clipper after Sally took off. "What's going to happen to Jacob?" she asked.

Clipper bowed his head. "I haven't a clue, but we're not giving up."

"I hope we will see him again," Reno said sadly.

Clipper gave a mournful sigh. "I do too."

JUST AS BEFORE, I LAY ALONE IN THE SNOW. SALLY LANDED NEXT to me and sat down.

"You know, sitting like a dragon is a lot different than how I've always done it, yet it feels natural now."

"What do you want?" I huffed.

"The same thing that Clipper wants. We want to find the pieces to the portal together. I know you don't want to go to your home world alone. You need to be with your friends and maybe soon your family."

"My family will die if I find them. I'll live on Elsov alone," I growled.

Sally snorted. "You're funny. By the way, I don't know if you're hungry or not, but we're not far from a good source of food. Have something to eat, and then you'll feel better. You know, I didn't realize how cold it would get here. It's kind of strange to see this much snow this early in the year. But it is beautiful here in Utah, I must say."

"I wasn't aware we were in Utah," I said in an expressionless tone.

"Well, we are. I believe we're near the first piece, as a matter of fact. We better get going before your friend comes back."

I didn't respond. Sally glared at me, her emotions evident in her dragon face.

"You know, when you got that message from the fairies all those months ago, you were very excited. I could hardly keep you in your scales. Now look at you. You're dull and lazy. Was it because of the train crash? Clipper told me about that."

I stood up and roared at her. "You have no voice in that! I did some disgusting things there that I can't forgive myself from doing them, so just leave me alone!"

Sally lowered her horns and lurched forward. Her powerful horns knocked me off balance, though not quite off my feet.

"I'm your friend, you idiot! I'm not going to let this misunderstanding ruin you. I'm going with you and that's final. That goes for Clipper and Reno, too."

I blew a flame at her. "I said leave me alone! I'm a darkscale! Maybe Syntare's right. Maybe I should— I should—"

I couldn't bring myself to open my feelings to Sally, so I left her on the hill. I again was in the air, wanting to lose her and the others. My anger and guilt were forcing me away from my friends, but my strong ties to them were pulling me back. There were two forces dragging me in opposite directions. I wanted to free myself from that bondage. Flying for about five minutes, I hissed and huffed from my emotional chaos. In the air, a second white knoll caught my eye. I landed on the gentle slope.

"They're probably following me," I fumed.

Having others find me and never leave was starting to annoy me. I began searching for somewhere to hide. As luck would have it, I found a small cave in the ground. It was dimly lit by an unknown source. I figured I could hide in there for the time being.

I brushed some flakes of snow off my snout and crept in the hill's cavity.

What if they find this cave? I wondered. I didn't want that. I was just about to turn around when a soft whisper reached my ears.

"Jacob."

The voice sounded like the spirit's, only this time it was an actual sound that traveled through my ears rather than a feeling. Still intent on leaving, I tried to turn around. But the voice again reached my ears. It was only a faint, gentle voice.

"Jacob. Jacob Draco."

In the wintry weather, I felt a warm, comfortable breeze coming from inside the cave. I wanted to leave, but curiosity got the better of me. I folded my wings tight against my body and decided to explore deeper.

"Sorry Clipper, I did the best I could," said Sally when she returned.

Clipper licked the base of his long fangs, reining in his feelings of grief. "Oh, I don't know how to get him back now. I don't want to lose him for good. We were planning to revisit Pearl Forest together. We now know how to get back and I don't want this to stop us."

He looked down to find Reno's eyes glistening with tears. She rolled onto her side. "I don't want to see him go. What's happening to us?" she said forlornly.

The three sat still, each saying a personal prayer. After Clipper finished, he looked up into the sky. His eyes suddenly widened. A strange, dim green ball of light was floating above his head.

"Do you see that?" he asked the others.

Sally was mesmerized by the mysterious sight. "It's a green light. Look, it's getting brighter. What is it?"

Sally and Clipper were prepared to run, but realized that there was no real threat to them. Other lights became visible in the woods beyond. Clipper suspected what the lights were. The one above their heads darkened. As it did, a figure appeared.

"It's beautiful," said Reno. "I don't think it's dangerous. I wonder what it is."

Clipper gazed at the mysterious being. "I'm sure I've seen someone like her before."

Sally, dumbfounded at the sight, said nothing. She watched as the figure, about the height of any human, approached her.

The figure's fine gown and clear wings left no question in Clipper's mind as to what she was. He remembered the fairies from his vision of Elsov. The memories of the plains and Pearl Forest came back to him. The fairies had informed him of the three different worlds. He also remembered the peaceful feelings while there and how his wounds had been healed. All fear within him turned to hope. This land was indeed enchanted!

"Be calm," the fairy said in a soft voice. "I am one of many here."

"What is it?" Reno asked in awe.

"She's a fairy," Clipper whispered back. "I never knew they were on this world."

"We have seen your friend in his grief," the fairy said to the three. "The dragon of old is ready to speak to him. Wait here until your friend returns. This is an enchanted land. Strong magic lives here, both light and dark. Seek the light and beware the sorcery. Where the first piece lays, the sorcery of cold reigns. This answers your question to the premature snow. The weather should not be as frigid as it is now."

"We have to battle against cold sorcery to find the first piece?" Clipper asked.

The fairy nodded. "You have the power of knowledge. You know this is a special land. I know your other friend holds the viewing ring. But if you collect the first piece, your sense of direction will guide you to the rest. The first piece will be difficult to acquire. Have courage. Do not run. As I leave, the Militia will protect you."

Clipper was about to ask what the Militia was when the fairy vanished. The bright green light was gone. The lights in the distance faded as well. The three friends were back in the bright morning. Each dragon in the group stared at the others, all sitting stunned and wide-eyed.

"That's the first time I've seen a fairy," said Reno, taking deep breaths.

"Oh, Jacob," Sally sighed. "She said the dragon of old is going to speak to him, wherever he is."

"I certainly hope the spirit can get to Jacob," said Clipper.

CHAPTER 22

ELEMEK'S VISIT

The voice called my name again. It was a very faint call.

"Jacob Draco."

I tried to squeeze my wings through the darkening tunnel. For a small hill, the tunnel was a lot longer than I expected. I soon came to the end where I was met with a snowy wall. The tunnel widened into a small, shallow room. I was surprised to find that the walls here were bathed in a dark blue light. But where was the light coming from? It should be completely dark in a cave like this, though I would still be able to see with my keen eyes. I found my answer when I noticed, embedded in the opposite wall, a small bright object that gave light to the cave. I crept up to it and inspected it. It was a crystal, a bright blue crystal. I lifted a paw from the ground and was about to touch it. When my claw was just an inch away, I felt an uncanny wind brush by me. I heard the voice again. This time it was much closer and clearer, as if someone was right next to me.

"Jacob Draco."

I had no idea where the voice was coming from. In my depressed state, my first desire was to turn and leave. But before I could, the voice said something more than just my name.

"Jacob Draco, do not leave. This is a sacred spot."

I wanted to leave before the voice spoke again, but something prevented me from doing so. It sounded like the voice of a dragon, as calm as a dragon's voice can be. I turned around to face the crystal and decided to reply to it.

"Are you the same spirit who was with me before?"

"*I am the same spirit, yes,*" said the voice. "*I have guided you along your path. Now it seems you need me again. I come when needed. Do you want to know my name?*"

"Yes," I said in a low tone.

"*Very well, I have been called by many names. My name at birth was Yosutan. I have had many other names as well, but that was when I served the ruthless monarchy during the first Vesuvian war. When I discovered life beyond that tyrannical crown, I took a more appealing name: Elemek.*"

"You want me to call you Elemek?" I asked.

I heard a deep, rasping inhale before he gave me an answer. "*Yes, I am Elemek. I am one of the few who have come to this earth from Elsov. Many stories and legends have sprouted from my existence and the existence of my kin. Some are good, most are not.*"

"So that's why some people have knowledge of the other world," I said.

"*Yes, some know of Elsov. You may remember the old man who showed you the carving in the stone. Knowledge of the second earth is scarce, but it's not extinct. Some of these people who know may help you find the six pieces. For most, the stories are in fragments. Since I have discovered the people of the first earth, I have helped them. After I left, my enemies spread the reputation of the darkscale, mostly over the land of Europe. Unfortunately most of their stories are true.*"

"I can easily see that," I said. "Dragons are awful creatures, I've come to notice."

"*When I hatched from the egg, all dragons were darkscales. We were not called darkscales at the time, for we were all dark at heart. I was evil. I lusted for power. All I trusted was my greed and pride, and never did I care about others. That all changed when I was rescued by fairies after being wounded. On a day I will never forget, I had planned to attack a human village. I had killed many humans before at this point. My life changed when I noticed one man at this particular village was a professional dragon slayer, and had a rare, ice arrow. I should have remembered the enchanted weaponry crafted by ancient warlocks, but I was too foolish. I was shot in the chest, just below my lungs. Other arrows pierced my wings. After the failed attack, I landed in the mountains, no longer able to fly. When the fairies nursed me back to health, I still had my young desires. I was no older than you are now."*

"The fairies taught you their ways?" I asked.

"They did. As a juvenile, the fairies did not let me go home to my kingdom. Each time I lost my patience, I would try to attack one. With their unpredictable magic, however, I fell into humiliating traps. Once they even made me fall out of a tree, into a river. When I realized how powerless I really was, I sat on the riverbank in anger and despair. I felt the same way you feel right now. I clawed the ground and began weeping. My heart melted and became tears in my eyes. For the first time in my life, I had no desire to hurt anymore. Even the local grøls began to wander closer to me. I still remember their famous 'yips' when they ran off after I growled at them. There I sat, for days and nights. The fish swam freely in the river; I did not care. As I was overcome by hunger, one of the fairies appeared above my head. She spoke of the rewards of wisdom. That was when I realized I had to change. The feeling in my heart was an experience I would never forget. As I reached the end of my life, I was placed under a spell that works like this: if my offspring followed my new path, they would differ from those we now call darkscales."

"And lightscales exist today," I said. "You can easily tell I'm not one of them. Look at me. Look at what I've done! The black dragon has the worst fury of any dragon and I know that. I don't think there's a way to save me. I caused a train wreck, and I did other horrible things! How can I possibly forgive myself?"

"You seem as upset as I was," said Elemek. "It seems now you are in need of some counseling before you become what Yosutan was. Yosutan had counseling from the fairies, and now he is Elemek."

I turned back to the tunnel. "I can't be helped, Elemek. Sorry. There's no return. How many homes were destroyed? How many lives were lost? I can't possibly deal with that burden!"

I continued into the tunnel, but then the small breeze became a sudden strong wind. Crystallized snow blew all around me. The mighty wind pushed me to the ground and back into the room. The awkward position of my tail made the impact with the ground even more uncomfortable.

At that point, Elemek's voice roared into my ears, *"Did I not guide you when you became who you are? Did I not help at all? Did I not give you the visions? I am not going to leave you until you are ready, Jacob Draco! You can overcome the darkscale within you! Stop your selfishness and resist the hardening of your heart! Soften your heart, Jacob!* **Do NOT let the cunning Vesuvius deceive you!** *Did you not notice that you couldn't hear me until now?"*

The spirit of Elemek struck me down with more power than I ever imagined. His voice physically pressed me to the ground. The joints in my wings and tail were stretched until they hurt. Elemek's power engulfed me, causing me to lose control of my emotions. Tears poured from my eyes. My chest ached from all the sniffling. Something crept inside me, though, into my darkening heart. I felt it changing me!

I soon began to breathe normally. I stood up and turned to face the bright crystal. I blinked many times. The blue light had turned into the color of brass. Looking at the brass color lifted my spirits. I felt at peace for the first time in weeks. I was finally free from the awful guilt. Free!

Elemek spoke softly to me once I was calm. *"Jacob, you are not evil. It was not your fault, yet you fell into Vesuvius' trap. I saw the entire incident from the third earth. If you continue to live the way you have before the incident, you will be granted a peaceful afterlife. But you must let go of the natural dragon. Let it go, Jacob, before it's too late!"*

His words struck me like lightning. The darkness and dread inside me brightened into light of joy. Tears trickled down my snout, this time for different reasons. I lifted my forepaws from the ground and stared at them. My scales were as black as night, no change there. But that was only my physical appearance. I knew that I was not evil. Elemek was right, I had to let go of the natural dragon!

"*Your black scales tell you nothing about who you are,*" said Elemek. "*You must know this. Through the power of an ancient spell, you were born with the appearance a darkscale. That does not mean you must follow their ways.*"

I blinked away another tear. "I know. I may look evil, but I'm not. Oh, I'm sorry I ever doubted you, Elemek. I'll do better. I'll be the dragon you want me to be."

The brass light covered me. Elemek made a low hum of satisfaction.

"*Oh, Jacob, I'm helping you find your way back to your home. I will come if you need me. Right now, you have many challenges ahead of you. Finding the six pieces of the portal will not be easy. You must battle the fires and the cold. The first piece lies near the tallest peak of the mountains north of this valley. You are closer than you think. Be aware that the piece is heavily guarded by the ice warlock and those who serve him: ice dragons.*"

"I've been told about ice dragons," I said. "They were little ones who were kidnapped and cursed. They don't know who they are or what they're doing."

"*You're right,*" said Elemek. "*They will stop at nothing to do what their warlock requires of them. The warlock's name is Glaciem. He creates the enchanted weaponry that can pierce through a dragon's scales, the ice blade.*"

"Yeah, I've seen ice blades in the hands of our enemies before. Even Triathra used an ice blade. Clipper was badly wounded because of it."

"*Indeed, it is dangerous, but you can succeed. Fight for right and I will be with you when you need me. I will help you back onto the bridge above the abyss. There will be enemies after you. Some will tempt you. Their words may sound convincing, but remember my words: do what you must. I will help you when you need me, Jacob.*"

"*I will help you when you need me, Jacob.*"

His voice disappeared as softly as it had come. The crystal began to darken until it was no longer glowing. There was little light in the cave now, but I found my way out with my pupils dilated. My grief and sorrow were gone. They were replaced with relief. With my tears drying, I made my way out of the cave. Now that I could spread my wings, I took flight, ready to find my friends who did not give up on me when I needed them most.

"Clipper! Sally! Reno! I'm coming!" I called when I saw them.

It was Reno who first raised her head. The three were standing close together. The second she heard my voice, Reno spread her wings. We both collided in midair and fell to the ground next to Clipper and Sally. Neither of us were hurt.

"You're okay!" Sally cried in relief. "What's gotten into you?"

It took a moment for me to find the right words. "I'm sorry for how I acted," I said, swallowing. "The recent events really bit at me. You won't believe this, but I spoke with the dragon of old. He said his name is Elemek."

"Elemek," said Clipper with light in his eyes. "He told you his name? The fairy was right about him. Elemek... I never even considered his name."

"I didn't know a fairy visited you," I said, fighting more tears of emotion. "I believe we all have much-needed help. Look, I understand now that the train crash was a tragedy, and I still regret doing what I did to that darkscale. All I can do now is to remember my past and either learn from it and improve myself or sit in grief and have it destroy me. Let's go create that portal. I'm sorry I left you all behind."

"Don't worry about that," said Clipper, smiling.

"We're together now. That's what matters," said Sally.

I felt a little embarrassed at what I had said, but I didn't care much about it. Grief was no longer dragging me down. I knew the fairies were on my side. I knew Elemek was on my side

CHAPTER 23

The Blue Blade & the Lightscale

William and Henry were frustrated because they were unable to help as much as they wished. Their parents, however, did not remain idle. Charles and Franklin, along with Henry's parents, went to the library to gather more information on past and present dragon sightings while the boys stayed home, waiting in the living room in Franklin's house.

"Two different worlds, yet we know how they come together," Henry said to William.

"You know, my dad told me what he knew about Elsov now that we've met the dragons," said William. "He admits that he doesn't know everything about that world, but I say he knows a lot more than most people do. He told me that the monster that attacked Jacob and Clipper was a Unitaur, which is a female *Mino*taur."

"Are you upset at all that he didn't tell you anything about Elsov until recently?" Henry asked.

"No. The only reason why he did tell me now was because I had already seen the dragons. This whole situation was a need-to-know basis, and by chance I needed to know, along with you. We can't tell anyone, just to keep others safe. So no, I'm not upset."

"That's good to hear," said Henry.

Emily soon returned home from her music lessons. Setting her flute case at the end of the couch, she joined the two boys who were waiting for her.

"Were you two talking about the dragons?" she asked.

William felt the hair on his arms stand straight up. He didn't expect Emily to ask him that. He knew she was aware of the sightings, but how did she know he and Henry were talking about them? William asked her that very question.

"How could I not guess?" she said. "I knew something strange was going on in the cabin, but I didn't think much of it at first. When I started hearing about the dragons being sighted around here, and remembering the sergeant inspecting the house before Joshua moved in, it got me thinking. Even after that big fight by our house, I still wasn't sure."

"But you know now," Henry told her.

Emily shut her eyes and shook her head, as if she suddenly remembered an old pain. "When I was in town, before my music lessons, I noticed something different, and not in a good way. Everyone seemed… scared. The streets were empty, except for a few police cars. It's like everyone had taken shelter for an upcoming gunfight or something. It was eerie."

"Do you think it's linked to the dragons?" William asked.

"What, with that fight in our yard? Yeah, I think there is a link. Isn't that why our parents are gone?"

William was lost in thought for a moment. Emily might have been right about the connection. If that was true, then the people could be sensing something else coming! Could it be another Minotaur? A swarm of goblins? A cult of wraiths? The undead rising? With his father gone, William began to feel unsafe. Only one logical idea came to his mind. He pointed out the window. "How about we look around where the fight happened? Joshua said he wouldn't mind if we go in his yard."

Emily was still nervous, but she and Henry followed William outside. They crossed lawns and approached the cabin, which was almost completely repaired. William grew determined to find answers at the site of the Minotaur's battle.

Henry understood what William wanted to do. "Look for anything out of the ordinary," he suggested. "If there's something that looks the least bit strange, show it to the rest of us."

The three friends began their search, keeping their eyes on the ground. William ran his eyes along the foundation of the house while Henry ran his hands over the newly laid grass. They went their own directions about the yard.

After a few minutes, Henry went over to where William was looking. "We haven't found anything yet," he said. "There's nothing here. I think if there was something, it's been removed by now."

"I'm sure if anyone else got their hands on any magical object, they'd be questioning it," said William. "They wouldn't know what it is."

They continued searching around the southern perimeter of the cabin. After a few more minutes, Emily called the boys to the backyard. Henry and William ran to her, both shocked at what she had found in a pile of disturbed soil. It looked like a blue sword.

William took a closer examination of it, though he was strictly cautious. "What is it?"

"Do you think I know?" Emily replied. "I saw it slightly buried here by the house. Just the tip of the handle was sticking out of the ground. Suppose this weapon was forged by 'evil magic'?"

"A sword that could harm a dragon?" Henry guessed.

William admired their hypotheses. "Since when were you two into the subject of 'evil magic'?"

"I don't know," said Emily. "You saw that book I had about elves when you came here. That's the most I know about magic, and that book is more than likely irrelevant with this sword."

"All right, so this blade could be enchanted," said Henry.

William crouched to get another close look at the sword, wondering what sort of power it had. He held his finger over the icy tip to give it a feathery touch. After just one tiny prick, he immediately withdrew his hand.

"Ah! It's so cold! My finger stings!"

"Are you all right?" asked Emily. "You're bleeding!"

Even though William had barely touched the blade, a nasty wound appeared on his finger. He pinched the spot to stop the bleeding.

"If it can slice flesh like that, I wonder how it affects dragon scales," he said.

Careful not to touch the blade again, William took another close look at the blue-flowing weapon. The more he stared at it, the more confused he was. The silver cloth-bound handle looked harmless. But the blade... what kind of blade was it? What was it made of?

Joshua came home not long after Emily found the ice blade. The three friends returned to the front yard to meet him. Like Emily, he also seemed tense.

"Hey guys, what are you doing here?" he asked.

"Show him the sword," said Emily. "He might know a little more about it."

Joshua followed them to the backyard where the ice blade lay.

"Emily found this half-buried here," said William.

Joshua's uneasy mood worsened upon seeing it. Though astounded, he carefully picked it up by the handle and leaned it against the wall.

"Jacob told me about swords like this," he said. "They're very deadly."

The lonely sound of the seashore was suddenly broken by an approaching car. Joshua peeked around the corner to the front and then immediately ran for the back door.

"We've got to get inside! Hurry!" he ordered.

The urgency in his voice told the kids something was terribly wrong. Joshua led them in his house and slammed the door shut. He then went into the living room and peeked out the front window as the car drove past. With a sigh of relief, he closed the curtains.

"What's going on?" Henry asked nervously.

Joshua was about to answer when another sound came from outside, as if someone was knocking on the door to Franklin's house. Joshua held up a finger to indicate silence. He cracked open the front door and peeked out, then quietly closed and locked it.

Emily began to hyperventilate, unsure of what had scared Joshua. "Just what is going on?" she asked.

Joshua led her and the boys upstairs into his study. In that room was a small couch. Joshua let his visitors sit there while he took a seat in his desk chair.

Beads of perspiration appeared on the boys' forehead. They didn't know what was out there, but they knew it was something threatening. Emily could hardly take in what was happening. She continued hyperventilating while her face turned pale. Henry and William tried to calm her as she took an inhaler out of her pocket.

"I'm sorry, I'm not meaning to scare you," said Joshua, "but this is serious. I was at the bookstore before I came home. I overheard the cashier and some man talking about Franklin."

"My dad?" cried Emily.

"Keep quiet!" Joshua warned. "He's still out there. Anyway, the man was aware of Charles staying at Franklin's house. He said something about Charles knowing the 'traitors'. The cashier then talked about the recent dragon sightings that have been happening nearby. Then the other man said something about the fall of the Monolegions. I left as discretely as I could after that. I knew they didn't know my connections, but I didn't want to look suspicious."

"That bookstore is run by Mr. and Mrs. Ellis," said Henry. "Do you think they're aware of the dragons as we are?"

Joshua shook his head. "I don't know, but it's possible."

"What are Monolegions?" Emily asked after catching her breath.

"They were the last Nibelung dwarf tribe on this earth," said Joshua. "They were the reasons Jacob and Clipper came here in the first place. For the most part, the Monolegions have been disbanded, so I've heard, but I think there are many dwarfs still out there. They must know about Charles and that he's here."

The sound of the doorbell interrupted Joshua's story. William, Henry, and Emily jumped at the sound if it.

"Be calm and hold still," Joshua whispered.

The doorbell rang again. Nobody in the study moved. William didn't know for sure if it was the same man Joshua had talked about. If it was, and if he was a part of this Monolegion tribe, then everyone in the house could be in a lot of danger! The tension grew when they heard the doorknob jiggle violently. Had Joshua not locked the door, the man could have come inside!

The doorbell kept ringing and the knob kept jiggling for several minutes, which felt more like several hours. At last there was silence. Joshua slipped downstairs first to check if it was safe. He brought the kids down when he knew for sure the coast was clear.

"I knew it," said Emily. "There is something wrong. William, someone is after your dad; and mine too! And Joshua, you said he was at the bookstore? That's right next to the library! That's where our parents are right now!"

"Well, clearly he didn't know that," said Joshua. "If he was knocking your door and ringing my doorbell, that must mean they're still looking for them. Don't worry; your parents will be safe."

"That may be, but I don't think it's safe for us to go outside for a while," Henry said. "What should we do in the meantime?"

Joshua made sure the ice blade could not be seen from the window. "You three can stay here until your parents come home. When they do, don't mention the ice blade to anyone or give hints about it. I'll talk to them about it when the time is right."

William could tell his friends were scared out of their wits. They had a good reason to be. This was no longer just a matter of meeting friendly dragons for the first time. This was now a matter of life and death with forces he couldn't even begin to understand! William did not know much about the Monolegions, but he believed they were a serious threat, even if they were ultimately defeated. He didn't think Henry or Emily were in the same danger that he was in, but he didn't want them to get caught in the cross-fire. As of that evening, William knew he and his father were in a dire circumstance, and the only thing he could do was wait it out and hope for the best.

CHANG PEERED OUT OF THE WINDOW OF THE CHARTER AIRPLANE over the mighty Rocky Mountains. His friend, Duncan, piloted the plane. Chang knew he could not stay at home after losing contact with all of his friends, especially since he had the viewing ring. It took him a while to find an opportunity to fly to St. George, but he was on his way as soon as the chance came. Duncan had been Chang's trainer over the summer, and the two of them had grown to be good friends. Duncan was unaware of the six pieces, however, but he could tell by Chang's mood that the flight to Utah was a matter of grave business.

"So why is it you have to go to St. George?" Duncan asked Chang about halfway into their flight.

Chang thought for a moment. "Jacob and Clipper are there looking for something. They need my help." He didn't mention to Duncan that we were the dragons everyone was talking about.

"What are you going to do once you find them?" Duncan continued.

Chang hesitated before answering. "That's personal. You know how it is."

Upon hearing the word "personal", Duncan chose not to ask any more questions. He instead began to talk with Chang about more appropriate subjects in flying until it was time to land. Once on the ground, Chang gave one last goodbye to his trainer before limping out of the hangar. He was glad that he no longer needed his crutches.

As Sally had done during her search for the Guarded Forest, Chang researched dragon sightings before he left. In a car he had rented in St. George, he headed for the most recent sighting, which was not far from Cedar City. When he made it to the reported location, he found the landscape was painted with the common autumn colors of red and orange; along with the abundant green of junipers. He eyed low clouds covering the higher peaks. The weather itself was cloudy and cool, which Chang found pleasant. With the help of the viewing ring, he made his way east of Cedar to the head of a hiking trail in Dixie Forest. Parking his car, he started up the trail to see if the red in the ring grew any bigger. After an hour or so with no luck, he decided to sit down on a bench and elevate his foot. The rest gave him some time to enjoy the fresh, clean air. No place offered such an appreciation for life as much as a forest did in Chang's opinion.

The whisper of the peaceful breeze was interrupted by footsteps behind him, off the trail. Chang stiffened as he slowly turned his head. He first thought it was another hiker, but then he knew otherwise. He carefully rose to his feet and moved quietly away from the bench. He stepped off the trail, into some thick brush. Not a moment later, he heard the footsteps getting closer, along with raspy breathing. When the creature was close enough, Chang lifted his head to see what it was. To his surprise, it was no common animal. It was a dragon! The beast suddenly noticed Chang and growled. Chang backed away, trembling in fear.

"Stay back or you will regret it!" the unknown dragon hissed.

"Who are you?" Chang replied. "If you've come for my friends, they're not here. How did you know where to find me of all people?"

The dragon huffed. "So you can speak the language? What is it called again, Anglish?"

"English," Chang corrected. "Now you stay away! I'm one of few who know about creatures like you."

Chang knew he couldn't run with his bad foot. He wouldn't outrun the dragon on healthy feet anyway. All he could do was stare into the creature's green eyes. Green eyes! Chang remembered what Fenson had told him about the most major physical difference between darkscales and lightscales.

Still feeling threatened, he said, "Who are you? I know you can understand me. Are you a lightscale? Are you from Elsov?"

Now it was the orange dragon who took a step back, only this time it was out of surprise rather than fear. "Yes, I am a lightscale," he said. "How do you know about the other world? I was told humans like you are not aware of the second earth."

Chang felt a bit more at ease. "I have friends who are from your world. As a matter of fact, they're trying to find a way to return. Tell me how you were able to get here."

"I've come to help the portal seekers," the dragon answered. "The Grün-hære is after them and I wish to offer preparation."

It was "portal seekers" that caught Chang's attention. "You're helping Jacob and Clipper? They're my friends! We're both looking for the same dragons! How do you know them?"

The dragon looked Chang up and down, obviously becoming nervous. "I was told there was only one who knows about the portal seekers, and that I should only speak to that one. What is your name?"

"Lewis Chang."

"You are Lewis Chang? I was told about you!"

"Hold on, you still didn't answer my question. What is *your* name?"

The dragon stood straight and tall. "I'm Auben."

He gently raised a paw from the ground and held it up for Chang to shake.

"Auben," Chang said, "nice to meet you."

After the hand-paw shake, Auben huffed anxiously. "We must find Jacob and Clipper! We must leave right away."

Auben spread his wings. Chang cleared his throat before he took off.

"Slow down, Auben. We have to be careful. We shouldn't attract attention to ourselves. We can share information and understand each other as we travel. Just hide in the thicket if somebody comes by."

Auben took a deep breath, fighting his impatience. "Agreed, but we must hurry. Many of us have left our homes to help Jacob and Clipper. Monsters will be stirring back on Elsov. I don't want my friends and family to be harmed."

"I'll do the best I can," said Chang.

He and Auben continued up the trail. There was much to talk about between the two of them.

Jordan B. Jolley

CHAPTER 24

PIERRE

Auben's prediction was correct. Monsters from all over Elsov were making their presence known, now that the news of the black dragon was spreading far and wide. Trihan also knew this would happen. There was a tangible sense of fear across the land and he felt the weight of it upon his shoulders. That afternoon, he decided to go for a walk to clear his mind. He first made a quick stop at the stable to feed Fenson's mare before pressing on into Pearl Forest. The fairies' magic that was everywhere helped ease some of Trihan's stress as he walked. He soon decided to take a seat on a fallen log where he could let the magic sway around him for a while. As much peace as there was, though, there was one particular thought that would not leave the Keeper's mind: Auben.

"As I've feared, Elsov is different," he said to himself. "One fact is certain: I shouldn't have left poor Auben to wander the halls of my castle. He found my portal and was too stubborn to wait for his friend. The first earth is completely new to him. If he was experienced like Jacob or Clipper, I would trust him. But he is young, prone to mistakes. I don't want him to do something that will cost him his life." Lifting his scepter to eye-level, Trihan took a deep breath. All he could feel was regret. "I need to send someone who the young dragon can trust," he decided after a moment of thinking. "Yes, he needs a companion. Of course, that companion will be just as lost as Auben, but two are more likely than one to get by."

Trihan remained on the log, wondering who he should send. It didn't take long before he thought of a worthy companion; make that the perfect companion! Indeed, it was perfect! But as Trihan stood back up, his concentration was interrupted by a low howl that came from the denseness of the woods. It was a howl that would haunt anyone new to Elsov. It echoed throughout the woods, making it impossible to tell exactly where it had originated. All of the fairies' magic seemed to disappear in an instant. Trihan shook his head, unsurprised. He knew what kind of creatures could make such a howl. It wasn't wolves, but ogres, and not even in the swamplands!

Trihan made sure his scepter was tight in his hands before going into the darkness of the thick forest. Some time later, he paused and listened carefully. He had taken only a few more steps when he heard rustling from nearby bushes. Trihan tapped his scepter on the ground. The jewel on top began to glow like a lantern. A thin screen of dust arose from the ground as a result of Trihan's magic.

"Come out, whoever you are, and identify yourself as friend or foe," he ordered.

There was no answer. Trihan prepared to cast an even greater spell. Before he could send it forth, a large green mass suddenly rolled out from the bushes. Trihan jumped out of the way just in time. The mass rolled past him and stopped dead at a sturdy trunk. Trihan turned to find that it was an injured ogre lying on its back. The clumsy creature got to its feet; its face was battered and bruised, which made his already ugly countenance even more unbearable to gaze upon. The ogre grabbed the Wizard by the shoulders and gurgled something in a disgusting language, obviously panicked. Trihan created a force from his scepter that pushed the pleading ogre back. The green lumbering monster fell again and this time it went to sleep. Trihan knew that whatever had sent it rolling was an experienced fighter, one who was no novice. It could only be the perfect companion Trihan was looking for! He knew its kind were currently in the woods.

"Whoever you are, come please. I won't harm you."

To Trihan's relief, the odd creature stepped out from the shadows. It stood at about the average height of a dwarf and had light-brown fur over its stocky frame. It also had broad, firm feet; a thick, yet flexible tail; and straight, pointed ears that ended with soft black tips. Its large eyes were round and dark which contrasted with its long white whiskers.

When the creature realized that it was Trihan the Keeper standing there, it bent forward and started panting. "G'day, Trihan," it said between breaths. "I sen' me apologiez fer the in'erruption, good wiza'd. These nasty ogres n' such are actin' more strange'n us'al. They're leavin' the swamplands and wanderin' round me home, causin' trouble. Their nonsense has forced our troop to take refuge in this curs'd forest. I've never been this far from me home. I'm cold an' I'm wet an' the insects're drivin' me bloomin' crazy...! And what brings you away from your castle, eh?"

"Your troop was what I had in mind," said Trihan in a pleased voice. "Could you tell me your name please? There is something important that must take place and I need the help of one of your kind."

The creature scratched one of its feet against a stick that stuck out from the ground. He tried to slow his panting before speaking again. "I'm sorry, Trihan. Teachin' that ogre a lesson 'as worn me out. Me real name's somethin' you can't say with your tongue, sadly. The elves call me Jawé. You may call me Pierre. I quite like that, y'know, Pierre."

"Oh, Pierre! Forgive me. It's you who I am seeking."

"Ha! Only we kangrui are able ta tell the diff'rence a'tween each other. So why would you be a-lookin' for me personally?"

Trihan paused, wondering how he should make his request. "I have a... problem with a young lightscaled dragon. A friend of his called him Auben. Do you remember a dragon of that name?"

"Auben? How could I forget me ol' friend?" cried Pierre. "He's kind to all. Good friends with elves, too. I r'member one elf. Loster, if I r'member his name correctly. Sadly, I don't see lightscales much anymore these days. They live far from the plains, y'know. What's wrong? Is Auben in trouble?"

"Well, either answer, a yes or a no, may be right. I have done something foolish…"

Pierre laughed in his kangrui way. "Yak-a-yak-yak-a-hoo-hoo-hoo!! I find that hard t' believe! You've a kind heart, Trihan. You r'spect everyone an' everythin'. I'll help with the power of your magic… eh, spectre or whatever that thing you hold is called. I don't think you've fooled yourself. A wizard never would."

Trihan was not convinced. He explained to Pierre how he had let Auben go to the other world alone. This left the kangrui flabbergasted.

"Er— Trihan…? Eh— I don' know what t'say 'bout this. Not your actions or anythin' o' the like, but in'er-world travelin'? That's somethin' else! I've heard many a legend o' this black an' red dragon, y'know. I was aware they're on the other world. Phew! I fear for Auben's life now! I have little knowledge o' humans, 'cept you're one of 'em. There's no way to know what those on the other world'll do if they see a dragon. You say he's alone?"

"Last I knew," said Trihan. "I'll check back on him once I get home. This is a serious request, Pierre… Will you go find Auben and take care of him? If you decline my request, I will understand."

Pierre lightly stamped his right foot. "Must ya tell me I'm on me way to the first earth? Normally I'd refuse, but this problem n' all. I can't— I want to— I— I don't know the answer. I want t'help Auben. I'd love to return a favor, y'know. But in a world full o' humans? That's a little extreme if I may say."

"I know this is a great thing I ask of you," said Trihan. "Don't think that I'm forcing you. I'm giving you a choice."

Pierre was silent. An expression of sadness crossed his face, which slowly changed into confidence. He took a single hop forward. "If any human attempts a kill, he gets a kick. If he attempts t'lay harm, he gets a set o' me claws to his face. Give me no knife. I will travel lightly if ya please."

"Now you shouldn't look to harm anyone. Only fight in defense," Trihan directed. "Your quest is not simple, but it is very important. Find Auben and help him. Help him find Jacob and Clipper and the others. The Militia, led by the Kuslan Losdir, is currently engaging the Grün-hære."

Pierre clenched his paws. "We kangrui enjoy a good weapon now an' then. But for now, the lighter the load, the better. I need no armor, nothin'. Let me firs' tell me troop where I'm a-goin'. When I return, I'm off."

Even though Trihan felt a little relieved at finding Pierre, he was still concerned for Auben's safety. He did not believe Auben had much experience fighting whatever monsters were roaming the first earth. The Grün-hære was not the only group of enemies there.

CHAPTER 25

ICE CAVERNS

Another day passed. I slept all day to make up for the past grueling days. My grief no longer kept me awake, thankfully. As before, to lessen our chances of being sighted, we flew during the night rather than the day. I remembered Clipper saying we were already in Utah. I didn't care which state we were in just as long as we were close to the first piece. We did not have the viewing ring, but we knew that whatever we were looking for was close by. Elemek said so, and I trusted the wise spirit.

The morning landscape was covered with thick snow, much thicker than it was when Sally and Clipper had found me. We circled around the wild, winter wonderland in order to find a clear spot to rest our feet. There was a steep pass between two valleys that provided just the ticket. As we hovered over the bottom of the cleavage, the wind from our wings created a misty whirlwind of sparkling white snow. Clipper was the first to land. He found that he sank an entire three feet before reaching solid ground.

"The snow's a lot deeper here," he said, digging small a pit around himself. "This might be a good sign."

I landed next to him and created a sloppily-crafted snowball in my paw, tossing it in the air only to have it splatter on my face. Reno found herself nearly lost in the disturbed flurry, so she decided to nestle on my back. I felt her claws grip just above my tail. Her wings, at this point having a span of several feet, gave her extra balance.

"You're getting heavy, Reno," I chuckled.

Reno puffed out a small cloud of smoke and snuggled closer to my wings.

Sally was still circling low in the sky. "I really want to go with all of you, but before Chang and I separated, I told him I would try to find him," she called. "Reno can stay here if she wants to."

"Be careful, Sally," replied Clipper. "Jacob's little friend, Syntare, might be out there. You might be able to smell her if she's nearby. I don't think she's very happy right now."

"I'll be fine! Don't worry about meeeee!" Sally yelled as she flew off.

I took a deep breath after she was gone. Reno blew a long flame around me which melted a section of the snow bank.

"Syntare," I said grimly. "She'll be tracking us soon, but I have a feeling she'll have help this time."

"It's strange," said Clipper. "I lost her scent when you were speaking with Elemek. I wonder if she stopped looking for us."

"Any other creatures you think we should be on the lookout for?" I asked.

Clipper thought for a moment and then cringed. "Ohhh…! You won't believe what I saw, Jacob. After you left the train wreck, I saw this strange animal. It looked like a bat, but it was much bigger. It was the same kind that landed on your shoulder. I saw it bite a person on the neck. The scariest part is what happened to the victim. The saliva was poisonous or something."

"Did the victim die?" I asked, concerned.

Clipper shook his head. "Worse… he became one of them."

I lifted my lips into a snarl. "How so?"

Quivering, Reno dropped her head beside the spikes on my back. "I'm scared. Are they after us?"

"I don't think so," said Clipper. "We shouldn't worry too much about them. Using fire can easily ward them off; I speak from experience. Right now, I think Syntare may be our current threat."

I gave a single flap, sending the snow dancing once again. "Then we best get moving and find that first piece. This is a mountainous region, and we have a lot of territory to cover."

The day slugged along. Our minds were too active to rest, so we continued our search for any clue as to where the piece could be. Searching on foot was becoming very tedious. We looked in every crack and crevice in the mountainside while avoiding human contact, which really wasn't that hard. We explored white slopes dotted with black boulders, green conifers, and crystal ponds that glimmered in the icy land. When noon came, I finally decided to rest within the pass. There was a soft, northern breeze. That meant we were downwind from Syntare. There was no scent of her all that day. Because of that, we decided that splitting up would be the best choice. We agreed that we would rejoin in the pass that evening.

I was back there before the sun began to set. Clipper soon found me and told me about a flock of sheep that he had found near a rural community in one of the valleys.

"When Reno comes, we can have a small dinner. I hope the shepherd won't mind sacrificing some of his keepings to the lords of fire," he said, snickering at that last remark.

"Any clue to the piece?" I asked, intently watching the sky for Reno.

Clipper shook his head. While we waited for Reno, he and I discussed the best parts of a sheep to eat and how to avoid that awful taste of wool. We continued talking about sheep, yet Reno did not arrive. I was beginning to worry that she was in trouble. But as I was about to take off to look for her, I saw her circling around a mountainside. She glided toward me after spotting us. I folded my wings as she dropped between me and Clipper. She excitedly blew a small flame in the air and explained why she was late,

"While I was flying by a cliff, I found a cave with light coming from inside!" She paused to catch her breath. "It looked like light of ice."

"Light of ice?" Clipper questioned, his eyes widening. "What do you mean?"

"Sounds interesting if you ask me," I said. "You have a good eye, Reno. Good job. Maybe we're in luck if this ice has 'light.'"

Reno didn't say anything else. Clipper jumped from the snow and let his wings do their job. "How about we have Reno lead the way?" he suggested.

Reno lifted herself up and passed Clipper before I could even take flight. She led the way with Clipper behind her. I took up the rear.

"Let's not fly out in the open for long," I said. "We don't want Syntare to spot us. There's no need for an unnecessary fight right now."

We continued to follow Reno, who soon circled over the mouth of the cave she had mentioned. She landed next to the rock beside the entrance. "This is it," she said.

I stuck my head inside. Reno was right; there was some sort of light emanating from deep within. It resembled the cave where I had spoken to Elemek, only this one was slightly brighter and much bigger, and it did not feel welcoming in the slightest. The interior walls glittered with the familiar blue light. Stalactites and stalagmites enclosed the smooth path like a dragon's teeth. Everything that met the eye was either made of rock or ice. I took one cautious step forward. I could hear my claws crack the frozen crystals under my feet. I took another step with the same result. There was no obvious danger so far, but I could feel something in my bones.

"Be careful," I whispered. "This place doesn't feel safe."

Clipper followed close behind me. Reno marveled at the ice. "It's so beautiful in here," she said in awe.

"It sure is," I replied, "but be careful. Sometimes beauty can be deceiving."

We continued on into the cave. Eventually we came upon a fork in the slippery path, winding off into two separate directions. I paused, unsure of which path to follow. Clipper stepped up and took the lead. He sniffed the right path and then the left. He then sat down to ponder for a moment. Sliding the tip of his tail across the cold floor, he lifted a paw and pointed to the right.

"Let's try this way."

We followed his hunch and continued down the right. I could tell Reno was nervous. With her eyes narrowed and pupils as skinny slits, she moved in close to me. I didn't blame her. The air was much colder in here than it was outside. A spooky atmosphere seemed to close in upon us. I felt like we were being watched.

"I think someone else is in here," Reno quivered.

"I know this place is creepy, Reno," I said, "maybe we should—" My ears stood straight up. I squinted my eyes. "Did you hear that?"

Clipper was alert as well. Neither of us liked what we heard. The sound was a deep lamenting moan, as if came from some large creature. In a way, it reminded me of a dying cow.

Reno shivered. "W—What was that?"

I puffed smoke from between my teeth. "I don't know. Maybe that means we're on the right trail. Just keep your eyes open for anything. I know Vesuvius has sent more than just goblins and dragons after us. He wants the six pieces to be guarded."

I tip-clawed along with caution, scanning for anything threatening. To my bewilderment, we came across perfectly cut blocks of ice hanging from the ceiling. They were about half the size of me or Clipper. Reno could have easily fit inside one. We also saw large dark spots in the center of the blocks.

"What are these?" Reno asked, mystified.

"I don't know," said Clipper. "Let's not touch them and keep going."

After a few long minutes, the moaning died away. That did not sooth Reno at all. I didn't like it myself, but we continued on. I tried to slow my breathing to stay quiet. The cracking of the ice beneath our claws was the only sound we could hear. Suddenly, Clipper brushed my tail with his head. I halted, staring at him. He lifted a claw.

"Look down there. The cave opens up just ahead."

We reached the place where he was pointing. The pathway did indeed end in a short but wide cavern. The light was slightly brighter here than in the rest of the cave. I stopped at the edge and looked down. The center of the cavern was lower than the rest of the slanted floor. Looking up, I saw something that I believed was a source of the bright light. Hanging above the center point, a crystallized sphere, azure as the ice, gave an ethereal glow to the rest of the cavern. Nothing else in the cave matched its beauty. It was even more dazzling than the blocks we had seen earlier. It was beautiful!

"Is that what I think it is?" Clipper asked in excitement.

"I don't know for sure," I said. "It might be… You know, I *do* think it is the piece!"

Reno flapped her wings while jumping up and down. "It looks like a round diamond! We found it!"

Clipper was also celebrating, but abruptly stopped with a dark expression. "If this really is what we're looking for, shouldn't it be guarded or booby trapped or something like that?"

We all became quiet. I grew concerned as well. Suddenly, the ground began to quake. Reno yelped, jumping back. The shaking began with a low rumble. This made balancing on the slippery ground even more challenging. I lost my grip and slid on my feet, rushing down with no control. I slid down the decline to the middle of the cavern. One of the walls at the end began to groan and crack. It then burst apart in a small blizzard. I shielded my eyes to avoid any shards. To my horror, a demented being emerged from the wall. He materialized as if he originated there. Chunks of ice fell all around me, causing me to fall again. The personage looked like a cross between a sorcerer and a blue goblin. He was also tall, about seven feet in height. He wore a whitish-blue shawl while his pale skin made him look as if he should have died from hypothermia days ago. He had no Master Scepter, but he looked like he had strength I was not ready for. The being tapped his bare foot and the ground rattled again.

"Hmm, dok dregon, eh?" he said in an oddly smooth voice. "Creature o' fire 'az dezided to tes' 'eez fate against my power, lord o' zee blizza'd. Majes'y knew you ver comeeng. Ah'm dreadflee zorry, zir, but I mus' protect my prize from zee." He had to have been new to the English language.

"You must be the iceman Elemek warned me about," I said, expressing a show of courage that I did not feel. "What's your name?"

My enemy glared at me with eyes that would freeze even the deepest depths of hell. "A'm Glaziem, warlock o' zee blizza'd. I rule zee cold. I am at right hand o' Keen' 'zuvia, an' I've comm 'ere becauze o' zee. Zou art zee dregon traitor!"

Fenson and Elemek were right about Glaciem. He was one of Vesuvius' loyal dogs. Since he was here, then the diamond above my head *had* to be the first piece. I recalled what I had seen in my most recent dream of Vesuvius; he *had* mentioned a diamond! Why else would Glaciem be here? And if he was guarding the piece from me, that meant the lives of me and my friends were at stake! Glaciem had to fall if we were to succeed. His disgusting appearance caused my blood to start racing. I felt my heart beat faster and faster. My fury once again returned, but this time I would not let the darkscale control me; everything was done with my consent. I jumped back to my feet and let out an open flame. Glaciem took a step back, bawling like an exorcised demon. The fire had to have weakened him significantly! As I prepared for another scorching breath, I could not help laughing. Holding back the warlock was not as difficult as I first anticipated. This will be easy!

My opinion changed on a dime when hard flakes of ice pelted my face like bits of glass. I remembered Glaciem had control of what he loved: the winter. Successfully blocking my advance, I felt his pale hand strike me below my mouth. He was strong! I was knocked off my feet again, sliding back to the center of the cavern. I stood back up as quickly as possible.

Clipper saw what was happening and readied to join the battle.

"Clipper, get the diamond! It's right above me!" I roared as I held Glaciem back the best I could.

Clipper spread his wings but then folded them back up. "Reno," he said urgently, "I'm too big to fly up and grab it with Glaciem down there. You might do it. I need you to grab the diamond while I help Jacob."

Reno's ears drooped. "I don't think I can do that."

There was no time for a speech about bravery. Clipper bumped Reno forward with his horns.

"Reno, hurry! If you want to see Pearl Forest, then you must do this! Never mind Glaciem. Jacob and I will hold him back. You have to show courage now. You've got to get it."

I didn't hear Reno's response. I was going to say something to her when Glaciem struck me with more shards of ice. Again, my fire was affective, but I needed more to bring him down.

Clipper left Reno and dove into the scene of battle. He skated down the decline just as he did at the hockey rink. With no trouble, he stopped just behind Glaciem and stuck his claws in the ice. He bared his fangs and jumped onto Glaciem's back, sinking his long sabers into the warlock's arm. Glaciem grunted. He attempted to fling Clipper away. I got up off the ground and cast another wave of fire. The cavern that held us captive was getting soft and wet. I felt tiny water droplets dripping on my back. That meant my plan was working! I just needed more time to defeat Glaciem! If I continued to use fire, we would have the diamond. Glaciem was bigger than the average human, but he was not as big as me or Clipper. Size meant nothing in my fury, anyway. My fire gave me a true upper hand. I prepared another breath of fire when I felt something strike me between the horns. Whatever hit me was hard enough to make my head throb. I looked down to find the shining diamond, which was about the size of a softball, sliding across the icy floor in front of my feet. Glaciem was still trying to get rid of Clipper when he too saw the diamond. He cast another arctic freeze upon me. I coughed the snowy dust from my throat when I heard something crack above my head. I looked up to see a large boulder crashing through the ceiling of the cave. Like the diamond, it fell directly on my head, though the boulder was much bigger and heavier. As it split in half on my horns, I fell back onto the floor. I was still conscious, but dazed. I watched as the warlock backed up and smashed Clipper into the wall. Yelping, Clipper slid on his wings down the wall and came to a halt next to me. He lifted his head to find his worst fear in front of him. Using his power, Glaciem had created the dreaded blue blade. Clipper stared but did not move. There was nowhere to run; so instead, anger took hold of him. He picked up the diamond beside me. Looking to his right, he threw it to Reno, who was perched at the edge of the cavern.

"Reno! Get the piece of the portal away from here! I'll keep you clear!" Clipper cried.

Reno picked up the diamond with her teeth and fled. Clipper blew another burst of flames at Glaciem before shaking me.

"Jacob, he has an ice blade!"

I groaned from the terrible ache in my head. Clipper ran a claw above my nose.

"Jacob, he has an ice blade! He can kill us!"

My sluggishness vanished in an instant. My heart skipped a beat at the sight of the ice blade descending toward my neck. Pure reflex took over. I jumped to one side; the blade crashed down right where I had been. Clipper raised his front paws, his claws at the ready. He clamped down on the grounded blade and held fast. He roared in fury as the force of his claws broke the blade in two. Both pieces of the blade faded to black, the liquid blue color was gone. Jumping forward, he bit down on the remainder of the sword and at the same time spewed bursts of flames. Observing his wrath allowed my energy to fully return. Roaring as well, I charged at the vile Glaciem. I sent him to the ground and sent another rain of fire over him. By that time, water was everywhere. The ice below my feet was even more slippery than before.

"Go now!" I called to Clipper. "Go help Reno!"

Clipper did just that. He flew back up to the edge of the cavern where Reno was perched in the exact spot she had been before, the diamond still in her mouth. Clipper urged her to go.

Reno set down the diamond. "What about Jacob?" she asked.

"He'll be okay," said Clipper. "Grab the piece and go." He turned around and started to run. Reno scooped up the diamond and ran right behind him, slipping and sliding along the way.

I remained behind, holding Glaciem back. He was weaponless and, where he was now, powerless. My back feet held his arms to the ground while my front paws held his neck. Despite his struggling, I held him tight. Not once had I ever really wanted to take a life (while in control of myself, of course), but I had been in this situation already. I knew if I kept Glaciem alive, he would roam free on the first earth. There was no telling what would happen to the people in the nearby towns and cities. They would continue to suffer through eternal winter, not knowing the cause of it. I figured that if I was not dead, Vesuvius would never let Glaciem return to Elsov. Closing my eyes, I prepared to make the kill.

"Zou vant to retu'n to zee second earth," Glaciem groaned under his breath. "'zuvia vants me to prevent zat. I mus' not let zee take zee diamond."

I reopened my eyes to find a violet beam of light flash high above the cavern. I growled, bending down to Glaciem's ear. "What did you do?" I hissed.

"I've zummoned my ice dregons," he said. "Even if's I die, zey vill not. Zey vill never stop until zey slay zee."

I recalled what Fenson and Bluepond had said about ice dragons. The young ones who were stolen from their families had been awakened! With my anger nearly overpowering me, I let out a flame that sealed the fate of the warlock. His cold skin melted beneath my claws. I was now pinning an empty, wet shawl. Glaciem was dead, but his ice dragons weren't. I had to rescue Clipper and Reno before it was too late! I flew out of the cursed cavern and ran after them. Running was my only option since I was unable to fly through the falling ice. What was once perfectly quiet, save the eerie lowing, was now loud with crashes and shatters, as if the cave was about to collapse upon me. Up ahead, I saw Reno looking back.

"Clipper, stop! I see Jacob coming!" she shouted.

Clipper slid on the ground below the many clean-cut blocks of ice as I sprinted toward him.

"Get out of here!" I cried.

One of the blocks detached from the ceiling and dropped just a few feet from him. It shattered, exposing the dark blur inside. Out emerged a beast about the size of Reno. It had crystallized blue scales and a blood-thirsty glare on its face. Its horns were curved in a forward curl, like a ram's; far different from the smooth, straight horns the rest of us had. Reno stared at it in horror. In defense, she spat a small flame and hid behind Clipper. The ice dragon screeched like a banshee and jumped on Clipper's hind leg. Clipper hissed, blowing a flame from his nose. The ice dragon squealed and rolled to the side. Clipper pounced and stuck his claws into the ice dragon's chest. The creature squealed again, then dropped dead. Other blocks began to fall one after another, freeing more and more ice dragons. They all emerged from their frozen prisons and attacked Clipper. One by one they covered him, ignoring Reno. The young brown dragon was too afraid to move.

The sound of falling rock and ice was nearly drowned out by the sound of the screeches and squeals of the ice dragons. Clipper grew more agitated by the high-pitched noises they made. He spewed fire in every direction, hoping to stop at least one. But they kept coming. They jumped onto him and began scratching and biting him on every part of his body. The wounds on his wings reopened and began to bleed again. Just as he was about to be overwhelmed, I caught up with him. I planted my feet into the ground and skated right into him, knocking away the blue parasites. I charged, flamed, clawed, and bit any ice dragon I could reach. Clipper and I fought the ice dragons for several grueling minutes. Water rushed over my paws while steam rose from my nostrils.

"Let's go!" I cried. "This has to be the first piece. The first step back to Elsov is ours!"

Reno glanced left and right before heading up the small river with the rest of us following her. More blocks of ice were still falling above us. I slapped my tail to the ground, causing it to splash in the shallow water. "How many of them are there?" I huffed.

The frontline of the ice dragons before us blew the strangest of flames. It wasn't fire at all. Instead of heat, I felt a freeze biting into my legs. Clipper wasted no time using his hot fire. The ice dragons melted in front of our eyes. Despite his visible need for survival, Clipper shed some tears. He had a good reason to feel bad. All these creatures were once infants enjoying life on Elsov. My heart sank at that thought, yet there was nothing I could do about it.

The path in front of us was clearing out, but more blocks of ice were beginning to fall. Clipper and I knew we could not hold off all of them. The next best thing to do was escape. Reno nearly swallowed the diamond when she ducked beneath blocks that still hung under the ceiling. Sure enough, she saw one of them about to drop right in front of her. She had no time to stop. Lowering her horns, she prepared for the impact. The block cracked one more time and fell. It broke open on Reno's back. Luckily she was not hurt.

To my surprise, the new ice dragon did not attack us. It was not even an ice dragon at all! The creature lay on the ground beside Reno. It may have been covered with frozen crystals, but I could tell they were not scales. When the block fell on Reno, whoever was trapped inside was freed!

"Who is he?" said Clipper, flabbergasted.

I took a brief second to look at the young one. As curious as I was, I knew we were still in danger. "We can find out who he is once we're out of here. Take him with us," I said.

The little dragon was unconscious. Clipper gently but quickly lifted him up and placed him just above my wings. When I felt his claws gripping my sides, I raced up the cave with the ice dragons close behind us. They continued to squeal and growl in anger, each filling the others' short intervals.

I never thought I would be so happy to see sunlight again. The second we were out of the cave, all three of us took to the air. Since the sleepy dragon on my back was in front of my wings, and light enough for me to hold, flight was not a problem. The real problem was who would be following us.

"Clipper, the ice dragons will come out of the cave!" I called. "We need to find a way to block the entrance!"

Clipper turned around. He hovered above the mouth of the cave. Before the ice dragons could emerge, he shot a flame at a cluster of rocks that clung to the mountainside just above the entrance. Following a noisy rumble, white, gray, and black chunks of rock and snow covered the mouth. The ice dragons were trapped inside, but for how long? We continued to fly away from the valley, landing in a field several miles away.

"Clipper, how are you wings?" I asked him.

He flapped them carefully a few times. "They sting, but I can still fly."

Dropping the diamond on the ground, Reno pressed a paw full of snow against his wounds in an attempt to stop the bleeding.

"Thank you," said Clipper. "That feels much better; and look what we have! I can't believe it! We have the first piece!"

We all gazed at the glittering diamond that lay in the soft snow. With it being outside and under the sun, its dazzling glimmer intensified tenfold.

"I'm relieved too," she said, licking her lips, "but who did we rescue?"

She moved around me to get a better look. The young creature lay quietly in the snow, trying to unfurl its wings. The crystals on its scales continued to melt. Smoke escaped with every deep breath it took. It slowly opened its amber-yellow eyes to look at Reno. This dragon was a darkscale.

CHAPTER 26

FRIENDS COME TOGETHER

Chang took a deep breath while on a bench that rested between two golden-red cliffs. The fresh, forest air felt soothing in his lungs. A low-hanging fog blocked most of the view, though he knew he was in one of the most beautiful locations in Dixie Forest. When Chang felt fully rested, he stood up and limped back to Auben, who was waiting for him to see if the coast was clear. The two started down the rocky trail that led into the woods. As they walked, Auben studied the life around him. He kept his ears open as he listened for sparrows, squirrels, deer, and other woodland creatures.

"This land is home to many. I can smell them," he said. "The trees and the stones, the water and the air, and the animals who dwell here are speaking to me. Can you hear them, Chang? This place is full of magic; magic that neither you nor I can ever replicate as mortals. And despite the colder climate, I feel like I am home."

Chang stopped again to ease the pain in his foot. "Where exactly are you from, on Elsov I mean?"

Auben blinked. "Is it not obvious? I was born in the north-east region near the coast. It is much warmer there, even in winter. It's subtropical if you wish to put it that way. But I have never lived in a permanent home. I am always on adventures. That is how I am able to see my friend Losdir often. He was in the subtropics when I hatched. I've also visited Pearl Forest, the Skalisk Canyon, the long plains, and many more regions. I have made many friends in these places, explored many cities and wildernesses, and yes, listened to what each form of life was saying to me, no matter what form they were."

Chang was impressed with the lightscale. "If you're from Elsov, how do you know English? That's a language from this world. Fenson and Bluepond speak it as well."

"There are many different languages and cultures," Auben explained, "and our worlds share many of them. That is why I can speak English. It is the only outside language I know. Have you not heard the stories? After one of the first lightscales traveled to this world, he learned many different languages and customs. Some were brought back to Elsov. I can speak English, Kuslan; which is a form of traditional elven; and my own native language, which I doubt you can speak with a human tongue."

The only languages Chang knew were English and Mandarin. Auben's ideas were intriguing to him. If it weren't for the first lightscales on his world, and the influence they had taken back with them, he wouldn't have been able to talk to Auben.

"I understand that many animals are similar between our worlds," Auben continued.

Chang nearly laughed in wonder as Auben went on comparing and contrasting various animals. "This is very interesting," he commented. "I have a doctorate in zoology at the University of California. Well, I would be studying there had I not gotten mixed up with Larson and the six pieces. But as a zoologist, I *would* like to see Elsov for myself, especially Pearl Forest. The way Jacob and Clipper describe the place makes me want to visit."

"My world enchants you as yours does me," said Auben. "According to stories told by my elders, the dragon of old traveled all over this world, particularly in the land of Asia. I believed in those stories as a hatchling, but I gave them up as I got older; that was until a scholar at the University of Krigsansby showed me documented records that proved this world to be true. And now I'm here! This world… a world that I used to think was only in fairy stories… is real! And I'm in it! I'm in a fairy story!"

Chang loved listening to Auben. He discovered many similarities between the two worlds. "It *is* fascinating," he said.

"And it is fascinating for me to be here," said Auben. "It is usually against the rules for another creature to travel to another world. However, I knew your friends were in trouble. I and Losdir received special permission to use the Keeper's portal."

Chang and Auben said no more as they approached a bend. Auben abruptly stopped in his tracks with one foot in the air, like a dog.

Chang stopped as well. "What's wrong?" he asked, feeling nervous.

Auben sniffed. "There is something nearby. I smell it. And just now, I heard it."

Chang swallowed hard. He didn't notice anything at first, then came a shrilling roar directly ahead. It was definitely a dragon's roar. Chang thought Auben was going to hide, but he didn't. He moved in front of Chang just as a bright blue dragon flew into view. Auben stepped back. He glanced into the other dragon's eyes and bowed his head.

"Sorry if I scared you," he said. "May I ask what you're doing here?"

The other lightscale had an expression of shock. She shifted her head so she could look behind him. "I'm keeping a promise," she answered. "Do you want to explain this, Chang?"

Auben did his best to appear friendly, but it was obvious he was ill at ease; which was evident through the smoke rising from his nostrils.

"Sally, this is Auben," Chang said, pointing to him. "He's a friend from Elsov. He says there's an elf leading an army of dwarfs and nymphs somewhere around here. We're being helped and we didn't even know it. Just think about it Sally, there are elves here. Elves!"

Sally bared her teeth in frustration, though not because of Auben. She did not seem surprised to hear about elves either. "Can he take care of this little fellow down the path?" she asked. "I don't know what it is, but he does love to kick and claw. I didn't have the heart to hurt it."

Two words piqued Auben's curiosity. His ears lifted. "Kick and claw, you say?"

"I was merely defendin' meself, I was!" the creature yelled. "Can you understand that? I see you're a lightscale and I didn't mean to attack! Allow me to approach and we can talk this out!"

Auben's lips lifted into a grin. "A kangrui? What is one doing here? I didn't know they were on this earth as well."

The creature stepped into view, rubbing the long whiskers on the side of his face with a wet-licked paw. "Auben, Trihan said you'd be here. We've met b'fore. I'm Pierre. Remember? Jawé?"

"Pierre? Is it really you? It has been ages! What are you doing here?"

"Why, comin' ta rescue you o'course! You must've guessed it was me that'd come here. I was battlin' many ogres n' such around the Keeper's castle when he met me. He told me you were in trouble and off I went! I mus' say I find this world quite disgustin'. Too many trees an' steep hills n' such. Worse off than Pearl Forest, I say. At least it was warmer there; if ya even consider that place warm enough, which it isn't!"

Chang blinked. He studied the strange animal's fur, ears, tail, the whiskers on its face, and most especially the large feet. Chang found he quite liked the kangrui. He also found his manner of speech quite proper; not precise, but proper. "He reminds me of a cute wallaby, except he's bigger than I would expect," he muttered to Sally.

Pierre made a light growl. "Wallaby? You call me a wallaby, eh? I'm no wallaby, y'know; whatever a wallaby is."

Chang was at a loss for words. He didn't expect the creature to react in such a way.

"Pierre's kind only recently learned to speak," Auben said. "The elves taught them, just as they taught our species long before that."

Chang kept his eyes on Pierre. "If you don't mind my asking, just what are you?"

"He is a kangrui, as I've already mentioned," Auben answered on his old friend's behalf. "His name is Pierre. And I too am surprised he's here. I met his troop when I visited his region at a very young age. I met Pierre when he was still in his mother's pouch. Since then, we've been great friends, but then I had to leave. Pierre, I still cannot believe it is really you! Look at how you've grown!"

Sally made a low, rumbling snicker. Pierre glared at her.

"Y'should be so lucky as to know 'bout us," he said. "We are lovin' and kind creatures and are intensely loyal to our kin."

Chang tried to hide his smile. He figured that Auben believed Pierre's claim, but he didn't think Sally did. "We need to focus on what we came here for," he finally said. "Right now, we need to find Jacob, Clipper, and Reno."

"We also need to find out where Losdir's army is located," Auben added. "They could be anywhere. Trihan told me they are trying to keep the Grün-hære away from Jacob and the others."

"Ptah! Some plan," scoffed Pierre.

Sally held up a paw. "Wait a minute, didn't Fenson or Bluepond say this *Trihan* knows where everyone is?"

"Yes, he's the new keeper of the three worlds," said Chang.

The four continued up the trail in a party of two dragons, a kangrui, and a human. Chang couldn't help but observe Pierre as he strode along. The kangrui occasionally hopped like a kangaroo, but most often he walked with one foot after the other. Chang brought up the rear of the group, hoping they wouldn't come across any hikers on the trail.

CHAPTER 27

RAZDEN AWAKENS

A sense of unease spread over the citizens of the isle. Vesuvius, on the other hand, expressed no concern; he merely sat on his throne, unusually calm. The Sorcerer Heitspel entered, performed the salute, and then reported the events that unfolded in North America so far away. Vesuvius growled lightly when he learned of the death of the warlock, but still showed no true anger. All he said was, "It seems Glaciem has failed to guard the piece."

For the first time in his high position, Heitspel noticed that his leader's voice was quiet. Vesuvius often spoke with a booming voice.

"Could it be the army you sent is not strong enough?" the Sorcerer asked.

"Our royal 'anarchists' are not the ones who failed," said Vesuvius, "though they are not where they're supposed to be. Something is impeding their advance. You say the little dwarf army is there also? That must be what is occupying them." He fell silent for a moment, thinking of an idea. "With your power, you have informed me of the location of the dragon traitors. The only darkscale who is somewhat following them is Syntare. I must discipline her, though. She doesn't fight, but talks. Heitspel, inform the dragons who are with the Grün-hære. Order them to attack any enemy they see. They will remain and dispose of the band of dwarfs led by that silly elf. I must also prepare to attack the traitors myself. I will take great pleasure in subduing them on my own. One of their precious pieces lies within a house a few miles from Mt. Ellen. My royal line has not used the portal on Ellen in years. As it prepares for my coming, the land will change. The water will become poison. The ground will rumble. The air will turn to smoke. Then I will rise. Cowardly man-folk; they are lucky I am not seeking their deaths this time."

"The people of the first earth will be dealt with in due time," said Heitspel. "I will once again grant you the ability to communicate with your servants."

Vesuvius released a cloud of smoke. "I will reign! The people who study their world may predict my coming, but unlike my usual visits to the first earth, I will minimize my attack. My interest lies with the traitors."

Heitspel bowed his head in deep respect for his leader. He and Vesuvius left the great hall. The Sorcerer was ready to begin the first steps in creating the destructive portal to Mt. Ellen, in southern Utah.

RENO LOWERED HER HEAD AND PRESSED HER NOSE AGAINST THE side of the sleepy stranger.

"Is he awake?" she asked in a whisper.

The last bits of cursed ice dripped off the dragon's scales, exposing a reddish-orange color. I placed a gentle paw on his horns. They felt much like Reno's horns: sharp but still growing. He also seemed to be about the same age as Reno. As he slowly blinked his drowsy eyes, he made soft grunting noises. I didn't understand what he said at first, but I knew he was trying to speak.

"Don't be afraid. We won't hurt you," I said.

"We're friends," Clipper added.

The young darkscale moaned like a bear cub. He continued making strange sounds before finally muttering a few intelligible words on his forked tongue, "I am... here. I am here."

"He's okay!" Reno cried joyfully.

The little darkscale's joints popped as he stirred.

"He hardly has any energy in him," said Clipper. "Let's not rush anything. The ice dragons aren't a threat right now. Let him adjust the way he needs to. There's no telling what he went through."

I twitched my nose in disgust. "Poor thing. He smells like a frozen carcass. That would make sense, I hate to say."

The young dragon yawned. I could see the glow of reignited fire that circulated from within his lungs and to his throat.

"Wh— Where am I?" he whimpered.

"Everything's fine," said Clipper. "You're safe. You just came from the cave."

"Glasssiem," said the worried darkscale. "I rebelled againsst Vesuviuss afore I wass taken here. I refusse— *refuse* to follow him and sso— so I was moved to the winter peaks. Glaciem imprisoned me in the icy tomb. As you said, I wreak of a stench not even I can tolerate. That is all I remember. My mind is in a fog."

Reno blew a small flame over the stranger to help warm him while I slid my paw under his belly to help him to his feet. His legs wobbled as he tried to keep his balance.

"Do you know your name or where you come from?" Reno asked him.

"I… I was born in a nest of evil," the darkscale confessed. "I was raised believing Vesuvius was some sort of god. They cut the tip of my tongue, as you can see, to show I am a true darkscale. But I remember one day I wandered off. I traveled for a very long time. In my travels, I thought about the nature of Vesuvius' Kingdom. I started to realize the lies that I was told. Instead of returning home, I decided to search for a new home."

"You ran away?" I asked.

He practiced a few more words before continuing. "Yes. Sometime later I met a fairy. She told me how to find a Kuslan city. Krigsansby was the name of it. I learned the ways of true happiness. I changed how I spoke too, even though it was difficult with a tongue like mine. Sadly, a group of royalist dwarfs captured me. They sent me to the isle by ship. I did not see Vesuvius, for he was addressing other matters. Rather, I confronted his pet sorcerer. He was enraged by my actions, so he banished me to the Winter Peaks where Glaciem rules. He turned me into an ice dragon against my will. My last memory is of Glaciem casting his vile spell over me, and the next thing I see is you. Oh, please do not send me back! I beg of you!"

Clipper shook his head. "Don't worry. I know we are darkscales ourselves, but, like you, we're not evil. You're free now. You no longer have to worry about Glaciem *or* Vesuvius."

I tried to wrap my mind around what "Kuslan" or "Krigsansby" meant. "The fairies were guiding you to a city?" I asked him.

"Krigsansby. Kusla is a nation founded by elves, but now populated with many different peoples. I… I never made it there." The dragon wearily set his head back on the ground.

"An elf city on Elsov?" asked Clipper. "How long ago was that?"

"I don't know. I may have been an ice dragon for only a few moons or many decades. Am I still at the Winter Peaks?"

"No," said Reno. "You're on another world, the first earth. It's the human world, but humans are not to be trusted."

I silenced her with a mild hiss. "Reno, not now. Okay, little dragon, do you know your name?"

"If I do, I don't remember what I am called," the darkscale sighed. "My life, as I remember, is dark. I don't want to go back to that life. I want to be a lightscale."

"Don't worry," said Clipper. "I know you're scared. You're not even on your own world, but we'll get you back to Elsov. We're finding the scattered pieces of a portal." He picked up the glittering diamond in his claws. "And here is piece number one. We have it."

"Ah… I wish to reach Krigsansby," the dragon said dreamily. "Let us find what we need."

"That reminds me," I said, "Sally's with Chang, and he still has the viewing ring. We can use it to help find the second piece."

"Then let's go," Reno said. She lifted a paw and helped the dragon to his feet again. "Do you remember how to fly?"

The darkscale stretched his wings. "I do."

"Great. You can fly with me while Jacob and Clipper lead the way."

As Reno had suggested, I took flight with Clipper beside me. Reno jumped into the air next, and finally our new friend. It seemed that Reno had taken a deep liking to him, which filled me with delight. In a matter of minutes, the remaining clouds in the sky floated away and the day was bright. It was nice to feel this way after my weeks of sorrow.

"It feels much warmer now, even if there still is a lot of snow below us," said Clipper.

"It feels great," I replied. "I think the harsh winter conditions were Glaciem's doing."

Reno and her new friend were having their own conversation behind us.

"You must have a name," Reno said to the darkscale.

"I believe I must," he responded.

"Well, I like your scales. Their color reminds me of rusted metal. I hope that doesn't offend you."

"No, that was the clue I needed. I know I look like a rusty old sword. In my native tongue, it's called razden. It means 'rusty'."

Reno thought for a second. "Do you want to be called Razden then?"

"I would like that! Razden... I would like it very much, thank you. What about your name? You haven't told me. I heard your friend say it, but I don't remember."

Listening from up front, I knew Reno was going to be shy; as she often was.

"My name? It— It's... Reno."

"Reno? I love that name. It really suits you."

Reno fell into a bashful silence, but Razden seemed not to have noticed and continued asking her questions. I decided to leave them be and instead went to search for a source of food. It was not long before I found an inland lake. At that point I knew the snow was Glaciem's doing, for there was dry ground under us now that we were far away from that dreadful cave.

"Clipper, look," I said, pointing to the lake. "There must be fish in there."

"Fish?" Razden repeated from behind. "I must say I am very hungry."

"Fish sounds good to me too," laughed Clipper. "I love fish! To think I hated them once."

We all descended down to the lakeshore. Sure enough, our lunch was waiting for us beneath the fresh mountain water. I snapped my jaws around a rainbow trout, swallowing it whole. We all fished for quite a while. After catching our fill, we were back in the sky, heading east in search of Sally. Reno and Razden were again talking to each other.

"I think Reno likes him," Clipper whispered to me.

"I think so too," I mumbled back.

We continued flying. I was sure Reno had not felt this happy in a long time, especially with the strong grudge she held against humans. I knew the pain she was feeling. My heart was broken after the disaster with the train. That all changed when Elemek spoke to me. Now we had found the diamond, and were on our way to find the second piece. One thought lingered in the back of my mind, however: Syntare. The wind was against us, meaning she may be following our scent. What confused me was that if she was indeed tracking us like she should, wouldn't she have caught up to us by now? Why was she holding back?

CHAPTER 28

TRAHERN'S CHARGE

The Militia had retreated following the first battle so there would be no more unnecessary deaths. Because it was not a large army, every casualty was a costly blow. The soldiers mourned for the loss of their fallen friends, but they could not mourn for long with danger still present. They buried as many bodies as they had time to, ally and foe alike, before resuming down the road of war (trail of tears would be a more appropriate name, actually). Most of the wounded, covered in soaking red bandages or strips of cloth, lagged behind while being escorted by the nymph medics while others who had immobile or amputated limbs were carried on stretchers. Every time Losdir ordered a rest, the medics attended to those who were sick or hurt. Some had already died since their last treatments about two hours before. On their next break, Trahern and Bluepond sat down next to a fir tree while Fenson lay in a patch of soft grass with his eyes closed. One of the nymph scouts reported to Losdir that they were near an open park that had a granite memorial on top of a hill. The scouts also mentioned the park had only a small family within it, nothing more.

"Can we at least build a small campfire, Konmester?" one of the dwarfs asked Trahern. "The chill is setting in and many of us are hungry."

"Our last meal was only a couple of hours ago," said Trahern. "We need to grow accustomed to low rations. We cannot have the town's folk feeding us all the time. We will manage, now I don't want to hear any more whining."

"Oh, this is not what I expected!" the soldier wept as he listened to the moans and occasional screams of the wounded. "We were supposed to distract the Horde, not engage them in a full-on battle."

"I told you no whining!" snapped Trahern. "If you keep it up, I will have a cloth tied over your mouth while you run as a punishment! I know this isn't easy and you are unaccustomed to going without a warm supper. But if we are not silent, we will be discovered. I don't want anyone to spot our entire army, do you?"

Fighting more tears, the stunned dwarf silently left Trahern's sight. Trahern placed a hand on his forehead. He felt bad for snapping at the dwarf since he understood exactly what his people were suffering through.

"Our first battle was only a small victory," Bluepond said softly. "We have lost an alarming number of our own force. You said some were your close friends. I will not let it be for nothing, Konmester. Those goblins and ruthless dwarfs will pay for the blood on their hands. I would especially like to wring their leader's neck. That goblin is smart and has no empathy for anyone. He must be brought down."

"The Grün-hære may fall under anarchy without him," said Trahern, trying to keep a positive note.

A nearby dwarf spoke up, sniffling a little, "He slew my closest friend in such a barbaric manner. I will not rest until that general is slain himself. However, Konmester Trahern is right, we must remain hidden. We must protect those who are not involved in our war."

From then on, the Militia only whispered back and forth. The honk of a car horn in the nearby park startled the band of soldiers. Fenson woke at the sound.

"My loving tulip, that gave me a fright," one of the malaises said, laughing a little.

Losdir took a deep breath as he looked up. The thick pines and firs limited his view of the cloudy sky. All was quiet. That was until the swish of wings interrupted the serenity from above.

Vocal growls or roaring were absent, but Losdir knew what was present. His throat tensed at the thought of an attacking darkscale. Just battling one would be ten times worse than fighting the Grün-hære!

"Konmester, threat from the sky!" he shouted.

Others gazed up at the sky as well in response to the sound of wings. In horror, they all saw the darkscaled dragon circling the sky like a vulture above them. This time it did not look like it was merely monitoring them. It was going to attack!

Fenson took cover under a fir. "Oh, no! What can we do now? We can't outrun it!"

"Follow me," Trahern calmly ordered the Militia.

He drew his sword and headed out of the campsite. The other soldiers did not hesitate to follow. Trahern continued until he stopped at the edge of the park where the monument stood on top of the hill. Trahern did not dare lead his troops out into the open.

The family in the park seemed to have heard the swishes too, but had no idea they were the wings of a dragon. The front line of dwarfs watched anxiously as the family casually returned to their car. They took their time leaving, unaware of the monster that was getting even closer.

"They must move faster if they want to escape," a nymph said.

"No," replied a second nymph. "If they try to rush their escape, they may excite the dragon and attract it to them. We do not want that."

Losdir kept his eyes on the darkscale. "I have my doubts it is after the family. It's after us. It knows we are here. As much as I wish otherwise, we must show ourselves and fight it, to the death if we must."

"It seems we have no choice," said Trahern. "Losdir, I would appreciate it if you will align the nymphs and prepare a ranged attack. The arrows will not kill him, but hopefully they will force him to land. Aim for the wings. I will take the front line and attack, face to face."

Losdir placed a hand on his shoulder. "Trahern— I mean Konmester— with no enchanted weaponry we cannot slay it! It will be *you* lying dead on that hill! We have no source of magic. We have no wizard, no enchanter, nothing."

"We must accept what we have," said Trahern frankly. "We will fight whether we want to or not."

Losdir said no more. He returned to his nymphs. "Hold position in the trees!" he shouted. "Load your arrows and stand by to fire!"

Unfortunately, the violet darkscale heard Losdir as well. Turning his head toward the thickets where the Militia was holding ground, he finally gave out a long screech and changed his direction.

Losdir saw the terrible beast swooping down. He swished his sword in a forward arc.

"Fire!"

The nymphs loosed their strings. The space above the treetops came alive with angry arrows. Sure enough, several bounced off the dragon's scales while one or two punctured his wings. The darkscale bellowed and started to dive. He whirled through the air and struck the marble monument, demolishing it entirely. Trahern surveyed the rest of the park, relieved that there was no one else around. The family was long gone. Safe. Unlike his people. The Konmester held his own sword high in the air.

"Now we will advance, my dwarfs! Charge!"

The frontline advanced with the rest watching with hopeful hearts. Gunfire once more filled the air.

"He will not leave victorious! This will be a day for him to remember!" yelled Trahern as he led the charge. "Fight for freedom for this world and ours!"

The darkscale shook his back to let the damaged masonry roll off his body. Looking ahead, he glared at Trahern's charging group. He took a deep breath, preparing to cast fire at his enemies.

Trahern noticed the glow in the back of the darkscale's throat.

"Dragon fire! Take cover!"

The dwarfs jumped aside just as the fire roared past them. Trahern felt the intense heat mercilessly biting at his face. There was no place to shield himself. The darkscale shook his head back and forth to let the flames burn wherever he wished. When the beast was out of breath, Trahern's soldiers stood back up and reformed their line as they were trained to do. As frightened as Trahern was, his courage was even stronger. Each dwarf reloaded and fired point-blank. The darkscale took a step back, lowering his horns. He growled as he surged at one of the dwarfs. The needle-sharp points of keratin struck the rifle's barrel, breaking it clean off. With remaining power, the short yet dangerous charge sent the dwarf flying backward. Next, the dragon swung a set of merciless claws at the other dwarfs. They caught two. With anger growing, the darkscale fought more brutally. Before long, several of Trahern's men lay wounded in the singed grass. Trahern expected his remaining troops would perish by more fire, but the darkscale did not breathe any. Trahern now believed the beast wanted to play with his people before killing them. That changed the matters of battle.

"Take a step back! Be careful!" Trahern called.

The darkscale growled again. Trahern knew his time on earth was put to the test the moment he returned his stare. Sweat soaked through his heated shirt. Unsure of what was going to happen, he watched the darkscale preparing to pounce. He pulled out his sword just as it jumped. Next came the horrifying cry of an angry dragon in pain. The two were separated only by the steel blade. The heavy weight pressed Trahern down. His back felt stiff as the strength in his arms started to wither. The Konmester finally understood what true terror was. All his previous fighting experience had been against silly, dim-witted cave goblins. He never imagined he would fight against the Grün-hære, let alone a dragon! His heart wept as the darkscale opened his jaws. Every one of his senses told him this was the end. The stench of the darkscale's breath poisoned his nostrils. The steaming wet saliva dripped on his forehead, burning his skin. Trahern's eardrums could not bear the loud roar, and his eyes could not bear the two sabered fangs that hovered inches above them. He was expecting the darkscale's teeth to sink into his head. Trahern shut his eyes, waiting for his nightmare to end. The darkscale waited so Trahern could suffer even more. All hope seemed to have gone. Trahern's arms were about to collapse under the intense weight.

Bang!

The weight suddenly tumbled away. A dwarf had shot the darkscale in the side of the face.

Trahern's arms shook with weakness, but the sword that saved his life was still in his hand. The blade was badly bent. The darkscale beside him held a paw over his ear where the lead bullet had struck him. He had another paw over his chest where the blade had pressed against him.

"Thes-sille no-tha vinise!" the darkscale hissed. The words were so slurred they barely sounded like words at all.

Trahern's accompaniment was about to charge again when the darkscale suddenly jumped back on his feet and flew away. The fight was brief, but four dwarfs squirmed from cuts and bad burns. Miraculously, no one was killed. Trahern eyed the damage. It was a terrible sight to see. Plumes of smoke rose from the blackened grass. The monument lay in ruin. Nymph medics came rushing out to the injured dwarfs. Some applied cream on burns while others stitched claw-wounds shut.

Trahern was grateful for the dwarf who had shot the darkscale. "You saved my life," he told him. "I am forever in your debt."

The dwarf offered to shake hands, but Trahern went with a large hug. Losdir and the rest of the Militia came out of the thicket once they knew the darkscale was gone for sure.

"Are you harmed?" Losdir asked Trahern.

"I can barely hear a thing," Trahern groaned. His ears were ringing; his forehead was red and sore.

"You are safe now," said Losdir. "There will be no losses today."

Bluepond arrived at the scene. "Sir, I kept my eyes on the beast.

I saw him escape to the east. He will certainly think twice before he returns. I do not know why he left, though. He could have stayed and fought."

"To our luck he did not stay," said Losdir. "But if he came from the east, that must mean the Grün-hære is over there as well. The darkscale has exposed our location, and now their general knows where we are. We must move out immediately."

The dwarfs that charged with Trahern held their sides, arms, heads, and wherever there was pain; but they could all walk in line. The Militia left the park as quickly as possible, eager to leave before the Grün-hære arrived. As Trahern marched behind Fenson and Bluepond, who guided his army with their map, his mind began to wander. He wished he was back in the mountains near Shiloh's Pass, where he could lead his men to work. Homesickness washed over the Konmester. He reminded himself why he was so far from home. He had a mission to complete.

"No one will stop us," he said to Losdir. "We will do everything in our power to stop the advancing devils."

Losdir only nodded in agreement since his mind was also elsewhere. Trahern puffed out his chest in bravery as he led the Militia onward. He considered his survival to be a Divine miracle.

CHAPTER 29

Under the Mound

Sally was spellbound by the wealth of information that Auben had shared with her. Chang also told her of his flight to St. George. Sally then mentioned the train incident and the reunion a few days ago. As time passed, she became concerned about other matters.

"Chang, I'm worried about Jacob and Clipper," she said. "I really have a bad feeling. Up where they are, it's all snowy. If I were still a human, I would have frozen. But look where we are now! It's warmer here, and we're not that far away from them. Something's wrong."

"If you're worried, you should go find them. You found me and you know I'm safe," said Chang.

"I think I'll do that. You have the viewing ring to locate us. Also, you have Auben and Pierre with you. Be safe and watch for danger." She said a quick goodbye and left.

All Chang could do was wave. "Auben," he said once Sally was out of sight, "you and Pierre should stay with me. I can guide you through this world. But I need to rest first. My foot's killing me." He made his way to another bench on the trail where he elevated his foot.

"I notice you limp," said Auben. "I wanted to ask this before, but I decided against it. What *is* wrong with your foot?"

"I broke it some time ago. I no longer use crutches and it's on the mend, but it still hurts when I spend too much time on it."

"Heh-heh. You broke your foot?" Pierre snickered. "I've never heard o' such a thing!"

THE TALES OF DRACO   307

"Now, Pierre, his feet are not as strong as yours," Auben pointed out. "Take off your bandages, Chang. I want to have a look at this broken foot."

Chang gave a skeptic glance at Auben before opening his boot. His foot was red and swollen.

At the sight of it, Pierre could not hold in his odd, kangrui laugh. "Breakin' a foot? Classic! I think it's impossible for a kangrui to break his foot! Hahaha! Fragile foot!"

"Be quiet, Pierre. I'm trying to heal him," Auben hissed. He took another look at Chang's foot.

Chang did not say a word. He didn't know what Auben would do. The lightscale sat down in front of him, brushing Pierre away with his tail. Next, he lifted up both forepaws. Looking at his right set of claws, he set them on top of his left wrist, away from important veins. Smoke escaped from his nose following a reluctant breath. He then pressed down with the dragon strength he had. Growling from the pierce, his tough scales gave away. Blood trickled to the surface.

"I thought only an ice blade could do that," Chang said.

"Yes, but we as dragons are strong. We have the ability to harm one another, you know."

The pale red blood flowed out. Auben let it drip to his other paw. He kept the fluid away from his claws as he reached out for Chang's foot. Then he let the blood drip onto it while Chang watched in distress. As the blood was absorbed into Chang's skin, the swelling deflated like a balloon. The red color faded. Chang winced, rubbing his foot.

"Take a step," said Auben.

Chang stood up. As he put weight on his bare foot, he was shocked to feel no pain. He took another step, but did not limp. He then circled the bench a few times.

"Auben, what did you do? My foot feels better! Thank you! How did you do it?"

Auben licked his minor wound. "Lightscales' blood has healing properties. The blood of a lightscale can heal many wounds, depending on the severity."

"What about darkscales?" Chang questioned.

"It is a fact their blood does nothing if it touches you, but there is a superstition among many who believe that darkscales' blood will curse you."

Chang's curiosity was again aroused. "Is that all the magic you have?"

"That depends. Many of us receive magic with the help of wizards or enchanters."

Chang wiped his forehead. "Wow, so much to learn. Well, I'm certainly glad you were here to heal me, Auben. Thank you." With delight, he jumped up in the air.

Pierre scoffed, waving a paw. "Ha! You call that a jump? Ya hardly left the ground. I'll show you a *jump!*"

Pierre crouched down, taking a deep breath. With his powerful legs, he jumped as high as he could. He reached a maximum height of a good six feet before landing back on the ground with a hard stomp. Chang felt the ground rumble for a brief moment.

"Now *that's* how someone should jump," said Pierre haughtily.

"Show some manners, Pierre," Auben snapped. "Chang may have abilities you can't even dream of."

Pierre picked up a small rock and tossed it in the air. "Mmm, sure he does. Well, when that blue dragon came about, I almost sent her to the side of a cliff, y'know."

Auben glared at Pierre before turning back to Chang. "The mountains here look gorgeous if I do say so myself," he said, deliberately changing the subject.

Chang took a deep breath of fresh air. While doing so, he decided to pull out the viewing ring and look through it, but with little hope of finding what he was casually searching for. The color green engulfed his surroundings. As he slowly turned in a circle, he was surprised to see a bright red spot over a small dirt mound not too far from where he was standing. He did not expect to be so close to the thing he was thinking of.

"Interesting… what's over there?" he asked himself.

He knelt down and began to unearth the mound to see what it was.

NIGHT HAD FALLEN BEFORE SALLY FOUND US. FROM WHAT SHE HAD told me, I realized we were much closer to Chang than I thought. That was a good thing. If all went well, we could meet up with him the next day. Fate must have been on our side that night. We built a small campfire (with very little effort) and curled up on the ground next to it. Now that we were farther east, there was much less snow. There was no sign of Syntare either. I didn't know where she was. This concerned me. I didn't want to admit it, not even to myself, but I worried for her.

"It's interesting how snowy it was back west. But here, it's not as bad," said Sally. "I'm really glad that that ice warlock you told me about is no longer around. Now we have the first piece of the portal. I can't wait until this is all over. Not only will I become a human again, but I'll also get to see Pearl Forest."

"Let's just hope that will all happen," muttered Clipper.

Sally nodded and continued, "I wasn't born a dragon like you were, but now...well I just feel like I need to join you."

I gave Sally a warm smile. "Look at you now. You can breathe fire, spit venom, and you have sharp claws like the rest of us. And let's not mention your horns."

"Yeah, but it's not who I truly am."

"If you come with us to Elsov, we'll do everything in our power to turn you back into a human," I said.

Sitting upright, I looked over and saw Reno and Razden sleeping side by side. I couldn't help chuckling a little. "That's sweet; and it takes a lot for me to say that," I whispered to Clipper

"I think she liked him the moment she laid eyes on him," Clipper replied. "Look at them. They're both sound asleep."

The sight was peaceful to see. We each lay back down to try to get some sleep ourselves. Eventually I stood up, stretched my back, and walked away from the others. My contagious yawn spread to Clipper. "Jacob, where are you going?" he asked drowsily.

I scratched my neck with a foot. "I just need to spend some time alone. Don't worry, I'll be back in a few minutes. I need to think some things over."

I stepped over the fire and away from the camp. I found myself in the dark of the night. There I scanned my eyes left and right. I kept thinking about Syntare, wondering where she was.

"*Don't worry. She won't find you tonight,*" an inner voice whispered.

My ears stood up. I looked around but saw nobody.

"*We have met before,*" the voice said in my mind.

"Oh, Elemek. It's you. I'm glad you're here."

"*I cannot tarry. I am only here to warn you and to prepare you.*"

"Warn?" I asked.

"*The dragon you call Syntare is getting close. However, what you have been told is correct. A lightscale is with one of your friends.*"

"Can you help me find a clue to the second piece?" I asked hopefully.

"*Sadly, I can't. You and your friends must find the clues yourselves. I only knew where the first piece was hidden because it was guarded by Glaciem. It is not the only piece that is guarded, however. Your enemies do not want you back home. If you and Clipper are able to end the Nibelung threat, you two may be helpful to Kusla, Kathoyen, and the Free States.*"

I closed my eyes, remembering the days of Triathra and his dwarf tribe. "I understand why I was sent here," I said. "That's the connection between the Monolegions and Vesuvius. If Triathra was a sorcerer, he must have served the Higher Crown."

"*You are right. The dwarfs on this earth lived under the Crown. They have longed to have power here. Control on the first two earths will grant true power. Vesuvius believes that only the strong should* reign freely. *The meek should not inherit. When there is one nation, the strong and the powerful will be the leaders. If the weak are not productive, there is no reason for them to live.*"

"I've heard of that belief before," I said. "It sounds like ethnic cleansing if you ask me."

"*It is. The Vesuvian Crown does not understand why we live at all. Don't worry, Jacob. Once on Elsov, you will be instructed on what to do with Vesuvius. Do what you must and all will be well. I will help you if you need me.*"

I began to imagine Pearl Forest again. I wanted to hear more from Elemek, but the voice was silent. Elemek was gone. Feeling in good spirits after talking with him, I returned to the campsite where my friends were waiting. Clipper was already asleep.

"Good thing you came back," said Sally. "I feel a breeze. A small storm is passing over us."

I looked into the night sky to see the clusters of oncoming clouds. "It doesn't look that bad," I said.

"Well if it rains, it may help us. It's easier to track a scent with moisture in the air, I've come to realize. Wait until you meet Auben and Pierre. Auben looks young, a few years younger than the rest of us. He looks a little like Razden, only with pure orange scales."

"And you said Pierre's a kangrui?" I asked her.

"Yeah. He bears a small resemblance to a wallaby. You'll meet him soon enough."

"He sounds interesting," I replied. "I'm looking forward to meeting him."

Sally continued talking with me for a few more minutes before sleep started to overcome us. I stood over the fire and stomped it out. In the dark, we nestled down and closed our eyes. As I drifted off to sleep, I dreamt of Pearl Forest.

CHAPTER 30

RENDEVIOUS ATOP THE CLIFFS

We decided to leave early that morning, knowing Syntare would be tracking us soon. Sally had flown back to Chang to let him know where we were. Later that morning, Clipper and I sat at the top of a frost-covered mountain. A light flurry of snow brushed about in the high altitude. This was where Sally told us we were to meet Chang's party. With the mountain made up of high cliffs and steep slopes, the summit was accessed only by a series of switchbacks.

I was sitting on the ledge, waiting for my friends to come while Clipper sat patiently away from the high drop. Waiting near Clipper were Reno and Razden, who kept a sharp eye on the polished blue diamond that glittered even without being exposed to direct sunlight.

"I have very limited knowledge of this world," Razden said to Reno. "I always believed this realm was a mere myth. Under the Vesuvian regime, I was taught that someday all creatures would bow to his crown. I figured this world was only mentioned metaphorically, but I always imagined what this place would be like. I remember in school learning that humans were as tall as elves. Yes, there are plenty of humans where I lived, but I never thought much of them; at least until now."

"Humans are untrustworthy," said Reno. "They can be cruel and greedy. I've been kidnapped by them and held in prison! The only ones I'm friends with now are Chang and Joshua. Sally was once a woman, but she's one of us now. It was Sally who freed me."

"It sounds like most humans here are terrible people," Razden said sympathetically.

"They are."

Reno's attitude irritated me every time she brought up the subject of humans. I didn't want her to say things like that to Razden, so I finally stepped in. "Reno, I know what Larson did was wrong, but not all humans are bad. The Captain was just doing his job. He didn't know anything about us. He must've been scared of the unknown. We all are. And what about Joshua and Chang, like you said? Or even Sergeant Nelson? If you don't forgive Larson, what makes you any better than him?"

Reno did not answer. She immediately stood and walked away in a huff. Razden followed her.

"Reno, don't be angry," he said. "Jacob has a point. I must admit, I fear humans as much as you do. But look at where we are. We are surrounded by trees atop a beautiful cliff. It is the second most beautiful thing I see." Razden gazed deep into Reno's eyes.

Reno turned away bashfully. It was the first time anyone had ever said something like that to her.

"Th— Thank you, Razden," she whispered.

Razden touched his nose to Reno's. "I would not worry. Soon we will see Pearl Forest. It will be lovely for the both of us."

Reno gave up the rest of her frustration, which was manifested by a smile. "Pearl Forest. That's where Jacob and Clipper said they went in their dreams. It really does sound lovely. Occasionally I dream of a place like that. I've always wanted to meet the nymphs and the grøls. I was told that grøls live in trees."

"The fairy once took me to a small hill near a grøl village. On that hill is a little waterfall that empties into a bright, sparkling pond. There are Lili-pads, frogs, fireflies, and much more. At night, under the starry sky, the frogs croak and you can hear fairies and other magical creatures sing. Their voices ring throughout the forest. In the hill is a little cave where you and I can live when we grow to adulthood."

Reno's heart melted. "Oh, I would love to go there!"

"When we go to Pearl Forest, you and I can live there forever. I will be there for you and you will be there for me."

A tear formed in the corner of Reno's eye. "I— I don't know what to say… We can live together in peace; together with a family. I really would love it."

Razden reached out and touched Reno's paw. "Enough is said. I promise you with all my heart that we will go to Pearl Forest. We will live together… forever."

Clipper listened nearby, blinking away a few tears. He quietly slipped away from them, joining me. "I believe Reno has found love," he whispered to me. He tilted his head in confusion when I leaned over the edge of the cliff.

"What are you doing?" he asked, keeping away from the cliff.

"I think I see him. Wait… Yes! I see Chang! And… I also see Sally and the other lightscale in the distance! Look at him, he's a bit smaller than Sally."

"What about Pierre? Do you see him?"

I squinted my eyes. "I don't see him just yet. I'm actually interested to see what a kangrui looks like. Right now I think I should give Sally and the others a signal so they know where we are."

There was no challenge in that. All I needed was a deep breath and a ten second, fifty yard flame. Sally's head turned up toward me. She said something to Chang and then, taking flight, she began to spiral up the cliff-side. Keeping my eyes on the path below, I soon saw Pierre marching into view. His stride looked just like any other traveler's. From a distance he looked exactly as Sally had described him earlier that morning: short, stubby, and with tan-colored fur; except his feet were a little smaller than what I had expected. I also found it odd seeing him swish his tail forward and hold it in his paws.

"Oh, there he is," Clipper said, pointing. "The kangrui's catching up to Chang. They all see us. Oh look, Chang's waving at us." Clipper waved back.

I smacked a rock over the cliff with my tail. "This'll be interesting for sure."

Clipper looked at me, snorting in amusement. I watched the small creature stomp the ground with his foot. After every few steps, he took a long hop forward.

"He should have no trouble fitting in," I said. "People will probably think he's a kangaroo or something like that."

Clipper snorted even louder. I thought about what I had just said. Even from this distance I could tell Pierre had distinguishable features that a kangaroo didn't have. Besides, kangaroos didn't live in such a region. The kangrui would stand out no matter what, especially when it was walking amongst men.

Sally reached the top. She landed between me and Clipper, taking a few deep breaths. "Huh-huh-huh— Chang and Pierre are on their way up. Huh— They found the path that leads up here."

She collapsed onto the ground, taking another deep breath. Auben arrived a few minutes later. He stared somewhat fearfully at me.

"Eh… Good day to you, sir. I assume you're Jacob Draco?" he gulped.

I nodded as passively as I could, trying to put him at ease. "Yes I am. It's nice to meet you, Auben."

The orange lightscale took a few deep breaths, no longer alarmed. "Forgive my uneasiness. I assume Ms. Serene has told you a little about me. I am the one who overheard Vesuvius' plan concerning the Grün-hære."

I could tell from his foreign accent that he was not from the first earth. In my opinion, it sounded somewhat like a broken German accent. I bowed my head in respect. Auben bowed as well.

"You've come a long way. Welcome," said Clipper.

Auben turned and bowed to him also. "You must be Mr. Clipper. It is a pleasure to meet you both. The reason I have come is to warn you about the Grün-hære."

"Yeah, Sally told us about them," said Clipper. "Maybe while we're waiting for Chang and Pierre, you can tell us a little more about them."

"Before that, Auben should meet the others," I mentioned.

Sally rose to her feet. "Great idea. It'll be awhile before Chang and Pierre make it up here."

Having caught her breath, Sally exhaled deeply, which caused a flame to escape her throat. It jumped over to a nearby tree and sizzled away. Sally placed a paw over her mouth.

"Sorry. I didn't mean to do that."

Auben took no notice. He had his eyes on Reno and Razden, who had their eyes on him. He realized he and Sally were the only lightscales present, but he did not seem to mind. The six of us waited all afternoon. I didn't think they would arrive until early evening, considering the climb and Chang's broken foot. As time went by, we sat in a circle and discussed future plans.

"I've been wondering about Fenson and Bluepond," Clipper said thoughtfully. "I haven't seen them since we left the house in California."

"Fenson and Bluepond?" Auben repeated. "Trihan told me about them. He said they were traveling north-east, last he knew. They should run into the small army my friend Losdir organized. Trihan planned it that way. They are here to keep the Grün-hære occupied so you can search for the pieces. Quite frankly, we are concerned how well you can handle the Horde on this earth. Being anarchists, they fight in such a manner that there will be as many civilians as possible suffering. We dragons are also destructive creatures, always drawing attention to ourselves. These two bodies would be a terrible mix in a land of innocent people who know nothing of us. I can imagine how terrible a conflict that can be. Losdir's army is meant to minimize the Grün-hære's influence on the people."

"Distracting our enemies; clever," I remarked. "You said they're keeping the Grün-hære busy? I believe we've met a few of them, from the Horde I mean. One has managed to follow us here: Syntare. She's the one that resembles me. Glaciem was also here. He was supposed to guard the diamond, but he's dead now."

Auben's ears suddenly rose. "You *killed* Glaciem?"

I took a step back, hoping I didn't upset him. "If I hadn't, he would've killed me, Clipper, and even Reno. That's when we rescued Razden, the young one next to Reno. He was an ice dragon until we freed him."

Auben's eyes widened in amazement. "Jacob, I mean Mr. Draco, Vesuvius is an ally to the ice warlock of the south. Glaciem, as he is always called, is responsible for the deaths of many innocent people with curses of long winters, often causing famine and starvation. Many have said he could never die at the hands of another being. They say the ice dragons could never be freed either. If I dare say, Jacob, you may be a worthy opponent against Vesuvius."

"A worthy opponent?" I replied. "I've seen him in my dreams. How can I stand up to someone like him?"

"Do you realize how long he and his royal line have spread terror over Elsov? Since the murder of King Landon and the fall of the ancient nation of Marin-sulae, Vesuvius' lineage has held the throne. If the current King, Vesuvius III, is removed from power, you will be remembered as a true hero indeed."

I thought about what he told me. I had never met Vesuvius face to face physically. But in my dreams, I knew he was a true adversary. If Clipper and I could stop an entire dwarf tribe, a sorcerer, and an ice warlock, then was it possible that we were of some concern to Vesuvius? That must have been what Elemek was telling me, even if it sounded impossible. But then again, Clipper and I needed help from this "army" Auben had mentioned to fight the Grün-hære. How strong was I against the Grün-hære and Vesuvius? The only way to know was to fight them. The problem was, it scared me to think about it.

"I don't know how worthy of an opponent I can be," I finally said.

"Not much by yourself," said Clipper. "It will take me and many other friends, friends that you already have."

"All of us," I finished. "Right now, we need to find the rest of the portal. A group of us can go after the other pieces, the other group can aid the army." I turned to Reno and Razden. "This is going to be a dangerous journey. We can leave the diamond here to make sure we don't lose it. Can you two keep it with you?"

"Us? Together?" Reno asked in excitement.

"We may be apart, but we'll be working together."

Everyone in our group agreed. We were determined to fulfill our duties. As we formed our plan, Chang and Pierre finally arrived, both breathing heavily. They came much sooner than I had expected. First, I greeted Chang. He was quite relieved to see me, as I was him. As he greeted Clipper, I noticed he was not limping in the slightest. But even on healthy feet, he was exhausted. Sweat ran down his forehead while Pierre panted like a dog.

"Chang, how's your foot?" Clipper exclaimed, surprised as I was.

"You can thank Auben for that," said Chang. "His blood can heal wounds. I told Sally not to tell you because I wanted to surprise all of you."

As he sat down on a dead log, Pierre walked around him. I gazed at the kangrui. Not once had I seen a creature like him. The animal stared back at me as he blew a leaf off his nose.

"You mus' be Jacob Draco," he addressed me in a formal tone, though he looked somewhat fearful.

I nodded and bowed my head to let him know that he could trust me, the same way I had with Auben. "You're the kangrui Sally told us about. Pierre," I said.

"That I am," he replied. He turned to my friend. "And you mus' be Mr. Clipper."

As Pierre spoke with Clipper, I told Chang about the train incident and Elemek's visit. Apparently Sally had already informed him of our recent experiences. He in turn told me about his arrival in St. George and his meeting with Auben. When we were both up to date, I explained our plan to retrieve the remaining pieces of the portal and to help Losdir's army.

"Perhaps you can go with Chang then," I told Pierre. "He can fly back home and get help from Sergeant Nelson. If the Grün-hære runs the threat of harming innocent people, I want him to know. I'm sorry about coming all this way and going straight back, Chang."

"If it's for a good reason, I don't mind," Chang said. "I can call Joshua and let him know I'm coming, then I can bring the Sergeant back up here. Hopefully, with his help, we can protect innocent people. There's only one concern I have; what if I run into Captain Larson again?"

I felt a tinge of annoyance at the mention of Larson. "Just tell him you need to talk to Sergeant Nelson. You'll be fine. Nelson is one who can accept a kangrui's appearance."

Pierre turned to glare at me at my last remark. "Appearance, eh? What d'you mean? Jus' what's wrong with me appearance?"

I tilted my head back. "What? Nothing. I'm just saying you can't show yourself to those of this world. That's it. I wasn't trying to offend you."

Pierre clenched a furry fist. "Jus' watch what ya say, Mr. Draco. I have a powerful kick, y'know."

I wasn't sure why Pierre was so upset. Perhaps he had read into my words more than I had intended, or maybe he wanted to show that he was not afraid of me.

"Jacob was not insulting you, Pierre," said Auben, walking in between us. "He's your friend. He knows how humans think."

Pierre gave me a sidelong glance and walked away with a snort.

"Okay Chang," I said, shifting my attention from Pierre, "can you go back home and find Sergeant Nelson?"

"No problem," Chang nodded.

"I can take Auben and find Losdir and his group," Sally suggested. "But how do I find this Losdir? He could be anywhere."

Another thought crossed my mind. "Remember that Fenson and Bluepond were heading north? They couldn't have traveled farther than we have. Maybe you can keep your nose open for them as well."

Sally's ears drooped. "That's a lot of land to cover, but we'll watch for them too."

"That leaves you and me, Jacob," said Clipper. "We can go after the next piece while Reno and Razden guard what we have. Does anyone have any other ideas? We don't mean to order everyone around." Nobody objected.

Reno carefully picked up the diamond with her jaws. She placed it at Chang's feet with care, as if it were a Faberge egg. The sapphire color danced in my eyes. It dazzled me every time I gazed upon it.

Chang mused, taking it in his hand. "So that's the first piece. I'm glad you found it. Now let me show you something I found under a mound."

We all turned our eyes to Chang. He carefully returned the diamond to Reno, then pulled something from each of his pockets. The first was something familiar that I hadn't seen in months: an albore made of fine wood with a golden rune etched in the handle. In his other hand was a piece of tattered cloth.

Sally took a closer look at the albore. "You didn't tell me you had that!"

Pierre took the tool of magic and held it in the air. "'Tis obvious an albore like this'd be part of a portal, bein' magic n'such. I was told it took one o' those wizard sticks with the other pieces, includin' this here albore, ta take someone between here and Elsov. An albore can most certainly boost the power o' the staff, y'know. Makes sense if I say so meself."

"I tried to teleport myself here, the same way Princess Rohesia did before," said Chang. "But I can't do it; I don't know how. That shows we've got a lot to learn about magic."

"How did you find it?" I asked him.

"I used the viewing ring, looking for the second piece. Like I said, it was under a mound."

"That means we now have *two* pieces!" said Sally. "Now we're getting somewhere. But we should probably get moving if we're to get the third."

"Only a few days here for me, but you're right Sally," said Chang.

"You and Auben can go," I said to Sally. "But before you do, we should look at that cloth. It might contain another clue. It'll be good to have everyone on the same page."

Pierre eyed Auben nervously. "The blue dragon and Auben are goin' by themselves, huh? Trihan gave *me* the task of lookin' after Auben."

"And your service will be greatly appreciated," Auben told him. "However, you cannot fly. You said Trihan sent you so I would not be alone. I won't be alone if I'm with Sally. But that does not mean your quest will be in vain. You will help Mr. Chang in many ways."

Sally and Auben looked at one another. We bid each other farewell and good luck, and they took to the sky. I felt confident as I watched them fly away. Everyone knew where everyone else was going, rather than being lost in a confusing mess.

"You guys can rest for as long as you want before heading down the mountain. Take in the sights if you wish," I said to Chang and Pierre.

Clipper and I were about to leave, again bidding the others farewell and good luck. Everything was organized. Chang was taking Pierre back to the lonely beach and going to look for Nelson, Sally and Auben were on their way to this "little" army, Reno and Razden were going to stay and watch the diamond, and Clipper and I were going to get the next piece. Four groups of two. No one was traveling alone. Simple and easy. Oh, if it were only simple and easy! The sound of a growl bouncing off the cliffs gave me a clear reminder why this wasn't going to be simple and easy.

"Pleased ta meet all of ya!"

CHAPTER 31

BATTLE ATOP THE CLIFFS

I looked up only to find myself blinded by fire.

"Syntare!" hissed Clipper.

"Shame ya didn't leave any sooner. Yer trail didn't betray my nose. What do they call ya, Clipper? An unusual name."

Syntare wasted no time. After landing, she immediately lowered her horns and charged at me. The powerful force sent me tumbling backward head over heels, over the cliff's ledge. Despite the intense ache in my chest, I calmly spread my wings and pumped them. My *descent* turned into *ascent*. As I battled my way back to the top, Syntare had charged into Clipper as well, but she didn't send him over the cliff. Clipper sprang back to his feet. He retaliated with the savage weapons of tooth and claw. Clipper may have not shared my level of fury, but that didn't make him immune to the dragon's rage. At the same time, however, Syntare, being a black dragon, fought with twice as much fury. She managed to pin Clipper to the ground in six seconds flat. In her dominant place, where she always loved to be, she sank her teeth into his wings then jerked her head back and forth. Clipper wailed from the disgusting sound of his wings ripping. They weren't disabled yet, though several thick rivers of dark blood began to flow down them. I returned to the top just in time to butt Syntare off my friend.

As I issued my own attack, Reno plucked the diamond from the ground and ran to the edge of the cliff under Razden's cover. They both leapt off and sashayed to the ground. At least the diamond was safe.

Pierre stood quivering as he watched the brutal fight unfold. He handed the albore back to Chang. "Here, use this while I defend meself me own way!"

Chang took the albore from Pierre's paw. "I don't know if this will help," he said nervously. "I've never used an albore before. I don't know how to cast a spell, let alone one that I can defend myself with."

Chang hung the albore at his side. His head and shoulders were covered with cold perspiration.

Gashes and scrapes were exchanged among us darkscales at a liberal rate. Flares of fire sprayed in various directions. Though Syntare was outnumbered, she fought with a terrible wrath. It was overtaking her as it was with me and Clipper, making the fight even more vicious. After sending me off the cliff again, she charged a second time at Clipper. Her horns knocked him against a fir, destroying the tree in a sound of wooden thunder as it twisted around its neighbors' branches before smashing onto the ground. With Clipper down, Syntare grabbed his left wing with her claws and squeezed, freeing more hot blood. Clipper roared and squirmed.

"Yer at my mercy, traitor!" she taunted. "What's yer name again, Clipper? *Ha*! As they would say in our native tongue, ye-svenise voss-thleass! Yer time fer death!"

Chang couldn't bear it any longer. He decided to try using magic, despite his fear. He lifted the albore to the tip of his nose. There had to be some spell he could cast! And he had to do it now! Chang closed his eyes, deep in thought. He felt the albore's power pulse in his hand. He tried to think of a number of spells. Each time the albore did nothing. He had never been taught how to use one. It was a hit or miss trial, a trial that needed to be resolved in the next five seconds. After thinking of another spell, his mind in full concentration, he opened his eyes to see a surge of energy form above Syntare. Whatever it was, it zapped her and threw her off Clipper. Syntare stood back up and growled at Chang. Her teeth were bared; her eyes were glowing. The pulse in Chang's hand intensified.

"An inexperienced 'uman practicin' magic, I see!" she snarled. "Let us see 'ow ya do."

Syntare charged at him. Frightened as he was, Chang tried to think of another spell off the top of his head. A cloud of dirt and grass came to life in front of him. Syntare was blinded by the swirling debris, yet she managed to get past the cloud of earth. By then the pulsing in Chang's hand felt as if it were breaking his bones. Syntare, only ten feet away, took in a deep breath. The glow of fire illuminated from the back of her throat. In panic, Chang summoned another spell. An invisible shield materialized just in time. Syntare's fire was unable to reach him. The fire didn't roast him, but he could no longer bear the pain in his hand. Syntare lowered her horns, released a deafening roar, and charged again. Chang's force field shattered like glass from the impact. He was exposed! He couldn't stand casting another spell either!

I saw Chang at Syntare's mercy when I returned to the top. I had to get her away from him! Chang looked like he was suffering terribly. I didn't want the albore to break either, since I still didn't know what the consequence would be if that happened. I tried my best to distract Syntare. I spat venom that landed on her horn, which did nothing. I blew small flames and began hovering above the ground. My wings beat back and forth, causing a wind to blow debris everywhere.

"Hey Syntare! You want me? Come get me!"

Luckily she did as I wished. She spread her wings to take off. But before she could, Pierre emerged from where he had been waiting. He threw a harmless rock at her and chattered in a strange, animalistic manner. With one foot down and one foot up, he kicked Syntare in her rear thigh. It didn't do much except knock her off her feet. The kick must have been hard, though, for she tried to limp away. Pierre gave another potent kick in her tail that caused her to slip off the ledge.

"Good work, Pierre," I said.

"An' that's why ya don't mess with a kangrui!" he laughed.

I turned my focus back to Syntare. She had fallen about half-way before regaining control. I blew a small flame down the cliff, beckoning her to follow me. I wanted to get her as far away from Chang or Reno as possible. Grimacing, Clipper found the strength to join me.

"Heights or no, I'm coming with you!" he yelled.

CHANG AND PIERRE WERE LEFT ALONE ON THE MOUNTAIN, SAFE and, for the most part, unharmed. They both eyed the fallen trees and uprooted ferns. The ground all around them had been torn up. Fire smoldered in places that were not damp. Pierre leaned forward and rested his front paws on the ground, panting. Chang sat next to him, addressing his throbbing hand.

Pierre tried to talk while cooling himself. "Hh-Hh-Hh— Such a… Hh-Hh— dazzlin' show… Hh— Mr. Chang. Hh-Hh— You should beware of a dragon's wrath, y'… Hh— y'know. Hh-Hh— On a normal day… Hh— you'd be cooked or torn to shreds or sometin' like that. Hh-Hh-Hh—"

"It was the albore that saved me," said Chang, "except my hand hurts right now. Ah, it hurts bad!"

Pierre slowed his breath. "No matter your hand. Hh-Hh— Ya handle an albore like a wiza'd. Hh— *ahem*! Mmm, sorry. Y'know, when someone uses an albore for the first time, they'd be iffy an' sloppy, tryin' to find the right spell that doesn't exist n'all. Takes much knowledge ta know what spells're valid and what aren't. You defended yourself very well, Mr. Chang."

"I hope Jacob and Clipper are holding up right now," Chang said, sighing.

He stood up and peered over the edge of the cliff. He didn't see anything, but he heard the cries and growls ringing throughout the mountains. Chang cringed. Someone was bound to hear it. To them it would sound like this land was haunted by vengeful spirits.

"If I was a wizard, I'd use much more magic with this albore," he said aloud. "But I'm not a wizard. I don't know much about magic."

"That's not stoppin' you," replied Pierre. "If ya practice magic n'such the right way, you can do anythin'. You already know much more 'bout magic than I do."

Chang wanted to think about what Pierre had said, but his throbbing hand kept his mind on one thing. "We need to get down this mountain as soon as possible. Reno and Razden are down below."

"Don't worry. Jacob an' Clipper'll whip ol' dragon-lady worse than yer thunder bolt." Pierre cackled with laughter.

Chang tucked his sore hand inside his shirt. "You're probably right, but we're wasting time. Let's head down and find Reno and Razden. I think I should keep this albore for now in case we run into any more danger."

"A plan's a plan, y'know. Again, I mus' give ya a compliment with that albore. Takes a talented being ta handle it the way ya did."

"Thank you. Now let's hurry."

With the advantage of two against a leg-injured one, things turned for the better. Clipper fought bravely until his torn wings got to him. Reluctantly, he backed off. Syntare and I, though not in as bad a condition as Clipper, showed battle wounds ourselves. The pains I had were minimal (not to mention no injured leg), so I had the upper hand. I used my horns to strike her to the ground. Fatigue finally overcame her, much to my satisfaction. She sat there, staring up at me. No longer was she in a defensive stance.

"Ya fought like the true black dragon this time. Ya didn't fight like that before." She let out a light huff. "'Tis a shame ta see ya waste yer gift."

"Don't tempt me," I hissed. "I know what you're trying to do. We are evil creatures, but I still have freedom to choose. I chose one path, you chose the other."

She took a snap at me, missing. "Dragon traitor! That shows yer weakness!"

She faced Clipper and discharged venom from within her throat. Taken completely by surprise, Clipper cried out while holding his paws to his eyes. From my personal experience, I knew his world transformed into something of false flashes and distortion. Angrier still, I gave Syntare a solemn glare. Syntare stared at me with a sly expression.

"Ya see what I mean, Jacob? Yer a traitor to the 'ighest dragon on the throne."

I didn't respond that time. There was another rusty noise coming from her throat. More venom was about to be discharged. Knowing where she was aiming, I dodged it.

"You're *not* going to change my mind!" I yelled.

Before I could strike her with my horns, she jumped out of my way. I charged into the side of the cliff. A rumble rang throughout the side of the mountain. The energy from my horns spread across the rock, causing a small boulder to collapse from where it rested. It fell down the steep slope and landed between Syntare's wings. The hard stone pressed her to the ground then rolled to the side. I walked up to my ferocious attacker. Her tail twitched as she groaned.

"Yer destined to return to yer 'appy woodland," she groused, stretching her wings.

"I'm going back to Pearl Forest. That's a promise," I answered.

What Syntare did next made me jolt backwards. I didn't understand what was happening to her at first. She started howling and rolling around on the ground, obviously frightened. Her sudden fit worried me. She began addressing an unseen being, "Thentize mi, Keng Vesuvius! E zoth von no…! Ahh! I apologize! I'll speak the other tongue while I'm 'ere as ya wish… I know about the ice dragons, yes. I freed 'em afore I came 'ere. They've gone to the northern 'ighlands… No, do not punish me! I beg o' you, o' Great King!" She paused for a moment. "I followed the dragon traitors to the east. 'eitspel must've showed ya what 'appened. I did the best I could."

I stood like a statue, astounded. I was there, right in front of her, yet she seemed to be staring straight through me, as if she were looking at someone behind me.

"I'm sorry. Please show yer mercy, migh'y King! I simply wanted 'em ta be loyal to yer sovereign power."

"What's going on?" I asked her, brushing my tail over her nose.

She did not respond to me but rather to her invisible superior. I couldn't bring myself to attack her in such a vulnerable state.

"Yes, I will. I'll succeed this time. I'll go where ya told me, yes. The one called Ellen. I will 'ead there immediately. Thank ye, great King, fer offerin' another chance ta me!"

Syntare shook her head violently, snapping out of her trance. She looked back at me again. Her eyes were not glowing as they had been earlier. Her pupils were mere black dots. I saw no hostility in them at all. They seemed sorrowful, as if she were afraid I would get hurt. In an eerily strange way, she seemed as delicate as a flower. It was odd to see her this way, considering how aggressive she had been not even a minute before.

"I have ta go," she said.

I watched her fly in an upward spiral before disappearing over the summit. She didn't tell me directly who she was speaking with, but she mentioned Vesuvius. The thought of his voice in such close proximity to me left me completely unnerved. I didn't know what to think. He must have commanded Syntare to leave. Stranger still, all Syntare said was that she had to go. She didn't use any hostile tone, only a quiet mutter. Her voice sounded a lot gentler that time; and gazing into her eyes before she left, I almost felt sorry for her.

I began pacing back and forth once she was gone, talking to myself. "I can't believe it. It was *him*! I couldn't hear him, but his voice was there!"

I walked over to where Clipper lay on the ground. He slowly got back to his feet. He rubbed his tongue over his fangs as he looked around.

"Oh, I hate getting that venom in my eyes," he huffed. "Those hallucinations aren't pleasant. Ah! And my wings! Huh-huh— don't worry. I think I can still fly once the stinging stops. You know, as much as it hurts, it doesn't hurt as I thought it would." He pulled down one of his wings and licked the tears. "What's wrong with you, Jacob? You look like you saw a ghost. And where's Syntare?"

"It was Vesuvius," I said. "He knows what's going on. He sent Syntare away. I heard her mention someone named Ellen."

"Ellen? Huh. That teaches us one thing about Vesuvius."

"What?"

"There's a lot we'll have to learn about him."

I blew out some smoke to clear my lungs. "I know. Ever since I first dreamt of him, it's been hard to go to sleep. You might say they were just dreams, but I think there's more to it. During one of these nightmares, he *admitted* that he haunts me often. It's very hard to comprehend."

"Well, at least we know that. The more we know the better."

Reno and Razden emerged from behind a cluster of ferns.

"Is the coast clear?" Reno asked, shaking like a leaf. "We heard the fighting. It sounded bad."

"It's safe. You can come out," I said.

"I told you they would defeat her," Razden said to Reno. "I'll never let you be harmed."

Reno scratched the dirt under her claws. "Just as you promised."

Clipper and I exchanged smiling glances. I noticed Reno didn't have the diamond in her mouth. She must have known I was wondering where it was.

"I buried in a hollow," she said, pointing to where she had emerged. "It's in a place that's easy to remember."

"Well, two pieces are ours and we know Syntare went to… Ellen, whoever she is," said Clipper. "It's a good thing Sally and Auben left before she came, except having extra help would've been nice."

For the next half-hour we rested. All of us were exhausted. When I heard Chang and Pierre's faint voices coming nearer, I made a chirping noise to call them. They had to push away lots of branches to get to us. Chang was shocked after seeing our battle-ridden appearances, especially Clipper's wings.

"They sting right now, but I think I can still fly," said Clipper.

I explained to Chang about the last fight with Syntare and why she had left. He was relieved that the battle was over for now. We all were.

"So where do we go from here?" Reno asked.

Chang pulled out the cloth from his pocket. "Maybe this can help." He carefully unfolded it and read what was written: "Journey to the dead mines. Kimberly; Piute County; north-east of here; hour's flight? Within the gray stone is the Gateway. The Fairies are always present."

Chang reread the text.

"Kimberly? I think that's the name of a town; in Piute County," Clipper guessed.

"Hour's flight? That doesn't sound too bad," I said. I studied the words over again. "It says the fairies are always present."

Chang ran a finger over the ink in the cloth. "It says the next piece is the Gateway, and it's in a dead mine in Kimberly." He pulled out his trusty map and unfolded it on the ground. "Here it is. You just have to cross this land here. Like you said, Jacob, it doesn't look that hard."

"The Gateway," I repeated. "I wonder how big it is."

Pierre cleared his throat, indicating that he wanted to speak. "When I used the portal to come here, I stood on some sort o' square stone thingummy. Trihan used his master whatever to sen' me here. The platform seemed flat enough on the ground, 'bout the height o' two o' me paws, y'know. I'd bet a corn ear this stone square's the Gateway."

"In a dead mine," I said. "It sounds like it's hidden in an *abandoned* mine. This part of the country is rich with mining history. I wonder how a piece to a portal wound up in such a place."

"An abandoned mine in Kimberly, eh?" said Clipper. "I guess that's where we're going."

I shook my head in mock frustration. "Well, we can't carry a paper map. Pity that."

Chang, knowing what I meant, reached into the pocket where the cloth was. "I can give you the viewing ring. It's with me right here. It sounds like you know what you're doing, but what about other people? How close is this mine to civilization?"

Clipper made a small huff. "People or no, we still have to do this. Don't worry about us, Chang. We'll find a way."

"Exactly, don't worry," I replied. "You can go home and see if you can clear the air with Larson. And you can take care of our little furry friend here."

Pierre sniffed. "Careful, Jacob. You don't know how dangerous I am. You saw me kick that other darkscale over the cliff, didn't ya? Prime example."

"Reno, Razden, stay here and make sure nobody finds the diamond," Clipper told the young ones. "Chang can keep the albore for now if he wants to. I think it can be useful to him. Jacob and I will head to this mine."

Chang placed the viewing ring on the ground for me to slide my claw through. With this, finding the third peace shouldn't be too difficult.

WE WISHED EACH OTHER LUCK BEFORE SEPARATING. RENO AND Razden were left together. They made their way to the hollow where they had buried the diamond, keeping an eye out for people and animals.

"It's nice being here with nothing to worry about," Razden said. He looked up at the cloudy sky. "I never want to be trapped as an ice dragon again."

"I've experienced captivity, myself," said Reno. "That's how Jacob and Clipper found me in the first place. They told me I was in a basket guarded by a sorcerer and the Monolegion dwarfs. This all happened last spring; I can barely remember it. I already told you about that last time I was in prison. That's why I don't like humans."

"I believe you have had interesting experiences, good and bad. You say some humans have imprisoned you while others like Chang help you."

"I know… Maybe I have been too prideful. If I don't forgive, then it doesn't make me any better. I guess humans aren't so bad after all. Some are better than others, just like dragons."

"It's best to forgive if you are to end a conflict."

Reno's growling stomach interrupted the conversation.

"It sounds like you are hungry," chuckled Razden.

"I think I am," said Reno. "I remember seeing a pond. We can eat some fish. If we can't, we could try to find a cow, or maybe a deer."

"I don't remember the last time I had good food," said Razden.

"Did you eat anything as an ice dragon?" Reno asked.

"I don't know, but I'm quite hungry now. I will stay here and guard the diamond while you eat, and then when you return you can guard it while I eat."

"That's a good idea," said Reno. "We'll eat and return here. We can talk about our past adventures, and maybe even our promise. Oh, Pearl Forest… I'll keep that promise. I won't let anything get in our way." She sighed dreamily.

CHAPTER 32

No Easy Journey

It was a tiring flight to Kimberly, but we arrived at the edge of the ghost town early the next morning. The cold was trying a second time to overtake the region, this time without the help of a warlock. There was no snow yet, but rather a thin layer of frost. Despite the mild weather, I was pleased we didn't have to travel far. We had made several stops during the night to rest and eat any edible prey we could find. Because of his wings, Clipper especially appreciated those rests.

There was not much to see when we reached Kimberly. The town (or what was left of it, anyway) was made up of rotted sheds and decrepit houses. I could have destroyed a shed if I sneezed on it, even without the help of fire. The condition of the town lost in time meant nothing to me, though. What mattered was the third piece.

We trotted through the meadow to the top of a grassy hilltop. There we found a cluster of old foundations. A small, muddy road ran below the hill and through the ghost town. Sitting down, I slid the viewing ring from my claw and pinched the rim with the scales on my fingers. I held the ring up to my left eye, closing my right. The world around me became a hazy green. Slowly scanning the horizon, I soon found a scar of red to the northwest. It didn't seem that far away.

"Did you find anything?" Clipper asked.

"Yeah, I see some red over there." I pointed with my other paw. "It doesn't look that far off."

"Are we talking a mile or so?" Clipper spoke with trepidation.

I lowered the ring from my eye. "Maybe a half a mile. I think we can walk to it. You don't sound well, Clipper. What's wrong?"

"I'm not sure what to expect," he huffed. "We had to fight Glaciem and his ice dragons last time. What do you think will be waiting for us in the mine? There's bound to be something there."

"That's true." I wanted to sound casual saying that, but what came out of my voice sounded rather tense.

I slid my claw back through the ring where it was secure. There wasn't much of Kimberly to hold our interests, so we went on past it. The windy road beyond had been washed out to the point that I hardly recognized it as a road, but more of a deer path. The gray clouds above us began to darken even more. The moisture in the air told me this next storm was not going to be as big as the last one. Never mind the rain, I told myself. It wasn't the storm I had to stay cautious of. There was no threatening scent for the moment, though I knew I would find one sooner or later.

"We should be getting close," Clipper said, twitching his nose.

We traveled along the bottom of the hill until we found the entrance to one of the abandoned mines hiding behind some lush foliage, sealed up as if it were a tomb. I pulled off the viewing ring and again looked through it. The inside, behind the barricade, became a revealing red. The tunnel looked wide enough for me to fit into comfortably. There was a silver lining there. I then took a quick look around and noticed the small beaten path bending past the entrance. Examining the poorly maintained trail, I found footprints; fresh human footprints. No silver lining there.

"It looks like someone has been here," said Clipper, sniffing the tracks. "Whoever made them can't be far off. I think we can make a quick swoop inside. I just hope whatever is waiting for us in there won't put this person in danger."

I blew smoke from my nose. "Why would anyone be out here alone? No matter. One of us can stay near the entrance of this mine and keep watch. If somebody comes along, don't show your face, but do whatever you can to keep that person from entering. Flap your wings, kick up the wind, roar, blow fire, do anything. That way they'll know something is nearby, yet they won't see you. Use venom if you have to."

"The other one of us can sneak inside," said Clipper. "Just find the platform and hopefully get away. Pierre said this platform shouldn't be too big. I hope he's right. We'll need to hide it with Reno and Razden until it's time to use it." He stretched his wings and moaned. "Ohh...! Ah! I think I'll be the one who stays out here, that way I can rest my wings. You better hurry."

"Sounds good. Wish me luck," I said.

Clipper stepped behind a boulder that rested near the entrance. I heard him sit down. I made sure the viewing ring was still secure on my claw before bashing the barricade with a bump of my horns. An icy breath blew out of the mine. A chill ran down my row of spikes. I became engulfed in darkness the farther I went in. My pupils dilated. I was able to see as if it was a clear, moonlit night. The mine smelled musty and earthy from the strong fragrance of minerals, just what I imagined a mine would smell like. I looked carefully around to make sure I was not near any wooden braces, then I blew a ball of fire. That only lit the way for a few seconds. I moved along and blew another flame.

Venturing deeper, I tried to think of a way to entertain myself. I cleared my throat and made a cackling noise no other creature could mimic. I heard my call bounce off the stone-hard walls. I blew another flame. The platform's got to be down here somewhere. I hope I'll know it when I see it, I thought, wondering if I would have to use the viewing ring again. I blew another flame and cackled again.

I expected silence after the echo, and was spooked when there wasn't.

I heard a series of chirps responding to my call, followed by a long, loud screech. I froze in mid-stride. The noises played around in the tunnel before dissolving away. I swallowed nervously, unsure of what made the sound. I sniffed the air, discovering the presence of another creature. It was nothing I could identify. It smelled dank like the mine itself, but I could distinguish a difference.

I was not alone in this mine.

"It might've been a bat," I concluded. "No bat can scare me away."

I had strong doubts the mine was haunted. I continued forward, using my fire to light the way. As I ventured even deeper into the old mine, I heard droplets of water coming from the ceiling. Soon after, I heard the screech again, this time even closer.

"No bat will scare me off," I said aloud.

CLIPPER OPENED HIS EYES AS THE MILD STORM LOOMED OVER THE highlands.

After this there will be only three pieces to go. We're halfway there, he thought.

He closed his eyes again, letting the tiny raindrops drip over his body. He began daydreaming about life in Pearl Forest again. His rest came to a sudden end when he heard something snap nearby, possibly a twig. Clipper popped his head up from the ground. In the rain, he could smell the strong presence of man. He could also hear the sound of footsteps along the nearby path. Standing up and leaning against the boulder, he kept his eyes on the mine's entrance. As the footsteps became louder, a lone man, wearing a worn outfit and holding an unlit lantern, came into view. He hummed a simple tune and stopped in front of the mine, staring into the darkness. From behind the boulder, Clipper unfurled his fangs, hoping the man would not enter.

Unaware of Clipper's presence, the man inched closer to the entrance. Clipper had a good eye on him. He knew he had to keep the man from going inside. Trying to think of some way to distract him, he blew a wave of fire that barely missed the wet trees. The man turned in response to the flames. He seemed to have noticed the smoky cloud where the flames had died out. The man waved a hand in front of his face before turning back to the mine. Clipper then made a low but noisy grunt. The man again turned around.

"Is someone there?" he asked.

In response, Clipper growled. He saw that the man now looked uneasy. He expected him to run down the path the same way he had come. Instead, the man turned back to the mine and ran inside.

"No, you're not supposed to go in there," Clipper huffed in annoyance. He jumped over the boulder and chased after the man. "Stop! Don't go in there! It's dangerous!"

Clipper saw the man come to a halt. He stepped back into the shadows to keep from being seen. He heard the man cry out, "They have found the right place!"

The man pulled out a matchstick and struck it on the rough wall. Opening the lantern, he then lit it. With his way now illuminated, he continued down the mine. Clipper followed him.

THE DRIPPING NOISES STARTED TO PLAY MIND GAMES WITH ME. I blew another flame. From what I could see, the dark tunnel led into an open chamber. Several other veins broke into various directions. I was also standing near the top of a mineshaft that sank into eternal darkness far below. When my fire died out, I blew another to take its place. That time, from the corner of my eye, I thought I saw some sort of engraving on the wall to my right. When the firelight faded, I lifted a paw and ran my claws over it. I felt carved characters a few inches in height. They felt like written words. Just above and below the inscription, I could barely see grooves in the wall. I clasped the space between the grooves and pulled. What came out were a flat piece of square stone and a shower of pebbles. I blew another flame, noticing that the square stone had a smooth surface. I couldn't read the runes around the rim, but that didn't matter to me. I remembered Pierre saying the platform wasn't very high, and this slab wasn't very high at all; it looked to be only an inch or two thick. With the viewing ring, I checked to make sure this was the piece. Sure enough, I made out the red in the darkness. I had found the platform! The third piece! I flapped my wings twice with excitement before restoring the viewing ring to my claw.

"Halfway there," I told myself. "Now to get this out of here." I spoke aloud to provide myself with a little comfort in a somewhat creepy environment. I believed the mine would have been far more spooky if I were still a human.

Using my paws, I lifted the platform from the ground. It was not nearly as heavy as I expected. I balanced on my rear feet, the way a bear does, and picked up the platform. I took a few steps forward. Walking on two legs was something I was not used to anymore, but was still possible once I found my footing. I had reached a satisfying pace when I heard a shout from ahead. There was a flicker of light in the distance. I set down the platform, returning to all fours.

"Who's there?" I asked. "Speak up, please. I won't hurt you."

To my surprise, a man came into view, holding a lantern in his hand. Clipper was visible behind him.

"Jacob, I'm sorry! I tried to scare him off, but he ran in here and not away."

The man did not see my wing. He ran straight into it. With a painful grunt, he fell to the ground, his arms held over his face.

I stared at him and then at Clipper. "Why didn't you catch up to him?" I said. "You're much faster than he'll ever be."

"I didn't have the chance," Clipper replied.

I glanced at the broken lantern lying beside the man; the flame inside it was still alive. The man slowly got back to his feet. Several trickles of blood ran down his face from where he had hit my wing. He slowly backed away until he bumped into the far wall. He kept his eyes on the both of us, but in excitement rather than terror. His expression baffled me.

"Great, now he's seen us face to face," I muttered.

The man pointed at the platform. "You came to the right place," he said in a peculiar Russian accent. "Don't worry. I know of Elsov."

If the man was not frightened, I wondered if I should be. "How do you know about Elsov?" I asked him.

"I'm one who knows," he answered.

"We met someone like you in Atlanta long ago," Clipper told him. "Just how many of you are here?"

"Not many," replied the man. "But there are legends, old legends, from Siberia to China and elsewhere to beyond. Few know of these dying legends. Even fewer know of the truth."

"And you knew the platform was here?" I asked.

"Yes. That is why I'm here. When I heard about the sightings, I knew where to go. I was the one who buried the albore and laid the clue that led you here. You must have found the albore if you are here now."

"So, people like you have laid the clues, not fairies?" Clipper asked.

The man shrugged. "Not exactly. As I and my friends have said, fairies are among us. Triathra has fallen. A great evil on this earth is now behind you. Now you are seeking various pieces of a portal to take you back home. How many pieces have you found?"

"Three, and we have three more to go. There are six pieces total," I told him.

"Six pieces you say. Were they easy to find?"

I shook my head. I was about to say something else, but I was interrupted by the screech I had heard before. The man covered his ears in fright.

"The devil, it can't be!" he cried.

Clipper gulped. "J— Jacob, look right above you!"

The three of us gazed up. We beheld a terrifying, bat-like creature. Its teeth, as sharp as my own, dimly glimmered from the lantern's flame like a tiding of damnation. I knew it was the monster Clipper had seen earlier on the night after the train incident, and the same one that had landed on my shoulder before that.

"Lilinge!" the man gasped. "I didn't know there were any left on this earth!"

The man had called the monster a lilinge. It must have been guarding the platform as Glaciem had the diamond.

"Oh dear God, please no!" Clipper shivered.

Before I could blow a flame at the lilinge, it swiftly descended onto the man's shoulder, and immediately sank its teeth into his neck. The man yelled as he smacked the lilinge away. Seconds later, his face became pale. He dropped to his hands and knees, breathing as if he were being strangled. It all happened so fast.

Clipper's eyes widened with horror. "Oh no! He's becoming one of *them*!"

There was more screeching and clicking coming from the different veins deeper within the mine.

IT WAS EARLY IN THE MORNING WHEN CHANG RETURNED TO CALifornia. Duncan's airplane landed on the runway at a regional airfield just before dawn. It was the same airfield Chang had used when he left for St. George. As he took his first steps off the plane, he felt grateful for two healthy feet. He took a deep breath of the warm, ocean air.

"It feels good being warm again," he said.

Pierre had been hiding in a crate during the flight. After Duncan left, Chang had it brought to his car where he opened it. Pierre emerged, clutching his stomach with his paws. "Ohh… I can tell I'm not afit for flyin', y'know. My insides feel like they're tryin' to jump out o' me mouth. If I may ask, why are'ya not ill, Mr. Chang?"

"I'm used to flying," said Chang, looking left and right. "Now I need to talk to Sergeant Nelson and hopefully Captain Larson. Nelson is the only one who can help us bury the hatchet. I did call Joshua before I left St. George, so hopefully he's contacted Nelson. But before we talk, I have to hide you, Pierre, maybe at my house. Joshua can look after you."

Pierre slapped his tail on the ground. "Look after me? Do I look like a pet to you?"

"For the umpteenth time, I'm not saying anything like that. We've discussed that exposing you to people is not a good idea. Now don't worry about it. Let's get you stowed away. First let's get in my car."

"Ptah! Car. Lazy way to say 'carriage' if I may say," Pierre snorted.

"If you would cooperate and stop complaining, we can get through this with a lot less trouble. Now let's go." Chang was pretty sure Pierre's sick stomach was causing his bad mood.

Chang opened the rear door for Pierre, who grunted as he figured out how to climb in. When Chang showed him how, he looked doubtfully at the seat.

"Mr. Chang, I don't think I'll fit in there with me legs an' me tail."

Chang said nothing. He did his best to fit the kangrui in the car. It was no easy task with Pierre's size and shape.

"Now be careful, Mr. Chang. Mind me tail… Ah! Kindly please. I don't want any broken bones when this is done! Youch!"

"Sorry, just hold still please," said Chang.

He finally managed to fit Pierre in the back. He closed the door and then climbed into the driver's seat, clicking his seatbelt. He started the car and was soon on his way back to the cabin. While he was on the road, he turned on the radio. He caught a news report instead of music. He listened closely to the broadcast: Unusual activity had been reported at Mt. Ellen in eastern Utah. There were earthquakes, mass migration of wildlife, and bad-smelling water. There were also more sightings of "the black dragon". The red one had not been seen.

"Syntare!" said Chang under his breath. "If they haven't seen Clipper with this black dragon, then it has to be her. And did he just say Mt. Ellen? In Utah? So Ellen's not the name of a woman, but the name of a mountain! That must be where Vesuvius will come. Oh, this is bad, very bad!" He turned off the radio. He couldn't stand listening to more of these "signs" that Vesuvius was coming.

Behind him, Pierre did his best to sit comfortably but to no avail. The kangrui groaned. "Ohh, it feels—" Before he could finish speaking, he dropped his head and vomited on the back of Chang's seat.

Chang cringed at the foul smell. "Pew! What do kangrui eat?" He dreaded cleaning it up later.

They soon arrived at the cabin on the lonely beach. The house itself was completely repaired. Chang helped Pierre out of the car and hustled him to the front door. Pierre wandered around the porch while Chang cleaned up the disgusting mess in the car. The kangrui looked at the rays of the sun as it peered over the horizon. He then turned to the right and viewed the outline of the distant yellow cliffs.

"This's where ya live? Just b'side a sandy beach an' the open sea? I've never seen a seashore b'fore. I mus' say, Mr. Chang, it's not so ugly as I'd expected."

"Let's get inside before somebody sees us," Chang said, returning from the car.

Pierre sniffed testily. "Yes, yes, I know. B'fore I'm seen. Ya've said that many times already."

Chang rang the doorbell to the house. A few minutes passed before Joshua answered it. He looked as if he had just woken up. His hair was tousled and his eyes were bloodshot and wide with shock.

"Chang, you're back! I can't believe it!"

Chang stepped in and looked around. "This place looks great. It's as if the Minotaurs were never here."

"It took a while, but I got it repaired," said Joshua. "The insurance covered most of it, except they didn't know they were covering Minotaur damage." He eyed Pierre. "Who's he? I don't think he's from around here. Is he from Elsov?"

"Of course," said Chang. "His name's Pierre. He's a kangrui. He's kind of cute, isn't he? Listen, I need you to keep him here for a while. I want to work things out with Larson. My last hope for that is Sergeant Nelson."

"Speaking of which, I did as you asked," said Joshua. "I talked to Nelson. He's coming over sometime today. Before he comes, I can hide Pierre."

Pierre squirmed around Chang as he explored the house. "Interestin' place ta live if I say so meself. So big and luxurious! 'course we kangrui never build things like this. No need to, doncha know. Don't worry, I won't touch a thing. I know I don't belong here. I'm not even here, if ya know what I mean."

Joshua gave Pierre a long look. He noticed the small black dewclaws at the end of Pierre's stubby fingers. "Do you use your claws often?" he asked.

Pierre gently ran his claws through the fur on his face. "Last time I used them in battle was when I came across a dead-hearted dwarf. He said he'd have my head and began swingin' his silly little ax. I'm sure his friends still laugh at him for havin' five red marks on his face. Heh, and that was b'fore I gave him a good kick to the rump he won't soon forget. He broke his tailbone too. Hah! Fit for a lark's humor, y'know."

"He can be dangerous when he's angry," Chang warned. "Don't underestimate his claws *or* his kicking."

Pierre explored the rest of the house while Chang told Joshua all that had happened since they last parted.

"Jacob and Clipper are after the third piece?" Joshua repeated from Chang. "That means you're halfway there."

"*They're* halfway there," Chang corrected. "Elsov is *their* home."

"I'm going to miss them when they do leave," said Joshua. "That includes Sally. I hope she can find some way out of her situation. Life won't be the same without them. I still remember Clipper twisting my arm to play hockey with him. I could beat him in table hockey but not on the ice."

"I remember studying with Jacob for exams," said Chang. "He was a very bright student. I don't think I would've excelled without him."

"They sure have made life interesting. If it weren't for them, we would still be graduate students in New York. I can't believe that our friends were hatched as dragons on another world."

"It's so hard to comprehend, even now."

"I know."

For a moment there was complete silence. They both knew what would happen when all six pieces were found. Chang was right: it was hard to comprehend all that was happening.

The silence was broken by the squeaking of car brakes outside. Pierre looked out the front window, tapping his foot on the floor.

"Eh— I hate to in'errupt the heart-felt moment n'all, but I see company comin'."

Chang peeked out from the window in the wide double-doors. Two men were crossing the yard: Captain Larson and Sergeant Nelson. Chang grew tense. "Uh-oh, we need to hide Pierre."

"Okay, Pierre, you can go upstairs," said Joshua "Come on, we have to go now."

Pierre sighed as he reached the staircase. "I know. I know. Hurry, Pierre, you can't show yourself. Hurry, Pierre, ya've got to hide. Hurry, 'cause humans can't stand a little fur." He placed a foot on the first step. "Y'call these useful stairs? They're so steep!"

"Hurry up!" Joshua demanded.

Pierre struggled his way up the stairs. Chang placed his hand on the doorknob. "Putting this off won't help," he said. "I want to end this here and now."

Before Joshua could join Pierre upstairs, Chang opened the door and walked out.

"Well, Mr. Chang," said Larson, grinning, "I didn't think it would be this easy to find you. We want to talk to you. I know you're not guilty of anything, but we want to ask a few questions."

"We can work this out. I have the time," said Chang.

He turned back to the house, inviting Larson and James to the living room. Once inside, Chang told his story about the cemetery, the Minotaurs, and the search for the six hidden pieces.

"What motivated you to go after Draco and Clipper in the first place?" James asked Larson.

"It was after the incident at the cemetery," replied Larson. "I knew somewhat about these dragons, so I knew I had to take action. The evidence pointed to them. The part that confused me the most were the bodies we found. We couldn't identify them."

"That's when we came on the scene," said James. "Knowing Draco and Clipper's story, I felt certain this incident had something to do with them."

Larson held back his argument. "Can you explain the bodies, Sergeant?"

"I can't confirm anything at this point, but I feel sure Draco and Clipper were defending themselves. And yes, that included claws and fire."

"Those enemies were ex-Nibelungs," Chang clarified. "We've also had to put up with goblins."

"Goblins?" Larson scoffed. "I know about dragons, but there can't be goblins, can there?"

James didn't answer Larson. "Chang, I've received a report that some people in south-eastern Utah claimed to have seen the dragons *and* people described as goblins. These 'goblins' were certainly not friendly, and they seemed to be attacking another group of unknown people in the Manti-La Sal Forest. Civilians described them as medieval warriors. I don't know how medieval they really are."

"That has to be the militia Auben mentioned." Chang thought for a moment. "Where were these sightings?"

"Monticello. What's more is that even before this fighting began, various citizens there reported seeing two suspicious men, one of a dwarfish build and one of an elfish build. That's my guess as to who they were, at least."

"Monticello, huh? Do you know if it's near Mt. Ellen?"

James appeared confused. "Yes, it is; just a few hours' drive. Why?"

Chang's eyes widened with wonder. "Mt. Ellen. Syntare. I knew it! Something bad is going to happen there. Oh, and there's one more thing I need to tell you, Sergeant. Do you remember Sally Serene?"

James nodded, and Chang explained to him what had happened to Sally and how she had been with Auben for the last few days.

"You mean she's a dragon too?" asked James when Chang finished.

"She was the blue dragon from before. She went through a similar stage that Jacob and Clipper went through when they became dragons. She wasn't *born* as a dragon as Jacob and Clipper say they are. Oh, and I found this." He went to the mantle and grabbed the albore. "I'm sure this will help. I just recently found it."

James touched the tip of the albore with his finger. He inspected the rune in the golden handle. "This might be just what we need," he said. "I remember bullets can't kill dragons."

"Jacob told me ice blades can pierce the scales of any dragon," said Chang. "The trouble is that we can't make an ice blade. Maybe an ice warlock can."

"Ice warlock?" said Larson, almost laughing.

"I'm wondering if you can find this militia you've mentioned, Chang," James said, fully serious. "I don't know how much magic they use. However, being from Elsov, they may be able to help."

"They came here to keep our enemies from interfering with Jacob and Clipper," Chang explained.

Larson shook his head in disbelief. "Sergeant, can you tell me what he's talking about?"

James briefly told him of the events of the past several weeks. "Captain, I know you don't understand this, but you must keep this a secret. This is classified on a need-to-know basis. Don't tell *anyone*. Do you understand how imperative this is? I'll travel with Chang and search for this militia."

Larson stood up. "I don't mean to object, Sergeant, but I don't think this is a good idea. If this militia is made up of dwarfs or whatever they are, it would not be under your direct authority. This could go against all regulations."

"We don't have standard regulations when we're fighting something from another world. I know things many other people don't. We must do what we can to make our own world safer. I know you don't believe in magic, Captain, but it's real. You've seen Draco and Clipper and their young one, haven't you? You have to trust your senses now."

Larson groaned. Chang figured there was no need to hide Pierre anymore. He called the kangrui's name. Pierre didn't bother to use the steps properly. He took a long bound and thudded on the wooden floor, slipping off balance. The whole floor shook from the landing. Standing back up and shaking his head, Pierre looked up at Larson and James with unsure eyes. Larson stared in shock at the strange animal. He blinked and shook his head.

Chang walked over and patted Pierre's shoulder. "Gentlemen, this is Pierre. He said he's from the Odno Plains. That's on Elsov."

Larson left his jaw hanging low. James chuckled and winked at Chang, who winked back. He turned back to Larson. "I'm trusting you, Captain. I'll take Chang. As I've said before, please don't tell anyone about this."

Larson rolled his eyes as he saluted. "Yes sir, Sergeant."

James shook Chang's hand, promising he would return soon, and followed Larson out the door. Chang, Joshua, and Pierre were again alone.

"That went well," said Joshua. "Making peace with Larson is something you can cross off your list."

Pierre yawned as he stretched his short arms. "That's nice t'know, but I haven't slept at all since I came t'this earth, 'specially in your little airplane machine. I still feel like me innards're upside-down. Well, I wish a good day to you both. A good *night* to you is what I should say."

With a single hop, he jumped up on the couch and dropped on all fours. As he curled up like a cat, his tail hugged against his body; the tip over his nose. Joshua and Chang returned to their rooms.

Chang knew he needed sleep as well despite the morning hour. He slipped in his pajamas before crawling into bed. Home sweet home for at least one day, he thought.

CHAPTER 33

ESCAPE FROM KIMBERLY

Neither Clipper nor I knew what to do. The helpless man was on his hands and knees, hyperventilating violently. Sweat ran down his face as he scrambled for his lantern. He continued to foam at the mouth. My heart ached for him.

"Lilinges...? Here...?" the man gasped, trying to swallow. "I... never knew they dwelt in our world. You know more than I do. But I do know that my time draws nigh."

Clipper examined the small purple bite marks on the man's neck. "Poor person. There's nothing we can do. It's too late," he said.

"There really is nothing?" I asked desperately.

Before Clipper could answer, I looked over my shoulder. I heard the clicking calls of the other lilinges coming from within the bowels of the shaft.

Clipper pushed the platform in front of me. "I told you that I saw one of them bite someone on the night of the train wreck," he said. "It only took a few minutes before he became one of them."

"Became one of them," I said uneasily. "Do you think they can get us? I'm not in for a second transformation."

I looked back over my shoulder. Actual bats were flying out of the shaft and above my head, fleeing in mass numbers. Just behind the colony were several more lilinges. Many of the bats had become the hideous vermin, I assumed. I looked back down at the man. I watched in horror as black fur began to grow over his skin. His ears became pointed and his teeth sharpened.

"Leave… now… while you can…Don't mourn for me," he mumbled with the ounce of strength he had left. "Go to Mt. Ellen…east of here…"

His body shrunk in size. His arms became wings that draped with thick, opaque skin. Climbing out of the shirt that once belonged to him, the new lilinge glared at us with blood-red eyes. He began screeching with the rest of the lilinges. The others heard it and began circling me and Clipper. What used to be the unknown man joined them.

Tears were in Clipper's eyes. "This isn't good!"

I blew a flame under the swarm. All but one were able to avoid the direct flames. With the second to spare, Clipper decided to leave. The space from wall to wall was wide and high enough. Taking advantage of the tunnel's size, he kicked off the floor, flying only a few feet in the air. With his back feet, he grabbed hold of the platform. He frequently kicked off the floor with his front feet to regain his flight. I blew another flame at the lilinges then followed him. It was not long before we could see daylight.

"Almost out," Clipper panted.

He flew out of the mine seconds before I did. Outside, the mild storm had cleared; the late morning sun unveiled its bright face. Clipper landed, taking a heavy breath. "I knew something would be guarding the platform," he said. "It happened with Glaciem before, now this; and I'm guessing it'll happen again."

I turned back around to face the mine. The angry lilinges were still inside, clinging to the shadows whilst screeching and clicking at us like dozens of imps. I bared my teeth and hissed in return. They retreated back down the tunnel.

"I don't think they like the sunlight," I said once they were gone. "Well, we have the third piece now; oh, but I feel sorry for that man! The people he once knew will never know what happened to him. That's heartbreaking."

"It is a shame," said Clipper. "He knew why we were here. He wrote the clue that was with the albore, but now there's nothing we can do for him. We're safe enough for now, so let's have a look at this platform. He wouldn't want our search for the six pieces to end because this. He told us to get out. Besides, it'll keep our minds off what we saw." He lowered his head to the ground as he examined the mysterious writing on the rim of the stone slab. "I don't know what language this is, nor do I think it's native to this world."

"Could it be the language a wizard used for this portal so long ago, or whenever it was last used?" I pondered.

To test the strength of the platform, I hopped on top of it. It was not a large square. I had to inch my feet close together, but the stone managed to hold my weight just fine. I nodded to Clipper. Looking down at its top, I found four small holes on each of the four sides of the gray stone square. Two of the holes, opposite of each other, were of the same size. The third hole at the back was somewhat bigger, while the one in the front was the smallest. It sat just behind an inch-wide depression. Peering in one of the holes, I could see a dim glimmer of something. I didn't know what it was, but I assumed it powered whatever fit inside each hole. I figured the smallest hole was where the albore was supposed to be. It seemed to be about the right size. The other three holes were a mystery to me, and I was unsure what the diamond did to help the portal become active. Perhaps it sat in the depression.

"This part of the portal has to be the biggest," I said.

"It's well-crafted," Clipper commented. "I think you're right. Wait, do you hear that?"

I lifted my ears. There was a peculiar buzzing noise coming from the sky.

"It sounds like an airplane," I said.

I looked around. I didn't see an airplane, but I noticed the clouds appeared to be gathering in angry numbers once again. A mass of darkness began to blot out the sunlight. The rain began falling again. In horror, Clipper grabbed the platform with his feet.

"Jacob, the sunlight's gone!"

I turned back to the mine entrance. The lilinges had also noticed the returning storm. They burst out of the mine, coming straight toward us. I blew a short blast of fire at them. Unfortunately, I didn't burn a single one. The angry parasites continued to hover over me like angry hornets. I jumped up and snapped my jaws, snatching one by the wing. I repeated the action, grabbing another. But I was still overwhelmed. Feeling them landing on my back, I beat my wings furiously to keep their fangs away from my scales. Rage was building up inside me. I cast more fire then gave a vengeful roar. The flames were big enough that it consumed several more lilinges. However, there were still over a dozen left, viciously trying to bite me and Clipper.

I managed to get myself into the air just in front of him. We flew for one, maybe two miles trying to escape the lilinges. A few minutes later, after looking over the hilly landscape, I noticed Clipper was not behind me. I didn't think he was bitten, or else he would have warned me. He must have landed somewhere. I knew if he still had the platform, I could not let the lilinges pursue him.

I continued to ride a thermal wave, doing my best to stay ahead of the lilinges. I also saw the plane in the distance. I was flying much faster than it was, and I was quickly catching up to it. I lowered my head below my feet and sprayed a long stream of fire to keep the lilinges from catching up to me. They couldn't fly nearly as fast as I could. Before long they were out of sight. With them gone, I wanted to land and find Clipper. I had no idea where he was.

I eventually caught up to the tail of the airplane. The pilot didn't seem aware that I was behind him. I slowed and lowered myself under the plane, then closed my wings. I fell like a rock, only to open my wings again just before I hit the ground in a rough landing. Believing all was well, I decided to rest for a moment. I looked up as I sighed in relief. The sound of the airplane slowly faded away until I could barely hear it at all.

I waited in cover until I decided it was safe to move. But before I left my spot, I realized what I had done. The lilinges were loose!

If the man in the mine had become one of them, then what would happen if he and the other lilinges caught up to the plane and bit the pilot, or worse; what if they attacked a town? That would worse than a plague! I had to kill each and every last lilinge. It was a little unnerving just thinking about the consequences if one bit me. I had to destroy them no matter what.

With wings spread, I jumped back into the air. There was still no sign of lilinges after me in the sky, so I again flew toward the airplane. There they were! Just as I expected, following the plane were the winged vermin. When I felt I was close enough, I let out a roar. I didn't want to risk burning the plane, so I didn't cast any fire. I flew closer to the lilinges, cackling loudly. This time, more than half of them turned back toward me. I gave one last roar. The rest of the lilinges spun around. Now that they were all after me, I made a steep dive, straightened my flight, and then made a sharp turn the other way. My wings felt a little strained flapping so many times in the rash turn.

Now for the risky part. Stretching myself into a vertical position, I took another rough landing. I broke through branches and thudded onto the ground. The thump sent a searing ache through my legs, but I had no time to wallow in agony. I straightened myself, looking toward the sky through the damaged trees. The lilinges descended in mad helixes, all landing upside-down on different branches. Each and every one glared at me with their red eyes. Toxic saliva dripped from their fangs. I waited for them to attack, but they didn't move. They simply stared at me. Maybe they were waiting for me to make the first move. I was readying a breath of fire when I felt something gentle touch my back. One of them had landed on me; I didn't even hear it! It was going to bite me! I threw myself to the ground and rolled, springing back to my feet a second later. The lilinge was lying on its back, obviously injured. It took one claw to finish it off. The moment it gave its last dying trill, the rest of the lilinges attacked at once. Their high-pitched squeals drove me crazy. There was little time left. My fury, that even *I* feared, was beginning to overcome me once again. Only one logical solution came to mind. I jumped in the air, my jaws open. On my way up, I snatched one of the lilinges between the wings. One bite squeezed the life out of it. I ran a few feet to escape the remaining ones. I stopped and jumped again. I missed the first time, but caught one by the wing the second. Then I ran again.

It took longer than I had hoped, but finally there were only three of the little monsters left. They still hovered above me as if they were a few in a million. The screeching of three was far more tolerable than that of a dozen or so. After a few more leaps, I caught another one; then the last two began to fly away. With the fury I had left, I drew a deep breath. I threw a flame far enough to scorch them both. Each went down in a smoky fireball. I heard no more screeches after that, and nothing was hovering over my head save a few harmless insects. I again made sure the viewing ring had remained secure on my claw throughout all the acrobatics.

"They're gone. Good riddance," I huffed.

I sighed in exhaustion, taking a moment to let my anger subside. Luckily this time I hadn't done anything regretful. The lilinges guarding the platform were gone, no longer a threat to me or anyone. They had finished their pestilence with the poor man back in the mine. Now I had to find Clipper who, hopefully, still had the platform. I knew I had been flying eastward to escape the lilinges, so I retraced my path. I decided to walk so I wouldn't miss Clipper's scent. My wings felt strained, anyway. It didn't take long before I sniffed out a fresh trail he had taken. I made a chirping noise from the back of my throat, expecting Clipper to respond. I heard nothing, but I could still smell his presence. I continued to chirp as I followed his trail. I felt the comfort of friendship when I heard another chirp in response. Making my way through the thick spruces and brush, I found Clipper sitting on the platform. I sat next to him, panting.

"Jacob, I'm glad you here," he said. "I was really worried when I lost sight of you. You were gone for quite a while."

"I figured I should kill those things so they couldn't bite anyone else," I replied. "You saw what they did to that man."

"I assume you weren't bitten?"

"No, thankfully."

I was glad we made it out, but I felt very sorry for the man in the mine. It would have dragged me down more-so had I not remembered Elemek's words. Drowning myself in sorrow was not going to help. Clipper was right: the man would not want that. The lilinges were no longer a threat. That thought made me feel a little better.

Clipper turned his attention back to the platform. He sniffed around the rim. "The third piece is ours," he said proudly.

"It'll take a few hours to get back to Reno and Razden, then they'll have this and the diamond," I said.

We decided to rest until sunset, during which we found a herd of range cattle. This provided a filling supper for us. Afterward, with the platform secure in Clipper's grasp and the viewing ring in mine, we left Kimberly behind us.

CHAPTER 34

BATTLE OF MANTI-LA SAL

Chang woke at around ten the next morning. He hadn't slept for days prior to last night, which made the much-needed sleep all the more refreshing. After going to the bathroom and getting dressed, Chang went down into the kitchen to prepare a piece of toast for breakfast. Joshua came down a few minutes later.

"Good morning, Josh," Chang said to him.

Pierre stirred awake at the sound of his voice. "Yaahhhh... Ohhh... Ah... Mr. Chang, good mornin'. So ya say this Nelson fellow'll come, huh? I see. Your friend Joshua told me 'bout him an' what y'went through b'fore ya met me. This was after y'went to bed." He let out another sleepy yawn. "Yaaahhhhh... Mm! Pardon me. I know how the cap'n b'trayed you n'all. You still trust him after all that?"

Chang took a bite of his breakfast. "I can't afford not to," he said.

Pierre twitched his ear, saying nothing more. Chang continued eating his breakfast while Joshua went over to the counter and cracked some eggs into a bowl.

"I didn't bother asking you last night since it was so late," said Joshua, "but I remember you told me you found an albore. You said it was the second piece, right?"

With a smile, Chang placed his toast on the table and took the albore from his bag. "Yes. I found this with the viewing ring. It's the second piece."

He placed the albore on the table. Joshua twisted it to get a better view. "An albore," he said, mystified. "This is the first time I've seen one. Do you know what the writing on the handle means?"

"I don't."

Joshua slid the albore back to Chang. "I would have no idea how to use something like that."

"It works when you speak to it with your mind, but I've only done a few spells." Chang held the albore at breast-height, thinking for a moment. In the kitchen, one of the doors to the cupboard opened. He then caused an unoccupied chair to slowly tip backward then right itself.

"Impressive," said Joshua. He could think of nothing else to say.

"Ptah! Properties of an albore are nothin' new to me," laughed Pierre.

"Well, I've never seen one until now," said Joshua. "In fact, I've never even heard of a kangrui until Chang came home with you."

"I 'spected that anyhow," said Pierre. "Never really had a love o' fame, y'know."

It was half-past eleven when James arrived. Chang answered the door the moment he heard the knock. He didn't bother hiding Pierre again.

"Good morning," said James. "I hope you had some good rest?"

"Yes, sir," said Chang.

"Good. Well, we don't have any time to lose. I've arranged a flight to an airfield outside Moab. We can drive to the Manti-La Sal Forest from there."

"Great. More flyin'," Pierre groaned.

James looked down at the kangrui. "I'm sorry… Pierre? You're not allowed to come with us. Only Mr. Chang and I are to make the trip."

Pierre testily tapped his foot on the floor. "What d'you mean I can't come? What's holdin' me back? If ya leave me here, it'll only be much harder for you to fight off the goblins an' darkscales n'such. I can offer you folk much help. I could knock a goblin clean over this house if I had the chance."

"I know how much help you could be, Pierre," said James. "But I don't think coming will be a good idea. You must understand the situation at hand."

"Situation? Ha! I can understand organized tactics n'all. You yourself said you don't have common regulations with these matters. I don't know how victorious your army's been throughout the years, but I'm sure y'never had t'fight a horde o' Elsovian monsters. And it's the darkscales you should worry about. It's nearly impossible for us to kill 'em alone."

"That's exactly my point. You're the only kangrui on this world. I can't risk having you get hurt. So no, I won't allow it." James was firm in his voice.

"The only one on this earth?" Pierre stamped the floor, rattling the entire house. "I'm the only one here 'cause me people's on a *different* world. For Saka's sake, let me come!"

James placed his hand over his forehead. "Point taken, Pierre… If you insist, I'll let you come. Just promise me you won't get hurt."

Pierre sniffed. "No promises, Sergeant. Now let's go. Thank ya for changin' your mind. Trust me, I'm more dangerous'n ya think."

JAMES AND CHANG REACHED THE AIRFIELD A FEW HOURS LATER. From there, they traveled by jeep through Moab and soon onto a trail through Manti-La Sal. Pierre sat passively in the back, his ears pinned flat against his head. When they reached the designated point, on the slope of a hill, James gave Chang and Pierre a stern look.

"I have to warn you, we have found bodies here," he said. "There's no telling what's lurking in those trees."

Chang pulled the albore from his bag. "Hopefully this will protect me."

"I can smell dwarfs," said Pierre, jumping out of the jeep. "They don't smell like enemies. Let me go first an' sniff out the area."

While Pierre searched through the forest, James and Chang began searching around the hill. At the top they came upon the remains of what was once a monument. Chang felt a chill run down his spine. Not only were there chunks of marble lying about, but the ground was torn up and there were clear signs of fire. It reminded Chang of the damage on the cliff top after Syntare's attack. He picked up a small piece of marble.

"How did this happen?" he asked.

"I'm not sure," said James. "I see some burnt spots in the grass. I'm guessing a dragon is responsible. But which dragon? Your friends were never here, were they?"

Chang circled around the damage. He found it difficult to walk through the mounds of mud and torn grass. There were no true signs of Losdir or his troops, no fallen bodies or anything.

"Do you know where Losdir's militia is now?" he asked the Sergeant.

"This was their last known location. I've been told that each time someone sees a suspicious person and gets close, they disappear like ghosts. I can understand why."

"They know how to keep cover if any trouble happens to come along," said Chang. "I'll see if I can find them. I can't imagine them being too far away."

"I have my doubts you can find them, but you can try," said James.

Chang bit his lower lip. He walked down the gentle hill into a thick bunch of firs. He couldn't find a sign of anyone. "Losdir? Pierre? It's me, Chang," he said aloud. "You don't have to worry; I know about Elsov. Jacob and Clipper are my friends. They're the portal seekers you came to help."

Still there was no response, but Chang knew he wasn't alone. Sitting down on a dead trunk, he decided to wait for any activity. About a minute later, he heard footsteps nearby. He got to his feet, turned, and was greeted by a man of different features. Chang, feeling slightly shy, assumed he was Losdir. The Kuslan removed his red cap in respect.

"Don't be afraid. My name's Lewis Chang, as you've probably heard. I'm a close friend of Jacob and Clipper. They're the dragons you're looking for."

"Jacob and Clipper you say?" asked the elf. "That is good to know. I am Losdir, welcome. I lead the Elsovian Militia, along with Konmester Trahern. Fenson and Bluepond are here too. They have told us about you. You are a very worthy friend, Mr. Chang."

"Thank you," Chang replied. "We also have other friends, two lightscales, coming this way. Have you seen them?"

"No, I have not seen any lightscales," said Losdir.

"Your friend Auben and one named Sally are on their way here. Have you met Pierre, the kangrui?"

Losdir nodded. "Yes, only minutes ago. He said you would come. He is now off to tell the nymph scouts of your arrival. And you say Auben is on his way to meet us? That's wonderful to hear, thank you." He turned around and called out, "All is safe! It's Mr. Chang!"

One by one, members of the Militia emerged from their cover. Chang watched in awe. He felt as if he was on Elsov already. He was the only native human in the group, but he didn't mind. He was unafraid of the men of all sorts who surrounded him. Chang was the tallest among them. Losdir was second by only a few inches. The dwarfs were short but well-built and the nymphs, dryads and maliaes alike, were the smallest. Fenson and Bluepond appeared from the line of emerging soldiers and hugged Chang.

"It has been a while, my friend," said Fenson. "It's nice to see you again with all your limbs."

"We are *both* happy to see you again," Bluepond added.

Trahern, with the burn still visible on his forehead, emerged. He stood next to Fenson. "This is the first time I've met someone of this world, Mr. Chang," the Konmester said. "You remind me of a wizard. Do you possess any magical power?"

"To be honest, I don't know," Chang answered. "I used an albore to hold back a darkscale not long ago, but I think my skills are terrible compared to an actual wizard's."

"Darkscales, goblins... lilinges... and other dwarfs," said Trahern, cringing. "The Horde is nearby. That is why we're hiding. We have avoided human settlements as well lately. We don't want innocent bloodshed, let alone the unnecessary the deaths of our own people."

"Each death is painful for us all," said Losdir unhappily.

More and more Elsovian folk appeared and joined their ranks. It was good that they did, too. Chang couldn't be amazed at the Militia for long, for the sound of a nymph scout's shout alerted them all.

"Goblins! Darkscales! Spotted in the east! Goblins! Darkscales! Spotted in the east!"

A moment later, Chang saw Pierre running toward him with wide eyes and chattering teeth.

"They're comin'! They spotted the Sergeant. He's hidin' in broad daylight!"

The members of the Militia drew arms. Fenson stayed behind the front lines while Bluepond rushed up a fir to join the other dryads. All Chang could do was lift his albore.

"Keep calm," ordered Losdir. "We must prepare ourselves. Panic will be counterproductive."

"How can we *not* panic?" Fenson cried from his protected spot. "We've been fighting the Horde but haven't even made a scratch against the darkscales! This time we'll all die for sure!"

"Silence!" Trahern yelled. "Now's not the time to run like rabbits! Prepare to fight! We will make the cowards run 'til they drop!"

"The goblins will be coming from the ground," Chang figured. "They'll have to go through the woods to get to us. Your army can fight them off, Losdir. The darkscales, I'm not sure how many there are, will be coming from the air." He eyed the albore doubtfully. "I sure hope I can do this again, and against more than one dragon."

Chang squeezed it tight in his hands and disappeared back up the smooth hill. Despite the fact that he had survived Syntare, he didn't know if he could withstand this time.

LOSDIR STOOD ANXIOUSLY NEXT TO TRAHERN IN THE FRONT LINE. He knew the Horde would come in view at any minute. Bluepond sat in his spot in the thick fir, prepared to fire his bow. From his spot, he watched the goblins advancing with spears and shields. Aiming carefully, he shot his arrow. It soared straight toward his target, only to be stopped by a wooden shield. Bluepond fired a second arrow, this time striking the goblin in the calf. Trahern's dwarfs fired a barrage of bullets before charging with bayonets. After another volley of arrows, Losdir advanced, yelling at the top of his lungs. Bayonets and swords clashed with spears and shields. The Grün-hære's advance suddenly staggered.

From his position in the rear, Fenson caught sight of the activity on the open hill. "It seems Mr. Chang and the Sergeant are in trouble!" he shouted up to Bluepond.

"As are we," said his friend from the branches. "We have lost two dryads already."

"We can't help them now," Fenson said grimly. "We need to hold off the enemy. Hopefully Chang can deal with the darkscales with his albore."

Holding up a pistol that was given to him, Fenson continued on his way into the fight. Bluepond watched with despair as he saw what was happening in the front. Soldiers fell on both sides. Neither army was losing nor gaining ground.

WHEN CHANG REACHED THE TOP OF THE HILL, HE NOTICED JAMES scanning the sky.

"What took you so long?" James asked. "I spotted two dragons. There may even be a third. If there is, he held back. Now's the time for you to use the albore."

"If I did this once, I can do it again," Chang said to himself, taking deep steadying breaths.

"Just keep your eyes open," said James.

Chang realized the only weapon James had was a bolt-action rifle. It could be affective against goblins or royalist dwarfs, but not darkscales. James had to have known that, but he kept his gun at the ready anyway.

"I'll do my best to keep them away from the Militia," said Chang.

Both he and the Sergeant heard a roar from above that echoed throughout the surrounding forest. One of the darkscales had spotted them and called for the other. Chang and James both shuddered when the second dragon flew into view.

"Here they come. Get ready," James said grimly.

The first darkscale, red in appearance, dived after them. With its sabered fangs, it looked almost exactly like Clipper. Chang felt sure it was the one who had tricked Sally.

Just as the darkscale was low enough, James fired his rifle. Crying from the shot in its wing, the darkscale swooped on past. Chang wasted no time. He thought desperately for an effective spell. There was a glow on the albore's tip soon enough. In response, the darkscale's flight was slowed to the point where it could go no farther. It screeched and decided to land.

"Ye vass-nel a thleass-el sevez, ye felose homose!" the vile dragon hissed.

Chang didn't understand what it said, but with the albore he gave it a good shock. The darkscale was stunned, but unharmed. James took another shot at it, this time between its horns. That must have done it. The darkscale yowled in pain and flew away.

Now Chang had his attention on the violet darkscale that remained in the sky. It glared down at Chang and prepared a storm of fire. James quickly reloaded and fired. The bullet, with all his luck, grazed the darkscale's left-hind leg, causing the dragon to roar terribly. Though not critically injured, it lost control and began plunging to the ground. Chang was aware the darkscale was high enough to regain its flight before it was too late. With the albore, he kept the falling dragon from spreading its wings. It took all his attention and stamina. He could see the darkscale trying to fight his magic. As it plummeted toward the ground, it started squirming in panic. It was falling from a dangerous height! As Chang held the albore tight, he felt the awful pulsing in his hand return. The darkscale roared one more time and spread its wings despite Chang's efforts. Chang began to sweat. His magic was too weak! Just before the darkscale hit the ground, it opened its wings into a glide. A final great pulse in Chang's hand caused him to drop the albore. The pain must have been the dragon fighting his magic. Unlike his fight with Syntare, Chang lost.

The scarlet got to its feet, noticing its comrade had landed within the ruins of the monument.

"Vase yass ye veness?" the darkscale said as he rushed toward the crater.

Chang stared at the albore on the ground. "I couldn't do it!" he growled. "I tried to freeze his wings, but he fought me…"

A tide of terror rushed over him. He and James stood motionless. The violet darkscale appeared angrier than ever. The red one stood beside it. Both had steaming saliva dripping out between their bared teeth, and smoke spewing from their noses.

"They're mad," said James, raising his rifle.

Chang gulped. "I got too confident. You caught him off guard by shooting and I thought I could deal with him."

James was still staring at the dragons. "Not so loud. Don't feel too bad. You did what you could."

The dragons hissed simultaneously. The red one took a step forward with a nasty glare in its glowing yellow eyes. Chang felt this was it. He was going to die.

The scarlet again hissed its strange words. "Fess no thive tha albore or ye-viss thleass!"

Chang did not move. There was no way he could escape. Even James Nelson, an experienced soldier in the United States Marines, dared not move a muscle. Both remained still. Chang hoped that he could be spared if he showed no hostility, though he highly doubted it.

The darkscales growled, each taking a step closer. The violet took another step. Its nose was inches away from Chang's. Chang felt the intense heat of its disgusting breath on his face. He knew the violet wanted to teach him a painful lesson. The toxic breath made him cough and gag. His nose started to bleed.

The darkscale made a chirping noise and then pressed its snout on Chang's chest, pushing him to the ground. The scarlet did the same with James. Chang felt the adversary's claws press him to the ground and tear open his shirt. The darkscales growled again. Chang felt the scalding-hot saliva drip on his exposed chest, making his skin sizzle. He couldn't help crying in agony. He understood they wanted to torture him and James before they killed them.

James could take no more of it. He quickly raised a boot and kicked the scarlet in the lower jaw between its fangs. With his hands free, he quickly pressed the rifle barrel on the darkscale's throat and pulled the trigger. Chang watched it cough cinders and fire from the point-blank shot. This time he could see blood.

Chang quickly stood back up. He jumped to one side, grabbing the albore. With a spell he did know, he zapped both darkscales. The violet made terrible gurgling noises and began to fly away. James fired at it again, only to have it turn its head and blow fire at him. James jumped away just in time.

"Chang, they're getting away!" he yelled.

Chang tried to freeze the darkscales' wings, but to no avail. They had perfect control of their flight as they disappeared over the treetops. Chang sat back down and wiped away the saliva. His chest was red and blistered.

"They're gone," said James. "Are you hurt?"

Chang inspected the tear in his shirt and the burns on his chest. "I'm hurt, but I'll live. I wonder why they left when they did. They could have killed us with one breath of fire."

"They must have had reasons we don't know of," James guessed.

Chang slid the albore back in his knapsack. Even though he couldn't freeze the violet's wings, the second piece had saved his life yet again. He knew he had much to learn about magic, however. He was not fully aware of its limitations and full power.

He and James were silent with shock as the shouts of the battle rang from the woods.

TRAHERN WAITED FOR THE NYMPH ARCHERS TO FIRE AGAIN. He didn't order his dwarfs to shoot, though. There was far less ammunition for his men now, and it had to be used conservatively. After the arrows were loosed, the Konmester and his dwarfs again advanced on the Grün-hære.

"Do not show weakness!" Trahern cried. "We're keeping the front of the Horde from gaining ground! Now's not the time to surrender!"

The nymphs agreed. They heard Losdir order them to ready more arrows. Trahern commanded his men to step back so the nymphs could fire. The dwarfs continued forward after the volley. Only a few gunshots were heard.

"Many of their men are falling!" a maliae cried. "We may gain ground this time!"

As the dwarfs stepped back again, Fenson discovered Pierre standing behind him. The kangrui was panting heavily but appeared unconcerned.

"What are you doing?" Fenson asked.

"I was in the worst of the fight, y'know," said Pierre. "Like I said, I sent many o' them t'the ground. I've come t'this world to protect ya, after all. Losdir was grazed by an unfriendly arrow, but he's fightin' like a warrior."

Fenson started running forward and Pierre followed.

"I was a bit worried for Mr. Chang and that other fellah," the kangrui continued. "But when I inspected them, I saw no darkscales. Looks like they're managin' jus' fine… for now at least."

Fenson was about to answer him when the fiendish yells of goblins pulled him back. "Well, we could certainly use magic on our side," he said instead.

"Leave it t'me," said Pierre. He quickly scrambled to the base of the hill and yelled at the top of his lungs. "Hey! Mr. Chang! Your friends down here need some help!"

"Not so loud," Bluepond advised from above.

Pierre didn't care. He was satisfied when he saw Chang running down the hill with the albore in his hand.

"The darkscales are gone, but they might come back," said Chang. "Sergeant Nelson left the hill and is on the lookout for others."

Chang then made his way to Fenson. Before the dwarf could speak, he heard the others running to the hill to gain the advantageous ground.

"The Grün-hære is retreating, thank God!" a dwarf yelled.

Fenson, Chang, and Pierre joined the remaining Militia. More guns were fired until the enemy was out of range.

The battle was finally over. The dwarfs dropped their weapons on the side of the hill and laid on the grass while the nymph medics cared for the wounded. Luckily, only few had fallen this time. The dryads scampered down from the trees and gave thanks to the maliaes. One of the medics cared for Trahern and Losdir, disinfecting their wounds and bandaging them. Another gave Chang a soothing cream for the burns on his chest.

Fenson stood with a broad smile hiding in his beard. "I may say, Mr. Chang, you have survived the wrath of the darkscales while we survived the Grün-hære. Today is a good day, believe it or not."

When the medic finished bandaging Losdir, the elf came over and shook Chang's hand. Each looked at the wounds of the other.

"Never mind my bandages," said Losdir. "I only have a few

cuts and bruises. It looks like you had a close encounter with the darkscales."

Chang rubbed more cream on his chest. "At least Jacob and Clipper will be happy to know you're helping them," he said.

Losdir's eyes lit up at Chang's comment. "Jacob and Clipper. Do you know where they are right now?"

"I think so. Jacob and Clipper should have left Kimberly by now. They overheard another darkscale mention Ellen. I later found out that's the name of a mountain. We're not far from there, in fact. But I do think Vesuvius may come through a portal there."

"A portal?" Losdir repeated.

Chang took a step back, not knowing if he had offended the elf or not.

"I should speak with complete honesty," said Losdir. "Do you know about limmamotas: mountains that explode with fire and ash?"

Chang hesitated before answering. "Yes, volcanoes. They're on this earth. But I don't think Mt. Ellen is one."

"No matter," said Losdir. "Throughout the years, you must know, Vesuvius' royal line would create many portals to this earth. When they attack, they enjoy doing it during an eruption. It helps mask their attack."

"That creates the perfect portal, because it's unrecognized," Chang replied. "But I don't know about Mt. Ellen."

"Whoever sees Vesuvius will die anyway," said Losdir.

Chang rubbed his forehead. He didn't like thinking about that. "Sergeant Nelson showed me an atlas before we arrived here," he told Losdir. "Mt. Ellen looked like a day or two's trek from where we are. That must be a part of the reason those darkscales left before killing me and him."

"How many men is Vesuvius willing to destroy to get to Jacob and Clipper?" Losdir asked.

"I don't know, Losdir. I don't know," Chang said sadly. "But do you think there could be a piece of our own portal near Mt. Ellen?"

"That is possible. It would make sense for a piece to be hidden there, otherwise Vesuvius would not have chosen this Mt. Ellen."

Chang felt a little excited to think that the next piece wasn't so far away. He thought about Pearl Forest again.

"More dragons! I see two in the sky!" a nymph warned, breaking Chang's thoughts.

The dwarfs quickly scrambled to their feet and looked up, expecting another nasty attack.

"We have no enchanted weaponry except for what our friend has!" a dwarf cried.

"Maybe Mr. Chang can do something!" a maliae suggested.

Chang held his albore out as he searched for the dragons in the sky. When he finally caught sight of them, he relaxed his hold on the albore. "One's blue and the other's orange," he said. "It's Sally and Auben! They've made it!"

The nymphs lowered their bows and the dwarfs dropped their guns. Losdir raised his arms upon seeing his dear friend healthy and safe. Sally and Auben landed beside him.

"You are well, I see," Losdir wept, patting Auben on the head. "Trihan told me of your sudden departure."

"I am well, Losdir," said Auben. "I must say, this world is very interesting."

Chang was happy to see Sally's blue scales as well. "You two made good time. You're as efficient as I am in an airplane; and all you had to use to find us was your nose."

Sally let her wings droop. "It's my speed I like the most. Maybe it won't be so hard finding all six pieces after all."

"Speaking of which," Chang said, gathering Losdir and Auben together. "I think I know where the next piece might be. Remember hearing the name Ellen? Well, that's the name of a mountain: Mt. Ellen. There's one problem, though. Vesuvius might be there."

Sally's jaw dropped. "Vesuvius? Here? That can't be! How bad will it be if he fights us?"

"I don't know," said Chang frankly. "We'll have to find out."

"If you think a piece is near Mt. Ellen, I can go find Jacob and Clipper," Sally said after a brief pause. "They can look for Mt. Ellen with the viewing ring."

"That's the spirit, me dear Sally!" cried Pierre, who had overheard the conversation. "If you're travelin' your own way, I'd recommend movin' as soon as you're refreshed."

"I'm refreshed to know all of you are safe," said Sally.

VISATRICE WATCHED THE REMAINDER OF THE GRÜN-HÆRE REGROUP. The goblins were in a fury. They had not expected a costly battle, followed by a cowardly retreat.

"Why did we run like fools, General?" one of his dwarfs asked.

Visatrice couldn't contain himself any longer at that question. "Hahahahaha! Oh hahaheeheeheeheeheeheehee! You have no leadership experience to speak of, do you spike-horn? I didn't pull you back because we were facing defeat. If we hadn't retreated, we could have slain all our enemies. We retreated for other reasons, as did our darkscales. Hahahaheeheehee! Retreat? You should become a jester, dwarf! Ahahahahaha!"

"And what are these reasons?" a goblin asked, trying to be light. "What d'you think the elf's army thinks of us for running?"

"Oh, never mind that," said Visatrice. "Vesuvius spoke to me. He said he was preparing to come. We will ambush our enemies at Ellen! I have also received word that there is something else that can be of use to us. The Unitaur that attacked the dragon traitors earlier is lurking nearby. The dumb beast was run out of the towns. Word of her spread like an illness and Heitspel beckoned her to go to Ellen."

Another goblin raised an un-groomed eyebrow. "I know how to give simple commands to beasts like Minotaurs," he said. "I will go find her."

"Good for you!" replied Visatrice. "Now, as I've said, drawing back was not a cowardly act. It was a smart move. If the Militia underestimates us, our victory will be even greater; think about it."

The General performed the salute of Vesuvius. The rest of the Horde repeated it and then shouted patriotic phrases, determined to do what they were commanded to do. They packed their weapons and supplies and moved out.

CHAPTER 35

ON TO MT. ELLEN

We made it back to Dixie Forest with no trouble. Clipper said the platform was a bit difficult to carry over all the mountain ranges without dropping it, but he was successful all the same. By the end of the day, we made it back to the bottom of the cliff, where Reno and Razden were waiting for us by the buried diamond. Both were grateful for our safe return. In those last golden rays of daylight, we all re-examined the platform. I discovered the diamond fit perfectly in the depression by the smallest hole.

The cold blanket of night soon fell upon us. I used my horns to push down a dead pine for firewood. With our claws, Clipper and I splintered it up into dozens of logs. Reno started the fire with a small breath of flame. We didn't really need a fire, but we all agreed we loved its cozy glow.

"We have three pieces," said Reno after the fire was crackling with life. "I can't believe we're this close."

"When we get to Elsov, I will show you the pond that I was telling you about," Razden told her with a smile. "You will love it. I know you will."

"I'd help Jacob find the lost nymph before we search for our parents," said Clipper. "When it's all over, I might decide to live in Pearl Forest. Well, that depends on where my family is."

"There are many beautiful places in and around Pearl Forest," said Razden. "When I was younger, I was told of the many regions around Pearl Forest. There was the Skalisk Canyon, the fjords, the snowy peaks, the Odno Plains, the rolling hills, and much more. That's just a few I know of, at least."

Clipper's ears drooped. "I wonder which of those places we're actually from. The fact that my parents could still be alive… I can still hardly believe it! Jacob and I could even have siblings, too."

"That is how I feel. I long for a home where I am free," said Razden.

"What else do you remember of Elsov, Razden?" Clipper asked him.

"I already told you how I was born in the Vesuvian Kingdom. My father raised me to follow Vesuvius, to do what the King ordered me to do. I never knew my mother, and my father was later killed by a dragon slayer. Without him, I felt powerless. I feared for my life, so I decided to leave. You know the rest."

Clipper sympathized with him. "Your father was killed and you didn't know your mother? I'm sorry to hear that. That reminds me of what happened to Jacob, only he knew his mother before she was taken away."

"My life seemed perfect when I was young," I said. "I had two loving parents and a great home. That was until my human father died in a storm and my mom couldn't take care of me. I have no memory of my parents on Elsov."

"I never knew my father. I was raised by my mother," said Clipper. "I haven't seen her since I left Saskatchewan. When Jacob and I met, we saw that we had similar trials in our lives. We both came from rural places and were lost in the big city. We never had true friends until we met each other. Now we're best friends."

"You knew nothing of Vesuvius?" Razden asked.

"Not King Vesuvius, no," I answered.

"I was one of the few who found the true character of him. Of course he feeds his people, but he only cares about himself. I refused to follow him, never knowing what the consequence would be." Razden leaned closer to Reno. "Because of you, I escaped with my life. I wish I could thank you more."

Reno bashfully turned away. I rubbed my nose against hers and smiled.

"Well, Razden can experience true freedom when we find the rest of the portal," said Clipper. "We need three more parts. Now the question is, where do we look next?"

"We had clues for the last few places," I said. "Right now, we have nothing to go off of except for the viewing ring. I checked with it after we'd landed, but I couldn't see anything."

Clipper tapped his fang, thinking about our dilemma. "We don't have a riddle or clue to where the next piece is except for 'Ellen', whatever that means. We're too close. I don't want to be misled now."

I pulled the ring from my claw and gave it another try. Scanning in a complete circle, I again found no red. I sighed in frustration.

"Where could the next clue be?" Clipper huffed.

I didn't know what to do next. None of us did. I would have sat in silence all night, wondering what "Ellen" meant, had it not been for the sound of flapping dragon wings above us. Following that sound came the rustling of trees, indicating that whoever it was had landed. I had no downwind scent to recognize it. I assumed it was either Sally or Auben. But just in case, I remained alert.

I let my guard drop when Sally stepped into the firelight.

"Jacob, Clipper," she said, relieved to see us. "It looks like you found the Gateway." She then went over to greet Reno and Razden.

"We ran into some activity," I said, "but thankfully it's all taken care of." I told her about Syntare's attack and our encounter with the lilinges.

"It's good to know you're safe," Sally replied. "It took a while for me and Auben to find Chang, but we did find him. That elf's army just finished a fight with the Grün-hære when we arrived. Chang said he even confronted two darkscales! One of them was the red dragon that fooled me into thinking he was Clipper. Chang and the Militia are all right, though. They were leaving the Manti-La Sal Forest when I left."

"How's Auben?" Clipper asked.

Sally chuckled. "He's okay. He does manage to get himself into trouble without thinking. He's young and very impulsive. Several times he flew low over a town. Oh, and you won't believe it! That name Ellen Syntare mentioned? She was referring to *Mt.* Ellen! She's a mountain!"

"Mt. Ellen!" I exclaimed delightfully. "That makes much more sense!"

"There is a catch," Sally went on. "Chang said he heard that there are strange things going on over there. After talking with Pierre, he suspects that those things involve Vesuvius."

I sat back on my haunches and blew a flame from my nose. "That's where Syntare went," I said.

"*And* that's where the fourth piece could be," said Sally. "That's why Vesuvius will be coming there."

"And he's after a few creatures in particular," Clipper said apprehensively, "someone who may be searching for that fourth piece."

My eyes lit up. "There *has* to be a piece there!"

"That must be a frightening thought," said Razden. "He is the most dangerous and he is after you two personally."

I tried not to show how nervous I was. I remembered each of my nightmares about the dreaded Vesuvius. Every time I woke up sick. "Auben was surprised when I killed Glaciem," I said. "He believes it's possible for me and Clipper to help defeat Vesuvius."

"That would be nice," Reno commented.

Clipper spread his tattered wings, taking a deep breath. "I guess we go to Mt. Ellen, then?"

"Right," said Sally. "Chang and Losdir's militia are on their way right now."

"At least we don't have to sit here anymore!" Reno chortled with excitement. "Now we can leave!"

"We can leave," Clipper echoed. "Unfortunately, I sense something coming. Elves, dwarfs, nymphs, goblins, darkscales; something tells me things are going to get nasty."

"Just remember, Clipper, that this isn't going to be two against a sorcerer," I said bleakly. "Vesuvius will be much more powerful than Triathra ever was."

Clipper tried to hide his fear, but I wasn't convinced.

"A battle for Elsov, we can't back down now," he said.

I placed each of my paws over Sally's and Clipper's.

"Whatever happens, no matter our fate, we will fight for Elsov," I said.

We did our best to feel confident, but it was futile. All I knew was that I was scared. There was the chance I might die.

CHAPTER 36

TENSIONS RISE

Vesuvius, after returning to the keep after attending to personal matters, summoned Heitspel for a private discussion. After receiving the message of his leader's request, Heitspel traveled by wagon from his castle in the northern region of the isle to the centralized location of the keep. Vesuvius was in his office of Kingship when Heitspel arrived.

"My Right Paw," said Vesuvius warmly, "you came. I assume you carried out your assault against the grøls in our borders on the mainland? Those little fools are a thorn in my hide. They give no loyalty to my nation."

"I have done as you ordered, your Majesty," Heitspel replied with a bow and a smart solute. "I have received your urgent message concerning the two dragon traitors."

"I am continuing with my plan," Vesuvius informed. "I'm not going to kill them just yet. I think I'll give them an opportunity to pledge allegiance to my Kingdom. If they don't, they will flee from me in fear. That fear will spread to their friends. When we begin our war, we can do what Triathra failed to do: that is to spread my reign to the first earth. The traitors will help whether they want to or not."

"But what if the traitors do not spread the fear?" Heitspel asked.

Vesuvius glared at Heitspel as if he were a simpleton. "If they return to Elsov, then I'll seek more than just their deaths. If there's no reason for them to help us, then there's no reason for them to live. We can go forth without them. Heitspel, I have brought you here to keep my land in order. Make sure no one leaves my keep. If they disobey, they will answer to the court. I've ordered Syntare to the portal where I will arrive. I can't let her pursue Jacob. She'll fail again if she does."

"Will you ever confront the dragon traitors yourself?" said Heitspel.

Vesuvius laughed, causing his entire office to shake. "Ha! Ask no more! I have a mission that I must complete! The situation on the first earth calls for my attention. The dragon traitors stand in my way. They must do as I say or they *will* suffer!"

He left Heitspel alone with the other advisors in the office. For Vesuvius, this was no little office. It was large enough for a mansion to sit inside it.

Heitspel knew he was in power while Vesuvius was gone. The fact that he was in charge of the entire nation gave him a sense of power. No land was more feared than this land!

WILLIAM PACKED THE REST OF HIS LUGGAGE. AS HE PLACED ITEM after item in his bag, various thoughts flowed through his mind. He loved his home on the Isle of Man. He had at one time believed his home was the only place he could be happy. But after his recent experiences, he knew there were other places just as wonderful as his home. He was in a special place on the lonely beach. His father had taught him that. When he finished packing, he looked around. The only thing he did not store away was his sketchbook. The paw was unlocked and his precious artwork was visible. William concluded that no matter where he was, there would be adventure waiting for him. He just had to look and find it. He had just closed and locked his book when he heard the door open behind him. He saw Henry standing there.

"I know you're leaving tomorrow," Henry said.

"It's been quite an experience," said William. "I've seen what I love most with my own two eyes. All my life I've wished they were real. I don't have to wish any longer."

"Will you be doing any more sketches of Jacob and Clipper once you're home?" Henry asked.

"I'll start them today. It will be nice to have sketches of 'real' dragons for once. I can work on them before I leave."

"Maybe someday I could visit the Isle of Man," said Henry thoughtfully. "I'd really like to see your home. But still, I think living near the home of three or four dragons is about all I can handle right now. Someday they'll make it back to their real home. I wonder what Elsov is like."

William picked up his book when Charles arrived.

"We need to go soon. You better say farewell to Joshua."

Charles followed his son outside, and they walked to the cabin. Joshua saw them coming and opened the door for them.

"I'm sorry you're leaving so soon," said Joshua after he greeted the two younger boys. "I sure hope you'll have a nice trip home."

"And hopefully we won't run into any monsters," said William. He was not joking.

Joshua frowned. "I hope so too. Maybe your dad will know what to do."

"I may know of Elsov, but that doesn't mean I can fight goblins or Minotaurs or whatever is out there," said Charles. "We shall see."

"Do you think we'll ever see Jacob and Clipper again?" William asked wistfully.

"I don't know," said Joshua with a shrug. "Just remember, anything's possible."

Joshua then went into the kitchen. He returned shortly with the strange blue ice blade. "You gave this to me," he said to William. "We don't want it to fall into the wrong hands. We need it to be far away, where no one knows where it is. Be *very* careful with it. You already know how dangerous it is."

Charles had a worried look on his face. "It is a big responsibility. This is a weapon that has never been in our hands before. If I didn't know better, I would not accept this. But I know the importance of your offer. I trust that my son will help me protect the ice blade." He took the enchanted sword. "We won't show this to anyone. We'll keep it safe where it won't do any more damage."

William said his last emotional farewells to Henry and Joshua.

"You came all this way to give Jacob and Clipper the clue to the diamond," Joshua told Charles. "Thank you."

"No need to thank me. I did what I had to," said Charles.

Before long, William and Charles had left the lonely beach. They were in the car with Franklin and Emily, on their way back to the airport.

"I'm going home and I won't be the same," William said to Emily.

Emily reached over and held William's hand. They both sat quietly after that. William didn't know how well they could keep the blade hidden, especially through airport security. What he thought about the most was the impact of having the ice blade in his possession. There was no telling what would unfold in the near future. He didn't know who or what would be waiting for him and his father back home.

It turned out they weren't going home so soon.

William continued looking out at the city when he noticed a sudden change in the weather. A cell of sickly-green clouds gathered overhead. At first, they looked like they were part of a mild storm. But after a few minutes, they began swirling directly over Franklin's car. They were about halfway to the airport when Charles told Franklin to stop.

"What is it?" asked Franklin, pulling over. "Did you forget something?"

Charles opened the door and gazed at the clouds in the sky. William felt uneasy. The green clouds circled over his head as if the storm was glaring directly at him. They were not natural clouds. There was no rain, only a freezing breeze. Before William could ask his father what it was, Charles climbed back inside and slammed the door shut.

"Go back home immediately!" he said firmly. "We're in danger!"

"Wh— what kind of danger?" William asked, trembling.

"I don't know. We need to head back right now."

Franklin gulped. Charles didn't say anything else, but sat with utter fright written all over his face. What could it be? thought William.

As the car sped back down the road, the swirling monster followed them.

THE FLIGHT WAS NOT A LONG ONE. SALLY LED US STRAIGHT THERE; I didn't even have to use the viewing ring. I figured it was early November at this point, but I wasn't exactly sure of it. The date wasn't my utmost concern. As we headed to the slopes of the designated mountain, Sally, Clipper, and I would take turns carrying the platform. Reno again had the crystal in her mouth. I knew Chang was already down there with the Militia and the albore.

We landed in a brush patch that was void of trees. My senses told me something terrible was about to happen. I knew *he* was coming. How powerful was he? How much harder would it be to fight him compared to Triathra or Glaciem? I had dozens of questions rolling around in my mind.

"Chang is around her somewhere," said Sally. "I'm sure glad we got here in good time. You know, I never imagined I could get used to these wings."

"That's how Clipper and I first felt," I said, trying to lighten the mood.

"I can't imagine you two as humans," Reno said from the rear of the group. "It's hard for me to think of that."

We continued through the sage and wildflower fields before I saw Chang coming from a side trail. He held up the albore to let us know it was safe.

"I see you're here in one piece," I told him.

"Hopefully we won't have to separate again," said Clipper, grinning.

Chang nodded. "I'm glad you two are here as well. Sergeant Nelson brought me and Pierre here, but he left. He's doing what he can to help us back in Moab. He already has this area closed off to the public."

He led us down the trail toward the Militia where a familiar creature glided to the ground in front of us.

"Auben, you're here," I said.

"It's good to see you, Jacob," he replied. "The Militia has been camped here all day. We've managed to stay hidden. I'm sorry to greet and fly, but Losdir is expecting me." With that he flew off.

Once we reached the camp, all of the dwarfs stared at us. Pierre was talking with the nymphs but fell silent with the rest. Trahern stopped a drill he was running. Losdir, Fenson, and Bluepond approached us.

"It's been a while, my friends," said Fenson, laughing. "It's nice to know you made it safely."

I tried to keep my tail from swaying as a sign of respect. "You warned me about the goblins, not to mention helping us find the viewing ring," I said. "We wouldn't be this far without you. Clipper and I are in your debt."

"Ha, and to think it all started with a ride through the forest," said Fenson.

"Once this is over, I'll find a way to properly thank you," I told him. "You truly are courageous for coming to a place so different from your home to help dragons that you didn't even know. That goes for Bluepond as well."

"Let us not forget Losdir and the Konmester's men," said Bluepond. "They have held off the Grün-hære. That takes true bravery. If not for them, there is no telling what might have happened."

"We needed the help of everyone," said Clipper.

We all expressed our thanks. When we were done, Losdir greeted us with a warm, elfish smile.

"You must be Jacob Draco and Justin Clipper. I'm pleased to meet you both."

I lifted a paw for Losdir to shake. Trahern approached us after dismissing his dwarfs. I shook his hand as well.

"Losdir. Konmester," I greeted formally. "I'm honored to have the help of your militia. Just hearing about how you left your homes. The fact that you organized an army... The fact that you fought and that some of you... oh, I can't put it all in words." I had a hard time holding back my tears. "I... can't express how grateful I am for what you've done."

"Do not mourn our sacrifices, Mr. Draco," said Trahern. "You have created a major setback for Vesuvius. You say you're in our debt, but the entire first earth is in yours."

"Whatever unfolds, thank you to you all," said Clipper.

I blinked away a few more tears.

The warm moment suddenly cut off. The ground shook mildly.

"Mother Earth is rumbling," said Bluepond, looking around.

"It's an earthquake," I said. "Vesuvius is coming. As scared as we are, we must keep calm. Losdir? Konmester? If something happens, keep the Militia away from the peak. I don't know what exactly will happen up there."

The ground trembled again; a large cloud spewed out of the top of Mt. Ellen. The dwarfs and nymphs looked up in awe and fear.

"We haven't found the next piece and Vesuvius is coming!" cried Sally.

"The devil of a dragon," muttered Bluepond.

"You, Auben, and Chang should go right now," I said, trying to not sound imperious. I slid the viewing ring from my claw and handed it to Chang. "No time to argue. Hurry, go find the next piece, and watch out for danger."

Chang slid the viewing ring into his pocket. Sally and Auben immediately took flight to patrol the area.

Clipper turned to Reno. "Can you and Razden take away the platform and the diamond? We came all this way to get these pieces.

We can't lose them now."

Razden butted the platform with his young horns. "Come on, Reno. If we want to fulfill our promise, we must move now."

"We'll do this together," said Reno.

I watched as they carried away the platform together. As they flew out of sight, I turned my attention back to the peak. The anger in my blood began to pulse. I was destined to go back to Pearl Forest. Nobody was going to stop me, not even Vesuvius!

"Get ready to fight," said Clipper.

I heard Pierre snort uneasily. "Our strength's put t'the test; all the way, me friends," he said.

The Militia stood in their strategic formation. The dwarfs stood up front with their bayonets and hand-axes (there was no ammunition left) while the nymphs formed a rear line with bows drawn. Pierre was at the front between Losdir and Trahern, ready for action.

"The Grün-hære is in sight!" a nymph cried. "They are coming this way! They may reach us within an hour!"

Sure enough, the army of darkness was advancing toward them, fresh and ready for battle. The Militia prepared themselves. Clipper and I were ready too. The ground shook again. This time I heard something else. It was a low growl that came from within the bowels of the mountain. The Grün-hære was coming. *Vesuvius* was coming.

CHAPTER 37

THE MILITIA & THE GRUN-HAERE

With the viewing I had given him, Chang set off back to his borrowed jeep alone. He took it back down the trail, onto the main highway. There he traveled north. It took a while, but he eventually wound up in the outskirts of the small town of Hanksville. He wasn't quite in the town when the viewing ring told him to get off the road, into a gravel driveway. To the side of the house, and several yards back, was a large barn. Whatever Chang was looking for had to be in that barn! The trouble was getting permission from the owners of the property to search it. Chang parked the jeep beside the house and went to ring the doorbell. No answer. He rang again. Still no answer. He peeked inside a window. Nobody was home. Chang ran his fingers through his hair in frustration.

"I guess nobody will be around to see what's going on," he said to himself.

He went around to the barn, holding the ring to his eye. It looked like the piece was in the loft. How did it wind up there? Chang thought.

Taking a deep breath, he opened the door. Inside, he was greeted by agitated livestock and a cowering basset hound. They didn't seem to be reacting to Chang, though. That meant something else was nearby. Chang pulled the albore from the knapsack, fully alert. He felt a tingle in his hand the moment he grabbed hold of it.

Crash! Chang nearly jumped out of his skin. From somewhere outside, there came the sudden sound of smashing metal and a terrible bellow. The cows and horses in the barn flailed about in panic; their wailing and lowing was worse than a man's scream. The basset hound shrieked as if it had been caught in a trap. Chang didn't know what caused such a horrendous noise. He leaned out the doorway, paused, then ran back inside in fright.

The cause of the sound was an enormous mallet that had smashed Chang's jeep. Bloodgutt, the female Minotaur! Chang could tell the beast was not very happy. "You again!" he muttered fearfully. He took cover behind a beam.

Bloodgutt slammed her mallet into the wall, demolishing the entire face of the barn. The animals couldn't take it anymore. They broke out of their stalls and galloped off as fast as they could. Bloodgutt didn't care about the animals (except maybe the cows). Chang scrambled up a ladder to the loft as Bloodgutt smashed out another wall. In his state of panic, he couldn't come up with a proper spell to handle her. He couldn't think straight with her furious bellows rupturing his eardrums. Then, to his horror, he saw Bloodgutt's flailing arms trying to grab onto the floor of the loft. It would have looked funny seeing a giant cow-like monster heaving herself up like that, but this was no time for humor. Bloodgutt kicked out her bottom legs and hoisted herself up. Chang, his eyes wet with tears, wanted to cover himself with straw, even if it didn't do anything to protect him. Once in the loft herself, Bloodgutt stood up straight, knocking out the roof with her horn. Her head was too high! She had to destroy more of the roof in order to find Chang. *Crash! Crash! Bash!*

Chang shivered as he hid in his spot in the corner. He had to find some way to defend himself and quick! He held out his albore, but the best he could do, amidst his panic, was to create a weak force-field. Bloodgutt swatted out more of the roof. *Crash! Smash!* She got closer and closer to Chang. He figured he would get crushed by her feet before her mallet came down on his head.

But as Bloodgutt's intensity grew, the loft started to groan. Before she could do anything about it, Bloodgutt broke through the loft and back onto the barn's main level. **Crash!** The fruit of her labors came showering down upon her.

Chang sighed, happy he was still alive. Using the albore again, he tried to drag the heavy beast out of the barn. Even with magic, it took a tremendous amount of effort and endurance of pain. Bloodgutt stood up in full rage after regaining her senses, bellowing much louder than ever before. Chang, shaking the pain from his hand, knew that was not a good sign. Thinking of a spell that would save him for good, he held up the albore once more.

"*Sleep*," he muttered.

Bloodgutt's bellow came to a sudden stop. She blinked her eyes, dumbstruck. Ten seconds later, she collapsed to the ground, snoring barbarously. Her fur was covered with sawdust, and a piece of tan leather was coiled around her horn.

Chang placed the albore back in the knapsack, grateful for his results. As he jumped down from the loft, he heard a screech in the sky. He cautiously stepped outside and saw Sally and Auben hovering over him.

"Down here!" he called.

Sally landed in a dust cloud, inspecting the damage.

"Chang, what happened here? Are you hurt? Your nose is bleeding."

Chang hadn't noticed the blood trickling out of his nose. He pressed his thumb over his nostrils. "I used the albore," he said. "It's not easy to use, but if I hadn't, I would've been finished. I made Bloodgutt fall asleep."

Auben joined them. He heard the last few words Chang had said.

"Mr. Chang, I must say you don't know your own skill," he praised. "You have power to put even a dumb Unitaur to sleep! You have much talent. If I didn't know better, I may have been fooled to believe you were a wizard."

Chang looked at him skeptically. "Like I said, it's not easy to use an albore. All I get in the end is a bad throb in my hand and a bloody nose."

"I think Auben's trying to tell you that you're very skilled for—well, for a novice," said Sally. "If you had a Master Scepter, then you'd be even more powerful."

Chang didn't know what to say. He felt amazed at how talented he seemed to be, at least in Auben and Pierre's opinion. He didn't think long about it, though. He brought the viewing ring back out of the knapsack.

"I believe there's a piece in this barn," he said. "That's why I came in here in the first place, just before Bloodgutt got here."

"It looks like you took care of her," said Sally. "But we came because the Grün-hære is closing in on the Militia."

Chang bit his lip. "I see. I better get back there then. Auben, can you stay here and keep watch of Bloodgutt?"

"I can do that," said Auben.

"Good. Just remember to fly off if the owners of this house come home. Sally, come with me." Chang held the ring to his eye. "It looks like whatever was in the loft fell to the bottom. It's right there."

He made his way through the debris and began digging through wood and straw.

"Please hurry," Sally whispered to him. "I don't want to leave Jacob and Clipper out there alone."

THE GROUND SHOOK AGAIN. LIGHTING FLASHED, BRIEFLY BRIGHTening the sky. It was only noon, but it felt like dusk. Clipper anxiously stood next to me. Not far off, we could see the Grün-hære approaching the Militia.

"They're coming together," Clipper said.

"You're right," I replied, sniffing the air. "I remember this scent from when those dwarfs attacked us in the cemetery."

The sound of a war trumpet bounced off the mountainside,

followed by yells and battle cries. Vesuvius had not yet come, so Clipper and I decided to offer aid to our friends for the time being.

Another voice came from the Militia's lines, "Nymphs, prepare to fire!" It was Losdir.

The nymph archers readied their arrows. There were no trees for the dryads to hide in, so they stood at the back. They knocked and drew back their bows, waiting for their targets to come into range.

"Fire as soon as they are close enough," called Losdir.

From the Grün-hære's lines, I could hear their leader Visatrice leading his Horde. His dwarfs looked almost exactly like the Monolegions.

"Launch the green arrow!" he ordered. "I want to see them burn before Vesuvius' arrival!"

One of their dwarfs in a horn-helmet aimed an arrow at the clouds and fired. The green arrow disappeared into the sky. Before it came back down, three darkscaled dragons swooped into view. One of them was Syntare. Clipper and I took immediate action.

"Careful, Jacob! We're outnumbered!" Clipper yelled to me in the air.

I paid no attention to his warning. My sights were on the violet darkscale. Preparing to spit venom while in flight, I felt it flowing through my throat. Aiming at the eyes, I let out the venom that was followed by a flame of distraction. My venom struck the dragon's eyes. Temporarily blinded, he lost control and plunged to the ground. I spiraled down myself. Syntare and the scarlet followed me.

"Clipper, do you think you can take care of the goblins while I hold off these dragons?" I called.

"I can!" said Clipper. He swooped to the right and headed toward the Militia's lines.

ANOTHER VOLLEY OF ARROWS SHOT INTO THE AIR. ONLY A HANDFUL of enemies fell, however. Most arrows either hit shields, armor, or the ground. Seconds after the arrows were fired, Trahern's dwarfs charged with their bayonets.

"Destroy them! Take no prisoners!" the Konmester roared.

Clipper shifted his direction and flew ahead of the dwarfs. Over the Grün-hære's rear lines, he spread a giant flame that wiped out a good number of goblins and royalists. Arrow shafts struck his wings during the attack, forcing Clipper to land. He snapped the wooden shafts with his teeth and shook away the arrowheads before leaping back into the air. He let out a roar that rang across the mountainside. Apparently, his own wrath was catching up to him.

I heard Visatrice taunting Clipper. "If you prefer that I do better, then I believe I should send an arrow down your throat!"

Drawing his rusty sword, he jabbed one of his dwarfs in the back. The dwarf knocked an arrow of his own along the string of his bow.

"Ritez nas 'e troth," Visatrice ordered.

The dwarf drew back his bow, waiting for Clipper to fly into range.

"Ritez nas 'e troth! Shoot it down his throat!" Visatrice repeated.

As Clipper dived, the dwarf took aim. But just as he fired, another arrow, shot by a nymph, landed dangerously close to his foot. Startled, the dwarf's aim was sloppy. He missed terribly. Visatrice kicked him with his boot.

"That stupid nymph almost killed you!" he sneered. Leaving the archer, Visatrice continued forward, wielding his simple weapon. He joined the other goblins in the advance. He made his way to the front line to give orders. But as he reached the front, he found himself facing of one of the Militia's dwarfs. In a very brief duel, Visatrice quickly pinned his victim to the ground, holding the sword point over his chest.

The dwarf shook his head bravely. "I know what you're going to do," he growled. "I know who you are. You won't kill me and live to see the next day!"

"Aha— and what is stopping me from living?" Visatrice cackled.

Just as he was ready to sink the old blade into the dwarf's heart, he felt the gentle touch of steel on the back of his neck.

Visatrice turned his head in shock. "Bah! And who is this gentleman?"

He found Trahern holding his own sword point to Visatrice's throat. The goblin only grinned mischievously.

"Heh-heh! You folk are an undisciplined bunch, you know. You're novices I've noticed, lacking skill and experience. What do you do for a living, sir; if you don't mind my asking?"

"Your words do not harm us," Trahern replied. "You have murdered many of my friends. Now you will pay the price."

Visatrice opened his mouth in mock horror. Then, in an instant's flash, he used his own sword to smack Trahern's away. The two began a tense duel. As skilled as Trahern was, fighting against an experienced general proved to be a true challenge.

I WAS IN THE AIR AGAIN, DISTRACTING MY ENEMIES WHEN I SAW that the Militia was locked in brutal combat. There was nothing I could do below until I got rid of the other darkscales.

We can get through this. I know we can, I thought.

The darkscales were now right on my tail. A brief flame blocked my view.

I dived to the ground before I crash-landed. Clipper flew over to help me.

"Don't worry, Jacob! I'm coming!"

With Clipper rushing to help me, I tried to regain altitude. But before I could, one of the darkscales snapped down on my tail. I started to fall, but the darkscale would not let go. We hit the ground hard and rolled for several painful yards. I scrambled to my feet to see who had bitten me. It was Syntare. She too stood back up and moved around her aching limbs. The other darkscales didn't come after me; Clipper led them off. It was just me and her.

"Appears ya aven't learned anythin'," she growled. "Ya still back away from me, not wantin' ta fight. What problem do ya 'ave? Ya shouldn't back down."

"I just don't want to… hurt you," I stuttered. I couldn't believe what I had said.

Syntare charged into me. She pressed her front paws on my ribs and struck me again.

"Yer a black dragon! We shouldn't fight! Yer bein' a coward!"

That was it. I couldn't take her needling anymore. I wanted my revenge, but something prevented me from doing so. One side of my conscience told me that she did not want to fight. She liked me more than she hated me, even if she didn't express it directly. The other side told me she was dangerous, and I had to fight back with all the strength I had.

"Join me or parish," she offered.

I didn't answer. My anger was rising, almost to the point that I could not control myself. The time had come for me to truly fight her. My mind was already made up; I was not going to join her. Despite our close resemblance, we were much different within. Syntare should have known I wasn't going to join her. I knew it would break her heart. She didn't want to kill me, but I could not let her drag me down into her ways.

I said three words that I knew would truly break her heart.

"So be it."

After a second or so, I could see her own anger strengthening against me. She spat venom at me; I moved my head just in time. The venom didn't hit my eyes, but struck me on my left cheek. That was the final straw. My fury overcame me. A battle with Syntare was the last thing I wanted, especially if Vesuvius was coming. I blew a flame at her then charged. My horns struck her to the ground. As she had done to me, I pinned her down with my claws pressing against her scales.

"Your beauty and cunning nature is not fooling me!" I hissed. "You're right, the black dragon does have a bad temper! And I've reached my limit!"

I raised my claws in the air and beat them down on her neck. She cried and pushed me off. We locked horns, bit, and clawed each other. I felt her pain as she felt mine. Fire flew in all directions. Syntare's eyes started to glow when I pushed her back once again. She stood up with her head swaying, blood dripping from her mouth.

"It's bad luck if the blood of a darkscale touches flesh or scales," I reminded her.

Syntare growled. "I first tried ta make a deal with ya. Now I'm goin' to make ya suffer. I wish you were with me, Jacob Draco. Sadly, that'll never be."

But before she could retaliate, we heard a screech in the sky. I saw the other two darkscales after Clipper, who was approaching us. Syntare caught me off guard. Our fight resumed; two dragons against three.

To the south, more goblins and royalists of the Grün-hære were falling. Losdir and Fenson were fighting back to back.

"The goblins are retreating!" Fenson shouted joyfully.

Losdir observed the opposing soldiers of the Horde fleeing to the smoky mountain.

"It's not because we are winning," he said. "Goblins fight to the death. They must be falling back for another reason."

"Vesuvius," Fenson trembled. "That must mean he's coming."

All of the Grün-hære soon abandoned the battlefield except for Visatrice. He was determined to finish off Trahern. As the duel continued, Trahern was becoming fatigued. His sword slipped from his hands. Visatrice beat him with the handle of his rusty sword.

"Hmmhmm, you make a swordfight most entertaining," he said. "You know, I've slain many dwarfs throughout my life, but you will be the most fun to kill. Congratulations, Konmester."

With Trahern at Visatrice's mercy, he couldn't bear to look into the black paint on the goblin's hideous face.

"Just kill me now," said Trahern. "Enough with your silly talk."

"Hmm… Just wait… Ah, yes! I just want to take a moment and enjoy this while I can. It feels wonderful! Let me savor this moment a little longer… There. Your death will be coming shortly, I promise." Did this goblin ever shut up?

"Do it! Either now or never. A new konmester will take my place if I die," Trahern said fiercely.

"A new konmester, eh? If you truly want a new leader, I can arrange that. Let's get this over with, like you wanted."

Just as Visatrice raised his sword above Trahern's heart, a furry foot kicked him in the rump. Visatrice tumbled head-over-heels, landing several feet away. Before he could stand up, the same foot pressed him down. Pierre bent forward and struck him with a set of short claws.

"If y'have fun slayin' the innocent, mayhap I'll have the same fun returnin' the favor."

Visatrice showed no sign of fear. "And what does a little kangrui do to have fun other than this?"

Pierre was in no mood for Visatrice's attitude. "I can break your ribs at any second, y'know. Laugh at that when I'm done!"

"Well, you're done now."

Visatrice suddenly jerked his sword, slashing at Pierre. The kangrui fell flat on his stomach. A fissure of blood began to form in his thigh. He tried to crawl away, but Visatrice pinned him down, causing Pierre to let out a high-pitched squeal. The goblin pressed the tip of his blade into Pierre's scruff.

The ground rumbled again, this time in a longer interval. Trahern, as he stood back up, observed that the royalists and other goblins had ceased to fight and instead began to retreat. Visatrice took no notice, however. He was determined to finish his business with Pierre. Trahern, upon seeing his friend at death's door, ran toward

Visatrice in a brutal rage. He leapt forward, tackled the General to the ground, and then boxed his face and stomach repeatedly.

Despite his pain, Pierre scrambled back to his feet. Trahern stepped back to allow him to administer a final blow to Visatrice. When the goblin stood up, dazed, Pierre gave a powerful kick into his side. Visatrice did not fall that time, but he did lose grip of his prized sword. Pierre immediately picked it up, pointing it at the goblin General. For a moment, Trahern thought he saw legitimate fear in the goblin's eyes, but that disappeared quickly.

"Make no mistake," Visatrice sneered. "If I can't finish you now, I'll finish you later. Believe me, little kangrui, we'll meet again."

Pierre tried to lunge at him, but Visatrice had already turned and ran off. The kangrui and Konmester knew they would never catch him. With the enemy gone, Pierre examined the wound in his leg. "He's such a coward," he told Trahern. "He lost his sword an' so he runs away. Real brave!"

"He had to follow orders," said Trahern. "I haven't ever fought a goblin like him before today, but believe me he is no coward. If he had all day, he wouldn't stop 'til either he's victorious or if he's dead, and he'd be determined to be the former of the two."

"Then why'd he run?" Pierre asked. "Looked cowardly t'me, y'know."

"Like I said, he was following orders. Notice how the rest of the Horde is leaving too? They are a highly disciplined people, but they are not cowards in the slightest."

Pierre ran a paw around his gash. "Huh, is that all? Strict orders jus' saved our lives. Now I jus' hope this wound don't b'come infected. I'd like to be alive an' kickin' tomorrow."

"Then let's get it looked at," said Trahern.

Up on the slope, I was still fighting Syntare with all my fury. After all that I had been through with her, it seemed as if she was finally weakening. I charged into her once more. She fell to the ground, too exhausted to fight. I jumped onto her back and pressed her down. She wasn't going anywhere.

"I finally have you under my own paws," I said. "I know you want me to join you, but that can't happen."

I was expecting her to say something back to preserve her pride. She didn't gloat, to my surprise. She instead wept. A sudden feeling of guilt overcame me. I jumped off her back and helped her to her feet. She was no longer a threat. After all the bad feelings we had against each other, I never thought she would cry in front of me. I lowered my head closer to her ear.

"What is it?" I asked in a neutral tone.

She sniffed before answering. "There's no way ta convince ya, is there? I came 'ere ta offer ya a choice. The only way for ya ta stay alive is if ye could join us. I really didn't want ta 'urt ya. You don't know 'ow bad I wanted ya to be with me."

My lungs felt heavy.

She sniffed again. "I wanted ya ta join me 'cause... I like you."

My ears drooped. "You know that can't happen," I said frankly. "We've chosen different sides. I had a task to do on this earth and I promised to do what's right. I'm sorry, Syntare. I won't change after all I've been through."

Syntare held her head away, not answering. The ground shook again, this time more violently. Another one of her tears dripped onto a trampled wildflower as she spread her wings. Before she flew off, she let out a growl.

"If yer not with me, yer against me. I told ya that. Prepare fer somethin' worse ta come!

"Goodbye an' good luck, Jacob."

She blew a flame at the ground and took off. I sat down, staring at the moist wildflower that had lived through our battle. The other two darkscales followed her, leaving Clipper. My heart grew heavy. No longer did I hate Syntare. I felt bad for her. I almost didn't want to see her go.

THE TALES OF DRACO   397

I spread my wings when Clipper joined me. "They're gone," he said, "the Grün-hære and the other darkscales. I spoke with Trahern about this. Apparently, they were ordered to leave. They can't even make a final kill if they're summoned. It saved Pierre's life."

I was glad to hear that Trahern and Pierre were okay. Now that Syntare was gone, my thoughts returned to Vesuvius. "Let's hurry and get this over with, Clipper," I said. "Elsov is waiting for us."

Clipper's tail brushed against the ground, kicking up dust. "I'm with you, Jacob," he said. "If we want to go home, we have to get past Vesuvius first. We have to do it together."

"You're right. This involves teamwork. We've been friends for a long time now. We're ready."

We nodded to each other. Clipper and I, best of friends, would fight our greatest battle; greater than with the Nibelungs, and even greater than with Triathra. We were ready, ready as a team to confront our nightmares.

The ground shook again. Rocks and boulders tumbled down Ellen's slopes. Each tremor was more violent than the last. A large, dark cloud towered from the mountain and into the sky. Vesuvius was about to come.

"If we live through this, we'll be ready to go home," said Clipper.

I blew a puff of smoke. "Home. Either we see Pearl Forest again or we die trying."

As we stood still, I heard Elemek's voice return.

"*You are not alone, Jacob Draco. I'm with you.*"

I looked into the sky. As cloudy as it was, I could see a small patch of clear blue sky. In that patch, I could see something hovering in the air. It almost looked like a fairy, maybe an angel, though I wasn't exactly sure. I felt comfort and hope. Elemek was with me, along with Clipper and our other friends. I felt more prepared than ever. It was time.

CHAPTER 38

COMING OF THE KING

Chang had to find another way to get back to Mt. Ellen. In a shed near the barn, he found a saddle and a blanket. That provided his alternative mode of transportation: horseback! Taking the riding equipment, he went out into the fields and managed to calm one of the horses before it ran away. With Sally's guidance, he fitted the saddle onto the horse, mounted the animal, and was soon on his way. Chang didn't take the road, which hopefully meant he would save some time. What worried him was that Mt. Ellen was over twenty miles away. He didn't want to arrive too late. But what other option did he have?

The piece Chang had found in the barn was a smooth black rod that was about four feet long and an inch in diameter. He didn't know what it was, but he knew for sure it was what he was looking for.

Bloodgutt was left alone, asleep outside the damaged barn. The piece of brown leather was still wrapped around her horn.

Sally accompanied Chang while Auben flew on ahead. "Do you know what that black rod is?" she asked from the air.

Chang spurred the horse onward. "I don't," he said. "But it was the only red thing I saw through the viewing ring."

Sally continued flying in silence; her mind was already full of worry. From the distance, she and Chang could see the smoggy clouds engulfing the mountains. The ground again shook violently, causing the anxious horse to rear back.

"There's another earthquake," said Sally. "I'm worried about Jacob and Clipper."

Chang looked left and right through the viewing ring before looking back up at Sally. "The other piece isn't anywhere around here, at least not in this area," he said. "But we have a bigger problem. If Losdir is right, Vesuvius could come at any moment. It may take an hour or so before I reach the Militia, though."

Sally stopped and hovered for a few seconds. "I can fly on ahead and go find Jacob and Clipper. You should maybe find the rest of the Militia. They've probably retreated down the mountain by now."

Chang agreed. Before Sally left, however, Auben flew into sight.

"Sally! Chang!" he called. "Vesuvius is here!"

Sally groaned. "We can't leave Jacob and Clipper all alone up there. We have to help them!"

The horse was disturbed with the two dragons shouting from above. Chang clicked his tongue to urge her forward. The horse reluctantly kept galloping.

Sally and Auben flew as fast as their wings could take them. Soon they could see the Militia at the base of the mountain. The lightscaled friends continued on. They landed on a rocky slope in the smog.

CLIPPER AND I KNEW VESUVIUS WAS CLOSE BY. FEAR PLAGUED OUR minds. None of us spoke until we heard Sally and Auben landing behind us.

"Did you find the piece?" Clipper asked them.

"Mr. Chang found it," said Auben. "I must ask, where are Reno and Razden? Do they still have the other pieces?"

"Reno and Razden left when the fighting started," I said. "They're keeping everything safe. Hopefully Chang can help them when he gets here. Auben, can you find Reno and Razden? You can tell them where Chang is. Clipper and I can't leave right now."

"But what if you have to battle Vesuvius?" cried Auben. "You may need my help!"

"We need someone to find them and make sure they're safe. We need you to do that, Auben. Besides, you could get hurt if you stay here. I don't want to risk that."

Auben huffed and flew back down the mountain. Sally stood next to a cluster of boulders out of the way, just in case she was needed.

Clipper and I sat alone in the open. I was sure he remembered his nightmares just as I remembered mine. Vesuvius was much larger than the both of us. And there was that long spike above his nose, as well as the many other spikes that covered his body. I was beginning to doubt if I was really prepared to see his fiery orange eyes. As scared as I was, I felt comfort when I thought of Elemek. Clipper and I were nearing the end of our journey. If we survived this, we would finally see our home again; home with our parents we had never known.

The ground shook yet again. This time, the tremors were strong enough to throw me off balance. A deafening blast was heard behind me. It was so loud I had to cover my ears.

"He's here," said Clipper when the quaking ceased. "Vesuvius is here."

I looked back up. Fountains of lava spewed everywhere. An unusual pyroclastic cloud burst from the mountain. I huffed at the terrifying sight. The cloud rushed toward me like an avenging god and settled right in front of me. After another loud blast, the silhouette of a large creature appeared in the cloud.

Clipper blew a small flame from his nose. *There he is.*

I stood up, ready for my first meeting with the fearsome dragon. I took a brave step forward. Lightning flashed all around us. A gust of hot air brushed past me; it was nothing like the calm, summer breeze I loved to feel. As I took another step, Sally emerged from the cluster of boulders.

"Why don't you find Chang and make sure he's safe?" I asked her.

"Chang's fine. I can't let you two be here alone," she said.

I looked around inside the cloud, remembering my dream of Vesuvius' keep. The land around me felt much like the mountain castle where he lived.

"I can't believe all this is happening," Sally shuddered.

Clipper unfurled his wings. "He's coming toward us."

He was right. Vesuvius was about fifty yards away from us. Sudden fear struck my heart. He was enormous, so enormous! How could I possibly go up against him? He was nothing like Glaciem. He was much worse! As he came closer, I felt like running. The worst terror I had ever experienced on the first earth could not even compare to Vesuvius' appearance! When the nymphs of Pearl Forest told me the black dragon had the worst of tempers, I thought I was the most powerful. That belief vanished in an instant. I felt no fury. All I felt was fear. Darkness and despair revolved around Vesuvius. Sally lifted her front paws and placed them over mine and Clipper's.

"So, it comes down to this," I said.

"Good luck," Clipper whispered back.

Vesuvius reached us, exposing his giant teeth. "Ah, you must be Jacob Draco," he said, looking at me. His voice made me want to cover my ears again. "It's been a long time, my friend. When I heard of your triumph over one of my sorcerers, I knew you were on your way back to Elsov."

He took a sideways step and looked down at Clipper.

"And you must be Justin Clipper. Welcome to my slice of the world. You, sir, have been alongside Jacob since you two were reunited on this wretched earth. I just knew you two would be together again."

He finally looked down at Sally.

"And you must be the friend who was born as a fragile human. The dragon is not your true form, is it?"

"Just get on with it…" I managed to say. "We know who you are. No matter what, you won't stop us."

Vesuvius glared back at me, emitting a low growl. "Your bravery is futile, Jacob. Do you really want to fight me? Are you prepared?"

I couldn't stand that question. I had to fight if I wanted to see Pearl Forest again. With a sudden burst of energy, I replied, "I was born to defeat you. And now I'll do it!"

I wasn't sure what I was doing after I said that. Before Vesuvius could reply, I jumped forward and landed on his back, latching myself onto his body to bite down on his neck. Roaring, Vesuvius tried to throw me off. My claws slipped and I fell to the ground. He then struck me with the spike on his nose. I felt the pain of the strike surge through my joints. When I stood back up, he struck me again. Clipper quickly took action after the second blow, followed by Sally.

"If you want to take one of us you'll have to take all of us!" Clipper roared.

Vesuvius didn't say anything. Both Sally and Clipper did their best to help me take down the giant beast. I stood back up, shaking the daze out of my head. Looking forward, I saw my two friends struggling against Vesuvius. Despite several open cuts and aching joints, I joined them as Clipper climbed onto his back just as I had done before. This gave me an idea. Lowering my horns, I charged for Vesuvius' legs. With Vesuvius distracted, he did not see me coming.

My horns struck Vesuvius with all the might I could muster. But he didn't budge a single inch. I stopped dead in my tracks. For the first time as a dragon, I had the most terrible headache. I didn't get it. I had destroyed several cars with my horns before. Clipper had once toppled a tank! But my horns had no effect on Vesuvius. Before I could shake the aching away, Vesuvius struck me for a third time. I again was tossed several feet and was rewarded with yet another open wound. It wasn't magic that was cutting through my scales this time, just pure strength.

From the distance, the Militia couldn't see the battle, but they could hear it. Everybody stood frozen in horror. Auben, who had brought Chang to Reno and Razden, stood next to Fenson and Bluepond.

"They don't sound like they are prevailing," he said anxiously. "Our friends are in danger!"

"How long can they last?" Bluepond asked nervously.

Razden and Reno both arose from their spot.

"I can't bear this! I need to help!" Reno said to Auben. "We buried the pieces, so they're safe."

"There must be some way we can help them," said Razden.

He and Reno looked around the mountainside. In the distance, they saw a portion of the Grün-hære in a line. Each soldier had his mouth covered with a rough cloth. Reno flew toward them.

"Over there! Maybe we can give them some grief."

Razden followed her. Most of the militiamen protested their departure.

"Reno, don't do it!" Fenson warned.

Reno didn't listen. She and Razden continued to fly toward the slope.

Auben watched the two head for the enemy soldiers. He took a deep breath before approaching Losdir. "My greatest friend," he said, "the two young ones are after the Grün-hære. I can't let them go alone. I must help them."

Losdir did not bother to stop him. "They need your help. Just be careful, Auben. Vesuvius knows who you are. He won't hesitate to punish you."

"I will take care," said Auben, and he too left the ground. As he followed Reno and Razden, he stared up at the clouds that hid the bloody battle. He figured he was needed up there more than he was below.

Sally left at an opportune moment to check on the Militia, at Clipper's request. She was relatively unharmed, unlike me. I felt

Jordan B. Jolley

Vesuvius' horn strike me a fourth time. He had just turned to go after Clipper when Auben appeared in the smoky sky. Vesuvius slowly turned his head, his full attention now on the lightscale above.

"You!" he steamed. "The foolish stoat who dared spy on me! There is a punishment waiting for you!"

Vesuvius left me and Clipper to tend to our injuries. I watched as Auben changed his course. That didn't help his escape at all.

"There's no water to hide in now!" Vesuvius laughed.

Looking back at Clipper, I saw him slowly stand up on shaking legs.

"Are you all right?" I asked him, worried.

Clipper groaned. "Ah... I'm fine."

With that reply, I looked back up at Vesuvius. I wanted to distract him from Auben before it was too late.

Clipper stretched his aching muscles just as Sally arrived again.

"Reno and Razden are gone!" she cried.

"Where'd they go?" I asked.

"You won't believe this, I just saw them flying after the Grünhære. I'm afraid they'll get hurt!"

Clipper sighed in disbelief. "Jacob and I can rescue Auben. Go help Reno and Razden as much as you can. I don't want anything to happen to any one of us."

With that said, Clipper and I joined the chase in the air while Sally headed for the Horde.

"Reno! Razden! Where are you?" she called once she cleared the smog.

It wasn't long before she spotted them. They were both circling over the Horde, spraying fire in every direction whilst avoiding flying arrows. In front of the Grün-hære line, Sally could also see some of the goblins and dwarfs jumping down a small hole. Wait, was that what she thought it was? It had to be! That hole was a portal to Elsov, no question about it!

"Sally, help!" Reno wailed.

Just as she cried out, an arrow pierced Razden's right wing.

"They got me!" he screamed.

Sally watched in horror. Razden's wings were not as developed as an adult dragon's. That single arrow ended Razden's flight then and there. He plunged to the ground, landing hard next to the hole. He was only inches away from the edge of the portal, surrounded by enemies!

"Don't worry! I'm coming!" yelled Sally.

With the fighting all around her, Reno was becoming overwhelmed. She saw what Sally was doing. "Sally, hurry!" she cried. She fearfully watched as Sally landed next to the edge of the portal.

Sally peered down. All she could see was a red mist. A completely different world was only a few inches away.

"Help me Sally!" Razden wept.

Sally saw that several members of the Horde were coming after her. Thinking quickly, she grabbed Razden with her rear paws. But before she could escape, the edge of the rim gave way beneath her. She began to slip down the hole. She quickly grabbed onto the side, and in doing so, lost her grasp on Razden. Sally watched him disappear into the mist.

Devastated, Reno rushed to the outer rim. "Razden, no!"

Her eyes filled with tears. Gazing down the hole, she found that Sally was losing her grip on the rock.

Sally was scared. She knew she would fall any second, and she was not prepared for life in a world completely new to her. Her life would forever be changed when she fell, and there was no going back.

"Sally, grab my tail," said Reno, lowering it down to her.

"I can't," Sally said. "I'm going to fall. Don't worry, Reno, I'll be fine. If you stay with Jacob and Clipper, you'll see me again. I must let go and take care of Razden. We'll see each other again in Pearl—"

Sally's words were cut short when her claws lost their grip. Reno watched as Sally fell down the hole, passing through the misty veil.

"No... Sally!" she wailed.

There was no time to sit for long. Reno blew a flame at the approaching enemies before taking off, barely missing ground-fire. She began to sob after landing about a mile away, fearing her friends were gone forever. Then she remembered what Sally had said. They *would* see each other again.

"Goodbye Sally. Good- goodbye... Razden," she wept. "We'll see each other again soon."

Despite her broken heart, Reno felt uplifted knowing that they were at least safe. Razden and Sally had each other, too. With those thoughts for comfort, Reno flew back to the Militia. There was nothing more she could do alone.

"What happened?" Fenson asked when she landed.

Fighting away her sorrow, Reno told him what had happened. She managed to give a warm smile.

"They're back on Elsov. They went home."

CLIPPER AND I FINALLY CAUGHT UP WITH VESUVIUS, EACH OF US wounded and exhausted. It was discouraging to see that the mighty dragon did not show any sign of fatigue. Our battle hadn't even fazed him!

As I tried to draw his attention away from Auben, I saw Losdir approaching. A piece of his shirt was torn off and tied around his mouth. He looked terrified when he saw Vesuvius closing in on Auben. After tightening the knot on the back of his neck, Losdir drew his sword. I watched as Auben's eyes met Losdir's, each happy to know the other was alive. Their happiness suddenly vanished when Vesuvius descended upon Auben. The orange lightscale crash-landed. Vesuvius landed on all fours next to him.

"And now for your punishment!" the King yelled.

It all happened so fast. I saw a large set of claws strike Auben with such brutal force. The young dragon was trying to squirm away when the claws struck him again. They tore through Auben's scales with little resistance.

I charged at Vesuvius, leaping onto his back. I bit down on his neck as hard as I could. Vesuvius grabbed me and tossed me aside with little effort. I was going to jump on him again when he suddenly moved off to one side. I met the rocky ground with a rough collision. Vesuvius struck me with his nose spike for a fifth time. Another bloody cut was formed on my back. I felt more pain when Vesuvius blew a flame at me. The wound became sheer agony as hot air seized it. There was much more fire than I could ever muster at my best. The intense heat made me roar. Vesuvius struck me again. I fell back to the ground. When the dust calmed, Vesuvius placed his rage back on Auben. The lightscale was badly wounded and gasping heavily. Losdir did not move from where he was.

Before Vesuvius could strike Auben again, it was Clipper who distracted him. Though he was weary, Clipper fought with all the energy he could forge. After biting Vesuvius' hide with his fangs, his claws lost grip and he landed beside me. We both stood in front of Vesuvius, weak but determined. The large dragon did not charge but rather blew another flame at us. Then he stood still, watching us pant in exhaustion.

"I'm impressed. I can see the strength within you two," he told us. "It'd be a shame to see it go to waste. Why do you continue to fight me when you can show loyalty to me? I will be merciful if you do."

I charged at him once again. I was met with more fire. Blinded, I was struck again. I had no fury left to keep me motivated after that. The next strike may cause fatal damage! I realized that I was too weak and hurt to fight. I was defeated. Clipper helped me back up while Vesuvius snorted.

"You cannot defeat me, you two. I can end your little lives right now."

I expected one last strike with his claws to end my mortality, but they never came. Vesuvius didn't want to kill me!

"I believe you need a lesson," he said. "Let this little battle of ours remind you that you are a small force against me. Provoke me again and you will experience something worse than this…"

Vesuvius growled and turned back to Auben, who was barely conscious. He raised his claws and brought them down on Auben one last time. Auben shrieked then fell silent.

"This is not the end," said Vesuvius. "You have chosen not to pledge allegiance to my nation. I will give you a warning. If you *dare* rise against me on Elsov, my armies will slaughter your friends and your family. Expect no mercy. No army can defeat my royal forces. No being can defeat *me*. You will experience something far worse than torture!"

He blew one last flame at us and then flew out of sight. The ground shook one final time. When it stopped, the smog lifted. The fountains of lava shrank until they were nothing. When I knew for sure he was gone, I took a deep, sluggish breath.

"It's done," said Clipper, panting. "We made it through. He never did want to kill us. He wants us to join him."

I blew a puff of smoke. "He wants us to fear him. He did say we would experience something worse than torture if we rise against him on Elsov. If we ever battle him again, it'll be a lot worse. I'm exhausted, Clipper. He defeated us like he does it every day. But one thing is for sure, *we're* not giving up. We *will* make it home. He won't find us in Pearl Forest or anywhere far from wherever he lives."

I was feeling quite satisfied that I was alive. That was until I saw Auben lying on the ground. He wasn't moving.

CHAPTER 39

CLOSER TO PEARL FOREST

Dust settled around us. All was quiet except for a whispering breeze that coaxed the filth in the air away. Everything else was silent and dead. Though I was grateful I had survived, my heart felt as lifeless as the mountainside. I lifted a shaking paw off the ground and set it near Clipper's.

"He's gone," I murmured.

Clipper didn't say anything.

Losdir crouched over Auben, his face still protected from the hazardous air. I walked quietly toward them to offer any help. I took in the gashes in the young dragon's body. They were much worse than my own. He was barely recognizable with all his wounds. Dense smoke came out with each breath he took.

"How is he?" I asked Losdir.

I could see the heartache in the elf's eyes. "His wounds are deep."

Clipper examined the lesions and frowned. "You're right, he doesn't look well." He glanced up at Losdir. "Can't he heal himself with his blood?"

"Not with his own blood, no," Losdir replied sadly.

Auben lay calm and quiet. He seemed to be at peace, yet he must have known he was going to die.

"I believe my time has come," he whispered.

Losdir's shoulders shook. "Oh, Auben! I've known you since you were a hatchling! How could I live at home knowing you are gone?"

"Don't worry, my friend," said Auben. "Remember the third earth. It is the world where souls of the deceased go. I will simply go elsewhere. Death is not the end of life, only a step. We all have immortal souls. Trust me, you will see me again." He slowly lifted his battered head and gave us a weak smile. "Jacob Draco. Justin Clipper. You were sent to this earth for a reason. Now you will return home. But I pray you will spread your good virtues. Vesuvius may be dangerous, but you are not afraid of him. Don't let his power overcome you. Remember that."

He took another deep breath. I knew his next would be his last. Auben used it to address Losdir.

"Farewell, my elf friend. We will meet again someday." With his final breath, he closed his eyes; a soft smile remained on his face.

Losdir let his tears drop onto his friend's scales. Auben had been Losdir's greatest friend. Though he was heartbroken, I could see acceptance in his eyes.

"We will meet again," he whispered.

Clipper and I decided to leave Losdir in peace. We flew back down the mountainside, over the desert land. In the distance, we could see the Militia milling about, unsure of what to do next. Chang and Reno were with them. The diamond and the black rod were on the platform next to them. It was a sad sight to see that there were only a few soldiers remaining: ten dwarfs and twelve nymphs, not counting Fenson and Bluepond.

"Auben has passed, and Vesuvius is gone," I said after landing in their midst.

"We have lost many of our own, as well," said Trahern sorrowfully. "They pledged to fight the Grün-hære and they have given their lives for the greater cause."

I thought about his words. Not only did they die for their people, they died for me and Clipper. It was a very selfless sacrifice. If it weren't for Elemek's visit to me, I wouldn't have held my emotions together. I was grateful for their sacrifice, and I promised to never forget their heroic deeds.

"Their deaths were not in vain," I told Trahern. "They fought for what they believed was right."

The Konmester wiped a series of tears from his eyes before patting my shoulder. He did the same for Clipper, who whispered a few words of solace to Trahern as well. When Clipper finished, he looked around.

"Where are Sally and Razden?" he asked.

I looked down at Reno. A peculiar expression crossed her face that I didn't understand.

Chang answered for her, "They're not here. Reno said that Sally was trying to rescue Razden when they both fell through a portal. Jacob, our friends are on Elsov even as we speak."

"I see… I think they'll be okay," I said. It was hard to comprehend that, but I didn't mourn for them. They were at least alive.

As I looked back at Chang, I noticed he was fidgeting. He stared at me in fear, as if he had never seen me before.

"Jacob, I first met you when we moved in together as undergrads," he said. "It's funny how you were a dragon the whole time and none of us knew it. But I'm human, someone who belongs on this world."

"What are you trying to tell me?" I asked him, worried.

"We both know that I won't be going to Elsov with you."

"Not all of the Grün-hære have gone," said Trahern. "There's no telling what kind of man or beast will be waiting for us. I told Chang it would be best if he were out of danger."

"I've been told I'm exceptionally good with an albore," Chang began, "but I can't follow you and use it everywhere. When the portal is built, you can all go back to Elsov together. If you need any help, Sergeant Nelson said he would be in Moab. That's east of here."

"We will stay nearby. You may visit us anytime you wish," Trahern told him.

Chang nodded. "Thanks. Goodbye Jacob. Goodbye Clipper. I'll miss you." He patted Reno on the head. "Goodbye Reno. Good luck to all of you. That black rod on the platform is the fourth piece, just so you know. You only have two more to find."

He picked out the albore and the viewing ring from his knapsack and handed both objects to us. Reno took them and placed them with the rest of the pieces.

"Good luck, Chang," said Clipper.

"Tell Sally and Razden I'll miss them when you find them," Chang replied with a catch in his voice.

Pierre, grimacing from the slash in his leg, limped up from behind Trahern. He shook Chang's hand. "Good luck, my friend," he said. "You're a great man o' magic, y'know. Now I'm the one with the limp an' you're the one with two good feet, eh?"

Chang shook Pierre's paw more firmly. Before he got back on the horse, Losdir joined them. He had tears in his eyes, but he smiled softly.

"Auben is resting in peace. Now let's continue."

Trahern shook hands with Losdir then addressed the Militia, "Back in your lines, soldiers. Our work here is done. Once we bury our dead, we will set up camp away from this ravenous mountain."

Chang waved to us one more time before riding away. With him gone, Clipper, Reno, and I flew back to the base of Mt. Ellen where dust still polluted the air. I figured a flight to stretch our wings would be good for us, considering what we had been through.

"Where do we go now?" Reno asked.

Clipper sat down, deep in thought. "We often had a clue where to go next. Chang found that black rod, whatever it does. The clue can't be impossible to find. Once we do find it, we'll know where the next piece is. The viewing ring can help us too."

I blew a stream of smoke from my nose and spread my wings. "Then let's go. Our fight did not go well with Vesuvius, but we should look past that. It's finished."

As we began to fly, Clipper and Reno blew waves of fire and chortled with joy. I, however, remained quiet; quiet enough for Elemek to talk to me.

"You have a brave soul, Jacob. Go in haste. I have faith in you, and so does Auben. He is with me on the third earth. Above all, don't be afraid of Vesuvius."

"Do you know what I heard?" I asked Clipper.

"No need to tell me," he said.

The three of us flew into the sky. Once we were out of the dust cloud, the cool air felt soothing to my wounds.

Clipper blew a cloud of fire. "I can smell Pearl Forest from here!"

"I can too," I said. "Now it's time to go there. For the enchantment! For the good of Elsov!"

I twirled in the air, roaring with triumph. We flew off into the clearing sky. I felt clear and free.

But still, Vesuvius was at the back of my mind. The Grün-hære had killed men of the Militia, and Vesuvius himself killed one of my friends in front of my own eyes. What bothered me most was his power. Clipper and I together were no match against him. I wondered how someone as powerful as Vesuvius could be brought down. There had to be a way.

EPILOGUE

The first thing William noticed upon waking up were the iron shackles bound around his wrists. So, this was his fate in the end! The last thing William remembered was when he made it back to Franklin's home with the evil cloud following him from above. Charles told everyone to get inside the house and lock it up. Poor William was left in confusion and distress as he got out of the car. His father hadn't explained to him what the green cloud was, or what it meant. When they went inside the house, they found a dozen or so men and women, dressed in black robes and faceless masks, waiting for them. There was a strong stench inside the house too. The fumes were so powerful, in fact, that when William walked in, he fainted on the spot. And now he was here, wherever here was.

With his vision clearing up, William looked around the chamber where he was being held. The place seemed big, but half-finished and forgotten. The only illumination inside the chamber, or dungeon rather, came from the pale moonlight peeking through the barred window up near the ceiling. William felt even more frightened when he discovered he was not the only prisoner being held captive! Lying at his left was his dear father, still unconscious. Beyond him were Emily and Franklin. There were many other people in here, too! Who was responsible for all this? William looked to his right. A young woman was shackled there, only she was fully awake. The woman seemed like a brave soul. She didn't seem scared one bit, but rather determined. Under a mud-caked blanket, she wore a decorated dress of purple silk and a tiara on her head. The only blemish in her appearance was her messy, drenched hair. Other than that, she looked like a princess! What was someone like her doing in such a horrid dungeon?

Upon noticing that William was awake, the woman placed her hand over his. "Don't be afraid. Help is on the way," she said.

"Where are we?" William groggily asked her.

"I'm not quite sure exactly where. All I know is that we are in the land of Utah."

William's jaw dropped. "Utah? How did we get here?"

"You were taken from your home," the woman explained. "You must know about the dragons if they wanted you and your family here. I know of the dragons myself. I was sworn to protect something for them, but I failed."

William didn't know what she was talking about. He took another look around the dungeon.

Seeing that he was shivering from the cold draft, the woman gave him her blanket.

"What is this place?" William asked.

"This is my home," she said. "My father rules this castle, but we are far from his land. The spell of time leaves many questions to be answered, I must say. This is the Castle of St. Cassius."

William's eyes returned to hers. "What's your name?" he asked.

"Princess Rohesia."

The Tales of Draco Glossary

(Second Edition)

The following are selected definitions of terms found in The Tales of Draco.

Locations

The Three Worlds (Or Earths):
- The First Earth: Our World
- The Second Earth: Elsov
- The Third Earth: The Spirit World

The Free States: A loose confederation of city-states spread across eastern and central Elsov.

Fjordsby [f/i/-y/oʊ/rd-sb/i/]: A major city in the nation of *Kusla*.

Kusla [k/u/-sl/ʌ/]: One of the two modern nations in eastern Elsov (Kathoyen being the other). Kusla is governed under a Constitutional Republic.

St. Cassius Castle (or, The Castle Of St. Cassius): A stronghold originally built in 8th-century England. The namesake comes from the castle's credited founder, Saint Cassius; and is currently ruled by King Adam I. (see "The Founding of St. Cassius" in the first collection of *Fairy Tales, Fables & Other Short Stories* to learn more)

Shiloh's Pass: The capital city of the *Free State* that is governed by *Konmester** Trahern. (*see People & Creatures)

Vesuvian Kingdom (formerly Marin-Sulae [m/ɛ/-r/ɪ/n-s/u/-l/ eɪ/]): One of the last surviving kingdoms of the "old world" in Elsov; currently ruled by Vesuvius III.

Objects & Relics

Albore [/aʊ/l-bōr]: A wand capable of casting magic spells. Its strength may vary depending on the strength of its creator.

Ice Blade: A weapon made of ice and enchanted steel that can take the form of a sword, an arrowhead, or even a bullet. It is most often used to pierce dragon-hide.

Master Scepter: A powerful, enchanted scepter that is most often used by *wizards* (see People & Creatures).

Portal: A transportation system consisting of six enchanted pieces. It is used for inter-world traveling.

Potion: A medicinal substance that contains magical side-effects.

People & Creatures

Dragon: (etymology: [Latin/Greek] *draconem* or *draco*, meaning "serpent") A serpentine creature capable of flight, casting fire, and spitting venom. They are mostly present on Elsov, but can be seen, though rarely, on *Our World** as well. Elsovian dragons are divided into two symbolic breeds:

> **Lightscale:** A descendant of the dragon Elemek. They are usually smaller and less aggressive than their darkscale counterparts, but they are still dangerous and easily provoked creatures. Common traits that a lightscale may have are its green-colored eyes and white eggshell before birth.

Darkscale: Nicknamed "the true dragon". The predominant breed of dragon not of Elemek's posterity. Darkscales are larger than most lightscales and are far more aggressive. The distinct features of a darkscale are its yellow-colored eyes and red egg-shell before birth.
(*see Locations)

Dwarf: A human, present on all three worlds, that is under the average height of 5"5' (1.68 M).

Elf: (etymology: [Germanic] "fair being"): A spirit or living being capable of strong magic. They are divided into several sub-races (only three will be defined in this current edition).

Fairy: (etymology: [Latin] *fae*, meaning "destiny" or "fate") A winged elf in spirit form that contains magic by means of an *albore* (see Objects & Relics). Even though they are supernatural beings, fairies behave upon their own free will. Some use their magic for *bene*volence while others may use it for *male*volence. Miniature fairies are known as "pixies".

Grøl [gr/oʊ/l]: A tiny, green-skinned elf that is commonly found in trees or under the ground. They can be mischievous, though they usually mean no harm. They are sometimes referred to as *gnomes* or *brownies* on *Our World*.

Kuslan: An elf from the land of *Kusla* (*see Locations). These sorts of elves are highly social and prefer to exceed in fine arts as well as industry. They get along quite well with humans, *dwarfs*, and other races of people. It is a part of their culture to treasure time with children, and thus they play a strong role in toy manufacturing and primary education

Kangrui [k/æ/n-gr/u/-/aɪ/]: (etymology: [Kuslan] *kan*, meaning "pouch"; [Kathoyenian] *degrui*, meaning "demon") A marsupial native to the deserts of Elsov.

Konmester [k/ɑ/n-m/ɛ/s-t/ə(r)/]: (etymology: [western dialect]

"*final master*") The head-of-state within the confederation of the *Free States* (*see Locations).

Lilinge [l/aɪ/-l/i/nj]: (etymology: [Kuslan] *li* is a root word meaning "to drink" or "to suck"; *ka-lingua*, meaning "*life*" or "*blood*", originates from a Kuslan proverb) A dangerous monster that resembles a large bat. They feed on fruit and animal blood. Their toxic venom, after infecting the host's bloodstream, is capable of turning the host into a lilinge as well.

Minotaur: (etymology: [Greek] *mino*, meaning "Minos" {King of Crete}; *taur*, meaning "bull") A highly aggressive monster that shares traits between a man and a bull. Males have two horns, which is typical for a common bovine. Females are sometimes referred to as *Unitaurs*, because they only have a single horn above the nose.

Nymph: A guardian of nature. Like *elves*, nymphs are divided into several sub-races (only two will be defined in this current edition).

Dryad: Wood Nymph; can be male or female.

Meliae: Flower Nymph; only female.

Warlock: Any man or creature under a spell that grants him strong magic. A female warlock is known as a *witch*.

Wizard: Any man or creature that has been educated and is capable of strong magic. Wizards who are seen as evil are sometimes referred to as *sorcerers*. A female wizard is known as an *enchantress* or a *witch*. The wizard who is elected Keeper of the Three Worlds is designated to watch and monitor each world that is mentioned above in the Locations section.

Note: This glossary will expand in future volumes in The Tales of Draco.

Rise of the Dragon
is the first book in *The Tales of Draco*

Join Jacob, Clipper, and the rest in
Book Three, coming soon.

For more information on
The Tales of Draco
and other works by Jordan B. Jolley,
be sure to visit
www.thetalesofdraco.wordpress.com
Thank you.

Lightning Source UK Ltd.
Milton Keynes UK
UKHW041145231120
373920UK00011B/686/J